D0442086

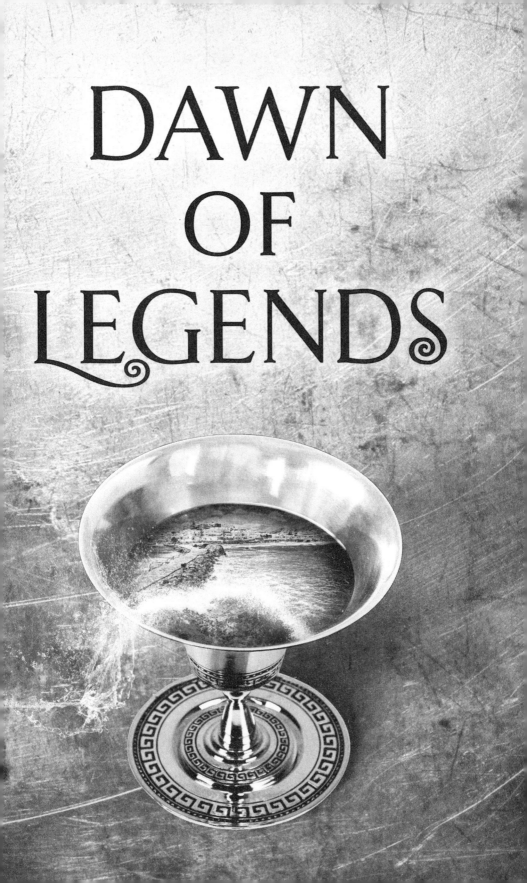

DAWN
OF
LEGENDS

ELEANOR HERMAN

DAWN OF LEGENDS

HARLEQUIN® TEEN

ISBN-13: 978-1-335-69998-5

Dawn of Legends

Printed in U.S.A.

To Starr Thompson and Pam Gilbert,
for their frustration and fury when each of the books in this series ended!

ILLYRIA

DARDANIA

ERISSA ●

MACEDON

● PELLA

● MIEZA
(Temple of Nymphs)

EPIRUS

● ORACLE OF
DODONA

THESSALY

AMBRACIA ●

Kat's Journey

GREEK
CITY STATES

DELPHI ●

ATHENS

CORINTH ●

OLYMPIA ●

SPARTA

CRETE

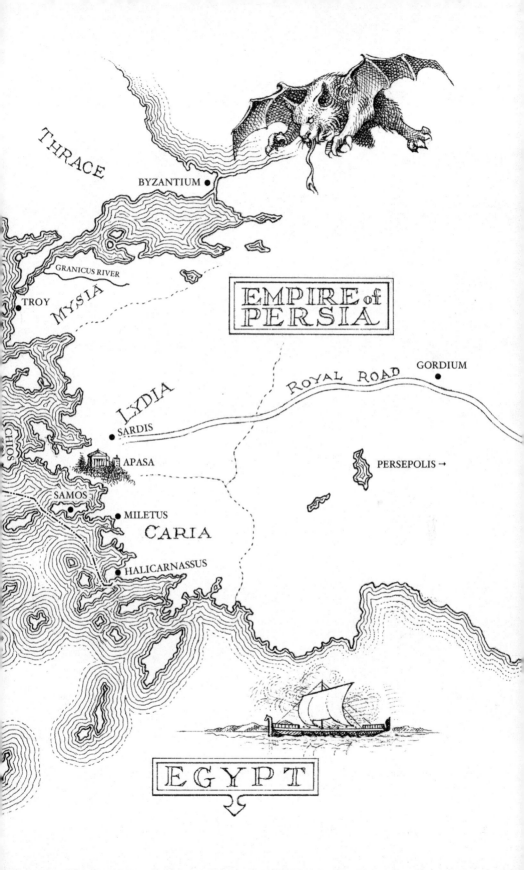

THRACE

BYZANTIUM •

GRANICUS RIVER

MYSIA

TROY •

EMPIRE of PERSIA

GORDIUM •

ROYAL ROAD

LYDIA

SARDIS •

APASA •

PERSEPOLIS →

CHIOS

SAMOS •

MILETUS •

CARIA

HALICARNASSUS •

EGYPT

ACT ONE

CATACLYSM

Great things are won by great dangers.

—Herodotus

CHAPTER ONE

JACOB

JACOB RUNS.

A hot pain radiates through his skull, blurring his vision—a nameless, wordless pain, the pain of a loss so great he cannot even think it.

Once, not so long ago, Jacob ran across the fields of Erissa in pursuit of a girl who raced gazelles. In pursuit of Kat. The vast sky loomed above him as large as his dreams.

Now his boots pound the labyrinth-like corridors of the Byzantine palace, three hundred miles from Macedon's countryside. Now *he's* the one being hunted.

As he races down the wide marble corridor on the second floor of the palace, strains of discordant music from the open windows wrap their eerie tendrils around him. He inhales the salt smell of the sea. Catches a glimpse of crowds on the docks below celebrating the royal wedding, and fishing boats bobbing in the crowded harbor just steps away from the palace.

He crashes through a small door at the end of the corridor into a winding servants' staircase, almost too narrow for his broad shoulders, and takes the steps down three at a time. He hears a loud, rhythmic pounding, but he's not sure if it's a wedding drummer or the pumping of his own heart. He explodes onto a wide marble hallway, hoping it will lead him to an exit—but it doesn't. Just more doors, more chances to make the wrong choice.

The queen.

Bright red blood. Silver-blond hair turning dark and matted.

He didn't mean to do it.

He didn't mean to kill her.

One of the many doors flings open directly in Jacob's path, nearly causing him to collide with it. A man and woman lurch out of the chamber behind, the man's mouth smeared with the woman's lip stain. The woman wears the sheer dress of the dancing girls he'd seen earlier; the man reeks of sandalwood cologne and wealth.

Something wild and angry lurches inside him—the carelessness of these people. The obliviousness. He should be grateful for it—for their distraction—but all he feels is a dizzying disgust. Shoving past them, Jacob finally spots an open door leading outside. He can make out the trill of a flute, the low hum of men's voices, and high lilting notes of ladies' laughter. There are smells, too: spiced wine, wood smoke, and the pungent tang of urine.

He may still have time to escape. It will be dark soon. If he can slip into the anonymous crowd of drunken revelers, he could find safety. He runs for the door, this time racing through the wedding guests, passing a man vomiting in the corridor and a boy playing the flute, and then—he's out.

A chilly wind off the nearby harbor ruffles his stolen red cape and snakes across his face with cold fingers. He turns around, disoriented; he has careened into a square central courtyard—four sides of turrets, balconies, and columns in green and pink and white marble. He curses. He's *not* out. He's wandered deeper into the palace complex.

The flowers are gone now, the ornamental bushes bare of leaves. But on the cobblestone paths, wedding guests huddle for warmth around brightly burning braziers in the last rays of the afternoon sun, pulling cloaks around them. A plump gray-haired manservant picks up fallen wine cups and places them on a tray. An old man with a cane walks slowly through the crowd, leaning heavily on a younger man's arm.

"Wine, my lord?" asks a high-pitched male voice in the soft accent of Byzantium.

Jacob turns to see that a servant boy has come up behind him, a teenager, his face a mass of red pimples. He's holding a tray of full wine cups.

"No." Jacob clears his throat. "No, thank you."

"But it's to their majesties' health," the boy replies earnestly.

Jacob hardly hears him. He needs to get down to the harbor and on the first ship out of here. But he can't risk making a scene. He reaches for the offered cup. Before his fingers even graze the cool metal of the stem, the boy lurches back. The goblet topples off the tray and clangs loudly on the cobblestones, spilling dark red wine clotted with black lees.

It takes Jacob a moment to realize what has startled the boy so badly. Then he notices his own hands—white-knuckled, caked in something dark and red. Blood.

Before the boy can recover, Jacob whips around and loses himself in the crowd.

How did he not notice before? How long has he run through the palace, his crime blazing on his hands for all to see? He is too overwhelmed to care. In the middle of the courtyard sits a marble fountain in the shape of a griffin, wings tucked against a lion's body, water foaming out of its open eagle's beak into a painted basin below.

Jacob stumbles toward it through the crowd and plunges his arms up to the elbows into the water. He can hardly feel the harsh cold of it against his slashed flesh as he scrubs, scratching and rubbing until he's sure the skin itself will peel away. Until the churning water has become cloudy and brown with his blood. He watches it swirl, overcome.

Jacob meant only to kidnap Queen Olympias—not kill her.

The plan was to hold her hostage. He had been planning to use her to lure out her lover, Riel the Snake. The last living god.

But when he went to her chamber, she recognized him. And then, smiling, told him she had savagely murdered his entire family.

She'd gone after his first love, Katerina, and when his family hadn't known her whereabouts, the queen had set their home on fire, had personally watched Jacob's mother and father and little brothers scream in agony as the soldiers butchered them and the flames devoured them. And from staring into her hard green eyes, Jacob had known she wasn't lying.

Now, as the water swirls before him, his dizziness returns; he replays in his head the moment he lunged for the queen and she swiveled on him, wielding her own two-pronged hairpin like the fangs of a snake, lashing out, and scratching open his arm. But she was too slow, too unprotected. He caught her slender wrist and snapped it like a twig. Then, without even thinking, he slammed her head hard against her cosmetics table. She slumped to the floor. He stared, stunned, at her limp, lifeless form, her blood draining into the cracks between mosaic tiles on the floor…before fleeing her private chambers.

Bent over the fountain and blinking to try to clear his vision, Jacob takes stock of the fact that he has lost the god, that the queen is dead, that his family is gone forever. If Jacob is caught, he will be executed for murder. But that's not even the worst of it. The plan he spent months pursuing—capturing Riel to satiate the Spirit Eaters with the flesh of the Last God—has been compromised by his own passion, his own rage.

Riel walks free.

And as for the Spirit Eaters—their evil and their hunger will only spread.

Once, Jacob knows, Riel had been good. He had, in fact, been humanity's savior in the battle between the gods and the

Spirit Eaters, who fed on magic. Who fed on *gods*. But in that ancient war, Riel lost much of his power. He became a fallen god, trapped in this world while the others fled, desperate to return to the realm of divine beings. He grew hateful, and for centuries he devoted himself to murdering his own kin. He had become a terror, a force of evil.

And yet, the Spirit Eaters were the far greater danger. Frightening, monstrous, they had been biding their time. That was all thanks to the Aesarian Lords, who had dedicated themselves to persecuting people with magic, capturing them…and feeding them to the Spirit Eaters.

For hundreds of years, that had been enough to keep the monsters satiated, contained among their caves in the Eastern Mountains. But now magic is running out. The Spirit Eaters are growing restless again.

And hungry.

They have begun to consume and destroy entire villages in the central regions of Persia, leaving only collapsed homes and bones sucked dry of marrow. Soon, they will come for the great cities. Then the empires, one by one, will fall, until one day the monsters will devour the world itself.

The long twin scratches on his left forearm from Olympias's hairpin throb painfully now, as if to remind him of the present moment. Blood still oozes from the jagged tracks in his skin. *A man never cries over a scratch*, his little brother Calas used to say, proudly sticking out his chest.

A fresh wave of nausea sickens him, and he leans over the basin, retching into the fountain. Cal is dead.

Cal is ash.

Because of the queen. She deserved to die.

"Too much worship of Dionysus?" a wedding guest calls, and a group of men nearby guffaw loudly.

Rage pounds Jacob's head. His heart, he's sure, is going to explode right out of his chest. He was the oldest son, the strongest.

He should have been there to protect Cal, to protect all of them. He wants to vomit again but there is no way to purge the real sickness—the grief. The guilt. He's gripping the rim of the fountain basin so hard he is shocked it doesn't crumble. He looks at the tormented face in the soiled water, rippling in the wind, causing his reflection to warp and scatter, unfamiliar.

Except it's not wind that makes the water shake and foam. Earth magic, the hot shame of it, is shooting up through his body, roaring through his veins, bursting into his knuckles and fingertips. Jacob just realizes what's happening before his mind shuts down, as the sickening fury—the raging pain of loss—goes still within him, and the power of soil and rock, of wave and wind, of the oneness of all earthly things courses through him, a scorching heat like the inside of the smith god Hephaestus's mountain forges. It burns, corroding his insides, singeing away all his anger. It pours from his hands into the stone of the fountain, crashing into the water and down, down into the earth below. It is horrible in its intensity, beautiful in its raw power. And then—

—it ends.

Jacob feels empty, liberated. Gasping for breath, he stumbles back from the fountain.

Slowly, he becomes aware of a silence in the courtyard around him. The performers' flutes have stopped, their final notes lingering sourly in the air. The chatter and laughter of the wedding guests have ceased.

The fountain trembles.

Suddenly, the pink-and-green-painted basin cracks open, releasing its water in a torrential gush. The griffin on the pillar lurches forward and dives toward the earth, falling in a deafening clatter on the broken basin, as water shoots out of the center like a geyser, five times the height of a man.

The ground, he realizes, is trembling. The world shifts suddenly and Jacob falls on one knee just as a jagged crack appears in the palace facade in front of him. The upper part of the wall collapses to the ground with a crash, revealing a dainty bedroom.

Someone screams. A plume of water gushes out of the ground at the other end of the courtyard, and three, four, five more erupt, pumping water higher than the palace itself.

All around him, water gathers on the ground, rising, rising to his ankles.

To his knees.

Somewhere in the distance, horses whinny in fear. All around him, people are screaming, tripping over one another to try to escape, some of them falling into the water and getting trampled. Braziers tip over, the burning logs and hot iron hissing when they hit the water, all the warm, flickering light becoming plumes of black smoke. The entire courtyard is plunged into the chaos of choking darkness and deafening noise.

Jacob pushes through the many-limbed dark, water filling his boots and sloshing into his clothes, weighing down the ends of his cloak. Somehow, he manages to make his way back into the building, which shudders and groans. Because of him. All of this, because of him.

He sent his rage into the earth.

The earth has answered.

He enters the rapidly filling main hall as people push their way toward the front door. He tumbles down the marble steps into the front courtyard and barely has time to register why everyone has frozen in place.

Then he sees it. Roaring up the Bosporus Strait from the Sea of Marmara toward the harbor at their feet is a towering wave, higher even than the palace on the hill, like the mouth of the coming night opening its massive jaws to an ever greater and more depthless dark. The setting sun, low on the horizon, colors the foaming white crests on its apex bloodred. And Jacob knows that evil—a magic far greater than most could ever fathom—has found its way to him at last.

CHAPTER TWO

HEPHAESTION

THEY HAVE KILLED A GOD.

But all Hephaestion can think, as Alexander brushes his thick light hair from his face, is that they have saved the god's son. The prince lives—wounded but rapidly recovering as he lies on the bed in this private chamber, high above the royal wedding festivities in Byzantium. And Katerina lives, too.

The prophecy has been fulfilled in ways Heph never imagined.

For months he held the secret safe from both of them: that Kat was destined to kill Alexander. It came true, but not in the way anyone would have thought. She killed him in order to save him. The spirit of their father, the god Riel, has fled Alexander's body, and if the prophecies are true, he is gone forever.

Now he watches the way Kat tends to her twin brother's wounds and knows that he was wrong to think she could ever *really* hurt him. Heph doesn't know how to feel—relieved, overwhelmed, and something else—a pang of jealousy. The two people he loves most in this world have a bond that he will never fully understand...and will never share. He will always stand outside that circle of love and light, a stranger to it.

But something else is bothering him, too.

It had also been prophesied that Riel could be killed only by an Earth Blood.

Heph once again picks up the ivory hairpin shaped like a snake, sticky with blood, that Kat used to stab Alexander, killing him—but only to release Riel's possession over him. There had *already* been blood on the deadly sharp hairpin.

Not just any blood. Earth Blood. Heph wonders whose it could be and where he or she is now. The needle on the Atlantean Mechanism in his hands swings wildly as if to echo his swirling thoughts.

Propped against large tasseled pillows on the ornate four-poster bed, Alex hisses in pain as Kat washes the scratches on his neck with wine. "Sit still," she commands, kneeling beside him. "I must clean it."

Pushing the ministrations of his sister aside, Alex slides off the high bed. He holds out a hand to steady himself, clearly dizzy.

"I'm fine," he says, as Kat tries to tug him back into bed. "Heph is right. We must discover who this Earth Blood possessor is."

As if the words themselves have conjured the response, the ground below them begins to tremble. Heph looks at Alex and Kat, whose expressions show the same surprise and alarm that must be in his. The floor continues to move beneath his feet. An oil lamp falls off a table with a crash as the ceramic shatters.

"An earthquake," Alex says. "We must..."

Kat, who has moved to the window, interrupts him. "Not just an earthquake," she says, looking out over the harbor below and into the strait beyond. "Oh gods," she whispers.

Heph is beside her before she can say what she has seen. It is like something from a haunting dream.

In the failing light, they see that the harbor is *empty*... It has no water.

All the little boats tilt at odd angles on the sand, which is littered with gasping silver fish. People who were celebrating the royal wedding on the docks moments earlier stand stock-still, gaping at the watery horizon. Coming relentlessly toward them from across the sea is a wave that, though still in the distance, must be taller than the Byzantine hills themselves.

"Our Earth Blood," Kat repeats, her voice soft with awe.

He should be horrified, but for a moment, Heph is filled with a wonder as wide as the sea. He learned about Earth Blood and their powers during his time on Meninx, the Island of the Lotus-Eaters. They are those who have the power to heal fatal wounds, melt metal, and make the earth tremble with their rage...and this particular Earth Blood must be *furious*.

Alex has joined them at the window. Despite the terror of what they're seeing, the prince seems to have the same exact thought Heph is having. "We need him," he says. He doesn't have to explain. An Earth Blood with this much power is someone they must have on their side.

Especially if they are going to take on the Spirit Eaters.

After all, there are no gods left on earth to help them.

Kat reaches for Heph's hand, and he can feel her own trembling. And then, seamlessly, she plies the Atlantean Mechanism from his grip. "Stay up here with Alex. I'll go..."

Heph grabs her wrist. "Absolutely not." He's not going to risk losing her, not when they've come this far. But just then, screams echo from the harbor below. Turning to the window, Heph sees crowds of people fighting their way toward the palace gates, others racing into the maze of narrow streets alongside the palace, madly dashing up the hill.

During his moment of distraction, Kat slips from his fingers and pushes out of the room.

He tears down the marble corridor after her, knowing that Alex is moving more slowly than usual behind him. "Kat!" She has always been so fast—*too* fast.

Two turns, three, down a set of stairs, and Heph is nearly bowled over by wedding guests scrambling *up* the stairs past him. He doesn't understand at first why he feels damp until he realizes the guests are all drenched, their garments flinging stray water onto him as they pass. They are fleeing an internal flood of some kind. He fights his way down to the landing, Alex not far behind him now, trying to find Kat in the mayhem.

The courtyard in the center of the palace is no longer a courtyard; he can see through the landing window that it is more like a massive pool, with water as high as Heph's waist.

Once again, Heph can't understand what he is seeing. He saw the coming wave—but it hasn't reached them yet. The water is coming up from cracks in the earth, he realizes, fountains of it, like underground springs exploding skyward.

Kat. Where is Kat in all this shoving, writhing, frenzied mass of humanity?

"I don't see her!" Alex yells, as men and women push past them in their desperate efforts to run upstairs.

On Heph plunges. Now he's level with this panicked mob, and he realizes his mistake: he can't see anything once he is *in* it.

"My wife is pregnant!" shouts a bearded man carrying a woman who looks as if she's fainted. "Help me get her upstairs!"

"Mother! Where are you?" yells a teenage girl.

Two men in front of Heph move away, and then he sees her, standing perfectly still as people jostle around her, like a mermaid emerging from the depths, her hair, wet now, streaming down her back. She is reaching out an arm to someone sloshing toward her—a man with broad shoulders and the red cloak of a Macedonian soldier. Jacob.

Heph remembers him. And with sudden clarity, he understands. He doesn't have to see the mechanism to comprehend where it has led Katerina—and why.

Jacob is the Earth Blood.

Cold water continues to flood from the courtyard, rising higher, making it impossible to run. They must swim. Those who cannot will surely drown. And though he can't see it, just outside the palace, the wave must be roaring ever closer toward them.

Something inside him twists sharply as he pushes his way toward Kat and Jacob, though he can't quite yet acknowledge what this could mean. Slogging through the rising water, forcing his way in front of panicked people, at last he thrusts himself between Jacob and Kat. He grabs the Atlantean Mechanism from Kat and looks at the needle. It has moved so that it still points at Jacob.

"Can't you stop it?" he yells at Jacob, gesturing to the watery chaos around them. "You did this, didn't you? So make it stop."

"I cannot stop an arrow I have unleashed on the field of battle." Jacob looks pale and terrified.

Heph's military instincts take over. "Down here," he shouts, pulling them toward the banquet hall, as he secures the mechanism in the pouch on his belt. "There has to be another stairway to the second floor."

They struggle through the freezing water and up the four steps to enter the empty two-story room where hundreds of guests recently celebrated King Philip's wedding. The water inside is shallower, only ankle-deep. Tables and benches are upended on the floor. Coals glowing orange in the central fire pit hiss and spit as water trickles onto them.

"Over there!" Heph clambers to the small door behind the two thrones set up on the dais. It must lead to a staircase.

He hears it first.

A low growl quickly rising to a roar.

And then he senses it. Though he has no magic in his bones like Kat and Alex with Snake Blood—or Jacob with Earth Blood—he feels the presence of something almost alive, and very, very powerful.

He steps toward a wide-open window facing the harbor and there he sees it: the wave, dark but littered with the sparkle of

white foam that makes it look, for a second, like a giant seg-
ment of fallen sky.

For a moment, it's as though the wave is alive, holding its
breath.

And then…it exhales.

Heph reaches for Kat, but his hand brushes air—Jacob has already pulled her to the door behind the thrones on the far side
of the hall.

And then finally, the water fist punches into the palace, shaking it to its core, exploding into the banquet hall through the
two rows of windows and down from the wide smoke hole in
the roof.

A cold blast from the lower windows hits Heph in the gut,
sending him hurtling into the wall behind him, and another
pours in through the higher row, pounding him into the floor.
A bench knocks him hard in the chest, taking the breath out
of him.

He climbs to his feet, sputtering and shivering, but before he
can inhale, another wave pounds the palace, followed by another,
until it seems as though the sea itself is intent on swallowing all
of Byzantium.

The freezing water is everywhere now, lifting Heph off his
feet and pummeling him into something hard. He can no longer
see the floor, can hardly tell which way is up. He sees Kat struggling, gasping for air, and calling to him for help. He fights the
roiling water to swim toward her, but more water rushes in and
suddenly he is below the surface, buffeted by strong currents.
He opens his eyes underwater, hoping to get his bearings, and
sees the huge iron chandelier…*below* him. Has it snapped off and
started falling to the floor, or has Heph floated above it? Or does
he no longer know what is up and what is down?

Somehow, he rises above the surface, coughing, and sees that
the harborside wall has completely collapsed, allowing in the
surging, sucking sea. Nearby, Kat's arms flail madly, while the

rest of her is underwater. A new wave pushes him toward her and he grabs her robe, trying desperately to pull her up, to keep her from getting pulled out to sea. But she is caught on something.

He takes a deep breath, plunges below the surface, and opens his eyes. He sees swirling greenness. Floating furniture. Kat's struggling body. And then...

Cold.

A cold so numbing that Heph wonders for a second if he is not in water at all but in ice. And below him, from the depths, comes a wide shadow. At first, he thinks it is a shark. He can't tell its exact shape—the water is too dark, the salt stings his eyes—but he has the strangest impression that the water itself has sprouted massive black wings, twin shadows, darker than the rest of the dark. No, it is four wings. Or...six?

Kat, instead of struggling, goes limp. Tiny bubbles escape her mouth as she loses consciousness and lets her last breath float out into the water.

Heph takes his dagger out of its sheath on his belt and starts slashing at the shadows that seem to be holding her down. An unearthly wail reverberates through the dark underwater world.

Heph's chest feels as though it's on fire, and his lungs scream. He needs air.

With one hand, he reaches for Kat, wrapping his fingers around her arm, and with the other, he holds his knife, slashing into the darkness again and again as the water roars, the sound low and warped.

Before he can drag her fully to the surface, something lunges into his gut, separating him from Kat. Her body floats upward and away, arms and legs spread, hair and robes swirling out. He fights his way to the surface at last, gulping in air that burns his throat and chest. Breathing is almost as painful as not breathing. He looks around. A gilded throne floats past him. No Kat. No Jacob, either. He panics at the thought that perhaps they have been sucked out to sea through the gaping hole in the wall.

Though his lungs still ache, he takes a deep breath and dives back down. But still, he doesn't see her in the murky depths. He swims this way and that, his numb, prickling limbs slow to obey, his head heavy and his thoughts scattered. They must be out there, in the churning ocean that Byzantium has become. Something hits him in the head, and pain explodes through him. Crying out, he inhales water. His lungs scream.

Raging waters push him down. He has no breath left.

An image of a girl with bright green eyes flashes in front of him. She's smiling...but not at him.

Wet darkness closes in on Heph as he stops fighting...

...and then...

A firm hand pulls him upward, yanking him into air. Someone throws him onto something solid and begins to hit him hard on the back.

Even as Heph tells himself to breathe, his waterlogged lungs don't respond. His entire chest is racked with pain and totally paralyzed. The hard blows keep raining down mercilessly on his back, and he knows whose hand it is by the strength of it, by the love of it.

Alexander.

The prince, only recently convalescing, seems suddenly stronger than he has ever been. He violently pounds Heph's back. "Come on, Heph! You can do it, dammit! Spit it out!"

Heph vomits an enormous amount of salt water and collapses as Alexander continues to beat his back. He throws up more water and, a moment later, more. When the vomiting stops, he gulps in air, his aching lungs making strange moaning sounds like a dying animal. His back is bruised. His abdomen throbs with pain. He's vaguely aware of moving on water, of being pulled away by a strong current.

Dizzy and shivering uncontrollably from the cold, he squints open his eyes. Alex has dragged him onto a giant slab of wood—

a tabletop. They are no longer within the palace. Everywhere is darkness and water and floating objects. Heph has the unnerving sense that this is what death looks like—endless and undifferentiated darkness, no ground, no sky. Then he has the horrifying fear that he *is* alive, but that this is what has become of the entire world. That the sea has consumed everything they ever knew.

He sleeps fitfully. When he wakes, he sees a full moon slipping from behind a cloud, and a horse swimming beside them, its eyes wide with fear. Sometime later, a canoe passes by, carrying a black goat calmly chewing its cud. Shivering, Heph hears a baby's cry, turns, and sees a wooden cradle floating by.

He wonders if they have drowned and are floating to the Underworld on the black and unforgiving River Styx, a place of unending nightmares.

The night is long.

The cold is bone-chilling.

He clings to Alexander for warmth, the two of them balanced on their raft in the middle of the nothingness, convinced that this is the end, that they have fought and won battles only to die this way, this young, stripped of everything, unmoored from the world.

But somehow, unbelievably, the dawn returns.

And with it, they are washed ashore, borne onto solid land once more.

CHAPTER THREE

TIMAEUS

DISGUST RISES IN TIMAEUS, SOUR AND STRONG, as he takes in the marble masterpiece in front of him, the pride of the Dardanian palace.

It's a statue of Aphrodite, bathing naked, each curve lustful and full. Or at least, it would have been a statue of Aphrodite, had not her head been hammered off and replaced with a carving of the Dardanian king's head.

The *late* king.

Whoever made this bust was talented—almost too talented. He'd perfectly captured King Amyntas's ridiculous grin, too wide for his narrow face. And even though Amyntas has been dead since last night, his painted pale gray pupils stare at Timaeus, unnerving him, seeming more alive than the overbright stare of the mad king himself.

Aphrodite's head is not the only one that has been replaced with one of King Amyntas. All the statues in the garden and in the Dardanian palace itself have suffered the same mutilation: Apollo, Zeus, Hera—everyone. Evidence in stone of the king's insanity.

"One of our first orders of business will be to replace all the statues," says High Lord Gideon in his deep, sonorous voice.

Tim looks away from the grinning head and toward the leader of his regiment of Aesarian Lords.

"Perhaps we should keep one to remind the Dardanians of life under their unfit ruler," Tim suggests, as they continue walking the garden paths. "Just in case they ever complain about Aesarian rule."

The brisk sea wind whips his black leather cloak around him. It feels so good to be in his uniform again, to feel the weight of his horned helmet on his head.

He is finishing up his tour of the Dardanian palace with the High Lord and has shown him, from the vantage point of the highest tower, the rich kingdom he has conquered for the Aesarian Lords. A tidy city of white limestone houses with red roofs wedged between rugged gray mountains and a sparkling blue fishing harbor. And beyond those mountains are towns and farms and mines.

"The people will no doubt rejoice," Gideon says.

Tim's chest swells. Everyone has always underestimated him just because he's approximately the size of a twelve-year-old girl. People have routinely overlooked him, bullied him, and called him names. Growing up, he developed his fighting skills to beat off village tormentors. Then, last summer, he competed in the royal Blood Tournament—held in Macedon's capital, Pella—for a chance to become a soldier, and was chosen because of his acrobatic skill to join the Lords, along with the tournament's victor, Jacob. But Jacob, his best friend, betrayed him, convincing High Lord Gideon to send him away from their powerful regiment to this sleepy little kingdom on the far western side of the Greek mainland. Tim easily infiltrated the Dardanian court— who would suspect such a silly, tiny man of being an Aesarian spy?—and became King Amyntas's court jester. The suspicious king gradually trusted Tim—or Papari, as he was known, a name that can mean *balls*. The name he chose because, while he didn't have height, he did have balls.

And it was exactly that trust that Papari had craved. Because it was just what he needed in order to enact the ultimate betrayal.

Tim flushes with an inner thrill when he remembers the events of last night. How he had brought towels and hot water, promising the mad king a clean shave under the full moon. How he lifted his sharpened razor...and sliced it deeply across the king's throat.

"However," Gideon adds, "it may pose a problem for us that the culprit has disappeared."

His dark eyes hold Tim's, and it's clear from his gaze that while *he* knows the truth—that Timaeus is the one who killed the king—the Dardanians can never know it. They would not take kindly to foreign interference. Which is why they have pinned the crime on the missing Queen Cynane.

Besides, if Cynane returns, there is a chance the people would see fit to have her become their ruler. Tim can't allow that.

Without a king or the possibility of an heir from the traitorous queen, the Dardanians will be grateful for the Aesarian Lords' protection.

Tim turns away from Gideon and looks out over the windswept garden, the twig-like bushes, empty flower beds, and dried leaves dancing in a breeze around the paths. A winter garden is not truly dead, not even at rest. Life, he knows, lies tightly coiled just beneath the soil, preparing itself to spring forth again when the time is right.

Boots crunch on gravel, and Tim turns to see Otus, a barrel-chested Dardanian steward, carrying a lead pitcher. Trailing behind him, connected by a metal chain and handcuffs, is his mute slave boy, Aesop, holding a tray with two cups.

Timaeus had convinced Amyntas to chain these two together, night and day, as the beginning of what he hopes will be a rewarding experiment. Aesop darts a frightened look at Gideon, but his glance lingers on Tim.

Timaeus smiles at him and the child smiles back. Aesop has

always been nearby, always watching. He reminds Tim of himself. Tim is overlooked because of his size, Aesop because of his muteness. They are both disregarded, underestimated, invisible. Which is why Tim gave Aesop the honor of being chosen first to test his theory.

Gideon takes a cup and hands it to Tim, and then takes one for himself. Otus pours hot spiced wine, and it steams slightly in the cold air as Tim inhales the aroma of thyme and rosemary.

"I salute you, Lord Timaeus," Gideon says, raising his cup. "I predict a great future for you among the Lords."

Greater than you can imagine. Tim clinks his cup with Gideon's and drains it rapidly. He hasn't told the High Lord about Smoke Blood yet, how he discovered the kind of Blood Magic mankind has forgotten.

He hasn't even begun to experiment with the magic fizzing and burning inside him. But once he knows more—knows how to control it—he will tell the Lords how they can stop the Spirit Eaters' destruction of the world. He will quickly rise high in the hierarchy of Aesarians. Surely, he will one day become Supreme Lord himself, ruler of all Aesarian regiments from the headquarters in Nekrana in Persia. Not to mention, the savior of all mankind.

All of it hinges on the mute slave boy.

Tim leads the way back into the palace, down a long marble corridor, and through a doorway into the odeon, an open-air structure of eight tiers of marble benches rising in circles from a small round floor and topped by a sturdy, brightly painted roof. Because of its acoustic perfection—a whisper can be heard on the highest row—the odeon is the location of all council debates.

Gideon and Tim stride down the stairs and onto the floor. Other Lords are already there—Turshu, the little bow-legged Scythian; Ambiorix, the huge blond Gaul; Gaius, the sleek Roman; and others. Dardanian nobles wrapped in furred cloaks crowd the benches, and their babble of conversation abruptly ceases as Gideon and Timaeus enter.

"Is it true?" asks the lean, bearded General Georgios, the late king's minister of war. "Is King Amyntas dead?"

Gideon nods. "It is—and by the queen's hand." He holds up his hand to quiet the burst of outcry. "Lord Timaeus, will you explain?"

Tim steps forward, relishing the height the tall horned helmet gives him, enjoying the awe in the eyes of those noblemen who scorned him only yesterday. He hears a few in the crowd murmur his false name, Papari. Well. He is Papari no more.

"It is as our High Lord says," he announces, taking in the room of gaping Dardanians. "Several months ago, the Lords heard of a plot by King Philip of Macedon to put his daughter on the throne of Dardania, not merely as queen consort, but as ruling monarch. The Lords placed me here, in disguise, to monitor the situation. And last night, just as my brother Lords arrived at the palace, I found the king's body in his bedchamber—his throat slit open."

"And where is she now?" a noble asks. "Where is Queen Cynane?"

Tim holds out his hands, waiting for complete silence before he says, "She's vanished—by magical means, one can only imagine. The woman was a known witch."

A murmur of alarm rumbles around the benches.

"We will offer a generous reward for her capture," Gideon says. "The Lords are experts in controlling chaos—and this woman has brought chaos to your doorstep. She must be stopped, and she will be."

Tim smiles inwardly. The wayward Macedonian princess with a tangle of black hair and an eye for the kill brought much more to the land than chaos. In search of Smoke Blood herself, she unknowingly revealed to Tim much that he hadn't known from the magic archives. As a sooty twist of smoke and ashes curls in his chest and wraps around his soul, he can no longer contain his joy and grins for all to see.

"It is true she hated him," says Kyros, the baggy-eyed minister of the treasury. "She wanted to dispose of him and had plans to rule in his stead—she told many of us so. But magic! Are we in danger of witchcraft?"

Gideon shakes his head. "Not with the Lords here. We have tools to detect unnatural abilities and...*methods* we can use to contain witches like Cynane."

"But what will we do now?" asks Simon, minister of religion, his huge barrel-shaped body rising from the bench. "Amyntas wasn't much of a king, that is true, but at least we *had* a king."

"And Cynane has not yet had time to bear an heir," Kyros adds. "Amyntas had no brothers and sisters, and no living cousins other than Eumalia, who ten years ago married the king of Crete. She has two sons. Should we ask her to send us the second one as king?"

"We don't want a child to rule us," General Georgios says angrily, waving his maimed hand as if swatting at an annoying fly. "And certainly not a Cretan child."

As the nobles begin to argue among themselves, Gideon steps forward. "As you know, the Aesarian Lords have a high code of honor. We do not pillage, burn, or rape. We do not murder innocent civilians. We do not steal. If you allow us, we will protect your kingdom for as long as your country needs."

Tim feels a rush of joy. This is it. His moment of victory. He sees admiration and jealousy in the eyes of the other Lords, much larger, stronger Lords, that he—a tiny fool, an acrobat, a comedian—can deliver a rich kingdom into the hands of the Aesarian brotherhood without a drop of blood...other than that of the mad king, of course.

"But there *is* no need," says a stranger in a commanding voice. A tall, dark-haired young man in military garb emerges from the shadowy doorway at the top of the benches. The crowd murmurs as the man makes his way down to the floor to face Gideon. "I am General Pyrolithos, late of Paeonia, but I was born in this palace, son of Nearchas, brother of Amyntas's father. By right and tradition, *I* am the king of this land."

Tim is hardly aware of the crowd's reaction because a rage he has never known kindles in his heart and burns outward, consuming him in a flash of red light. He wants to kill this man, this stranger who has shown up at the last moment to foil his lifetime of working and training to become *somebody*. If he were Lord Ambiorix, the brawny, brutish blond Gaul, he would cut off this imposter's head before anyone knew what was happening…but Tim's strength lies in his brain, not his muscle.

Think. He must *think*. Gritting his teeth, Tim steps outside his fury. Who is this man?

And why is there something familiar about him?

CHAPTER FOUR

PYROLITHOS

ON THE CIRCULAR WHITE MARBLE CENTER OF
the odeon, Pyrolithos looks up at the shocked faces of the Dardanian nobles on the benches above.

"Liar!" says Cilix, the hawk-nosed owner of the mountain
silver mines.

"Treason!" cries the brawny minister of the games, Branchios,
standing and unsheathing his sword. The rising buzz of conversation reminds Pyrolithos of visiting the palace beehives in that
other, vanished life of his.

He turns slowly, confidently, recognizing all the personali-
ties of the Dardanian court. But naturally, they don't recognize
him. He recognizes, too, the Aesarian Lords standing next to
him, eyeing him keenly, and hopes they can't hear the pounding
of his heart or smell his fear of them. The sight of High Lord
Gideon's proud, dark face, and the sound of his deep, rich voice
make Pyrolithos want to run out of the odeon as fast as he can.

For all his personal flaws, however, cowardice was never one
of them. "Hear me!" he says, walking around the edge of the
floor, raising his hands to quiet the outbursts of surprise. He
looks down at those seated in the first row, then up at those in
higher rows. "Hear me."

The odeon falls silent. His heart calms. He can do this.

"You know me—you all do. Do you remember ten years ago, a hunt in the Mantean woods?" He fingers the hilt of his hunting knife. "It was in celebration of the rites of Artemis during the fall equinox."

"I remember that day well," Kyros says, standing abruptly. "It was the hunt where Nearchas and Damia lost their ten-year-old son. His name was—"

"Pyrolithos," Pyrolithos cuts in.

"Yes," Kyros breathes. "We offered prayers and sacrifices in all the temples, but to no avail. No trace of him was ever found. I think the grief killed Nearchas and Damia."

Pyrolithos lowers his head in respect, forcing himself to remember the death of a parent, hoping the truth of his mourning will be etched on his face.

Slowly, heads nod up and down. A man with a long gray beard says in a trembling voice, "With no body, we burned Pyrolithos's effigy on the pyre to help him on his way to the underworld."

"For that, Damianos, I thank you," Pyrolithos says, enjoying the man's shock that he knows his name. "But as you can see, I've climbed back out of Hades and am here to reclaim my throne."

Pyrolithos lets the silence dangle, watching the nobles as they weigh his words. Out of the corner of his eye, he sees the Aesarian Lords standing rigidly, shifting their weight.

"Take off your helmet!" commands a man with long black hair. "We want to see you!"

Pyrolithos removes his helmet and pivots in a slow circle so all can study him. The Dardanians elbow one another and point. He starts to smooth his hair but drops his hand to his sword belt.

"But he looks just like Nearchas!" says Kyros. "And just like Nearchas's sister, Audata, who married King Philip of Macedon, and her daughter, Queen Cynane. The family resemblance is amazing."

"There are many tall, dark men in Greece, you fool," General

Georgios retorts, folding his muscular arms over his chest. "That means nothing."

"If you are who you say you are, where did you go?" asks a red-faced, white-bearded nobleman Pyrolithos recognizes as Phalces. This man, at least, seems ready to accept him. Phalces stands, pulling his thick gray cloak more tightly around him. "Why didn't you return?"

Pyrolithos stares at the floor. "Why, indeed," he says, almost in a whisper. "My parents had taken me to Delphi late that summer, do you remember?" He sees heads—white and gray and black, some bearded, others clean-shaven—nodding.

"After giving my parents prophecies, the oracle asked to see me alone, and my parents withdrew. The gods, the Pythia said, had a message for me, a warning. My cousin, Amyntas, heir to the throne and still a child himself, was jealous of my popularity at court and was plotting to kill me. She said I must do all in my power to thwart his plan."

He looks into the shrewd dark eyes of the Aesarian leader, High Lord Gideon, a frank, man-to-man look that he hopes conveys respect and sincerity.

"I asked the oracle how I was to avoid being murdered," Pyrolithos continues, sliding his gaze to the audience, "and she said that I must tell no one, not even my parents, and that I must flee Dardania. I was not to return until the gods sent me a sign that Amyntas's death was near. And so, I disappeared at the hunt and made my way to live among the Paeonians, telling no one my true identity. Then last month, when I sacrificed to Zeus in the main temple of Stobi, the high priest removed the organs for examination and found the goat had no liver."

"No liver!" The words repeated around and around the tiers of marble benches sound like a circling wind. Sacrificing an animal with no liver is the worst omen imaginable.

"This is preposterous!" thunders Memnos, the wealthy sheep trader, in his annoying high-pitched voice. "Are we really supposed to believe such nonsense? Who will take the time to travel all the way to Stobi and confirm this man's story? Clearly, he is an imposter!"

Pyrolithos casts what he hopes is a cool gaze around at the men in the odeon. But his courage begins to falter. What if he says the wrong thing? His throat seems to close. Angry at his weakness, he forces himself to continue.

"Perhaps," he says, slowly unsheathing his hunting dagger, "some of you will remember this." He walks up three steps and hands it hilt-first to Georgios.

Georgios fingers the hilt slowly. The ivory overlay is the winged lion of Dardania. "You could have had this made." He grunts, thrusting the dagger back.

Pyrolithos says, "Look again, Georgios. The wood beneath is seared with a thunderbolt of Zeus, imbued with his divine lightning."

The general looks, then pushes the dagger back at Pyrolithos.

Pyrolithos grins. Now he holds the dagger up for all to see, "Surely some of you here remember this heirloom? It has been in my family for generations."

"I remember it," says Tisias, a mild-mannered man who served as Amyntas's private secretary. "Upon coming to the throne, Amyntas had me search for it, but it has been missing these past several years."

Relief sweeps over Pyrolithos. They don't remember.

"Thank you, Tisias. Now, who else remembers this dagger?" he asks. "You, Phalces?" The old man nods. "You, Thrasullys? Vettias? Olus? Agamedes?" he asks, pointing at each one. "If I am an imposter, a liar, how do I know your names?"

"Someone could have given you the dagger and told you about us," Georgios says, but his voice is weak.

Pyrolithos cocks an eyebrow. "I remember the day you returned from fighting Labatean cattle raiders, Georgios, who, before you slew them, took two of your fingers and most of your ear," he says. "Despite the pain, you never cried out or even groaned. My father praised your bravery."

Georgios falls silent and stares at his knees.

Simon heaves his bulk off his bench, pushes past several men with difficulty, and clambers down the steps. "Welcome back, Pyrolithos, son of Nearchas," he says gruffly before embracing him. "Praise be to all the gods that kept you safe to rule over us!"

"Praise be to all the gods!" several men cry. "Praise be!"

Pyrolithos stifles a small sigh of relief. Because, though his people might be ready to accept him, he can still feel the tension of the Aesarians standing behind him. The small one, Papari-turned-Lord Timaeus, looks at him with unadulterated loathing. This act is not yet done. Pyrolithos will need to win the Lords over, too.

"Silence! Silence!" he cries. As the room settles down, he continues, "The Aesarian Lords are right about our need for their guidance and protection," he says. "Amyntas took no joy in training our armies. Let the Lords as our allies reorganize our defenses, train our men, and develop our strategy, together with our own brave General Georgios. We can all work together. And our first order of business must be to find the murderous Queen Cynane."

Something changes in High Lord Gideon's face. He steps forward, smiling slightly. "People of Dardania," he says in the sonorous voice that causes Pyrolithos to shudder. "It is clear you are beloved by the gods. You have found a new king from the old royal line. You are fortunate, indeed."

Lamps flicker in the spacious bedroom used by Dardanian kings. Warm tapestries line the walls, and the cabinets and chairs are of the finest ebony inlaid with ivory and tortoiseshell. But beneath the thick wool rug, Pyrolithos found bloodstains on the olive-wood floor. Evidently, no amount of scrubbing could remove them. And he is unwilling even to touch the wide four-poster bed where that cackling threat slept. The past few nights, he has been sleeping on a pallet on the floor.

Tomorrow is the day he has waited for all his life. The day he will be crowned and take up his rightful role as king of Dardania. Since earliest childhood, he wanted to be a king and a general of armies. Until a few days ago, it seemed impossible, a ridiculous dream, a childish fantasy. *No. Never. Not allowed. Take off that armor. Stop your military training. You won't be allowed to rule.*

They were wrong, all of them, wrong. He has achieved all his wildest dreams. He wants to let all his naysayers know what he has done, to rub their noses in his victory the way you housebreak a puppy by rubbing its nose in an ill-placed turd.

Frustratingly, ironically, he cannot tell a soul. Yet.

If he can ever tell anyone depends on tonight's private errand. For he could never trust men, who lie and plot and kill for their own advantage. He will only put his faith—his life— in the loyal hands of women.

Wearing a wool tunic, supple leather boots, and a thick cloak, he walks the windy streets of Dardania until he finds what he's looking for—an ornate door in an otherwise windowless wall. Aphrodite's Grotto, the most elegant brothel in town.

Two guards, broad and muscular—more like slabs of beef than men—stand in torchlight that flickers on the myriad knives in their belts. They look him up and down as he approaches, eyeing approvingly the cut of his cloak, and step aside.

Inside, he's met by a gracious dark-haired woman in shimmering robes, who smiles warmly.

"Welcome. I am Xanthe. First time here, sir?" she asks in a sultry voice, tilting her head and gazing at him through thick lashes. "I never forget a face. Are you looking for something in particular?"

"Alecta," he says gruffly, heart pounding. "I've heard...of Alecta."

The woman bows her head. "One of our most popular girls. You won't be disappointed. Won't you follow me?"

She sashays down a wide corridor and shows him into a small but elegantly outfitted chamber with two couches, a table, and a bed. A bronze brazier keeps the little room warm, and aromatic smoke rises from a perfume burner on the wall.

A few minutes later, Alecta sidles in, her red hair gleaming golden in the lamplight, her flawless skin rich and smooth as cream, her teal robe just sheer enough to tantalize rather than reveal. She has brought with her the delicate scent of violets, which caresses him like a gentle hand.

She doesn't recognize him, but he recognizes her. Her lithe beauty makes his breath catch in his throat. Smiling, the entertainer pours two cups of wine, hands him one, and takes the other. He stares at the red-and-white paintings of figures on the black glazed cup, clearly meant to arouse: naked lovers embracing. He sips it: a rich, expensive Chian.

Alecta has settled herself on a couch like a sinuous cat, long legs folded neatly beneath her. "It's not every day a handsome stranger asks for me," she says in a low, musical voice. "How can I serve you, my lord?"

Desire surges through his body, this strong, masculine body he has many plans for. Man's desire, he thinks, is so different from woman's desire. It is immediate and all-consuming, rather than the slow burn of a woman's secret yearnings. No wonder, he thinks cynically, prostitution has been thriving longer than perhaps any other business in the history of mankind.

But tonight is truly business. Lust must wait.

"I am here at Queen Cynane's request," he begins in a low voice.

Alecta's sensuous demeanor drops, and she sits up straight.

"But the queen's vanished," Alecta says, her voice much less musical and more practical. "There is a large reward for bringing her in alive."

He nods. "There is, but she did not kill Amyntas. The Aesarian Lords killed him and are blaming it on her. She is arranging the next step of her plan, and in the meantime, she has sent me here on her behalf."

"For what purpose?" Alecta asks, eyes narrowing.

Pyrolithos takes a sip of wine. "I am her ally and kinsman— and I am a general. She wants me to train the women of Aphrodite's Grotto to become her personal army. She doesn't trust men. Doesn't much like them, either." He smirks.

Alecta's stormy dark eyes take on a wary look. "Then why does she trust you?" she asks.

Pyrolithos feels his cocky confidence extinguished like a lit lamp wick in a strong wind. He wants to come up with a witty answer but cannot.

"Perhaps you are a spy sent by the Aesarian Lords, looking for an excuse to close down this establishment?" she continues, relentlessly.

He has always had a quick response. It must be Alecta. She does this to him.

"I think," she says, rising, "you had better leave."

This will not be easy, then. Yet even as he curses himself for his slow-wittedness, he can't help admiring Alecta's caution.

"The queen will send you a sign," he says, collecting himself and standing. "Gifts in preparation for your training."

"Goodbye, General. The guards at the door will expect full payment for my time."

Pyrolithos rises to his full height. He had not planned on revealing this, not yet, but perhaps he should. "Let me be clear. Tonight, I am a general. Tomorrow, I will be your king."

Alecta sucks in her breath. "My apologies. Shouldn't you be getting ready for your coronation tomorrow, your majesty?" she asks.

He's about to reply when he sees the mocking gleam in her eyes.

He bows his head. "Come to the main palace entrance tomorrow at midday. I will have your name on the list of guests for the banquet."

And before she can say a word, he leaves, making sure to pay the guard Alecta's due.

That night, when his dreams should be filled with the coronation, he dreams instead of long red hair and flashing dark eyes. And by the time he wakes the next morning, bathes, dresses, and appears for the ancient coronation rituals, he thinks he will explode with impatience.

He has plans, so many plans with Alecta and the other women, and aches to get started, but first he must endure long prayers on the high palace tower as dawn warms and brightens the land. Then he must take a ritual bath in front of the royal council.

"I wash my hands to clean them of all bad actions," he intones, plunging his hands into the steaming bowl of fragrant water.

"I wash my mouth to cleanse it of all falsehood," he says, drinking from a cup of warm spiced wine and water, and spitting it out.

"I wash my face to eradicate all shameful behavior," he affirms, splashing cold spring water on his face.

"I wash my feet from having walked in all false paths," he announces, stepping into a large basin of hot water and dried rose petals.

Servants robe him in a blazing white tunic and place a crown of laurel leaves on his head. Then they form a solemn procession through the streets to the shining Temple of Zeus, where a white bull is slaughtered, and the chief priest, after examining its liver, predicts a long and successful reign. The priest replaces Pyrolithos's laurel crown with a golden one, and when the new king steps outside between the tall columns, the jubilation begins.

In the amphitheater back at the palace, he watches the king's champion—he picked Lord Timaeus, who seemed honored at the request—defeat the masked demon of Chaos in a mock battle. Then, finally, comes the feast.

Seated on his throne in the banquet hall, he searches the hundreds of excited faces but doesn't see the one face he wants—*needs*—to see above all others.

Then he notices, in the back of the hall, a veiled matron standing as tall as a willow. Her eyes, dark as night in the pallor of her face, latch onto his with the ferocity of a predator pouncing on its prey. He feels their bite and sting. And then she pulls her veil over her head and walks back out the door, the very sway of her hips a challenge.

If he were not within view of his new nobles, Pyrolithos would jump off his throne and chase after her. As it is, he wilts with relief. She came. She saw him.

It's clear she still doesn't trust him, but that can be dealt with later. Maybe she will agree to work with him when she sees the gifts he sent the brothel: an oxcart full of swords, helmets, breastplates, shields, spears, bows, and arrows, all concealed under a canvas cloth. *A gift from the Queen*, was the message, *and her servant, the King. When do we commence our training?*

Pyrolithos endures the rest of the celebrations, waiting until most of the Dardanians drink themselves into stupors, and then he leaves.

After slipping into his room, he looks in disgust at the dead king's possessions. But he is king now, he can live where he chooses. In the morning, he will instruct his servants to move his things to Queen Cynane's old room.

A soft knock on the door interrupts his thoughts. The mute slave boy, Aesop, comes in, chained to his slave master, a bald, burly man with eyes that wander in two different directions. The boy's eyes dart nervously to the spot on the floor covered by the new rug.

"Yes?" Pyrolithos says, annoyed at the disturbance.

"A message for you, my lord," says Otus. He elbows Aesop

hard, and the boy, trembling, holds out a tiny scroll tied with a scarlet ribbon. Heart pounding, Pyrolithos unrolls it.

We give thanks for the generous gifts. We'll be sure to make good use of them.

Pyrolithos smiles a slow smile. Clearly, Alecta made her words coy enough that no one would guess at her true meaning if the message were intercepted.

He locks the door behind Aesop and waits. Waits until the hour of the night when even the whores have gone to bed, when the palace cooks have not yet arisen to begin the day. The hour of utter silence.

Quickly, quietly, he bolts the door and closes the shutters. Then he unsheathes his hunting dagger, the precious family heirloom that convinced the nobles that he was the lost boy, Pyrolithos. But Pyrolithos never had this dagger when he disappeared in the woods. It left Dardania soon after, when the boy's aunt, Audata, went to Macedon to marry King Philip, as part of her dowry.

Standing before the polished bronze table mirror, he lights a lamp. Then, carefully, slowly, he pricks himself in the fleshy part of his upper arm, just enough for a drop of blood to flow. Pain sparks, helping him to push the Smoke Blood through his veins as he concentrates. Not enough to last more than a few minutes. He feels the power of fire and glowing cinders spreading through him, reshaping his face, his shoulders, his chest, his hands. Just for a moment. Just to remind himself of who he really is.

In the mirror, Cynane smiles.

CHAPTER FIVE

OLYMPIAS

URGENT VOICES. WORRIED FACES. CAREFUL, prodding fingers. Tiny sips of warm spiced wine.

A world of gray and haze.

A cool cloth wipes Olympias's face, and she smells the clean scent of mint. *Mint water calms the ill.*

Her blankets are plucked off. She feels a cold rush of air and then heat radiating from a warming pan as the blankets are tucked back around her. Her eyelids are so heavy it takes enormous concentration to open them. But when she does, she sees the slight form of a girl bustling about a tiny room that dips and sways slightly. A small, high window lets in a shaft of light and a stream of frigid air.

She is on a ship.

It seems impossible, as she vaguely remembers being in a palace on the Bosporus Strait. A pang moves through her, a feeling of loss more jarring and heavy than the weight of her illness.

She feels as though she has been brought back from the dead—again.

Perhaps, in fact, she has.

She opens her mouth to speak, but her tongue and lips resist the formation of words.

"Your Majesty," the girl beside her breathes. Her pretty, pointed face seems dimly familiar. She places one hand behind Olympias's neck to support her head and tips a cup of sweet, rich wine into her mouth. It slides down her parched throat, warming her.

Olympias tries hard to focus her thoughts, even though the effort hurts her head. Memories and images blur and shift. She was sitting in her bedroom in the Byzantine palace, getting ready for the eighth wedding of the king, her husband, to a brazen blue-eyed girl: the eighteen-year-old Cleopatra, niece of Attalus. The wedding where, according to the words of the gods themselves, Philip was destined to die.

What of them now? Olympias had tried to poison Philip, had given Cleo a pot of poisoned lip stain, knowing the king couldn't resist the young temptress he'd chosen to make his newest wife—and knowing, too, that he wouldn't survive his toxic reaction to the rare Persian mulberry.

"Tell me where..." she begins, her voice like the scrape of one pottery shard on another.

"Don't tire yourself, my queen," the girl says, adjusting the slats in the shutters on the small window. "King Xander will take care of you once we arrive. I am sure of it. He will make certain you are safe from those who might mean you harm."

"Safe..." So, they are bound to Epirus, home to her brother, Xander, the stern, distant man she never really cared for, despite having named her son Alexander in his honor. Xander never protected her before—not when they were children and she was beaten and neglected by their cruel and coldhearted parents. Not when they were fair-headed teens, and she was sought after by a god.

Riel.

A cold dread moves through her. What has happened to the god who once loved her? He was at the wedding, waiting for her to do the deed. For the prophecy said King Philip would die at the wedding of Cleopatra by the hand of a lover. Riel and Olympias decided she would be that lover. He was waiting for her in the banquet hall, but she never made it downstairs...

She shudders hard, the chill suddenly unbearable, and desperately tries to tug at the blankets but realizes something is wrong with her right arm. She raises it and squints. Her wrist is in a splint, tightly bandaged. She puts her other hand to her head. That, too, is bandaged. She can't remember how this happened. "Who hurt me?" she croaks.

The girl shakes her head. "No one hurt you, my lady," she says. "You, like so many others, were injured in the great waves that Lord Poseidon sent to batter Byzantium. Then you developed a high fever."

The girl's words make no sense, and Olympias wonders if she heard her correctly. Questions just beyond her reach prick at her like small knives.

Then she remembers the truth: that peasant boy turned Aesarian Lord Jacob did this to her.

There was no one to save her from his rage when he learned that she had killed his family. She managed to slice his arm open with her hairpin, but he snapped her wrist and slammed her head hard onto her cosmetics table. She remembers waking in a jumble of blood-soaked broken glass and, terrified Jacob would return, crawling like a wounded animal into the servants' passage.

If there's one thing Olympias has learned on this earth, it is how to survive. Sometimes she thinks it is all she was built for.

"Why...Epirus?" Olympias manages to gasp out.

"Your lord brother worries that a fatal accident might befall you now that King Philip has taken a new bride," the girl says, pulling up a stool and sitting beside the bed. She holds a long strip of laundered bandage and starts to roll it. "They both survived the devastation unharmed, and King Xander didn't want Cleo adding anything *unusual* to your medications. He'd rather his own healers attend you in your childhood home."

Olympias shuts her eyes. Philip is alive, then.

And her brother—he doesn't care about her well-being. Only his fragile alliance with Macedon. He must be planning to use her in winning some advantage from Philip.

But how could Philip have lived? The prophecy of the oracle of Delphi—that Philip would die at the wedding of Cleopatra—was wrong...

The oracle...

"I know you," Olympias says, her voice sudden and harsh in her throat. She pushes herself up. Pythia. The oracle of Delphi. *That's* where the queen last saw this girl. During her and Riel's visit to Delphi, seeking answers.

Immediately, Olympias's moment of recognition morphs into the acrid taste of suspicion. Delphi is far from Byzantium. This can be no coincidence. "What are you doing here?" she snaps. "Who are you *really*?"

The girl drops the bandage in her lap, suddenly looking achingly young and vulnerable. For a second, the queen's suspicion makes room for something else. Something like pity. But it is gone before she can feel it. Olympias's life has no room for pity. No room for fragile, breakable things.

"My real name is Patra," she says.

Olympias sits up straighter, digesting this stunning piece of news. "Is that short for Cleopatra?" she asks, her voice harsh with rising excitement. For if so, here is another Cleopatra. Here is another chance.

"Yes," the girl replies, her voice low. "Too grand a name for a slave. Because oracles may be the voice of gods, but in reality, we are nothing more than slaves." She swallows and straightens her slender shoulders. "I escaped Delphi during the great earthquake, and I will never go back."

Olympias relaxes back on the pillows, fear draining like water as a wave pulls back out to sea. The girl's name opens a world of possibilities for the queen. And besides that, truth rings in her voice. A truth she recognizes because it was once her own. When she was a girl, her father ignored her. Her stepmother beat her. All she could dream of was running away.

She shuts her eyes, unwilling to remember any more. Unwilling to care.

"Patra," she says, raising her shoulders in a delicate shiver, "would you put more wood in the brazier and bring it over here? I am so terribly cold." The pull of the beyond has not yet fully released her. At any moment, she could still let go, could slip away. The burning, raging fever has broken. But is the coolness she now feels the chilling presage of death?

Patra pushes the portable brazier closer to her. She gathers sticks of wood from the tray below and places them in the elaborately carved bronze bowl on top. They catch quickly, and a sweet-scented smoke rises like curling white fingers. Patra coughs and stumbles. Olympias's eyes flash open. The smoke.

Smoke to an oracle is like sparks to tinder. Someone told her that once. Someone she loved dearly.

Helen. Who raised Katerina as her own daughter. The only friend Olympias ever had.

No. No more memories.

Olympias blinks again and watches as the smoke swirls around Patra's face. Her eyes are drifting away from the queen… They start to roll back in her head and muttered sounds move between her lips.

The few words Olympias can make out send a jolt of terror through her.

Patra shakes her head rapidly, flinging her hair from side to side. Wild tendrils are strewed over her face, which is as blank as new parchment. Her hazel eyes are flat and soulless as river pebbles.

"All gone. All dead," Patra murmurs.

"Who?" Olympias's voice is a raw scratch against her throat.

"The last of us. The last of us. The last of us. No more gods walk this earth. No more ever shall."

Riel. That chill of certainty moves through her again, the dull thud of a loss she cannot fathom, cannot allow herself to feel.

"Gone…gone…gone…"

And then Patra collapses, breathing heavily as the Voices of the gods leave her. She moans on the floor and curls into herself, but Olympias barely notices. The queen falls back on the pillows, light-headed, too numb to feel pain.

All that she possesses is a yawning emptiness.

She is an abyss.

An empty space.

Nothing.

Life before she met the green-eyed god had been unbearable. He gave her love, ambition, secrets, and plans.

Life with him was also hard. But even then, all those years when he had been trapped in snake form, she had had him close by her, knowing she would release him with a powerful spell as soon as the changing of the age allowed.

And a life without him now would be impossible.

A wave of raw pain rips through her, a wave as huge and destructive as any that hit the Byzantine palace. Tears prick her eyes—she cannot remember the last time she wept. It takes everything in her, every last fortress against disaster, every force of will that has kept her alive this long, to hold it in.

She is alone. Alone. Every single day, for as long as she lives, she will be totally, utterly alone.

But she has this. *She has this.* This will to live. This will to *win.* And, most important, the will to *get revenge.*

She opens her eyes and sees Patra distorted through the murk of her tears.

"My queen… The god is dead," the girl rasps, pushing herself up from the floor, her wild hair covering her face, though the fear in her voice is clear as a light breaking open in the sky. "But the monsters." She gasps. "The monsters are coming."

CHAPTER SIX

ZOFIA

THERE'S ONLY ONE WAY TO CHANGE YOUR FATE,
Kohinoor had said.

In the predawn chill, Zofia pulls her overlarge blue cloak tighter around her shoulders and hurries down one of the winding streets toward the center of Athens. Unspeakable dangers may lurk in the shadows all around her. It is never safe for a woman to travel alone—Zo, of anyone, should know that. But she is no mere woman—she is an escaped princess, promised to the great Prince Alexander himself.

And more than a princess, she's a pawn…in what could become the largest war the world has ever seen. The Assassins Guild is hunting for her, even now. She was not actually meant to wed Alexander but to be murdered by the Assassins, who would have made it look like the prince had done it, her death the planned catalyst to ignite war between Persia and Macedon.

And what none of them know—not Alexander, whom she has yet to meet, nor the Assassins, nor the Great King of Persia—is that she is with child.

But her secret has become more difficult to hide. Her hands automatically move to her belly, now taut and round, where she feels a stirring. Her child will live. Zofia will never stop running until she finds a way for that to be true. Until she understands what freedom is.

Not so very long ago, Zofia had been a romantic. She'd fallen in love first with Cosmas, the father of her baby, with whom she made love once in the Sardisian palace basement. Then she had fallen for Ochus, son of the head of the Assassins himself, Darius, chief advisor to the Great King of Persia. Ochus had promised to protect her, no matter what came. No matter if it meant disavowing his father and everything he'd been raised to believe.

That last sweet night with Ochus at the Pellan palace, where she had been waiting for her fiancé, Prince Alexander, to return from Byzantium, she told Ochus the name of her first lover and the father of her unborn child. When the first rays of dawn struck the gilded statues on the roof, Zo found Cosmas dead, murdered along with soldiers both Persian and Macedonian. Ochus had vanished. He had either fled, been captured, or died. It didn't really matter which fate he had met, because in each scenario, she was completely alone. Utterly without protection against the Assassins, who would kill her the moment Prince Alexander returned.

And so, she had run away.

She hadn't planned to come here. But once she realized her life was in danger in the Pellan palace, she had thrown gold coins, all her expensive dowry jewels, and a change of plain clothing into a pack, slipped out of the palace complex, and made her way to Lakeport. There she boarded the first ship out, which happened to be going to Athens.

For a brief time—and truly, for the first time in her life—Zo had a taste of freedom, though it was a perilous, precious kind of freedom, for she knew at any moment it could be snatched away again. Still, she hoped—hoped Athens would provide the safety she hadn't found elsewhere.

And, at first, it seemed to. She spent days in awe of the wonders Athens has to offer. She watched as bearded philosophers hotly disputed the nature of the human soul and sculptors chiseled gods from blocks of stone. She gaped at tanned, brawny wrestlers in loincloths grappling with each other as men wagered and shouted. She listened as a statesman called Demosthenes enraged crowds of citizens against the evil King Philip of Macedon, who threatened the freedom of all of Greece, the orator's powerful voice and persuasive rhetoric sweeping so forcefully into her heart that, as if in a trance, she found herself raising her fist and chanting against the northern tyrant who almost became her father-in-law.

But then, the shadows returned. Or maybe they had never left her. Lately she has had the feeling of being hunted, like a stag in the forest as riders slowly close in on her. Everyone she sees—the plump baker's wife, the cheerful wine merchant—could be an Assassin lying in wait. And what about the ones she doesn't see?

There's movement in the shadows of a lamp maker's shop, and Zo grabs the knife in her belt. But it's just a lean black cat, rising on legs stiff from the cold. It stares at her with glowing yellow eyes that make the hairs on the back of her neck rise, then turns to sniff the smell of frying fish. *It's just a cat*, she thinks, chiding herself for the heart-churning panic that shot into her so fast she could hardly stop it. That's been happening more and more. There have been darkly hooded figures in the eaves of doorways, watching her. If the Assassins have followed her here, she must move on.

But where can she find safety? Bound together with the urgent need to do something is the incapacitating fear of doing the wrong thing. What do the Fates have in store? Didn't all of this begin because of her desire to change her own?

A hooded figure staggers out of a low dwelling and pauses, staring at her. In the iron-colored early light, she can't see the figure's face, and the panic returns full-fledged, a stampede of hooves inside her chest. She blinks. The figure sways and the hood slips back, revealing a haggard painted face. A whore, Zo realizes, leaving the room of her latest customer. The woman slinks around the corner and into the purpled shadows of an alley. Slowly, Zo begins to breathe again. The city is full of women who sell their bodies—women like this who do so for a few obols, as well as hetaerae, the city's most elegant, educated, and expensive courtesans. She has seen them in the marketplace, wafting clouds of sweet perfume in their wake, their golden anklets tinkling like tiny bells.

Well-heeled prostitutes operate in every major city, Zo knows. But she has heard that in Dardania common prostitutes are training with military weapons, perhaps armed by the warrior-queen Cynane herself, who murdered her insane husband and disappeared. There have been rumors that women from across Greece have been leaving abusive husbands and flocking to a brothel called Aphrodite's Grotto. Men who try to take back their wives are beaten black-and-blue by the prostitutes.

These women, Zo knows, are searching for the one thing women are always denied: freedom.

The sun is about to rise, the sky brightening above her. Zo takes another breath and presses onward, praying that today she will get answers. She is running out of time.

The baby will not wait.

Neither will the Assassins.

Last summer, when she was held captive by rogue slave traders, Zo received a prediction from Kohinoor, an old soothsayer locked in the cage next to hers. *Your blood is fated to mix with that of Prince Alexander,* the violet-eyed crone had mumbled. *The only way to undo the threads of Fate that have been woven for you is to find the Spirit Eaters.*

Zo was repulsed at the thought of marrying Alexander, a cripple, it was said, with mismatched eyes. And so, she traveled deep into the Eastern Mountains to find a Spirit Eater and change her fate. She did briefly find one—or it found her and raked her back with its claws as she raced away on a flying horse—but she doesn't believe the encounter was one that could have changed her destiny, especially after Great King Artaxerxes packed her off to Macedon as soon as he saw her.

Every day in Athens she has visited at least one temple or altar, imploring the gods for guidance, seeking a divine omen to tell her how to change her fate, where to go, and how to protect the precious life growing inside her. In short, how to alter her fate. But none has given her any sign at all. Even the goddess of the biggest temple, the Parthenon, great Athena herself, was silent. The enormous statue, many times the height of a man, with robes of beaten gold and skin of gleaming ivory, stared down at her with cold crystal eyes. Zo left feeling smaller and more alone than ever before.

But yesterday Zo learned of another temple, this one outside the city, ancient and mostly forgotten, called the Temple of the Moirai or the Three Fates, and hope rose in her chest. Perhaps her best path now is to find the Greek goddesses who spin the threads of Fate and negotiate with them herself.

She cuts through the agora—the main marketplace—where shopkeepers throw open shutters with loud bangs and drag out tables of merchandise. Men set up booths and unload wagons of cheese and wine, olives and fish, glinting weapons, fine leather goods, and brightly colored carpets. In the center, wood has been stacked for a huge bonfire. Tonight is the winter solstice, and drunken people will dance around the flames, praying to the sun god to turn his face back toward them and bring longer, warmer days.

Smoke rises from shops and houses, mixed with the mouth-watering aroma of fresh bread, which makes her stomach grumble. She should have brought some food with her, but it was too early to go into the kitchen of Berenike, the kindly landlady who has been renting her a room.

The freezing wind is stronger in this wide plaza, beating her with invisible fists, and she pulls her dark blue cloak more tightly about her. It was Ochus's; he had left it on a chair in her bedroom the evening before her escape. She should have shrunk from touching anything of his, but in those last frantic moments before she fled the palace, she realized her own cloaks were embroidered with gold and sparkled with gemstones, far too ornate for her to blend into the crowd and escape.

She marches through Kerameikos, the famous neighborhood of pottery shops, with pots and cups in every size and shape, beautifully painted with scenes of gods, heroes, and myths. Then she is out the Acharnian Gate, fighting her way past wagons of produce headed to market. Something glimmers in the corner of her eye. She turns and sees the first rays of the sun strike the temples crowning the Acropolis, setting them aflame in shades of gold and orange. The enormous flat-topped hill, jutting straight out of the center of Athens, has become a familiar sight to her, yet she is constantly thrilled by the majestic beauty of its many-columned buildings and towering statues.

Athens was named in honor of the goddess Athena, Zo learned, because she gave the city the incomparable gift of the olive tree, used for food, oil, and wood. Now, as Zo trudges up the Acharnian Road, she passes through olive orchards as far as the eye can see, the thousands of leafless, silver-barked trees standing like burly armored soldiers on the field of battle.

She walks quickly to warm up, deftly avoiding steaming animal droppings and stepping out of the way of horses and carts. Then, a mile or so down the road, she sees the temple off to one side. At least she feels like she can breathe again—there are no mysterious hooded figures in the countryside. No one is following her. At least, not as far as she can see.

Then again, the deadliest enemies are the kind you don't see coming.

The Temple of the Moirai is nothing like the tall marbled masterpieces on the Acropolis. It looks centuries older and is made of wood, the black and red paint on its squat columns faded and flaking. And it is small, the size of a comfortable room.

Gnarled trees bend over it protectively, and the wind streaming through their leafless branches seems to whisper ancient lullabies.

An old man wearing the white vestments of a priest sweeps dust off the porch with a broom of bent twigs. He stops and looks up. As soon as his eyes catch on her swelling belly, his bushy gray eyebrows lift knowingly, as though this is not the first time a pregnant woman in need has visited their humble temple. Then he gives her a toothless grin.

Leaning on the broom, he lisps, "You've come to the right place. We help many girls like you here."

Zo hesitates before nodding. Then she steps carefully through the open door. Inside, the pungent smells of mildew and old wood smoke nearly make her choke. It's dark here; a few shafts of light slanting through high openings reveal cobwebs hanging from every beam and fat spiders spinning. At the far end is a wooden statue of three old women at a loom. Zo knows she has seen the image before, but she can't remember where.

"Come here, my child," a voice croons from the shadows. Zo follows the command to a screen in the corner and sees a figure seated behind it, though it's too dark to make out the old woman's face. Chills race up her spine and she considers backing out, but she has come this far, and something takes hold of her body, compels her to obey. She sits on a low stool. It is much colder in here than in the sunlight outside.

"The three goddesses have told us you would come." The priestess's voice sounds like fall leaves scuttling in a whirlwind. Zo shivers again, but this time, not from the cold. She could swear she *knows* that voice.

But that is impossible.

Still, the crone continues in that eerily familiar voice. "What is it you seek?"

To change my fate, Zo thinks. *To save my child*. But she hesitates. "I—I…" She shuts her mouth as a cold breeze winds its way up the back of her neck. She is suddenly gravely aware of how the temple doors closed shut behind her with a low, muffled bang, sealing her in. How hard would it be for her to open them? "I think I've come to the wrong place. I'm sorry. Thank you for your time."

She starts to get up but hears the priestess laugh softly. Again, that stirring familiarity—but not the good and trusting kind.

Once, Zo was a trusting girl. She trusted that Cosmas wanted to marry her. She trusted that love would conquer fate; that if she were righteous enough, people would listen to her, that they would do the right thing.

That men existed not to hurt each other—not to wage wars but to build cities, not to take advantage of women but to adore them.

That even wise old soothsayers like Kohinoor meant only to protect and never to harm.

She doesn't believe those things anymore.

"Less than four months, I think, before your child is born," the priestess says.

Zo swallows hard. Even through the screen, in the dimness of the temple, her situation is no longer a secret.

"I must go," Zo says again.

"And where is it you think you'll go next? How far can you run from them?"

Zo freezes. "What do you mean, from *them*? What do you know?"

The priestess is silent for a moment, and in that silence, a creeping awareness begins to take hold of Zo. She *does* know this priestess, somehow. It's more than just her voice that's familiar. It's the weight of her gaze; even though she can't see her face, she can feel how the woman is watching her, studying her. She hasn't felt this exposed, this uncomfortable, since she realized Kohinoor was healing the injuries from her fall off the Pegasus in her cave in the Eastern Mountains, not out of kindness, but to try to steal her child.

"Live with us here, girl. We will take care of you both," the priestess says gently. But her offer feels stifling, like a wet cleaning rag being stuffed down Zo's throat, choking her from the inside. She can't breathe. She can't breathe!

She bolts upright, the child giving a violent kick in protest, and the little stool falls backward with a crash. She pushes away the screen, its legs screeching against the floor like the harsh cry of hunting birds. There sits the priestess—her gnarled hands up in front of her, as though in surrender...as though she has been caught.

Zo squints.

The woman doesn't just remind her of Kohinoor.

She *is* Kohinoor.

Kohinoor: the woman whom Zo last saw *hundreds of miles from here.* First on the slavers' trails outside of Sardis, then much farther east, by the caves of the Spirit Eaters, and now all the way here, across the sea, in this tiny temple outside Athens. Has she managed, somehow, to follow Zo all this way? That cannot be. Travel even for royals can be difficult and dangerous, but it must be impossible for those as weak and ancient as Kohinoor, so poor she lived in a cave and scrabbled for food in the hills.

Only some work of dark witchcraft could have transported her here.

It *can't* be her.

And yet it is.

As Zo gapes in shock, Kohinoor smiles gently, her blind, violet eyes unblinking and terrifying. "Princess, you cannot escape fate," she says calmly. "On the longest day of the year, you will suffer your longest night."

The longest day of the year. Summer solstice. That is just six months away. Nauseous with fear, Zo stumbles toward the door and pushes her way out into the morning. She runs, even though her body aches, her belly taut and sore and resisting. The cold, slimy, creeping feeling still follows her; her breath comes fast and short.

Eventually she is forced to stop and throw up at the side of the road. Acid burns her throat. Why didn't she buy a roll in the marketplace for breakfast? She feels light-headed and wonders if she imagined the whole thing. It isn't possible she saw Kohinoor just now. She begins to doubt herself. And if it *was* Kohinoor, and the woman did manage, somehow, to track Zo here, then is *anywhere* safe?

She wipes her mouth with the back of her hand, takes a shuddering breath, and moves on.

It's not until she reaches the Acharnian Gate that she stops, leans against the thick walls, and catches her breath, sinking to the ground. She closes her eyes and inhales deeply to stop the hammering of her heart and the spinning of her head. She must calm herself and *think*.

Near her, wheels creak. Horses whinny. A donkey utters a cry of stubborn protest over a man's loud commands.

She opens her eyes on a chilly Athens morning with life going on as normal. But normalcy has fled from Zo's life. It's not just the Assassins who are after her, seeking her blood. Kohinoor is following her, too, for reasons she cannot fully understand.

All she knows, with a sudden certainty, is this: Kohinoor wants the child.

Zo clenches her eyes shut, remembering that day, three months ago now, when she wandered into a cave adjoining Kohinoor's living quarters in the Eastern Mountains and found ancient paintings brushed onto the rough walls. One of the paintings— crude, hand drawn—depicted three old women on a loom, she now remembers. That's where she saw that image before.

Another one was a dark-haired girl falling from a Pegasus— just as Zo had fallen after the Spirit Eater attacked her. She also saw the capital of Persia, Persepolis, burning, people falling from cracked and flaming towers. And a winged child, its tiny arms holding a wax tablet, rising from the flames. The pictures seemed to indicate that a child was destined to save the world from destruction.

Zo had had the dizzying suspicion that it was *her* child.

Then the worst memory: the object Kohinoor had been diligently constructing, all while drugging Zo to keep her complacent. It had not been a table, as she said, but a crib. And next to it, Zo had found an adult-sized cage.

She didn't understand Kohinoor's plan then, and she doesn't now, but the woman had shown an unnerving amount of strength and cunning despite her feeble appearance, blindness, and age.

Zo tries to concentrate. She needs to get out of here.

If she sold some of the royal bridal jewels sewn into her robe, she would have enough money to go any number of places— Egypt, Rome, Crete, Jerusalem, Bactria... All the places Zo has ever learned about flash through her mind. Should she lose herself in the black northern forests of the Gauls? In the eternal grasslands of the Scythians? Or in the hot jungles of Africa, with their empires of wild beasts and mineral riches? Where in all the world can she hide, when not even the temples are safe?

That last night in Pella, Ochus asked her where she would go if she could go anywhere, do anything she wanted. She said Babylon. She wanted to study at the famous Royal Library, learn important things to teach her child, things she never cared about when she was a gossipy princess who ignored tutors she found deathly boring. But Babylon, in the heart of the Persian Empire, is not terribly far from Persepolis, home of Darius and his Assassins. It would be like wandering into a lion's den.

She needs a sign. She needs the Pegasus, whom she named Vata for the Persian goddess of the winds. If Vata landed here, on the Acharnian Road, and Zo hopped on, the magical creature would soar high above Athens and wing her way to exactly where Zo needed to be. *Pegasus sees the strings of Fate. Pegasus is never lost. Pegasus knows the way.* Zo remembers with a pang how she used to tell her little sister stories about the legendary winged horses, stories that made Roxana's dark eyes light up with excitement. But Roxana is dead, and the last time Zo saw Vata was in Persepolis, almost two thousand miles from here. No one is coming to tell her what to do, to show her the way.

She opens her eyes just as four tall Ethiopian slaves wearing leopard-skin cloaks and wide golden collars stride by, carrying an ornate litter, and set it down not far from where Zo sits crumpled on the ground. A white hand flashing an emerald ring pushes open the curtains, and a low, sensual voice calls to the commander at the gate, a barrel-chested man who grins and strides over. He pokes his head inside the curtains and laughs, agreeing to an assignation that evening. As he returns to his post, the woman pokes her head out and waves farewell, her gleaming chestnut hair piled under a golden tiara. She is clearly a hetaera.

This one is a different class entirely than the woman Zo saw staggering through the streets earlier this morning, before the sun had fully risen. Zo marvels at the whims of Fate—how fickle and unfair it is that some can be beaten down and bruised, while others are carried high above the heads of men, in control of their bodies and their destinies.

And it's then that clarity hits her. *This* is the sign she's been looking for.

Suddenly, Zo knows *exactly* where she must go.

CHAPTER SEVEN

DARIUS

THE MESSAGE CLUTCHED TIGHTLY IN HIS HAND, Darius, leader of the Assassins Guild, hurries through the torch-lit corridors of the many-domed palace of Persepolis. The Great King of Persia must hear the news from Darius himself.

This matter, like some of the rarest and deadliest blooms in Darius's poison garden, is delicate, to say the least.

Around him, the noise of dancing revelers swirls through windows facing the Courtyard of Palms. A raging bonfire in the outdoor enclosure celebrates the longest night of the year, the winter solstice, a time for music and joy and light in the nadir of darkness.

Darius knew better than to trust his son, Ochus, who had failed in his first mission to kill Princess Zofia. That was why, nearly three months ago, when Artaxerxes sent the girl to Macedon as Prince Alexander's bride, Darius inserted additional Assassins into the princess's escort. Several soldiers, of course, but also two attendants no one would ever have suspected—a eunuch and a sweet young handmaiden—and a few Greek-born Assassins who enlisted as Macedonian palace guards.

If Ochus didn't kill her this time, these others were supposed to do the job. Darius had envisioned himself telling Artaxerxes of the girl's murder at the hands of Alexander, an affront to Persia that would force the Great King to break the alliance and declare war on Macedon.

At last.

But that is *not* the news Darius just received.

He takes the curling steps three at a time up into the tower, slipping into the viewing-deck room unseen. Artaxerxes has his back to him, his tall conical crown glittering in the dancing torchlight. The eunuch Bagoas, the Great King's other trusted advisor, stands beside him, looking out over the bonfires below.

"Sire," Darius says, his well-practiced voice sliding out as smoothly seductive as always.

"Grandson," Artaxerxes says coolly, turning. His onyx eyes glint, just slightly.

Darius freezes, his mind racing with calculations.

He knows.

It is possible Bagoas has told the king already.

Perhaps Bagoas heard from his own spies and persuaded him that Darius is a traitor. Darius flicks his gaze subtly to the eunuch for some sign, but the dark eyes under heavy makeup are inscrutable.

Artaxerxes turns back to the railing, the chill wind whipping his long purple robes and white hair. With one word from Darius, his Assassins could kill the Great King's entire family and place Darius on the throne.

There's movement behind him. Darius turns to see four of the king's bodyguards with spears outstretched emerge on the tower.

Without turning, the king begins to speak. "Do you know why, Darius, I like this vantage point?"

Darius doesn't reply immediately. There is something odd in the king's tone that begs caution. He glances at the sprawling complex below—the gardens and courtyards alight with bonfires and celebrations, the barracks and racetracks, the stables for a thousand fine horses.

"To view your power, sire," he replies smoothly.

"Ah," Artaxerxes says, "a good reply, but not the right one." He finally turns again, and Darius drops into a deep bow. While his eyes are down, he hears a familiar sound: the scrape of a sword unsheathing. Instantly, Darius prostrates himself on the ground, hating the nearness of the dirty paving stones to his well-oiled beard, worried about the dust grinding into his flawless, finespun black robe. But such thoughts are foolishness. The other boot lands on his neck, followed by cold steel. Being the Great King's grandson will not help him, he knows. This king has even strangled his infant brothers in their cribs.

"I come up here," Artaxerxes continues, "to remember how thin the line is between king and peasant, power and death. Someone has betrayed me, Darius. Someone close in my ranks has been purposefully thwarting my goals for peace."

The sword presses more deeply into Darius's neck.

"Is that someone you?"

Darius inhales sharply, waiting for the fierce bite of the sword into flesh. "No, my king," he says. His voice is thin, yet steady. Deceit is one of his greatest skills.

"Think carefully," the king instructs. "The girl bride I sent to Alexander of Macedon was accompanied by *your* most trusted escort."

"Yes, Most High," Darius gasps out, the king's boot increasing its pressure on his windpipe.

"And yet...the girl is gone. Your son is gone. And many in my military escort have been mysteriously slaughtered. Can you explain this?"

"Perhaps my son has rescued the princess from some Macedonian plot," he says calmly, as if he were sitting across from the king over hot spiced wine and not prostrating himself with his face pressed painfully into the stone floor.

"Oddly, King Philip and Prince Alexander hadn't arrived yet in Pella when Ochus and the princess disappeared. Perhaps *your son* stole her away to prevent an alliance with Macedon," the king retorts.

"I don't know what happened, sire," Darius assures him, hoping the king will hear the truth ringing in his voice. "But I do know this." He inhales for the speech he has prepared, but the crushing of his windpipe under the king's boot turns his voice into an unpleasant gasp. "No matter whom I sent to escort the princess, the results would have been the same."

"And why is that?"

"Because the gods ordained it so," Darius says with the last of his breath.

The pressure of the foot lightens on his neck. "Explain," the king commands.

Darius inhales, conscious of the fluttering of his heart, subtle, like a frantic moth. Nothing an observer would notice, of course. "My king, the gods have been against this alliance since the beginning," he says. "First Princess Zofia was kidnapped by slave traders before she could travel to Macedon. Then we sent three other princesses as brides, and they were murdered on the Royal Road. Miraculously, Princess Zofia flew into Persepolis on a Pegasus and, ignoring all the messages the gods tried to give us, we sent her to Macedon, where she has disappeared."

"Are those dire messages from the gods or from men?" the Great King asks.

"The flooding of Byzantium, my king. Is *that* a message from a man?" Darius replies, his voice rising along with his frustration. "Did a *man* shake the earth and send waves taller than any building to batter King Philip's wedding?"

The king's boot is no longer at his neck, nor is the tip of any blade. Still, Darius doesn't stir. "Even the Greek gods themselves are attacking Macedon," he continues, more hurriedly than he had planned. "Poseidon, Earth-Shaker, ruined King Philip's wedding and destroyed his newly conquered city. Their gods have made it clear they will not lift a finger to protect Macedon. Now is the time for Persia to attack."

Darius hears the king's heavy jeweled robes flap in the brisk wind and knows he is considering his answers. Then Bagoas speaks in his oddly high, silken voice.

"Lord Darius is right, Most High. Verethragna, god of war and victory, has told our priests the same. We must no longer ignore the signs and omens of the gods. If we do, they will surely punish our stubbornness with earthquakes and giant waves."

Darius waits for what seems like an eternity. Finally, he hears Artaxerxes sheathe his sword.

"Rise."

He pushes himself up on all fours, like a dog, then stands awkwardly and brushes the dust off his cheek and his fine black robe.

The Great King smiles at him. "I choose to believe you...for now. We will hold a council of war."

The king's words wash over him as Artaxerxes ducks to pass through the doorway, followed by the guards. As their footsteps fade down the stairs, Darius's heart continues its shameful battering. His eyes rise to meet those of Bagoas, which now sparkle with sly humor.

A cold understanding passes between them that requires no words. Artaxerxes, though sharp in mind and healthy in body, is in his eighties. His numerous heirs are either at each other's throats or drunkards or cowards or all three.

Who will be the next king of the Persian Empire? Who will be left standing?

Darius, himself, of course.

And when he is, he will surely reward his allies.

But in the meantime, there's a war to be fought.

CHAPTER EIGHT

ALEXANDER

DESPITE THE WINTER CHILL, SWEAT DRIPS INTO
Alexander's eyes as he sidesteps Heph in the training arena outside
the Pellan palace. Heph's ax comes slicing out of nowhere, cutting
through the cold dawn air, and Alex pivots just in time, hoping
his weak left leg won't buckle. He raises his own ax, his muscles singing with the effort. The two handles meet with a bone-
shaking *thud*. Alex feints to the right, but Heph doesn't commit.
He's springy, light on the balls of his feet, watching Alex coolly,
refusing to fall for any of his tricks. Suddenly Heph attacks, beating Alex back with calm determination.

Ever since Heph and Kat woke him from his possession, Alex
has felt…altered. Bereft. He no longer sees deep-buried secrets
in the eyes of men, no longer feels that heady transport from
the current moment into one of the past. And he can't help but
guess at the truth: that when Riel died, leaving Alexander's
body, he took all of Alexander's Snake Blood Magic with him.

Alex's magic is gone.

And twinning that loss is the disappearance of Kat. They never
found her after the waters receded in Byzantium. Instead, Alex
received a note from a beggar boy several days after their return

to Pella, which said simply, *She is too weak to travel, but trust that she is safe with me. She is healing.*

The note was from Jacob. The Earth Blood. Kat's first love. And it indicated he would pick up messages at a bakery near the Temple of Ares, behind the Byzantine palace.

Heph was worried, but Alex argued that if Jacob wanted to kill her or turn her over to the Aesarian Lords for her Blood Magic, why would he have written the prince to let him know she was safe?

Heph still wants to go back to Byzantium, stake out the bakery, find Kat, and bring her home. He has brought it up nearly every day since the note arrived, and Alex is sure he's still furious at him for insisting that they stay here in Pella, where they are needed most.

But for now, for this brief instant in the training arena, with sand covering his legs and shifting beneath his feet, all of the prince's focus narrows into the blade, into Heph's form as they circle each other. There is nothing but this moment. The dark, undulating memories of the Byzantine flood, which haunt his dreams, and the strange time of possession where he lost himself to the control of his father-god, Riel, have fallen away. The uncertainty about Kat. The loss of his Snake Blood Magic. The great emptiness yawning open inside him is, for these brief moments, disguised, and he feels alive.

Before he ever understood his magic, before he ever met his twin sister, before he woke up back in his own body at the disaster that King Philip's eighth wedding had become—before any of that, there was Heph. His oldest friend. His sparring mate. When Alex saw him floating, facedown, in the black swirling waters of the palace, a raw fear the like of which he had never before known sliced through him. And when the cold, corpse-like figure started to retch and cough, even as the table they floated on was sucked out into the foaming tide, Alex cried tears of joy and gratitude to the gods.

Now Heph's face is like the theater mask of a warrior—cold-eyed, tight-jawed, and absolutely imperturbable. His best friend has truly changed, Alex realizes, with a brief but not unpleasant flutter of surprise. Before, when they trained, Heph would show off, making the dazzling move, crowing with pride before he truly won, and often getting himself in trouble because of it. Now, he's pure concentration, all graceful skill and unyielding strength. He no longer bothers to comb that wild dark hair, and its disarray suits him, makes him seem older and more rugged. Familiar and yet different.

Heph's ax blade strikes Alex's as the clang of iron on iron rings out. Alex feels the strength of the blow shoot up his arm and into his shoulder, giving him a thrill of fear. Heph seizes the advantage, pummeling Alex's ax until it flies out of his hand and lands at an angle in the sand.

"Well done," Alex says, stripped of his weapon, breathless. He claps Heph on the back, his hand meeting the bulge of Heph's shoulder muscles.

Heph doesn't reply, and despite the physical release of sparring, Alex can still feel the tension in Heph's body—the fury, the frustration. And more than that. Heph is heartbroken over Kat.

"Are you thinking of her?"

Alex's question seems to startle Heph, and he nods. At least he hasn't lost the connection with his best friend—that feeling of two souls who are perfectly in tune with each other even without magic.

"If something was gravely wrong with Kat, Jacob would let us know," Alex says for what feels like the hundredth time, but his voice trails off. Despite his lost powers, the prince's bond with Kat is immutable, eternal. She could not leave the earth without him sensing it, without him knowing. "And in the meantime, we have to stay focused."

"Focused. So you've said." Heph sits down on a bench, opens a pot of beeswax, and inserts two fingers. "It's *almost* like you're testing me," he says and starts spreading the pale yellow lump on the handle of his ax to lubricate the wood—without a good coating of wax, winter would bring out all its splinters.

Alex sits down beside him, resting his arms on his knees. Watching Heph carefully massage the ax handle, he marvels again at how much his friend has changed. Before, he would have defied Alex, would have gone against orders to search the entire city of Byzantium for her, but now he's finally focused on *duty*. And his duty—*their* duty—is to protect Macedon and the world from its newest horror:

The Spirit Eaters.

Because the creature that attacked the wedding in Byzantium was a Spirit Eater, he's certain.

No, this isn't a test of Heph's loyalty. This is real. Heph said he'd seen something unsettling during the flood—a black spread of wings beneath the water, a shadow that seemed to morph like a cloud of claw and fang in the waves, reaching for Kat. And then there were the bodies...at least three corpses in the ruins of the palace itself that seemed to have been almost entirely devoured, and many others found in town. Based on everything he learned while possessed by Riel, combined with everything Heph learned from Ada during his time on the island, they've spent the last few weeks piecing together some semblance of a theory: the Spirit Eaters are, clearly, spreading their reach far beyond the Eastern Mountains, possibly north into Scythia and east toward Bactria. Some have found their way as far west as Byzantium.

Alex rubs his thumb over his ax handle, picks off a splinter, and flicks it away. "The prophecies warned that the world was poised between ushering in an Age of Men or an Age of Monsters. Riel would have allowed the monsters to rule the earth, and I would rule over the Age of Men. Riel is dead. That can only mean I will vanquish the Spirit Eaters." He feels like a broken marionette at this point, but adds, "What we need is a solid plan."

"What we need," Heph argues, forcing the cork back into the pot of beeswax, "is an *army*. The Spirit Eaters live hundreds of miles deep in Persian territory, and the last I've heard, the Great King's troops are poised to pounce the moment you get off the ship. It's a shame your father's skull is as thick as one of these," he says, handling the blade carefully. "Nothing gets through."

It's true—Philip has so far refused to believe anything they have told him with regard to the greatest threat to their nation. It seems the king prefers to focus on wars he knows he can win— wars with men, not monsters.

Dark smoke curls up from the blacksmith's next to the barracks, and the metallic pounding of hammer on iron rings out in the early-morning light. Even now, Brygos, the palace blacksmith, is making or repairing weapons for Philip's army, the army that has built Macedon from a hardscrabble land of feuding cattle raiders into a power strong enough to challenge Athens, or even Persia.

Alex shakes his head. "His pride won't let him accept the truth." That his own wedding was ill-fated, overtaken by a destructive force beyond the workings of nature. In fact, Philip becomes furious at the mere suggestion that people believe the disaster was a bad omen for Macedonian rule over Byzantium. His repeated defense is that the earthquakes and waves were caused by Lord Poseidon drinking too much in celebration of the wedding. If the gods were angry at him, he points out, why did he and Cleo emerge unscathed from their upstairs palace rooms while the waters killed and injured hundreds of others?

Heph smiles. "Maybe the goal shouldn't be to get him to believe us, in that case."

Before Alex can question his line of thinking, Heph looks at something behind him and closes his mouth.

Alex turns in time to see Straton, his father's elderly manservant, approaching, his dazzling white hair like snow in a sunbeam.

"My lord," says the man with a bow. "Your father would see you."

"This early?" Alex darts a glance at Heph. Ever since his wedding with the luscious young Cleo, the king has taken to rising quite late.

Straton nods, his coal-black eyes twinkling. "He says it's to do, my lord, with the disappearance of your bride."

Zofia. The woman promised to Alexander—the one who showed up in Pella while Alex was away, but disappeared before his return, almost as though she could sense from afar his disinterest in ever meeting her. Perhaps she had as great a reluctance to meet him.

Well, if it gets Philip to talk about Persia with him, it will be a fruitful morning. "We are on our way," Alex says, and Straton darts off quickly for a man of his age, dust and sand rising at his heels.

A chilly breeze swirls through the slatted shutters in the king's office, waving the bloodstained battle flags hanging from the walls. In between the banners are spears, shields, and swords, trophies of Philip's many victorious battles. Alex has always loved the king's office better than any other room in the palace. It is a man's room, a soldier's room.

Heph stands respectfully by the door as Alex walks up to the king's desk, careful to hide his limp. Philip drums his large fingers on the highly polished ebony surface, which smells of lemon and beeswax. Then he looks up toward the door and makes a dismissive gesture. "You may leave, Coxcomb," he says, using the nickname he gave Heph years ago for being vain about his appearance. "I want a private discussion with my son."

Without hesitation, Heph slams his right fist on his chest and walks out in long, smooth strides.

As Philip rubs his bushy red-brown beard, pondering, Alex studies the man he had always believed to be his father. He had, in the way of boys with their fathers, loved him, feared him, wanted to be just like him, wanted to be nothing like him, and wanted to be much better than him.

Now he is no longer a boy—and he knows the truth.

Still, some of Alex's earliest memories are of the king carrying him proudly in his arms at palace feasts, showing his beautiful son off to visiting ambassadors. Alex will never forget his excitement on his sixth birthday, when Philip gave him a hunting pup, the pick of the litter. When Alex was thirteen, the king took him into a skirmish—his first battle, really—against mountain cattle raiders, staying at his side the whole time to prevent him from being wounded.

There were also not-so-good memories. The time a ten-year-old Alex drank the king's best Chian wine, stumbled into the throne room when Philip was giving an audience to Persian emissaries, and promptly threw up in his father's lap. Philip took off his belt, pulled up his son's tunic, and whipped his bare bottom in front of everyone. Alex's humiliation hurt far more than the physical pain.

What would the king do now if he knew the truth?

"You trust him?" Philip asks, after the door has clicked shut behind Heph.

"With my life," Alex replies firmly.

The king grunts again, picks up an oenochoe, and sloshes wine into his cup. "You trusted that traitor Kadmus, too. By his own account, he was spying for Persia while serving as a general in my army."

"Kadmus only did it because Persia threatened to kill his family members living in the empire. He confessed everything to me, begging me to execute him as his just punishment." He clears his throat, remembering how Kadmus had confessed far more than regret or loyalty. "But I convinced him to make amends to Macedon by continuing to work as Persia's spy and reporting back to us. While you were in Byzantium, he was invaluable. But what does this have to do with my fiancée and her disappearing act?"

King Philip is silent. He plucks an ivory toothpick from his desk and digs in between his big yellow teeth. "The princess of Sardis was a pawn in a much larger game, it seems. My intelligence has it she was meant to be killed upon arrival, her murder blamed on us as a means to incite war."

This is a twist. "And presumably Artaxerxes is behind this plot?" Maybe convincing his father to take on Persia will not require as much work as Alex thought. And once in Persia, he will find a way to seek out the Spirit Eaters.

The king grunts and shrugs. "Perhaps Artaxerxes is playing a double game with us," Philip says, his words muffled by the toothpick, "or, he truly wants an alliance, but other forces within his great nation do not."

"So, the princess has escaped her fate," Alex says, thinking how glad he was to find he had escaped his, too. As with most royal marriages, neither the bride nor the groom in this one was eager for the wedding. When he first arrived in Pella from Byzantium and heard of her disappearance, he assumed she had run away in the chaotic aftermath of the guards' murders, grasping desperately for the freedom no princesses ever had. But now, knowing she is prey, the thought of the young foreign girl, alone, afraid, and hunted, touches something deep inside him. "Perhaps it is not too late to send investigators to detect her whereabouts," he adds. "She is in a highly vulnerable state, if what you say is true—and she could be an asset to us either way."

The king scoffs. "I'm not worried about the princess."

Philip's heartlessness irritates Alex. Kings must be brutal at times, he knows, but it would cost Philip nothing to try to find the forsaken girl. "If they find her, her own men will kill her," he protests.

"Her life doesn't matter to me. Listen, Alexander. There are many things for people to fear. But do you know one of the most feared? Us. Macedon. The Greek nations tremble in terror of us. They fear us, and they covet what we have. We cannot rush east, giving our neighbors ample opportunity to invade an undefended Macedon. We conquer the rest of the Greeks first—*then* we take on Persia."

Alex is about to argue back that to focus on the Greek nations could be a fatal distraction from the real threat to Macedon—Persia and the Spirit Eaters—but stops himself. He's right, Alex suddenly realizes. Of course, he is. How could he have missed it? A heavy weight presses on his chest when he realizes that, for the first time in a long time, he feels like the youngest cadet. There is no immediate gratification in war—only a long and steady journey of building up one's forces, gathering strength, and perfecting strategy. You don't get what you want overnight. Alex should know that by now.

"I will march with you, Father," he says, his heart speeding up and mind racing even faster. Once in Persia, he will find a way to make Philip see the truth of the Spirit Eaters, the magnitude of the danger.

As soon as they are actually equipped to handle it.

Philip tilts his head and studies Alex. "And your regency?"

"You can select a regency council to govern while we go to war," Alex says, thinking swiftly. "I need not be a part of it."

Philip strokes his beard thoughtfully as his single dark eye bores into his son. "Based on your recent victories against the Aesarian Lords," he says slowly, "I believe that you would be of more service to your country on the front lines. Alexander, I would be pleased to have you join me."

Alex is shocked at the thrill that moves through him. After all this time, his father's approval still matters. More than that: this is the greatest compliment Philip has ever—*could* ever—give him. Alex has inured himself to the king's gruff insults and harsh criticisms, but now Philip is willingly calling him a great warrior. It's a strange feeling.

"Thank you, sir," he manages to say with an air of confidence. "When do we depart?"

"We'll use the winter to prepare the army," he says. "And leave for Athens around the time of the spring equinox."

"Athens?"

"Yes," the king replies. "Only once Athens is crushed beneath our heel will we be able to defend ourselves against Persia. Demosthenes continues to stir the Athenians against me, and he will grow more dangerous if left unchecked."

The Athenian statesman, Demosthenes, Alex knows, is the greatest orator in the known world, whose powerful speeches could almost rouse the dead to enthusiastic applause. Unfortunately, he has devoted much of his talent into whipping the Athenians into an alliance against Macedon.

Alex nods and turns to leave.

"Wait."

Alex turns back. Philip steeples his large fingers, frowning, and says, "There are two other things I wish to discuss with you. They are…delicate matters."

Alex's heart starts to flutter, but he says nothing, nodding respectfully.

"The first one is this. It seems Cleo is, well, in a *condition*."

"Condition?" This is not the direction Alex was anticipating.

The king waves a dismissive hand. "Late in her bleeding. With child, they think. It is hardly confirmed, but I know she will go running that mouth of hers, and by dinner, the whole court will have heard. I wanted to be the one to tell you."

Alex feels cold as ice, unable to move, unable to breathe. Once, on a winter hunting trip with Heph, a snowstorm hit. Crossing a frozen stream, Alex tumbled in and got soaked, from his boots to his fur hat, quickly becoming too numb to feel anything besides panic. He is like that now, but worse. Philip knows the truth, and he will disinherit him for this child if it is a boy.

Still frozen with dread, Alex nods. "Excellent news, Father. Let us hope Cleo is indeed with child and carries a boy."

The king seems satisfied with the response. "It is a good thing for a king to have more than one son," he says. "And poor Arridheus, even if he turns up, could never be king."

A pang grips Alex's heart. Last summer, his twelve-year-old half brother, Philip's son from a servant girl, was kidnapped by unknown enemies and never found. Arri has the mind of a much younger child, and often Alex pictures him afraid, tongue-tied, abused, without the ability to escape or find help.

The king's gaze wanders over unrolled maps on his desk. "Second…"

So, there's more.

"This Katerina. Ever since the girl appeared at the Battle of Pellan Fields last summer, rumors have abounded. I hadn't planned on even dignifying them by discussing them, but still they continue." He fixes his eye on Alexander. "Who is she?"

Alex exhales, choosing his words carefully. "She is my sister, Father. My twin." He doesn't say, *Your daughter.*

Philip snorts. "How can you be so sure? As you know, it is treason for an imposter to claim royalty. It could be punished with death."

"Which is why someone who does so must have very good reason." Alex inhales deeply and tries to calm the hammering of his heart. "Look, Father," he continues, "when you were in Byzantium, I spent a great deal of time with Katerina. It was as if I found the missing part of my soul. We are so much alike. And she wants nothing from us. She even risked her life to go on a mission to Egypt while I was regent."

Philip shakes his head. "I just can't fathom why Olympias would have thrown this child away at birth and never told me. It's hard to believe that even she—a selfish witch with the morals of a Persian cutpurse—would do such a thing."

"You know how superstitious Mother is," Alex replies, ignoring the slur on Olympias—because of its truth, among other reasons. "Leonidas showed her a prophecy of ill omen."

Philip nods. "By all the gods, I most certainly do. I believe you, Alexander. But I don't want this ridiculous prophecy to get out."

"It's hard to stop rumors," Alexander says, thinking of the many that surround him. That he was born of a god. That he could speak with his horse. That he could practically read men's souls. But, of course, these are all true. *Were* true.

"Then we must attempt to quell just one—that your mother had Katerina by another man. It makes me look the fool, her the whore, and you, quite possibly, illegitimate."

He tilts his head, a smile playing on his lips. Alex feels color flood his face.

Philip *knows*.

The king pushes back his chair with a scrape and, to Alex's surprise, puts a muscular arm around his shoulder and whispers, "And we can't have that now, can we?"

Is Philip saying he knows but doesn't care? That he will keep Alexander as his heir? And if so, is it pride that will prevent him from disowning his popular warrior son? Or something else?

The king chuckles and goes to the window overlooking the palace's entrance courtyard. "We will say this girl is my daughter by another woman," he says. "Bastards only burnish a man's reputation for virility, after all. And it's not too late for her to prove useful to me—she is the perfect age for marriage."

Alex's heart sinks. "Yes, Father."

"Do you know where she is?" he asks, the eye boring into him.

"No, Father," Alex replies truthfully. "I last saw her in Byzantium, the day of your wedding, and heard that she survived the flood."

"Send a search party for her," Philip commands, turning toward him. "Let me know when you have found her. I will send an honor guard to fetch her here. Perhaps we can marry her into one of the top families in Athens. Or… No, come to think of it, I have a better idea."

The king does not continue, and Alex has to bite his tongue to stop himself from asking what plan he has in mind for Kat. Alex feels as though he's used up his allocation of luck for the day.

"May I leave?" Alex asks.

The king flicks his fingers in a gesture of dismissal.

Alex bows, then hurries from the office. He's resolved to send agents to learn Kat's whereabouts as soon as possible. But not to bring her home. To warn her to stay far away from Macedon if she values her freedom.

CHAPTER NINE

AESOP

IT IS THE DEPTH OF NIGHT. AESOP LIES STILL IN THE
slave quarters so as not to wake his master, Otus. Otus is chained
to him, wrist to wrist, and currently snoring like a pig in Aesop's ear.

With his unchained arm, the boy reaches down and feels for
the knife hidden beneath his tunic, his movements subtle and
quiet as the night.

Aesop's tongue was cut out when he was five. Now he is
eleven, which means he has lived more than half his life in silence, and all his life a slave.

But no more.

There are certain advantages to being mute. People say and
do things right in front of you as if you were their dog—things
they would never do in front of someone who could speak. They
mistake a lack of response for a lack of understanding.

But Aesop understands far more than anyone knows.

He knows about Queen Cynane and her invisible Smoke
Man. About the Blood of True Betrayal and the magic powers it brings. Hiding in the courtyard, he saw Queen Cynane
kill the Smoke Man, and the blood of his heart burst over her.

He saw the smoke and fire enter her body, giving her the magic.

And he believes that Papari, now Lord Timaeus, killed the mad king to get the same magic. He and Otus were walking by when he saw Papari enter the king's rooms with hot water and a sharp razor shortly before he raised the alarm that the king was murdered.

Though he blamed it on Queen Cynane, Papari must have killed the mad king, who'd cut out Aesop's tongue.

Is the enemy of your enemy your friend?

Cold wind howls down the smoke hole of the kitchens, where the slaves sleep. Several mutter and groan, clutching thin blankets. If Otus makes a loud sound before Aesop is finished, he will wake the others and Aesop will lose his chance. He must be swift, then.

Sitting up, he is careful not to move his left hand, which is chained to Otus's right one. Slowly, he pulls the vial Lord Timaeus handed him in secret earlier from beneath his belt and removes the cork with his teeth. Then he drinks it and almost retches. It is as bitter as gall. He feels as if he has inside him all the foul dead things of the world. It sears like flames down his throat and spreads across his chest. Once the urge to vomit has passed, Aesop braces himself. Though all the torches are out, and the shutters closed, he can see well enough to do the deed. A sliver of moonlight floats through the smoke hole above the hearth, and some coals still glow orange.

He positions the knife right above Otus's heart and then, using the full force of his weight, he thrusts.

The blade pierces through skin and breastbone and muscle into soft, palpating flesh.

Otus's eyes open wide and he gasps and gurgles, but not louder than someone murmuring in his sleep. The eyes stay open and gleam white as hard-boiled eggs as air rattles out of Otus's throat. Blood blooms on his tunic. Dark, red, and glistening.

The blood of betrayal. Blood spilled by a slave who has betrayed his master.

Fiery pain explodes inside Aesop, as if someone has thrown him onto a bonfire. Flames and smoke, ashes and soot coat his throat, choke his lungs, eat his internal organs, burn his skin. He cups both hands over his mouth to avoid crying out as he writhes on his sleeping mat.

And then, just as swiftly, the pain flickers out. Aesop, too exhausted to stir, curls up on his side and gasps for air. He faces Otus's corpse, ghastly white in the moonlight, the blood on his tunic almost black.

Suddenly, Aesop feels as if a strong wind carrying vibrant sparks is hurling itself through his veins. Power rises inside him, vanquishing weakness and fatigue.

Slowly, he sits up and sets to work on his slave master's hand, sawing through bone. Finally, he picks up the bloody hand and sets it on Otus's stomach.

It is over.

He is free.

Just as Lord Timaeus promised.

ACT TWO
ENEMIES & ALLIES

You will never do anything in this world without courage.
It is the greatest quality of mind next to honor.

—Aristotle

CHAPTER TEN

KATERINA

SHADOWS, WIDE AND BLACK WINGED AND MASSIVE
as clouds, engulf her.

The water pours over and around her, drowning out the pain. Her
screams are swallowed in the waves.

Something wants her. Something has its claws in her, tearing through
skin, through self, through soul. She feels torn and limp.

The world goes black.

Waters full of horror surround her, suck her down into a whirlpool of sad-
ness. Trapped in the dark, airless bottom, she feels all the death and loss that
anyone on earth has ever suffered. She is no longer Kat. She is Despair.

Through the blackness comes a flickering lamp. A cackling laugh. A
wrinkled face that becomes three faces.

An old woman. Or three old women, each rippling into the others.

Each unspooling a ball of yarn through the darkness.

Only it isn't yarn—it shines as silver and glows as the sharp knit-
ting needles that glint and clack, glint and clack. With each tiny move
of a needle, Kat feels a stabbing, feels pulled, twisted, entrapped in an
invisible web.

★ ★ ★

Now she is in Ada's abandoned palace in Caria—covered floor to ceiling in an intricate snare of spiderwebs. Her magic tugs at her from within as if bursting to escape. Her soul has scattered into the corners of the darkness, tiny spiders racing off in every direction, until she is nothing.

She is nothing.

She is nothing.

She wakes screaming.

Jacob appears in the darkness, real, though wavering, as if he has emerged from the sound of her voice. How long had she been screaming before he came? She reaches out weakly to touch his face. She must feel the warmth of him. She must assure herself that this is not another dream.

By some miracle, it is him. And he is here. They are together again. It must be a dream. He had gone forever, become an Aesarian Lord, Macedon's enemy.

His family burned. Because of her.

He hates her. Now he is her enemy, too.

No. He saved her life. Didn't he?

On the battlefield, he kissed her. She nearly died then, too, but something changed.

His lips had been warm and gentle against her own. A pulse, a wave of heat moving through her, connecting them… Bringing her back to life. She remembers.

Kat tosses in her sweat-laden sheets.

Now his strong hand is on her skin, brushing stray hairs, damp with sweat, from her face.

Yes. She takes a deep, calming breath at his touch. Yes, he is real. He will help pull her from the pain of despair, of death and loss.

He stays by her side until she falls back to sleep.

In her weeks-long delirium, images and conversations, real and imagined, swirl around her:

Heph on the island of Meninx, confiding his deepest secrets. Riel offering her the entire world if she would only betray Alexander. His hands around her neck, squeezing the life out of her.

The needle on the mechanism pointing right at...Jacob. The boy she had grown up with. The boy she had hunted with. The boy whom she had milked the goats and swept the kiln with.

He'd been there all along. An Earth Blood.

It has been a month since the flood, and still Kat's body is weak, her mind stuck and swimming in the darkness of her thoughts and memories.

The only thing anchoring her is this knowledge: Jacob is here. He forgives her. He is taking care of her. Through his touch, he has been healing the deep lacerations all over her body—her shoulder, her hip, both legs. She doesn't remember his healing her, exactly, only spasms of pain that are there and then gone. A warmth like a radiating light moving through her limbs at his touch.

Even as her physical body heals, the inner pain continues, a pain much worse than the cruel claws that raked her skin in the freezing maelstrom of the Byzantine flood. It's as if her spirit itself has been mauled and torn, pulled and sucked almost completely out of her. There is a sadness in her now, so strong and deep that she thinks it must be welded to her soul and she will never lose it.

She is grateful to Jacob, and yet...when she wakes to find him gone, out to get supplies or whatever he has been doing beyond the closed door of her little room, she wishes he'd just left her to die. Death would be better than this ache, this yawning, yearning emptiness at the heart of her.

She is afraid she will never be herself again.

She has been touched by something evil.

She wakes again, her mind clearer than it has been in a long time. Her hand goes automatically to her neck, searching for the silver lotus blossom pendant that had belonged to the woman who raised her, Helen. She feels its cool, smooth surface and smiles. She didn't lose it in the flood, then. She props herself up and glances around the little attic room. Today her forehead is cool.

Jacob is standing by the window, looking out on a cold gray day.

All she can do, lying weakly on the little bed, is drink him in. His height, the width of his shoulders, the strength of his legs. The broad, friendly face that seems handsomer now, chiseled by loss and longing.

This is—and has always been—her Jacob.

She has loved him since childhood, of course, for his kindness and sturdiness and laughter. But she overlooked him, too. She didn't really want to marry her childhood friend from the farm. She wanted someone completely new and exciting. Someone like Heph.

But now…

"Jacob," she says softly, barely louder than a whisper.

And when he turns, a smile illuminates his face so brightly that she thinks she can feel its heat from across the room.

He comes to her bed and sits, placing a hand on her forehead. She shivers slightly at his touch.

"The fever has broken," he says. He looks so happy that something inside her shatters all over again. There has been so much time lost. There's so much they don't know about each other.

She misses Heph—and Alexander. Her brother, her *twin*.

But at this moment, there is a comfort in being here—wherever they are—with Jacob. Just Jacob. The rightness of it being him. The power he exudes, partly the result of his Earth Blood blooming, partly because he has grown from a boy to a man. A stranger, handsome and hard and distant—but still her Jacob, the one person she knows the heart of better than anyone else in the world.

Over the next days and nights, they reacquaint themselves with each other. She learns that, in the aftermath of the flood, after they washed up on a nearby beach, Jacob hastily found a dry room for them on the top floor of this narrow, abandoned town house within walking distance of the Byzantium harbor.

He manages, somehow, to find that other attic room where she and Heph hastily left their belongings before they set out for the royal wedding, where the waves parted them. And he brings back her cherished sword and her bags, one of them containing some two dozen curious blue-glazed figurines shaped like little mummies—ushabtis. Kat saw the brawny warriors, all sharing the soul of the great Egyptian general Wazba, transform into the statuettes, and scooped them into her bag as Princess Laila's palace caught fire.

Gradually, Kat explains everything to Jacob—her trip down the Nile with Heph and the mechanism she and Heph created with the help of Aristotle and Ada of Caria. She tells Jacob how she discovered her true parentage—how Prince Alexander is her twin brother. And—though she pauses briefly, wondering if *Lord* Jacob should know—she tells him about her Snake Blood abilities. That Riel, the Last God, was, in fact, her true father, and with Jacob's blood on the hairpin, she killed him, freeing Alexander from his evil possession.

In turn, Jacob explains how his blood came to be on the hairpin, that after the queen told him she had murdered his family, he grabbed her wrist and she sliced his arm with it. Then he killed her.

"I'm not so sure she is dead," Kat says now, watching the oil lamp next to her bed sputter, threatening to plunge them into darkness. "When I arrived in the room, there was no sign of her body." The details are coming back to her more clearly now: the hairpin, the streaks of blood on the mosaic floor.

"Then," Jacob says grimly, tipping a bit more oil into the lamp, "either she dragged herself out of the room or someone else disposed of the body."

He sets the oil jug down with a hard click, squeezes his eyes closed, and hangs his head so low that his chin almost touches his chest.

When she found out last summer, Kat, too, grieved deeply for the family who had raised her. And she will always mourn. But Jacob's grief is fresher, sharper, like a dark living thing gnawing his insides.

He stares into the glowing lamp flame. "Dragged herself out of the room," he repeats, shaking his head. "She's one person I wish I *had* killed. Instead, I killed hundreds of innocent people."

He stands and starts pacing the little room. "My rage unleashed hell's deep. I am the cause of so much death and destruction, not just here, but in Delphi, too. Me." She can see how his entire body seems weighted with guilt.

"Jacob, it's not your fault—"

"It *is* my fault," he says, approaching her. "Thousands here in Byzantium were injured. I couldn't control it. But I can try to make up for it. Because it's my fault."

No.

It isn't his fault that he was born with this magic in his blood and that he was never taught how to use it. Just like it isn't her fault that her mother was the cruel Queen Olympias and her father the evil Last God, Riel.

Before he can resume his restless pacing, she takes his hand— so warm and strong—and curls her fingers around it.

"Jacob," she says. Because there is one thing she remembers more clearly than anything else—the reason she and Heph were searching for an Earth Blood in the first place. "Your powers *can* be used for good. We must destroy the Spirit Eaters, or they will devour the world. You can help us defeat them."

Jacob looks uncertain, but he allows her to pull him down onto the edge of her bed again. "Perhaps," he says, though he seems doubtful. "But in the meantime, I have been doing all I can to make amends."

He tells her about the past few weeks of agony as he tended to her, waiting for her to get better. How he left every day while she slept to ask those he met in the streets if they knew of injured people who required a skilled physician. Quietly, he visited them, healing their wounds. Slowly, he has been undoing part of the damage he caused, one survivor at a time.

"I want to help you," Kat says, sitting up in bed.

"Not yet, Kat. You are still so weak."

But soon, with his help, she grows stronger, begins to stay awake longer. Even sitting at the tiny table to eat is exhausting at first, but she forces herself every day to do more than the day before. Slowly, she begins to walk again, practicing in the small room, one hand against the wall. And just when she thinks she will die of frustrated boredom, Jacob deems her well enough to leave the house.

Kat bites her lip, fighting back a cry of pain as she pushes her way through the bedroom door and down a narrow hall. It has been six weeks, she realizes, since she's been outside, and her body protests loudly as she walks down the three flights of stairs. She sees waterlogged plaster and smells pungent mold.

"Are you all right, Kat?" Jacob asks, turning back to check on her.

"Yes," she says, forcing a smile. "At least, I will be soon."

He forces open the swollen front door to the street. As Kat carefully emerges into an icy wind, she gasps at the devastation all around her. Doors and shutters have been torn off the lower floors of the mud-caked buildings. A fishing boat protrudes from a second-floor window across the street, and a building on the corner has collapsed entirely. Part of her wants to return to their cozy nest on the top floor, the small attic room easily warmed by a brazier.

But she's not sure she has the energy.

"It was much worse right after," Jacob says, gesturing. "The streets were filled with boats, furniture, dead horses. I even saw a dolphin. Many people left the city, afraid of more floods, but they have started to trickle back now, ready to clear out the rubble and rebuild."

Kat sees a bonfire at the far end of the street. A sickly sweet, acrid smell fills her nostrils and she rubs her nose. "What is that?" she asks, pointing.

"A pyre." Jacob's mouth twists. "Whenever they clear out rubble, they find bodies…"

Kat shudders. Though the air is cold and the wind off the harbor brisk, she is assailed by the smells of mildew and rot and the lingering scent of burning human flesh. *Pain here.* So much loss and death and grief she is almost overwhelmed. She wants to sink to the ground and cry. Instead, she squares her shoulders and forces the despair back down.

Looking around, she sees that most of the properties are abandoned, but there are also signs of returning life. The city reverberates with the sounds of hammering and sawing, and the creaking of carts loaded with rubbish on the way out of town, or wooden planks and tools on the way in. A few bakeries are open, and a tavern, and Jacob points out a shop selling warm cloaks where he bought Kat's thick russet one, probably looted from an abandoned home, he said.

She nods, unable to reply as the exercise has made it difficult to breathe. Holding on to Jacob's arm, she feels slightly dizzy. He stops abruptly.

"This is too much for you your first time out," Jacob says. "Let's go back. There's time."

"No," Kat says forcefully. "There *isn't* time. We've lost so much already, it's unthinkable. I need to rebuild my strength. We have to be ready." She doesn't have to finish her sentence for him to understand what she means: they must be ready to fight.

When the monsters come.

He hesitates, then nods. Slowly, they make their way to the harbor. The gorgeous palace of pink, green, and white marble, of turrets and balconies, was heavily damaged in the flood. The banquet hall and one wing have completely vanished, and workmen crawl over scaffolding surrounding the remainder. All the long piers that jutted far into the sea are gone. Ships have anchored farther out, and Kat spies several rowboats, their white oars slicing through the choppy gray sea like the powerful wings of swans, ferrying people and goods back and forth.

Next to the palace complex, an entire block of houses and shops is gone. Men are still dragging away waterlogged wood and plaster and hoisting it into carts. But across the street, some houses still stand.

They visit several families, each one worse off than the one before. Each time, Jacob does his best to channel his magic to help the wounded. Even watching, Kat is awed by the raw power he possesses, the gentleness with which he wields it, clearly held back by something she recognizes: fear.

There is nothing worse than fearing what you, yourself, are capable of. Kat knows that fear all too well. The fear of a darkness bubbling in your veins, capable both of greatness and of terrible destruction.

As they leave the home of a young mother with a broken leg that healed badly, Kat knows she cannot enter another sickroom. It is as if she has absorbed all the pain and worry in each house they visited and none of the joy when Jacob left the injured person healed. Now, suddenly, the sheer weight of it hits her like a massive wave. She has been lost in her own sickness long enough, and she feels dizzy, overwhelmed, pushed to the limit. She can no longer bear the stuffy sickroom smell—overflowing chamber pots, sweat, and fear—along with the mold and mildew the waters left in their wake. The cold harbor breeze is what she needs, and the winter sun on her face. Perhaps the coldness and brightness will help clear away the dark thing growing inside her.

"I'll let you do the next one by yourself," she says. "I need some fresh air."

A look of concern crosses his face. "Are you all right?" he asks. She smiles. "I'm fine."

Jacob squeezes her hand. "Once I'm done here, I will see if there are any messages at the baker's."

He enters a neighboring house, and Kat walks to the water. She takes off her boots and enjoys the feel of sand between her toes, even if that sand is cold. Then she sits and watches a rowboat ply its way toward shore from a merchant vessel some way out.

Despite the nightmares, the dark, writhing memories of near drowning, and the unthinkable *thing* that came for her in the water—a Spirit Eater, she now knows—there is still something about the sea that draws her, calms her. It is as though a voice amid the waves is singing to her. For a moment, she could swear it was her mother, Helen, who died when she was only six. For a moment, she is back in time, a child in Helen's arms. They are safe, and she has not yet learned what or who she is.

The wind embraces her.

The voices ebb and rise within and around her, braiding together and then dissipating. They are the voices of infinite creatures in the sea, she realizes.

It is an amazing comfort how, after all this time, her magic comes back to her, easy and flowing, like a near-forgotten lullaby. She would cry with the relief of it, the blessed release, except that she is too tired, too lulled by its heavy calm.

Soon, the sounds of hammering, sawing, and men's voices fade entirely. Her breathing slows, and her mind drifts into the water, into darting fish and scuttling crabs and shellfish that drag themselves over sand with one muscular foot. She sinks into floating, pulsating creatures too tiny to see, her mind drifting, seeking that distant song. She has done this often with water— with the Aegean and the Nile and the North African sea off Meninx. Once, in Meninx, she thought she saw an entire civilization below the waves, a many-towered city with handsome people walking through the watery depths, their long hair and robes floating behind them. Atlantis.

But never before has she felt such a fresh, living wound, such lingering trauma. The creatures here, below this churning silver, were shaken first in a violent underwater storm, then pulled out, far out to sea, thousands of them left gasping for breath on harbor sand. Then they were cast into the air, somersaulting in the roaring power of the waves, and slammed into the city. Those that survived felt the horror and pain of the dying. Now, even six weeks later, having no sense of time, they tremble with dread. This unquiet sea is filled with fear.

Something else floats toward her, a bloom of tiny creatures almost lost in the tug and pull of the waves. The feel of them is foreign, alien, completely different from any creature she has ever inhabited. Curious, Kat slips inside the collective consciousness of the hundreds of watery forms. They are small; each could fit easily in the palm of a young child's hand. They are mostly transparent, with bright red centers and dozens of long, slender tentacles.

Jellyfish, but not any jellyfish. They are both young and old. Sinking deeper into their being, Kat feels herself age and renew, age and renew, again and again. The jellyfish have, by their nature, a kind of immortality, though something natural, crafted by the earth herself without magic. The parts of the jellyfish refresh themselves with new vitality, unlike the physical bodies of all other living things, which age, sicken, and die. Suddenly, Kat realizes the creatures are hundreds, possibly thousands, of years old. She has never before traveled into something so ancient, and the weight of their age nearly crushes her soul.

Floating on warm summer waters, she sees hundreds of black-sailed ships, bristling with men, sunlight glinting off their armor. But the ships and armor are nothing like anything she has ever seen in her travels. They aren't Macedonian, Persian, Egyptian, or Carthaginian.

Is this a recent memory of a different place, far away? Or is it from nearby, but long ago? The sun and moon rise and sink in the sky. Torches and campfires flicker on a beach. Men fight on a wide plain. Chariots clash together as horses and soldiers shriek in pain. Soldiers on high walls fire arrows. A city burns and collapses in upon itself, becoming its own tomb. Then, for what seems like an eternity, all is silence as the jellyfish glide past vacant beaches.

She feels a tap on her back and looks around. It's unsettling at first, to be in air, not water, and to see a human face peering at her. She blinks in confusion. It's Jacob.

"Found you," he says, his voice cracking as he seats himself heavily beside her on the cool sand. He looks drained, as if he has used every ounce of his Earth Blood Magic to heal the injured today. His powers are not inexhaustible, she knows, and it will take him some time to regain his strength. There will be no healing of Byzantium's injured tomorrow.

He reaches into his pack, pulls out three fluffy rolls, and hands her one, along with the cloth the baker wrapped it in. It is still warm. She puts a hand on his cheek, and he kisses it, his face brightening. "I've received another message from Timaeus," he says, pulling a small scroll from the pouch on his belt. "It seems that Spirit Eaters have spread as far west as Dardania. Farmers have been plucked out of fields, fishermen off boats. Archers now stand guard in fields and on boats, ready to shoot the creatures."

Kat shudders and holds the bundle of bread closer to her for warmth, though she is no longer hungry.

"My Aesarian regiment is leaving Dardania," he says. "For Troy. Timaeus has urged me to meet them there."

Troy. Kat has an icy feeling on the back of her neck. The ancient ships. The battles on the plain. The burning city. What she saw in the memory of the immortal jellyfish was the fall of Troy. It must be.

And it cannot be a coincidence that she has just had a vision of it, and now some new evil breeds in the ruins of Troy. She can feel the darkness in her bones. That is why the Lords have gone there.

"Why Troy?" she asks. "What's in Troy?"

Jacob shrugs. "I don't know. Perhaps it's just a meeting place where our regiment will join up with other Aesarian armies. He says there are orders from Nekrana for all regiments to combat the Spirit Eaters in any way they can."

"Do you trust Tim?" she asks quietly.

Jacob is silent for a moment. "I'm not entirely sure, actually. I suppose that's why I had him sent to Dardania. We were both always ambitious to rise above our humble origins, but...he changed. Became a bit too determined, somehow. And he—he knows. What I am. What I have." He looks at his hands, and Kat knows he is talking about his Earth Blood.

She looks out to sea again, wishing she could locate the jellyfish to learn more, but they have slipped beyond her reach.

Even still, she recalls that strange feeling of being drawn toward the water, toward distant shores. She cannot understand why, but there's something in this—something she must follow and uncover.

Besides, Kat knows she cannot return to Macedon. At least, not yet. The queen, if she is still alive, wants Kat dead. And Alexander sent her a message that King Philip decided to acknowledge her as his daughter by a servant woman and plans to use her in a marriage alliance with a rival nation. If she valued her freedom as much as Alex thought she did, she would keep clear of Macedon until he told her it was safe.

If not Macedon, where should she go?

She sinks back into her memory of the jellyfish, into the darkness of the ruins of Troy—now she's *sure* that is what it was. A strange and beautiful thought comes to her: perhaps she and Jacob, with their powerful Blood Magic, are the ones fated to bring light to that darkness. And perhaps, in so doing, she will bring light to the darkest part of herself.

"I think we should go there," she says carefully. "But in secret." Regardless of Jacob's feelings, she knows her own: she will never trust any Aesarian Lord but him.

She wonders if Jacob will argue with her, but he says, "Absolutely. I don't want them getting anywhere near you with their Hemlock Torch." That's right—the tool they developed to detect the presence of Blood Magic. A far more rudimentary form of the mechanism she and Heph built on Meninx. "You and I are both in danger, as far as the Lords are concerned," he goes on, "but they know me as one of their own, and I can handle myself around them. If we go, stealth must be the order of the day until I can find a way to speak to Timaeus alone."

His gaze slides to four men heaving a rowboat onto the sand, splashing through knee-deep water, then moves toward the numerous ships anchored near the harbor. "We will need to find a ship sailing for Mytilene on the isle of Lesbos," he says. "From there it's just across the channel to Troy."

For the second time that day, Kat feels like she could cry—whether from relief or joy or the terrible weight of not knowing what may come, she can't say. But the tears, like the waves, rise only to recede as she reaches out to Jacob—her oldest friend, her greatest love, her only reason, right now, for being alive—threading her hand into his, aware that she is only just getting her strength back and a great journey awaits them yet.

"I've been thinking," Jacob says late that night, unrolling his sleeping mat in the narrow space next to Kat's bed. They have packed everything else they can and will ship out tomorrow. "It is said that Earth Blood runs in families, though I don't think anyone in my family ever had it."

Staring at the ceiling in the flicker of dim lamplight, Kat mulls this over. "When Helen needed to hide me from the queen,

Ada of Caria told her to take me to Erissa. Perhaps she knew of an Earth Blood family there, Jacob. Your family. Maybe they learned to suppress it, knowing that if they didn't, the Aesarian Lords would take them away."

Though she can't see him from her position in the bed, she can hear his breathing, quick and short, as if nervous—or harboring an emotion he is trying, with difficulty, to hold back. "It's true that my father loved working with earth. Channeled all his skill into making household things—pots, bowls, vases, even the occasional little sculpture for me or my brother."

A wave of guilt and sadness engulfs Kat.

"It's my fault," she whispers into the near darkness.

"No," he starts.

"If I hadn't followed you to Pella, the queen would never have found out where I was—"

"Kat, no, you can't blame yourself—"

"—and your family would be safe—" Her voice breaks.

"It's not your fault." Suddenly he is no longer lying on the floor but sitting on the side of the bed, reaching out to her. She sits up and lets him fold her into his arms. "I'm the one who never should have left Erissa," he says. "I'm the one who was bursting with ambition. Father's kiln and the farm were never good enough for me. Now I would give anything to have them back…" His deep voice cracks.

She chokes back the heavy knot in her throat, touching his arm, his face, wanting to make it better, and knowing she can't. "To lose everything, everyone…" she whispers.

"Not my *whole* family," he says, lifting his head. "I haven't lost *everyone*, Kat." He looks into her eyes, and heat races through her body.

He puts a finger beneath her chin and lifts her face to his. She stares into his warm brown eyes and feels desire prickle and tease her. She parts her lips, and his mouth meets hers, as though he has been waiting to kiss her ever since that time on the battlefield, when he saved her life...or even before that. Since their first kiss, drenched in the pond outside of Erissa, urgency still coursing through her limbs from the hunt. It's as though every touch to heal her since has been leading to this moment. Her body feels like it is on fire, melting and shivering. His hand traces her back, pulling her to him as his tongue gently meets her lower lip, sliding into her mouth, making her want to pull him even closer. His body is hard against hers, guiding her back down onto the bed, and she clings to him even as she feels herself dissolving into movement and heat, into touch and breath and gasps.

The intensity of it burns through her until her whole body is aflame. But it is not just physical desire that consumes her—it is deeply rooted love, and the need to comfort him and to match his loyalty with her own, her magic with his, to bring everything within her together with everything in him.

And it is *right*. So very right. There are no doubts.

There is no holding back.

Outside their little room, the waters rise and pound the shore as the earth trembles and shooting stars blaze across the sky. Birds tucked into their nests for the night lift their heads and sing for joy, she is sure of it, and in the harbor, fish leap with happiness as the earth—the rocks and waters and wind—mix with the spirits of all living things, and the two halves of the world are one again.

CHAPTER ELEVEN

PYROLITHOS

MOONLIGHT FILTERS INTO THE LARGE CAVE through the sparkling veil of the waterfall, mingling with the flickering light of torches. Shafts of gold and silver light on Alecta's long red hair as she spins gracefully away from Pyrolithos, just out of reach. For a moment, the king is caught off guard by the sheer beauty of her movement. He lunges toward her and meets her shield; she sweeps her leg in an arc, pivoting and connecting with his flank. Pain radiates through him; Pyrolithos leaps to the side, out of her sword's reach, to regain his breath, watching from the corner of his eye as she lands on two light, deft feet. Her face is expressionless and ready.

He has been secretly training Alecta for weeks, training that Alecta takes back to the brothel and teaches the other women. Because, of course, no one must know that the new king of Dardania has been arming and training a group of prostitutes—the New Amazons, he calls them. At least, no one must know until he's ready to debut them as his new, most-trusted bodyguards. Then, he will lead troops out to capture surrounding territory. All his dreams are coming true.

It is, at best, however, an uneasy alliance. Though Pyrolithos never gave Alecta proof that he was, indeed, the representative of Queen Cynane, the shrewd redhead grudgingly agreed to the training. Prostitutes know better than most women that the world can be cruel, and men can be brutal, and there is no one to look out for them except themselves. Skill at arms could prove useful in any number of ways.

His plan was assisted when the bulk of the Aesarian Lords departed Dardania, headed, apparently, for Troy—called there on some important mission, High Lord Gideon said. He left behind a handful of men to help reorganize the army. Unfortunately, they were never able to ingratiate themselves with Pyrolithos by capturing Queen Cynane; no one has seen her since the night of the mad king's murder.

And none of them *will*—until the time is right.

Pyrolithos circles to the right as Alecta crouches slightly, slinking like a cat around him. "How are last week's recruits faring?" he asks, as he asks every week, his voice sounding like a stranger's, mingling with the rushing water beyond the cave.

She smiles, and he feels something light up inside him. He has been combing the streets of the capital, the mountain villages, and the fishing boats for strong young women to add to their ranks—those dissatisfied with their lot in life, with abusive fathers and husbands, with little or no freedom, poor wages, and secrets no one must ever know. In the brothel, they can choose either to entertain men or do household work when they are not training.

Alecta lunges at him, and he raises his shield just in time, feeling all the muscles in his abdomen go tense. "As if you care about those women," she says, laughing harshly.

"But I do." He doesn't blame her; if he were her, he wouldn't trust himself, either. In fact, he's not sure he *does* trust himself— at least not around her.

"What about the one from the mill?" He'd been worried about that one—too soft, too sweet to become a warrior. But he knew firsthand how that softness could streamline into strength with the right training. How the desire to please could be molded, carefully, into the desire to kill.

"The mill?" Their swords clang together, then separate.

"The one who uses lye on her legs." He couldn't get past the scent of it; even after bathing, it lingered. It was particularly strange for a mill worker who spent her days measuring grain into sacks, to bother with such hair removal tactics. But all women, he knows, have their little vanities.

Alecta lowers her sword and frowns. "What do you know about all that?"

Pyrolithos freezes. Men are not supposed to know the secrets of the women's quarters. "I...grew up with many girls," he says stiffly, hoping his voice sounds nonchalant.

"Hmm." Alecta narrows her dark eyes and raises her sword. Shifting light from the waterfall washes over her face, which is all angles, all skepticism. "Erika is doing well. She takes to the training, as if she has been waiting for it all her life. They all do."

"And the Persian with the swelling belly you told me about?" he asks, buffeting Alecta's shield with his own and leaping back. "I don't suppose she can do much for a while."

"She's stronger than she looks," Alecta replies, suddenly a blur of motion as a hard kick connects with Pyrolithos's elbow, sending his shield thudding to the ground. He curses under his breath. He really is a much better warrior than this, but he always loses his concentration when he trains with Alecta.

"It is a grave mistake to think that being capable of carrying a child makes us weak," she says, her voice steady as always, betraying no emotion, even when he wishes she would. "If anything, it makes us stronger. The Persian will do whatever it takes to be one of us."

Good. He knew that what he was doing would gain traction, but he had no idea just how popular it would be, or how quickly. Women from as far away as Athens have been coming to Aphrodite's Grotto for training and protection. It's getting so

crowded that Alecta has to train the women in two groups—
they can't all fit into the brothel courtyard at once.

"But to tell you the truth, the women have been…asking
questions," Alecta continues, feinting to his left. "The attacks
continue, and they seem to be heading west. It cannot be long
before they reach us here."

He knows which attacks she means. Everyone is talking about
it. In Eastern Greece, fishermen have been plucked off ships by
flying creatures. Swimmers have been pulled underwater, their
bones spit up on the beach at high tide.

"Last week, a woman asking for sanctuary with us told of a
village in Paeonia she had come through," Alecta says, thrusting her sword at his arm. He casually knocks it away with his
shield. "She was there when a shepherd ran screaming from his
fields, saying his entire flock was gone. The villagers returned
carrying bones with teeth marks in them."

Pyrolithos studies the outline of her body in the dimness of
the cave, catching the stray, fractured moonlight as she moves.
He's heard many of the stories from the east by now of creatures called Spirit Eaters, which were thought to have died
out thousands of years ago, if they were ever real to begin
with. Now people have begun to fear that the Spirit Eaters are
not only real but are on the rise, spreading west, and heading
straight toward them.

"First Byzantium, then Paeonia," he replies, lunging as she
gracefully springs back. He can't deny that they seem to be
headed west.

"Some of the Lords are fond of my girls," Alecta says. "As
I'm sure you are aware."

He simply nods, deflecting a parry. It's true that before the
Aesarian Lords left Dardania, a handful liked to visit the Grotto,
much to Pyrolithos's chagrin. He hates the idea of his warriors-
in-training entertaining those brutes.

"They've hinted to the girls that they knew something more

about the attacks," she says, lowering her sword and stepping back until she's almost entirely hidden in the shadows of a recess in the back wall of the cave, slick with moisture and thick moss. "Filled their heads with stories of creatures from the Eastern Mountains of Persia, hiding quietly for centuries." Her voice emanates from the darkness, but he does not make a move to corner her. "They said if we knew the truth, we would be terrified. But no matter how drunk the girls got them, they never said anything more than that."

"Then we'll have to become even more terrifying than the Spirit Eaters themselves. Wrestle," he commands, dropping his sword.

With hardly a moment of hesitation, Alecta leaps out of the shadows like an arrow released from its bow, and then she is on him, crying out as she thrusts a leg between his, hooking it around his calf, trying to make him buckle. She's strong, but this body of his is much stronger than it used to be. Easily, he grabs her arms, forces her to turn around, and holds them behind her back.

"What have I been telling you?" he asks, his lips close to her ear. "You cannot fight against a man's strength. Stealth. Charm. Playing at fear and incompetence. Those are your best weapons."

Alecta stops struggling and hangs her head, her hair a golden-red curtain across her eyes.

Pyrolithos releases her. And she swings around, landing her fist at the edge of his jaw, sending him stumbling backward.

"Like that, you mean?"

Pyrolithos spits blood onto the dirt. Then he looks up, catching those flashing eyes. "Exactly like that."

She crosses her arms and stares at him suspiciously. "You have a remarkable understanding of women's bodies." She pauses. "How to fight with them, that is."

He makes a little bow. "Thank you."

"It's strange, though," Alecta continues, tilting her head. "How did you learn to train women?"

"I've told you before—I'm doing what Queen Cynane asked of me. I risk my throne every time I ride out here and give you my time and expertise. What do you think the nobles would do if they knew what we were doing here?"

"Hmm," Alecta says, shifting her weight. "Why *are* we doing this again? Surely a new king could find pleasure doing other things at night..."

"Alecta, we've—"

"I want to hear it again. More slowly this time," she says, playing dumb, just like he had instructed her to.

He sighs. "I told you, Queen Cynane is being hunted. There is a reward for her capture, and she wants a new guard, one made up only of women. I, too, want such a guard, but I cannot reveal my new warriors until you are a well-trained, impressive force."

"And why do you want a female guard if you know the nobles will protest?" Alecta asks.

"Queen Cynane and I trust women," he replies. "We don't trust men."

"But you are a man."

He hopes she can't see his grimace in the shadowy light. "I can't help but notice, Alecta," he says, stepping toward her, the darkness suddenly too thin—nothing separating them from what they desire, "that in return for everything I do for you, all I receive are questions." His hands land on her upper arms and he easily sweeps her to the ground, straddling her.

He has never, he realizes, been this close to a woman's body before. Feeling her beneath him, he understands in a whole new way what it means to be female, to be both soft and firm at the same time. Tiny beads of sweat glisten on her face, and there is a smear of dirt on her cheek that he is intensely tempted to wipe away, or to lick. She looks up at him, expressionless.

It occurs to him that she must often find herself in this position.

Quickly, he rolls off her.

"I think that's enough for tonight," he says, rising. "It must be near dawn."

She brushes herself off and gets to her feet. "Thank you, your majesty." Her tone is suddenly brisk and distant. She moves toward the waterfall, about to pass through it, where, he knows, her tunic will become soaked through, but before she leaves the dark sanctuary of the cave, and its cool, minerally darkness the king has come to savor, she looks at him over her shoulder. "You will come to regret everything you've given me."

And then she is pressing herself against the side wall, slipping through the tiny opening protected from the water's spray, and is gone.

He has come to savor those parting words, the same every time. They seem to him both a threat and a promise. Even if it is the promise of betrayal, it keeps him coming back for more.

Approaching one of the burning torches, he summons the soot and ashes pumping through his soul and puts his right hand in it; he feels no pain. Then he pulls the flames out, like a cord, and twists them into a glowing bracelet around his other wrist, feeling the exultant rise of power inside him. The fiery glow subsides, and the bracelet turns into something hard and crystalline, like diamonds, just like the others he has made. Next, he calls on the torches for their smoke, and it billows forth, surrounding him as he coughs. Quickly, he channels it into a swirling column, walks around it, and, with a flick of his wrist, scatters it. He has been experimenting with his Smoke Blood, investigating what he can and cannot do. There is no one to teach him.

He paces the darkness for a few minutes, the smell of moss and river stone no longer enchanting, only cold and damp, until he is certain Alecta has made her way a safe distance. Then he moves through the slender opening at the lip of the cave. Splashes of icy water refresh his hot, sweaty skin. It's only the beginning of spring and the sun still has not risen, but he can tell it will be a warm day. The trees have begun bursting with green leaves and flowers. Grass and ferns have sprouted everywhere. Insects and birds appeared after their long winter hiatus, and now they rub themselves loudly, croaking at the coming dawn.

He squats beside the chattering stream, fills his waterskin, and drinks heavily from the flask. Through the thicket of trees, he can see the dark form of Alecta riding toward the road, growing smaller. Once she disappears on the strip of coastal road that rounds the mountain, he mounts his horse and follows.

There is little movement on the cliff-side roads, and the sky gradually lightens. He allows himself a moment of peace, sinking into himself, conjuring once more the stirring in his blood. He imagines himself a spirit, made of air and thought. The burn of Smoke Blood rises within him, coursing through his veins. His legs begin to tingle. After several moments, he realizes they have disappeared entirely, though from his hips up, he is still solid. He realizes he must look like a centaur from afar. He calls on the sooty magic within him to turn himself into a being of smoke, as Taulus was, but only his arms turn into gray wisps. His smoke hands still hold the reins; they could also hold a sword, he knows. But he doesn't have the power to turn anything more than a part of himself into smoke. It must take a great many betrayals indeed to do that. If only Taulus were still around, he could ask him for help.

But, of course, Taulus is not here. Without Taulus, Pyrolithos wouldn't have Smoke Blood. No—without Taulus's *death*. When his guilt becomes too heavy, Pyrolithos reminds himself that Taulus wanted to die, wanted Pyrolithos to end his agonizing existence. Otherwise, why would he have told Pyrolithos that, despite being a creature of shifting smoke, he still possessed a human heart, the last part of him to dissolve? When Pyrolithos plunged his sword into the swirling vapors of Taulus's chest, blood, red and hot, spurted all over him as his smoke dissipated.

He shakes his head as if to clear it from that atrocious memory and looks to the right, where breakers crash against the rocky beach; gulls cry and wheel above. By the time he reaches the city gate, he has regained his solidity, and the world has silvered itself awake.

He tightens his helmet strap—he's wearing the uniform of a palace guard to avoid recognition on the streets—and slows his horse as the gate guards wave him on. With his nosepiece and cheek flaps, they do not know their own king.

He picks his way around carts and pedestrians, past the many-pillared Temple of Zeus, and across the main marketplace where people sell fish, vegetables, and household goods. He takes a side street, past the walled town villas of the rich. Aphrodite's Grotto is on the edge of the wealthy section of town; the next street over, the neighborhood of artisans begins. He approaches the villa from its rear wall overlooking the courtyard and ties his horse to a tree, dropping a coin into the outstretched hand of Oikos, one of the brothel bouncers who guards the rear of the complex. Agilely, he climbs the tree, savoring the way his muscles pulse with use, and crouches on the corner of the wall, hidden by the leafy branches.

The brothel is closed to male clientele during training sessions, such as now. The women tend to use the hours no man would ever come seeking pleasure—those just before breakfast, when the drunks have staggered home to their own beds at last and the light has barely touched the sky.

Torches line the walls inside the courtyard, throwing flickering warm light onto the stones and the moving bodies within. Alecta is already on the far side of the pool, the splashing of its central fountain drowning out some of her words as she instructs some twenty-five helmeted women in the moves he taught her just today. Even the heavily pregnant one is there, awkwardly wielding a sword and shield.

They practice in stages, following Alecta in slow motion, and for a moment the whole vision from above looks to Pyrolithos like the incoming tide—all white tunic surf and flashing silver metal in the torchlight, as each one goes through the motions: raising the shield to pummel the opponent's chest, aiming it at the elbow of the opponent's sword arm to force her to drop her own, whirling left, then right again. He's not sure how long he's been watching them when something in the air changes. Every nerve in his body prickles with warning, and even the leaves unfurling on the tree surrounding him seem to freeze, the sea wind going still. The springtime warmth has vanished, replaced by a cold dread. The birds have gone silent, he realizes, like they do sometimes before a storm. But the women below don't seem to notice anything wrong as they circle and wrestle and spar.

Unnerved for reasons he can't quite say, Pyrolithos pulls on the branch and climbs over to stand on the wall for a better view. Clouds are moving across the sky in the distance, innocently enough. There's now a blazing line of orange gold on the horizon. Not a storm, then.

Before he has time to consider another option, an unearthly shriek rends the air.

Below him, the women look around and begin to point in alarm. At first, he thinks they are pointing at him—an intruder.

But no, he swivels just in time to realize they are screaming at something just beyond him.

Something dark is coming toward them from the sea, blotting out the just-rising sun. A dark smear dives toward the brothel, huge black wings outstretched. A thin howl turns his blood to ice.

In the swirl of movement, he cannot get a look at the thing, but it doesn't matter.

He knows what's coming.

"Get inside! Now! Run!" His voice, though strong and urgent, is muted by the women's screams and the slap and burble of the fountain.

Alecta, eyes wide and mouth open, catches his gaze. Their eyes lock for a moment. Then she pushes the women toward the many doors opening onto the courtyard. "Go!" she cries, shoving them hard.

The creature sweeps past Pyrolithos, the chill of it glancing off his body and sending an ache down deep into his core.

A Spirit Eater.

The creature dives into the panicked women in the courtyard, all the torches snuffing out at once in a billow of smoke. There is a terrible scream through the sudden smoky darkness as the creature dips and grabs onto one of the women, ripping her head off in one swift movement and spitting it out.

Pyrolithos has seen much horror in his life, but for seconds he is frozen in shock.

The creature swoops again and lands amid the chaos of the courtyard, flapping its foul black wings, then rips the bloody yellow intestines out of the dead woman's headless body and swallows them in awkward gulping motions, as a famished bird swallows worms. There is something shifting about its form, as if he were looking at it through a prism. One moment it seems to have two heads, then only one, and four wings, only to focus into two. He rubs his eyes.

"Swords out!" Alecta's voice—why hasn't she gone into hiding? "Sophonisba, throw us some spears!" she commands.

A tall dark-skinned woman begins tossing spears to Alecta and several other women. The creature raises its heads—no, just one head—from the bloody carcass, and sniffs the air. Its black eyes light on Alecta, standing at the front of the armed women, and Pyrolithos feels his heart trying to break out of his chest.

If his Smoke Blood Magic were more advanced, he could

appear at her defense in seconds. Instead, he jumps down from the wall, draws his sword, and tumbles across the courtyard, swinging his shield off his back as he runs.

The creature swivels toward him, and his breath stops in his throat. He could swear there's something distinctly *human* in the way it stares at him. A memory comes to Pyrolithos in that moment, swirling up and out of a past that feels too distant to be his own—a torture wheel. Axes and horned helmets and searing, constant, agonizing pain. Whispered conversations about witchcraft and magic—and Spirit Eaters. A murmured rumor— that they were once, somehow, impossibly, human.

The creature almost seems to smile, as if reading the king's mind, revealing sharp yellow teeth, dripping bright red blood. Hundreds of teeth in several heads... No, just one. It's a trick of the light.

Pyrolithos takes in the situation behind the creature. Most of the women have made it to safety inside. Alecta, Xanthe, Sophonisba, and a few others stand defiantly with spears outstretched.

"Get inside!" he manages to shout. "I can handle this." But it's a lie. For all his Smoke Blood, his powers are nothing against this ancient evil, this demon who reportedly ate the gods alive, ingesting all their magic and their knowledge.

An iron spear hurtles through the air and bounces off the enormous leathery wing as if it's only a feather. The monster hisses and turns back to the women. Its skin is like armor, Pyrolithos realizes in horror.

Two women run around the fountain to join Pyrolithos, surrounding the Spirit Eater. Alecta steps forward, sword raised.

Before Pyrolithos can scream at her to back away, the enormous wings send the women flying. Alecta is thrown into the fountain and rises, sputtering, still, amazingly, gripping her sword even as blood streams off her shoulder. One woman is thrown against the courtyard wall. Another hurtles straight into Pyrolithos, knocking him over.

The creature ignores the others, leaping with outspread wings toward the king. Pyrolithos has bravely fought many enemies larger and better trained than himself. But this is different. This causes his blood to become both ice and fire. He is no longer a body propelled by thought but pure muscle driven by animal panic. He scrambles to his feet and runs.

There isn't time to look back, but he hears the rustling of wings, hears the unearthly howl, feels the foul, freezing breath on the back of his neck. He crashes through the gate leading to the brothel's service courtyard, expecting agony to slice through him every moment as fangs and claws shred his flesh. Shouldering open a small door, he finds himself in what appears to be the brothel laundry and runs to the far side of a large bubbling cauldron in the fire pit, scanning around hurriedly for a weapon. A large wooden paddle rests among sheets in the cauldron; that would be useless. Then he sucks in a breath—the Spirit Eater has stopped in the doorway and stands perfectly still, blocking out the light, sniffing.

Hearing a muffled sob, he realizes there are two women huddled behind a pile of laundry in the corner: the pregnant Persian and a large middle-aged woman, who is probably the laundress. The creature steps inside the room and, now totally uninterested in the king, slinks toward the women.

Pyrolithos takes a breath and, with the razor-sharp tip of his sword, punctures the inside of his left arm. Pain radiates through him. Smoke, ashes, and flames roll through him as he coughs and writhes. He has no idea what he is going to do, only that it must be clever and it must be now.

As he straightens, his gaze lands on the fire beneath the laundry cauldron. He dives toward the fire pit and picks up ropes of flame, along with burning coals and feathery ash with his bare hands—it doesn't hurt. Instead, it seems to strengthen the smoke inside him, and he feels himself expand, not visibly but in power.

Using the full power of his concentration, he flings the flames and coals toward the Spirit Eater, who now seems to be a hydra of several heads, envisioning them forming a rope to lasso the creature, just as earlier this morning he played with making bracelets. His mind pushes the heat and light together, rearranging them just the way he has rearranged his own body.

A glowing orange lasso falls over the Spirit Eater's single head and shoulders. It turns, shocked, and stares at him.

Pyrolithos shudders with the magic flooding him now, dizzying and senseless and intoxicating. He can't stop, and he doesn't want to, funneling all his concentration into the burning rope as its many filaments become strands of heat and light. They crisscross one another until the creature stands in a *cage* of fiery coals. It grabs the bars with its long clawed fingers, shaking them with all its might and roaring in rage. But the bars are stronger than iron.

Slowly, the fire cools to a glowing, hard, glittering white.

Pyrolithos blinks. He is staring at a diamond cage. Made by his own magic.

And within it writhes something miraculous and terrible and unthinkable.

He has caught a Spirit Eater.

He wants to open his mouth and laugh.

Just then, Alecta and the other women from the courtyard clatter into the laundry, wielding spears. For a moment, the only sound is their heavy breathing as they take in the astonishing sight.

"What are you waiting for, you fool? Kill it!" Alecta's command cuts through the general awe. She lunges toward the cage, but instinctively, Pyrolithos steps forward, blocking her path.

He shakes his head, then turns back in wonder to the powerful creature he has caught.

Once, he knew hunger.

He knew patience, too.

He has learned the hard way—when he was a she, when she was Cynane—that the way to gain power is not to destroy it, but to harness it.

CHAPTER TWELVE

HEPHAESTION

FOG LIES THICK OVER THE BATTLEFIELD, MOVING across enemy lines, revealing only glimpses of the battalions lined up across the green fields near the town of Chaeronea, a two-day march from Athens. Heph breathes in the cold morning air. When King Philip wants a war, he gets a war: the Greek city-states have rallied at his provocations, and now it's time to show off Macedon's finest asset. Namely: their army.

There was a time when battle wouldn't have been necessary, but while the king was loafing about in Byzantium and Alexander was in the grips of a spirit-possession, chaos had spread throughout Macedon's neighboring territories, and Heph knows the king is right—that there is no way to attack Persia without more allied forces. And if the forces won't come willingly, then Macedon will just have to make them.

Heph shivers slightly at the haunting wails of the salpinx, a four-foot-long bronze battle horn, as the sound floats over the armies like the shriek of some spirit wrenched straight out of the earth. Heph's horse, Ares, a dun-colored stallion, shifts under him, flicking his long tail and whickering softly, sensing the tension of thirty thousand Macedonians staring across the plain of Chaeronea at thirty thousand allied Greeks led by the forces of

Athens and Thebes. The line of warriors stretches more than two miles, from the banks of the lazy Kephisos River just to Heph's left, to the foothills of craggy Mount Thurion on the right.

Next to him, Alex casually pushes a strand of blond hair back under his plumed, golden helmet. To others, he looks as calm as if he were planning on having a picnic out here on this fine spring day. But Heph can see the tension around his eyes, the nervous way he threads his fingers around the black mane of Bucephalus. This is their first great battle with King Philip, who has given his son the honor of commanding the left wing, while Philip commands the right.

In the far distance, a massive blue Macedonian flag with the gold sixteen-pointed star waves across the sky, raised high and then quickly lowered by a man standing on horseback. Soon after it, other flags begin repeating the motion until the battlefield looks like an undulation of waves crashing over one another. In front of Heph, rows upon rows of infantry lift their shields and lower their spears.

"Advance!" The mingled roar of thirty thousand men echoes through the fog as, across from them, the Greek allies blow horns, drop flags, and lower spears, too.

The foot soldiers on both sides launch toward the middle of the field, and within an instant they are clashing, screams of pain ringing out alongside the clang of a thousand spears. Moments seem like hours as Heph tries to see which side is advancing like a tide, and which side will cave.

It takes all his willpower to hold himself back, his entire body an arrow in a cocked bow.

The leather lining of his helmet grows slick with sweat. Ares flicks his tail and nickers in protest. The battle ahead has raised great clouds of dust; the heavy spring rains have not come this year.

"Telekles," he calls out. Telekles has the best eyes of any scout he knows.

Telekles raises a hand to shield his eyes. "All I can make out is dust and fog."

Phrixos, on Telekles's other side, leans forward and rolls his eyes. Even now, right before they race into a pitched battle, Phrixos's round, homely face has the look of someone about to tell a very good joke. "Is that all you can do, Telekles? I'm half-blind and I can see that much."

From somewhere deep within the yellow-brown whirlwind ahead of him, Heph hears three short bursts of a horn. *Advance!* The Macedonian infantry has successfully punched through the enemy lines. Now it's time for the cavalry.

Alex turns to Heph and grins. "Battle!"

"Battle!" he replies, the word pumping a surge of excitement through his veins. He has already kicked his horse into motion and, sword raised, he plunges headlong into the fray, Alex at his side. It is good, so very good, to be doing this with his friend. There is no other feeling like it.

Together they roar into pockets of battling foot soldiers, stabbing those carrying an owl shield or wearing an owl breastplate, treading on the bodies of the dead and wounded.

Somewhere out here, Heph knows, is the Sacred Band of Thebes, a regiment of one hundred fifty pairs of warrior-lovers, each fighting not only for himself but for his lover, which gives added reason for victory. They have such a fierce reputation, they are called the Immortals. Heph is not afraid of any warriors in the enemy army, except the Sacred Band.

Heph and the Macedonian cavalry thunder quickly through the remains of the infantry and now face the Athenian cavalry galloping toward them. He picks his man from a hundred paces out. The graying beard hangs below the helmet, and the man looks ill at ease galloping on his horse. As Heph approaches, the Athenian raises his sword but Heph pounds him so hard with his shield that the man falls off his horse and the alarmed animal screams in fear and bolts. Two Macedonian cavalrymen push in front of Heph, and he doesn't see the Athenian he just unhorsed. Clustered all around him are knots of men fighting on horseback, the clash of arms, the staccato braying of frightened animals. Where is the prince? He searches desperately for the unique golden armor.

There, about fifteen paces to his left. Clinging to a rearing Bucephalus with one hand, Alex plunges a sword into an Athenian, who keels off his horse in grotesquely slow motion. Then the prince whips around in a tight circle, looking for more enemies. Out of nowhere, three mounted Athenians surround Alex, and Heph kicks his horse into motion. As he gallops around the trio, he stabs one through the back and slashes another in the arm. The first falls forward, and the next yells in pain and gallops off. While the third man, startled, looks for his comrades, Alex decapitates him in one clean sweep. His helmeted head flies into a nearby scrum of battling, mounted warriors, who scream and race off. The headless body slumps forward on the horse, which panics before tearing off through the crowd, likely trampling more of the enemy as it tries to flee.

Alex pulls up next to Heph, smiling. He reins in a nervous Bucephalus, who paws the ground anxiously. "We've almost broken through!"

An arrow whizzes past Alex's face, and his eyes widen as he pulls it back a few inches and continues, "Time to finish them off." He means the rest of the cavalry, and with arrows. He unhooks his battle horn from his belt and blows two long blasts. From across the Macedonian left wing, other horns echo the blasts.

Heph and the other archers sling their bows off their shoulders, nock them, and, guiding their mounts with their knees, race around the battlefield, looking for remaining Athenian cavalry. Heph spies an Athenian horseman on his left, sword raised, heading for a small group of Macedonians trying to carry a wounded comrade away on his shield. The horseman is so intent on his goal, he sees neither Heph nor Telekles, his waist-length golden hair thick with dust and sweat, approaching on his other side. Heph looses his arrow with a *thwing*, and the Athenian falls to the ground as his horse bends down and nudges him. Heph gallops up and meets Telekles over the dead man, who has an arrow projecting out of each ear.

"My aim," Telekles says drily, leaning over his horse to study the dead man, "was a bit truer than yours."

Heph peers down at the dark-haired young man on the shield, his face white as a sheet, a blood-soaked bandage wrapped around his waist. "Get him to the hospital tent immediately. Guard these men on the way and then catch up to us."

"Yes, sir!" Telekles salutes.

As a shadowy mounted figure emerges from a cloud of dust, Heph nocks an arrow and raises his bow. He lowers it when he sees it's Alex.

"I think we've done our part," Alex says, wiping sweat from his eyes.

Three long blasts echo from the right. Heph's heart hammers in his chest. The signal for retreat. Philip's right wing of the army is collapsing, running away.

"Retreat!" Alexander begins shouting. "The king's side is retreating!"

The prince unhooks his battle horn and blows one short and one long blast. Across the field, others repeat it. Alex raises his sword in the air and shouts, "Macedon! Macedon!" as cavalry and infantry rally around him. When enough men have collected around him, he urges Bucephalus forward, Heph galloping at his side, the infantry running behind. They make a slow, wide horseshoe turn across the battlefield, killing enemy stragglers, and frightening many more who race away, throwing down their heavy shields to escape more quickly.

Several rows of men turn around to fight their surprise attackers with all the desperation of the doomed. Up front, some of the Theban cavalry wheel around and race back to rescue the rear. Then Heph sees King Philip's Macedonian flag pushing toward him through the opening. The Thebans are caught in between the Macedonian pincers, exactly as planned. Philip's retreat had been a feint to lure them into a trap.

With a whinny of pain, Ares rears, throwing Heph onto the hard ground. He sees his stallion race away, an arrow in its back. Scrambling, he finds his sword and shield and runs full tilt into the fracas. The Macedonians have the advantage tactically and emotionally. The Thebans, shocked and frightened, are being squeezed together in a death grip.

The fog is dissipating and reality setting in. Time slows. A drop of sweat trembles from Heph's eyelashes, for what seems like an eternity, before splashing onto his cheek in slow motion. A spear flies in slow motion toward his head. He pulls back agonizingly slowly, just in time to avoid his skull being impaled; the spear whistles only a hairbreadth past his nose. Feeling half-paralyzed, he pulls a dagger from his belt and throws it. It floats toward the man, head over hilt, enters his eye, and he drops writhing to the ground.

Now time speeds up as a panicked, riderless horse careens past him, heading straight for Alex on Bucephalus, who is facing the other direction, studying the remaining pockets of resistance. "Alexander!" Heph cries, but the warning gets stuck in his throat as he inhales more dust. He coughs and splutters as the frightened horse, large eyes rolling in panic, careens right into Alex, knocking him and Bucephalus to the ground in a horrible tangle of thrashing limbs. A cloud of dust wafts over them once more, and Heph can't see what is happening. He races toward them, crying, "Alex!"

"Hephaestion!" comes the reply. The dust settles, and to Heph's immense relief, he sees Alex nearby, standing tall, holding his sword and shield. Bucephalus is nowhere in sight.

"Are you all…" Heph begins but realizes that Alex isn't looking at him. He's looking ahead, his mouth open.

Out of the dust comes a group of some three hundred men carrying the double-headed Sphinx banner of the Sacred Band.

The Immortals.

They are the most enormous warriors Heph has ever seen, so tall and broad-shouldered they couldn't fit through an average door. Their tanned, oiled muscles glisten. The sun reflecting off their highly polished armor nearly blinds Heph. These are not men but beings of breathing bronze with death in their unblinking, flinty eyes. Several dozen Macedonian cavalry have amassed behind Heph and Alex, and the advance guard of the infantry has caught up, too.

He can't be sure how it happens, but suddenly Heph is in the midst of hand-to-hand combat so ferocious he expects to die every moment. He is surrounded by yells, grunts, screams, the metallic clang of swords on swords, the thumps of swords on shields, and dust. And everywhere, throat-clogging dust.

A muscular young warrior springs forward from the dust, sword outstretched. Heph meets it with his own, and the two swords do a ferocious dance. The warrior is an excellent swordsman; Heph has difficulty keeping up. The Theban's sword point slices Heph's biceps. He feels the sting and burn; hot stickiness slides down his arm.

Then the Immortal's sword swipes the leather strap of Heph's helmet, severing it. The helmet topples off him with a gush of cooling air. He groans inwardly. In battle, a head without a helmet is like a giant melon just begging to be sliced open. But the fresh air brings needed relief to his sweat-soaked head, and he feels a sudden burst of energy.

Ignoring the searing pain in his bloody right arm, he does a maneuver he learned from the Aesarian Lords last summer; he lifts his shield to pummel his opponent in the chest and at the same time plunges his sword underneath, stabbing the warrior in the thigh. The Theban cries out and backs up. Blood gushes from his leg as Heph advances, realizing he must have severed the artery. Still, the Immortal puts up a good fight with his sword. Heph has no idea how long it lasts, but finally, his opponent, weak from loss of blood, falls. Heph kicks his sword away and raises his own.

"You may not see an Immortal die," the man says, smiling despite the pain etching deep lines on his young face. Jerkily, he pulls his shield over his head. Heph raises his sword but hesitates.

"Damiskos!" a man shouts, rushing wildly toward Heph. The wounded man's lover—it must be. Heph has never experienced such a brutal assault. The other man is like an avenging Fury, full of venom and rage. He's so intent on fighting Heph, he doesn't see Phrixos casually walk up to Damiskos, kick away the shield, and send his sword straight through his leather breast-plate, into his heart. There's a sickening crunch. When Heph leaps out of the way of yet another sword thrust, the Immortal sees what has happened.

"No!" Tears stream down the man's dusty cheeks.

Heph has seen grief on the battlefield as men find dead friends, brothers, fathers, and sons, but he has never seen such pain and anger before. The Theban's gray eyes blaze with hatred as he stares at Phrixos, who, for once, doesn't look like he sees any humor in the situation. In a flash, the Theban has kicked the shield out of Phrixos's hand and, Heph notes, probably broken his wrist. He swings his sword as Phrixos, left arm dangling like raw meat, stands gaping stupidly.

But before the sword can come down, Heph has fired an arrow into the back of its owner's neck. The Immortal falls and, with his last ragged breaths, drags himself toward his lover. Heph and Phrixos watch in horrified fascination as he crawls on top of Damiskos and dies. It is a sight Heph knows he will never forget in the coming years, no matter how hard he will try. He feels it has ripped part of his soul right out of him.

By the time the spring sun has reached its zenith, the great battle is over.

Heph and Alex wander through the carnage with attendants

from the field hospital, searching for wounded and dead Macedonians. Greeks, too, scour the field, taking their casualties back to their own camp. Heph's arm wound throbs painfully; Alex bandaged it with the strip of cloth all soldiers carry on their belts to help their comrades stanch bleeding on the battlefield. But he said it was so deep the surgeon would have to sew it closed. Heph will wait a bit, though. The surgeons should tend to the more serious wounds of others before stitching this scratch.

Alex, despite having won ecstatic praise from King Philip, is grim, particularly when they search among the Sacred Band of Thebes; they find that many of the lovers died together. Periodically, Alex kneels to look at a face, feel for a pulse, or say a prayer.

"Gone," he says, unlatching his helmet and throwing it down in frustration. The feather is wilted, the patterned gold splattered with blood and dirt. "All of them, to the last man, dead. Courage, valor, devotion…" He spreads his arms wide as a tear trickles down his dusty cheek. "A waste," he says angrily. "Heph, all of this is a damnable waste. These heroes could have been our allies, could have helped us conquer Persia."

Heph hangs his head. "But the king was right—these same men would have invaded Macedon."

"Don't you think I know that?" Alex asks, his voice thick with emotion. He runs a hand through his stringy, sweaty hair and seems to come to a decision. "Be that as it may, these men will be buried together, and a monument to their courage built above to remember them forever. And in this way, the Immortals will remain truly immortal in human memory."

The sickly smell of charred human flesh still lingers in the night air as Heph and Alex leave the dinner in King Philip's tent and walk between rows of smaller tents lit by brightly burning torches. Heph notices that the pyres outside the Macedonian camp, on which some three thousand comrades were reduced to ash at sunset, still burn. Tomorrow men will shovel ashes into pots to be taken back to their families in Macedon.

He shivers. The temperature fell rapidly when the sun set, and the night is cool, almost chilly. Campfires burn as far as Heph can see, where soldiers huddle and relive the day's fighting.

Torches light the perimeter of the camp, where guards will patrol all night, ready to sound the alarm if anyone approaches. The Greeks, though they clearly lost the battle, suffered only about the same number of casualties, mainly because most of them ran off when they saw how badly they were losing. They could regroup and fight again tomorrow, though Heph doubts they will have the appetite for it.

They duck into their tent, where Basil, their servant, has lit oil lamps hanging from metal rods pushed into the ground. Heph and Alex rip off their shirts and wash off the filth and blood of the day in the large basin of water at the back.

As he plunges his entire head beneath the surface to get the dust and sweat out of his hair, letting the cold water roar into his ears and dull the ringing that has been in his head since combat, Heph holds his breath for a second, suddenly remembering floating in the ocean off Meninx, holding Katerina in his arms and kissing her for the first time. The way she moved against him with an urgency that surprised him, her reservations suddenly coming down between them.

He pulls himself up and grabs for a towel, gasping for air. This is the first time he thought of her today, which is unusual. Since they parted in the massive Byzantine flood some five months ago, he has found himself thinking of her the moment he awakens each morning—wondering if she, too, is awake somewhere, thinking of him.

Shirtless, he rubs his hair briskly with the linen cloth, allowing the night air to cool his chest, calm his tense muscles and racing heart. "What do you think Kat would have done in the battle today?" he asks, throwing on his sleeping tunic, careful not to disturb his wound-dressing. "Would she have had mountain lions race in to attack the Greeks or vultures dive down to take chunks of meat from their horses?" He blows out all the oil lamps except for the one between their narrow camp beds. When he looks up, he sees Alex, standing with his clean tunic balled in his hands. The single lamp casts a flickering light over his pale, taut muscles, which still drip from washing.

"You miss her," he says, finally getting dressed and pouring two cups of watered wine.

Every muscle in Heph's body is stiff and sore from the battle. He looks at his cot in the corner, with its fresh sheets and a clean woolen blanket—no bed has ever looked so inviting. But first, there's something he has to do—has to say to the prince. Something he has been holding in for too long. He has wanted to bring it up many times before, but somehow lacked the courage, or found that the moment wasn't right, or got interrupted after a few halting words. Something about today's battle, though— about bravery and fear, love and death—has made him realize he shouldn't hold anything back from Alexander, that doing so is a kind of lie between them.

Heph picks up his cup and sits on his bed. "On Meninx, I asked her to marry me," he says. His voice sounds weak to him, thin.

Swigging from his wine cup, Alex starts to cough. After a moment, he responds, his voice low, "What did she say?"

"She didn't really say anything. It wasn't yes. But neither was it no." He takes a deep gulp from the cup, his mouth feeling too exposed. "I was sure I could convince her in time, but then, in Byzantium, the waves parted us. It was almost as if…"

"As if Fate decided for you," Alex finishes for him, sitting down beside him, "and gave her back to Jacob."

Heph inhales roughly. Alex can finish his sentences for him. Word for word. Thought for thought. This, he thinks, is perhaps the true marriage. That's what Aristotle would have taught them: the marriage between two perfectly aligned minds and souls, the greatest connection one can seek in this life.

"And now they're in Troy," Alex says, looking so deeply into the dancing lamp flame it's as if he sees the smoking, broken towers of Ilium within it. Weeks ago, they received Kat's message that she and Jacob were living and working at the Temple of Asklepios, near the fabled ruins. "I can't say I understand it."

"Anywhere but Macedon," Heph says. "I shudder to think of your fath—the king—marrying her off to some petty princeling as part of a treaty. How many times has Philip asked you if you could locate her? Four?"

"Five," Alex says. "Though all this," he says, gesturing around them, "has kept him nicely distracted. For now."

The flickering lamplight casts moving shadows on Alex's face as he says, "I think such a marriage would kill her. Though, to be honest, Heph, I just don't know if Kat can be happy as anyone's wife. There is something about her that needs to remain wild and free, like the animals her mind can inhabit."

Heph wonders if that's true. Kat always seemed to be keeping a part of herself back. That was what had drawn him to her in the first place: the levels of mystery within her, the doors in her heart that he wanted to unlock, one at a time.

Heph lies back on the cot, staring up at the curved peak of the tent, swaying in shadow. "I think I could live with her marrying no one at all," he says, his voice scraping along his throat, "so long as I don't lose her to someone else."

Alex lies back beside him, their shoulders touching. When he rolls to one side, he looks at Heph with such compassion in his eyes that Heph feels suddenly raw, like an open wound. "Don't you remember what Aristotle always told us in school? Love is a kind of insanity."

Heph rolls toward him. He knows the prince is right, and

yet... "There's something about her that I can't resist, that I can never forget. She's so... She's so much like..." He stops.

"Like me," Alex finishes, tilting his head and looking at Heph, his blue eye gleaming in the lamplight, his brown eye hidden in the shadows.

"Yes," Heph agrees, feeling heat rise in his cheeks, though he can't imagine why. "My loyalty is always to you. Always. I was an orphaned beggar when you took me to the palace and made me who I've become. It's... What I feel, it's...it's more than gratitude. It has always seemed that you and I...well, that we belong together." He rolls onto his back again. "And then I met Kat and, though it took a while for me to realize it, it was like she was a female version of you. And I loved her." He clears his throat. "Love her. Hope she'll come back to me. Even though my first loyalty will always be to you." He releases a breath, suddenly humiliated with how much he has revealed. "It's just that sometimes I think I am in an impossible situation."

"Whether she comes back to you or not," Alex says, putting a hand on Heph's shoulder, "the only truly important thing to me is that I never lose you."

Heph turns again to find Alex staring at him and sees the same sparkling intensity he often saw in Kat's eyes, the same expression of intellect and passion. It's almost as if Kat is lying beside him, a hand, warm and soothing, on his skin. Heat floods through his body at the thought and Heph sucks in a breath, deeply and rapidly. Suddenly all the nerves in his body are alive and tingling.

He has the strangest, most disturbingly real feeling that he and Alex are going to kiss, here, now, in the flickering lamplight of a war tent.

Then his head clears, and the moment passes with a gust of relief.

"I should sleep," he whispers.

Alexander rises. "Me, too." He moves toward his side of the tent, then stops, and turns back. "Hephaestion."

Heph sits up, breath trapped in his chest, feeling a little dizzy. Is he going to acknowledge what almost just happened?

But Alex just stares at him for a second, his face unreadable. Finally, he sighs, offering a slight smile. "I understand what it's like." He swallows. "To be in an impossible position."

Then he leans over, pinches out the flame on the lamp, and climbs into his own bed.

CHAPTER THIRTEEN

ALEXANDER

ALEX WAKES WITH A JOLT. IT'S PITCH-BLACK INSIDE the tent. His first thought is that Riel has returned, trying to claw his way back into his mind, and his heart flutters like a sparrow beating against cupped hands. Then he searches inside himself and realizes there is nothing unusual there. Just himself, roused from sleep.

He listens carefully for the snap of a twig, the metallic note of a sword being unsheathed, or men's low voices, signs, perhaps, of a sneak invasion by the Greeks. But he hears only Heph's regular breathing.

Just hours ago, he and Heph had the strangest moment, where it seemed, briefly, like their friendship might have turned seamlessly into something else—into something *more*. He thinks of the Sacred Band of Thebes, the many pairs of male lovers who died together yesterday on the field. He cannot deny the unexpected thrill of it, the *almostness*. But it terrified him, too, unsettled him. Went against everything he thought he believed. Nothing can change what they have, nothing can risk their bond.

He wants their friendship to remain the same.

Or does he? Is that the reason he doesn't want Heph to marry

Kat, or anybody else, for that matter? Does he want Heph all to himself?

His muddle of thoughts is interrupted by the loud crunch of footsteps outside and two men arguing about a dice game—probably Macedonians sent to relieve the watch.

He punches his pillow and turns on his side. It's still dark out; he should try to fall back to sleep, to be rested for the challenging day ahead. But questions prick him. What will happen in the morning? Will the Greeks send emissaries to conclude a treaty? Or will they demand another battle? How will Philip negotiate? Alex worries that his terms will be so harsh that the city-states' pride will not permit them to accept. And more soldiers will die instead of swelling the Macedonian force to invade Persia.

If only Alex could still look into men's minds and use that power to persuade Philip and the Greek generals. Perhaps Kat, whose Snake Blood skills involve animals, could learn to travel into the minds of men. But she is far away in Troy. He wonders if there could be another Snake Blood in the Macedonian army, perhaps one who is unaware of his powers or hides them to avoid capture by the Aesarian Lords.

No, he can't sleep.

Quietly, Alex gets up and fumbles on the table for his flint set, strikes the iron against the flint, and watches as sparks fall on the tinder and blaze. Then he lights the wick of the oil lamp, squats down, and rummages in the trunk at the foot of his bed, careful not to make enough noise to wake Heph.

There, in the corner, wrapped in several layers of protective wool, is the Atlantean Mechanism designed to detect Blood Magic, manufactured by Heph, Kat, Aristotle, and Ada of Caria, on the island of Meninx.

In the Byzantine palace, on Philip's wedding day, Kat used it to find the Earth Blood who, according to prophecy, was meant to kill Riel, little knowing it would be her childhood friend Jacob. Heph had shoved it into the pouch on his belt as the waves came. Miraculously, he discovered it the next day in his soggy leather pouch. The water warped the wooden crank on the side—the part that gave energy to the spring beneath the dial—but Alex wonders if it still works. Was it the mechanism or Fate itself, as determined by the old prophecies, that led Katerina and Jacob to the Byzantine palace?

There's no doubt, at least, that the mechanism is unnaturally powerful. About the length of his hand, it gleams dark gold in the lamplight, as if lit by an inner fire. The little lever on the front is still set to a diamond shape, a symbol of Earth Blood. He winds the crank, which works more smoothly now than it did right after the flood, and watches the needle on the dial spin. It stops, pointing northeast. Perhaps that is Jacob in Troy, or some other Earth Blood in between. Then he changes the lever to the image of the snake for Snake Blood. The dial spins around again and points almost to the top of the device. Southeast. Alex pulls on his boots and throws his cloak over his sleeping tunic. He unpins the tent flap and ducks through, into cool night air, redolent of smoke, roasted meat, and charred flesh. The funeral pyres outside the camp have become a glowing, smoking crumble. High above him, a crescent moon scythes its way across the paling heavens.

He walks silently through the camp, following the needle on the gently humming mechanism. At the perimeter, where torches still burn brightly, he sees armed men patrolling and checks the device again. The closest Snake Blood is beyond the Macedonian camp, then, across the wide fields, though if he is one mile or a thousand, Alex does not know.

"No sign of the enemy?" he calls to the watch. Two men approach him, one holding a torch.

"No, my lord," the soldier says, his smile revealing several missing teeth. "I imagine them Greeks'll come to us, begging clemency soon as sunrise. Shouldn't be much longer."

The horizon beyond the river is a thin blue-gold line, a harbinger of approaching day. It was a foolish plan, he knows, to find a Snake Blood out here among the men, and he turns back toward the camp. But out of the corner of his eye, he sees movement on the dark road to Chaeronea. He turns back and squints.

In the distance, a tiny, solitary figure picks its way slowly toward the Macedonian camp.

"Someone is coming," he says, and the guards swing their bows off their shoulders and nock the arrows. "But it's only one person. Hardly the Greek entourage of negotiators and generals." They peer into the gloom. The dial on the mechanism moves in Alex's hands. By the torches' glow, he sees that it is pointing directly toward the traveler.

As the stranger approaches, the sky lightens. Something about his stride reminds Alex of... But no, that can't be. Heph said he returned to Athens, to his scientific experiments, unwilling to be mixed up in wars of magic and monsters. But as the first rays of the rising sun brighten the plain, Alex sees that he was right.

It's unmistakably him: the prince's old friend and childhood teacher. Aristotle.

Known throughout Greece as the wisest man in the world.

Sauntering straight toward a military camp as if he owns the place...

As if conjured by Alexander's need of him. Alex thinks fleetingly of Fate and its interventions—he has the uncanny sense that everything that has ever happened to him was determined infinite years before any of them were alive, a master plan, unseen by the eyes of men.

"Stand down," Alex barks at the guards, and he runs across the field, not even caring if the night watch sees his limp. The old philosopher, for his part, doesn't seem at all surprised to see Alexander racing toward him as the sun rises. His gray eyes twinkle as he stops walking and cocks his head. "Out for an early-morning stroll, my prince?"

"What are you doing here?" Alex grasps Aristotle's arms as if to be sure he isn't a figment of his imagination.

"All Athens could talk about was Philip and his young Alexander, come to conquer us." Aristotle smiles cryptically. "I thought you might need me."

"Why didn't you answer my letters?" How many had he sent the past several months? Three? Four? "Did you receive them?"

Aristotle nods, shifting the pack slung over his shoulder. "You have been through quite an ordeal." He scans Alexander closely, and, as always, seems to take in everything about him in a matter of moments. "Very well, then." He nods. "It's all right."

"What's all right?"

"What has happened to you."

All at once, Alex realizes he knows: Aristotle can see that his Snake Blood powers are really, truly gone, siphoned off with the horror of Riel's brutal spirit.

Aristotle looks at him pityingly. "Now you know firsthand the torment magic can bring. Better by far to rely on the power of your wits."

Alex shakes his head. "I'm not so sure. This morning the Greeks will probably send envoys to negotiate. Philip may refuse, may want to punish them. Athens fears he will turn them into a Macedonian colony. The war may continue, and who knows at what cost to our forces, or theirs, when the whole idea was to *grow* Macedon's army, not weaken us."

Aristotle looks at him shrewdly. "Let us walk to the river over there and sit. I am an old man and tired from walking all night."

As they walk, shadows retreat like water draining into the hard-baked ground. The fields around them glow orange pink, and the Kephisos River looks like a sparkling band of beaten gold. They stop in front of a large tree that bends over the river, its long branches touching the dappled surface. Alex kneels slowly, realizing how stiff and sore he is from battle. It's always this way: to survive the next second, you call on muscles you never knew you had, and the next day they make you pay the price.

For a long moment, they don't speak. Aristotle unhooks a waterskin from his belt and takes a long swig.

"I don't want to lose another Greek or Macedonian soldier," Alex says, choosing his words carefully, "for two reasons. The first is they are men, Greeks, with families. Why waste their lives?" He looks at Aristotle, who wears an expression of polite curiosity, one bushy dark eyebrow raised.

"And the second?"

"We will need them all in Persia." He tries to slow down the tumble of words that want to rush out. "And we can't afford to lose any more time. The Spirit Eaters are on the rise. Surely in Athens you have heard of their predations."

Aristotle stares at a pair of swallows winging their way over the river, swooping and diving for insects. "And King Philip's thoughts?" he asks.

Alex makes a little grunt of disgust. "He doesn't believe they exist at all. He does want to conquer the Persian empire, though he is no great hurry. I agree it is wise not to leave enemies at our gates when we go. But we both know my father." He stops at the word, constantly finding himself entrapped by it. *Father.* His real father was a god.

His real father is dead.

He clears his throat.

Aristotle nods and says, "You're afraid the king will draw this out, that he'll dally with these negotiations instead of crafting an alliance and preparing to march."

He watches the two swallows—he thought they were mates, but now it seems that one is fleeing the other. "Tell me what we can do to get a treaty signed. *Today.*"

Aristotle turns to him and says crisply, "I don't believe you have the necessary abilities to pull off such a thing."

It's as if his teacher has slapped him. "What do you mean? Yesterday I led half the Macedonian army to victory."

Aristotle shrugs. "That's all well and good, but bashing people on the head requires far different skills than conducting complex negotiations among enemies to forge peace."

Alex had almost forgotten how infuriating the old man could be. "What are you getting at?"

"Show me how you would negotiate terms. Prove to me you can."

"How must I..."

Alex trails off as he sees a falcon swiftly flying toward them over the river, scaring off the swallows. It dives down before them, and to the prince's astonishment, it lands, transforming into a beautiful naked woman. She has tan skin; long, shapely limbs; and thick black hair threaded with strands of silver. She rises magnificently before him, and stares at him, unblinking. Her black pupils are ringed with white circles.

"Prince Alexander," she says, smiling. Alex is struck mute but manages to scramble to his feet.

"Prince Alexander, this is Ada of Caria," Aristotle says, removing his battered traveling cloak and draping it around the woman.

Now Alex understands why Kat was so enthralled with this royal Snake Blood. She exudes wisdom, strength, power.

"I have heard much about you," he says, bowing his head.

"And I of you," she replies. Her skin is as smooth as a girl's, except for the lines on either side of her mouth, betraying her age—she must be older than his mother.

Alex realizes he still has the Atlantean Mechanism in his hand and looks down at it. The needle now points directly at Ada. Of course.

"Ah," she says, reaching toward his hand and stroking the device. "Katerina wrote me that this fruit of our labors found the Earth Blood and caused Riel's death. For that we must be infinitely grateful. But that was only the first step. Now I need your help."

"My help?"

"My brother Pixodarus has chased me out of Caria. The people are terrorized. I need an army to dethrone him and make me the sole ruler."

"And thus," says Aristotle, smiling and rocking back and forth on his toes, "begin the treaty negotiations."

Aha, so this is some sort of test. It doesn't surprise Alex—he's used to Aristotle's cryptic riddles and unexpected experiments. He stares at the two of them. He has so much to do—how will he have time to drive out a petty tyrant in Caria? He has the uncomfortable feeling, as he considers the question before him, that Ada is reaching into his thoughts, prodding the way an army surgeon probes a wound. Unnervingly, it reminds him of Riel, sitting in the corners of his mind like a raven in the rafters, listening, watching.

The prodding vanishes, as if she has realized his discomfort and left as a courtesy.

"I can help you, once we have fought our way into Persian territory and conquered the Spirit Eaters," he says. "Though there will, of course, be a price to pay."

Ada's black arched eyebrows rise up questioningly and Aristotle's lip twitches.

"What is that price?" she asks.

"You are unmarried, I think?" he replies. "No children?"

She shakes her head.

"Make me your heir," Alex continues. "Make it publicly known to your people that I will be their king when you die."

Ada strokes her long black hair and purses her mouth. She looks up into the sky, now a glorious blue with white puffy clouds scudding across. "It is a tempting offer," she says silkily, "but my people are devoted to my royal house. They would never accept a foreigner, an outsider with no family relation to us."

Alex's mind churns. If she were younger, he would ask for her hand in marriage. "If you legally adopted me as your son," he says, "would your people accept me as their prince and future king?"

Aristotle chuckles; Ada simply raises an eyebrow, but the suggestion of a smile plays at the corner of her lips. "I suppose, in that case," she says slowly, "they wouldn't have a choice, would they?"

Alexander grins.

"So, you'll help me, then? If I officially adopt you as my son?"

Alex shakes his head. "There is one more thing I require of you."

"We will agree to form a league, but we will not agree to King Philip as its leader," says Chares, general of Athens, standing in a semicircle with the other generals in front of Philip's impressive field tent. The midmorning sun has chased away the night chill, but still Alex shivers, wondering if his plan will work or just make him look like a fool.

The Athenian continues, "We will vote on a leader. Or take turns with different leaders. What gives Philip of Macedon the right to rule us all?"

Philip, splayed in his ivory-inlaid camp chair, swigs wine from his skull cup, leans forward, and roars, "The right of conquest, perhaps?"

Alex, standing to the right of the king's chair, hides his smile. Though he usually hates his father's boorishness, at times like this it can be effective. He glances over at Heph, standing with Parmenion and the other Macedonian generals, and their eyes lock with just a hint of shared amusement.

When Alex returned to their tent this morning and told Heph what had happened, his friend was deeply disappointed he didn't

get to see Aristotle—who is already on his way back to Athens—
and Ada. But he was excited about the plan they devised to seal
an alliance among these contentious warriors.

The red-faced General Theagenes of Thebes, whose army suffered the greatest number of fatalities in yesterday's battle, shifts
from one foot to the other. "He has a point, Chares."

"Fools!" cries the Spartan commander, Agis. Dark-eyed,
hook-nosed, and black-bearded, he seems as fierce as the reputation of his homeland's warriors.

"Why we ever came here to negotiate is beyond my understanding. You still have a strong army of twenty-seven thousand
men! With Sparta's aid, you would be back to thirty thousand!
Why let this one-eyed northern barbarian—he isn't even Greek,
technically—rule over us?"

"Bravely said by a man whose forces didn't even fight yesterday," Philip sneers, his formidable bulk rising from his chair.
"Who came to *observe*. And complicate the negotiations." Sun
glints off his golden diadem and the rondels on his leather breastplate. Despite his battered face and coarse ways, in this moment,
Philip seems every inch a king.

"Oh, we could give you another battle," he continues. "And
kill more of your men. And march into Athens and Corinth
and Sparta and burn your cities and rule them ourselves. But I
am offering to let you keep control of your cities as long as you
contribute to my army and follow my command."

He stands as tall and solid as an oak tree, hands on his broad
hips. A brisk breeze picks up his gold-bordered red cape. "I have
heard from spies that Persia is planning to attack Macedon. Do
you think they will stop there? Once on the mainland, do you
honestly think they would not rush down to grab the rich prize
of Athens?

"Chares," he calls, and the lean, dark-haired Athenian commander snaps to attention. "Has your city forgotten what the
Persian pricks did a hundred and fifty years ago? How they

demolished your Parthenon, killed your men, and stole your women?"

"And who was it that saved Greece from the Persian Plague?" Agis counters, taking a step out from the group. "Was it not the Three Hundred Spartans, led by my own ancestor Leonidas, who blocked Xerxes's armies at Thermopylae until the other Greek armies could arrive? Where was Macedon to help us then? Living in caves and stealing each other's cattle!"

Alex sees a vein throbbing next to Philip's missing eye.

"If we form a league to stop Persia," Agis continues, gesturing wildly, "I say Sparta should lead it! We earned that right from the blood and glory of our men!"

"If that right is earned by blood and glory against Persia, then Athens should lead," says Chares, squaring his shoulders. "We stopped the Persian army during their first invasion, at Marathon. And sank their navy after Thermopylae at the battle of Salamis. They have not attacked us since."

"You pack of jackals, asses, and fools!" Philip jeers. "Who cares what your ancestors did centuries ago? Where were all your fine, glory-coated forefathers yesterday when I defeated your armies in battle? Ashes in pots and moldering bones in fields, that's where they were! Yesterday I handed you a few thousand more, and right now I would gladly add to that number!"

Red-faced, the Greek negotiators reach for their swords, forgetting they had to turn them in to the guards on the perimeter. Agis balls his fists, and Alex fully expects them to begin throwing punches. Heph shoots him an urgent, knowing look. It's time.

He's right. Though Philip told Alex to stand silent and impassive next to the throne and watch, he must intervene. *Now.*

"It is for the gods to decide this," he says at the top of his voice, stepping in between the snarling generals and Philip.

"Sit down, boy!" Philip growls, pushing him aside. "I told you to stay quiet."

"Who is so impious he does not trust the gods?" Alex asks, holding his hands up to the sky. "You, Agis?" He points to the Spartan, who freezes. "You, Chares?" The steely blue eyes beneath thick dark brows meet Alex's, and Chares shakes his head.

"Is there anyone here who will not leave this to the gods?" he asks, walking in front of all the negotiators. No one says a word.

Phoebus, the red-haired Megarian missing a chunk of his nose, says, "Yes, we could ask the gods to decide, Prince Alexander. But how do they tell us the leader they want?"

Philip's single reddish-brown eye stares at Alex. "Yes, how?" he grunts.

"King Philip won the battle yesterday," Alex replies evenly. "He will sacrifice to the gods, and we will wait for them to give us a sign."

A few minutes later, Philip has sacrificed the lamb and placed its limp body on the oil-soaked pyre. Philip lights the wood with a torch. The fire quickly crackles to life.

"I have no idea what you're playing at," he whispers hoarsely to Alex as they back up from the heat of the blaze.

"Hold your hand up and call on the gods to confirm your right to lead," Alex whispers back.

Philip turns his scarred face to Alex and frowns. "What do you have planned, son?" The rising roar of the fire masks his words from the others.

Alex bows his head. "Trust me, Father." The exchange of terms: *father, son,* says everything.

"You'd better hope this works," Philip growls beneath his breath. He raises his right arm and cries in a deep voice, "Oh, gods of Olympus, show that you have chosen me to lead these armies against the foul barbarians of Persia! Zeus, Apollo, and Ares, give me a sign from heaven! A sign these idiotic Greek fools who rest on the honor of their long-dead ancestors cannot deny!"

Thick black smoke wafts all around them, making Alex's eyes

water and his throat raw. Philip, his arm still raised, casts him a scathing look. But then Heph points toward the river as his voice rings out. "A sign!"

A falcon wings its way toward them. The Greek generals mutter and shout, shading their eyes with their hands to see better. The falcon flies right over them, through the smoke... and lands on Philip's outstretched arm.

There is something in its mouth.

The king throws his head back and laughs loudly. The bird steps sideways on long black talons and deposits on the king's head a branch of laurel—the symbol of victory and anointing of humans by the gods.

The entire area goes silent.

The other generals look at each other in awe.

Then, one by one, the negotiators take off their helmets and fall to their knees, heads bowed, praying loudly. All except Agis, the Spartan, who stands with his mouth gaping open.

Alex, too, kneels, his golden helmet tucked under his arm. Brightly polished, it reflects the early-morning sun, and a new red plume waves bravely from its center. Ada tilts her head and slides her sharp yellow gaze from the helmet, to Alex himself, then across the entire assembly. Her beak opens, as if she, like Philip, is laughing. Instead, there is a piercing caw. And then, with a flapping of heavy wings and a whirl of feathers, she flies up and out over the plain. Back to her fortress in Alinda, Alex knows, where she will wait for him to rescue her kingdom, as was their promise.

Philip sits behind his camp desk, muscular booted legs propped up on the table, and belches. He has eaten and drunk much at the feast to celebrate the new League of Corinth, a name less likely to ruffle Athenian feathers than the League of Macedon. After the clear sign from the gods in the form of Ada, the other generals—except the Spartan—agreed to a treaty, and voted

Philip the strategos, the commanding general. This was enough: Sparta by itself is no threat against the combined forces of the rest of Greece and Macedon.

"Tell me how you did that," the king demands, throwing his crown on the folding camp table with a clatter and scratching his scalp.

"It must have been the work of the gods" is all Alex says, seating himself on a camp chair. The light from dozens of lamps flickers around the tent, and in the center, a small brazier of perfumed wood keeps the night chill at bay, its fragrant smoke drifting upward through the opening.

"You are a strange boy," Philip mutters, shaking his head. "And no boy of mine. If I didn't know it before, I know it now."

Alex feels his entire body go rigid, his blood turn to ice.

"I don't know how you did that thing with the falcon," the king goes on, "but you have always been…different. The way you tamed the wildest horse in the known world at the age of thirteen. I'll never forget it."

Alex cannot move.

Finally, Philip waves a large hand. "This doesn't change anything, of course." Now it seems as if it is the king who has the power to read minds. "Yesterday in battle and today in the negotiations, you proved yourself worthy as my heir. And, I suspect, your legacy will one day burnish my own."

Alexander sits back, dizzy with relief. And something else, too: something like real joy. Philip has never told Alex he loved him—has probably never said those words to anyone on earth—and his son never sought to ask it.

Now he doesn't have to.

Hatred and love are not, he suddenly realizes, opposing forces, after all. Perhaps they are folded into each other, inextricably tied up in the pain of wanting something you fear you may never receive.

Philip seems to feel the weight that has settled into the air between them. He lets out a rough laugh. "But your inheritance won't matter for a long, long time, boy, so don't get your heart set on having it anytime soon. I've got a lot of fighting years left in me!"

"May the gods grant it," Alex says with a smile. Then, after a long pause, "Now that we have an alliance, when do we leave for Persia? How quickly can you make arrangements?"

Philip swings his legs off the table and turns to Alex. "I will spend a fortnight seeing to the readying of allied forces," he says. "Then I will leave Parmenion to make the final preparations while you and I make a little trip west."

"West?" Alex says, much more loudly than he would have liked.

"What did I tell you about leaving enemies behind when you're gone?" Philip asks, his one eye twinkling with mischief. "They can take advantage of your absence to bite you in the ass."

Alex rubs his forehead. More delays. How can this even be possible? "What enemies do we have in the west, Father?" he asks.

"Oh, an asp of the most dangerous kind, especially now that Cleo is beginning to show signs of the new shape of things," Philip replies, leaning in to whisper in his ear. "Your mother."

Of course.

"The snake herself is currently nesting in Epirus with her snake brother, King Xander, who was never a great fan of mine." He gestures to a scroll on the desk. "Before we leave for Persia, son—" he smiles broadly, revealing yellowed teeth "—we need to solve the problem of these loathsome snakes once and for all."

Alex has a sinking feeling in the pit of his stomach. "She can't hurt you," he begins, but Philip gestures impatiently to silence him.

"Her brother has an army," the king points out.

"Epirus has never been allied to either Athens or Sparta," Alex counters.

"Epirus is currently not allied to Macedon, either," Philip retorts, "given the fact that I for all intents and purposes dethroned Olympias when I married Cleo. Father Zeus, I couldn't have those two women living in the same palace."

"What are you going to do?" Alex asks in a low voice. "Invade?"

"Oh, Hades, no," Philip replies, chuckling. "That would be a waste. I am going to convince Xander to join the League of Corinth in our invasion of Persia by using your mother's own weapons against her."

"And what are those?" Alex asks, uncomprehending.

The king laughs loudly. "You'll see. I enjoy little surprises as much as you, my son."

CHAPTER FOURTEEN

ZOFIA

A HOUSE OF SIN PRODUCES AN INCREDIBLE amount of dirty laundry, even on a normal day.

But one that secretly trains women in the martial arts is another matter altogether.

Zo can't help but grunt as she shoulders a basket of sodden sheets and exercise tunics through the brothel's service courtyard, a small, cluttered place housing the laundry, kitchen, gardening shed, and other work areas. Though separated only by a tall ornamental gate, this courtyard seems a world away from the luxurious pool and burbling fountain of the main courtyard, where women entertain clients by evening and refresh themselves with a swim in the cool of the morning.

No matter her level of exhaustion, every day since she arrived here in Dardania, home to the recently murdered mad king, the vanished queen, and this now-famed brothel, Zo has worked harder than she ever has in her life, despite the nightmares that leave her ragged at dawn, despite the unwieldy weight of her belly and how it makes her have to pee at the most inopportune times. She has to work hard—she knows she'd be kicked back out onto the streets if she didn't. More than that, she doesn't want to disappoint Alecta.

The day she knocked timidly on the front door, obviously pregnant, her faulty Greek bearing a heavy Persian accent, she expected Alecta to turn her away. But the redhead looked her up and down and nodded briskly. "I hope you're prepared to sweat" was all she said, beckoning Zo in. The relief and gratitude that flooded Zo then was enough to make her swear loyalty to Alecta forever.

But it's more than that. Working hard, throwing herself not just into chores but archery, spear throwing, and sword fighting—everything except for wrestling—helps her forget the heartache that tears at her from the inside. Helps her forget the fear of what may come, fear of the Assassins, of Fate itself, of the unknown.

Sometimes, on a good day, she pushes herself hard enough to burn away even the dreams that normally haunt her as soon as her eyes fall shut—dreams of the Spirit Eater, whose face morphs into Kohinoor's over and over again.

Yesterday she was practicing with a broadsword, and now, reaching up to hang the sodden sheets, one by one, on the clothesline, her sore muscles ache so much that her arms begin to quiver. She stops to catch her breath and rub her round belly. It has been just about nine months since Kohinoor told her she was with child, and Zo knows the baby must be coming soon.

Her heart snags in her chest. Cosmas, the father of the baby, is dead. Murdered. Kind, sweet, dutiful Cosmas. And yet—*what kind of person is she for thinking this?*—it isn't the loss of Cosmas that hurts. It is the loss of Ochus, the man she loved after him, and loves still. The man who killed Cosmas. Abandoned her without word, without a reason.

The same man who lied to her, who held her captive, who led her into the mouth of death more than once.

And yet...

He is also the man who *couldn't* kill her, who insisted on protecting her. And somehow, despite his roughness, despite how impossible it was to read his feelings, despite *all of it*, she had opened up to him, had fallen for him, hating herself the whole time but unable to stop herself from seeing what was good and brave in him.

And eventually, he had confessed that he loved her, too.

Sometimes, in the lamp-lit night, when the other women gossip about the pleasure men seek from the brothel house, Zo can't stop her mind from traveling back to that starry night in Macedon, several months ago now, when Ochus whispered promises against her skin, when he held her so protectively she could have sworn he would never let go—and then her legs and belly tingle and her knees go weak from a sensation that is most certainly not tiredness.

That was the night before he left her with no message, no explanation at all.

Why did he do it—kill Cosmas and betray her? What did he stand to gain? Was he driven by jealousy or just plain cruelty?

These are the questions she cannot answer, and it torments her even more than her fears of being followed, even more than her nightmares of the threads of Fate itself twining around her ankles like vines and dragging her into the dirt, burying her alive.

There is so much to fear, even in this haven of safety and satisfying work.

And yet there is one thing that she cannot find it in herself to fear:

The creature in the diamond cage.

She can hear it stirring restlessly even now, in the storeroom off the laundry. She's not afraid—even though she saw what happened, saw what the creature did, how it swooped down on them, darkening the entire sky. How it attacked a former tavern keeper's wife, and when it was done, left only a smear of entrails, bones, and hair.

In the bloody chaos of those horrifying moments, Zofia had run into the service courtyard and hidden in the laundry. Huddling there with the laundress, she had witnessed nothing short of a miracle. King Pyrolithos called forth fire and ash to ensnare the monster in an enchanted cage. He is not just a king, she realized, but a man of incomparable magic power. The brothel women, who were suspicious of him and his purported ties to Queen Cynane before, now accept him readily. Protected by a wizard with powers like these, they would have nothing to fear.

Except, of course, the Spirit Eater.

Still, she isn't scared of it, only oddly mystified. Perhaps that is because whenever she approaches, it seems to go quiet, as if watching her closely.

Zo gathers another basket of wet laundry from the cooling cauldron in the wash room. But instead of going back to the clothing lines, she steps into the storeroom, squinting in the darkness at the monster. The bars of its cage seem to glitter with their own light, a kind of magic Zo has never heard of before, powers possessed by King Pyrolithos and no other.

The Spirit Eater itself is impossible to describe, even trapped as it is in this too-small, gleaming cage. The creature is all shadow and movement, all cold wind and hissing, all fang and claw and black leather tongue, forked like a snake's.

Zo has heard of terrifying creatures before, those that have risen from the ashes of myth and are rumored to still exist, like the Hellion—which, it is said, Queen Cynane of Dardania once tamed and rode, back when she was a mere princess in Macedon. And, of course, Zo has seen another such creature, less terrifying but just as awe inspiring: Vata, the white-winged Pegasus, whom she rode through the clouds to Persepolis.

But the Spirit Eater is unlike any such beast of myth. It is somehow fleshless and shapeless, constantly shifting, sometimes looking like more than one creature, making her wonder if something is wrong with her eyes or the light. Or perhaps the creature itself is made of light and shadow, constantly changing and moving. Yet it *must* be made of flesh, because it devours flesh.

Then again, it is said that in the time before time, the Spirit Eaters also devoured the gods.

Now, staring at the creature, trying to take it in, to understand what she's seeing, Zo marvels at the strange synchronicity of fate. At Kohinoor's suggestion, she traveled far into the Eastern Mountains to find a Spirit Eater, in the hope of altering her fate, saving herself from having her blood mingled with that of Macedon's. She had never wanted to marry Alexander—she'd always yearned, simply, to be free to choose.

And yet, despite her unbelievable, excruciating journey, it is only *here*, on western shores, that she has found not only a Spirit Eater but also a fate of sorts that she likes. Fate is strangely circular, she sees now, like a snake eating its own tail.

"Can you change mine?" she whispers. A forked tongue—or is it two?—emerges from the Spirit Eater's mouth and licks its black leather lips. If that is an answer, she doesn't understand it.

Despite knowing now that Kohinoor can't be trusted, she still wonders what the old woman intended when she told Zo to seek out these shadowy monsters.

She bends down for her heavy basket and cries out as a pain rips through her abdomen.

Someone is at her side in an instant, holding her up.

"Is it time?"

Alecta. Her arms around Zo, guiding her, taking on her weight.

Another cramp seizes her and she gasps.

Now that Alecta stands between Zo and the cage, the Spirit Eater has begun to lash out, Zo realizes, releasing its unbearably cold breath, slashing its claws out between the bars. If Alecta noticed it had been strangely calm when she first entered the storeroom, she does not say.

Gulping in air, Zo straightens up. "No," she says. "I...don't think so."

Alecta places her hands on Zo's shoulders. "It is too much,

Zotasha," she says softly, using the mostly fake name Zo gave her on arriving. Anyone looking for the princess missing from Pella would be searching for Zofia.

Zo starts to protest, but Alecta shushes her. "Come, I will have Zara finish the laundry. You shouldn't be in here with the...*beast*...anyway."

Many of the other girls are terrified the Spirit Eater will escape and devour them in their beds, Zo knows. It is a reasonable thing to fear.

Alecta leads her to a door next to the garden shed, takes a key off her belt, opens it, and gestures for Zo to enter. It's a small room, lit only by the smoke hole in the roof. A girl Zo has never seen before sits at a table, chopping herbs with great concentration. She has a lovely profile, with smooth pale skin, thick dark lashes, and luxuriant black curls tumbling down her back.

"Yes," she says, not looking up.

"I have brought you the helper you requested," Alecta says. The girl turns and looks up expectantly. Zo gasps. The right side of her face has been ravaged by fire or acid. It's a mass of twisted red scars and lumps. The girl, staring hard at Zo, doesn't seem terribly impressed with her, either.

"Zotasha, this is Badri," Alecta says firmly. "You will do as she says. You will find this work less physically demanding."

Zo nods, and Alecta leaves them alone, locking the door behind her. Despite trusting Alecta, a shiver of uncertainty works its way up Zo's spine. Gentle as she was just now with Zo, Alecta could turn on her.

"Well, sit down and make yourself useful, if you *can*," Badri says curtly, in Persian, with a swift glance at Zo's belly.

Despite the girl's coldness, Zo finds it a relief, after all these months, to hear the elegant lilting music of her native tongue, even if it is spiced with nastiness. The Persian language is like a song, or poetry—medicine for her soul.

Badri pushes a small knife and a mound of dried roots toward her. Zo assumes the girl is preparing medications until Badri says, "Deadly nightshade."

Zo's heart skips a beat. Everyone knows deadly nightshade is one of the most poisonous plants on earth.

"Peel off the skin," Badri continues, "and once we have finished this pile, we will pound them with mortars. Don't touch your eyes or face. If you put your fingers anywhere near your mouth, you will die."

Zo stands there frozen for a moment. Then she swallows hard and pulls up a stool and sets to work, stripping the skin off the roots with the sharp knife blade. She works efficiently and wordlessly. Once she and Badri have finished skinning the roots, they mash them with mortars and pestles, creating a thick, gooey paste.

"What is this for?" she finally asks in Persian.

Badri eyes her with evident hostility. "Why do you want to know?"

"Well," Zo replies evenly, "I don't suppose I really need to. But the fact that Alecta brought me here means she trusts me. So, I think you can, too."

Badri blinks. "She might not know you for who you are, but I am not so stupid. Even Dardanians who speak Persian cannot tell a noble accent from one off the streets. They can't see that you are highborn." Badri scans her up and down. "Say something. In our native tongue."

"I don't know—"

But before she can finish, Badri cuts her off. "A high-ranking noblewoman is my guess. Maybe even a princess. So, tell me, what king or lord did not approve of his daughter's choice of lover?"

Zo can feel herself blushing furiously. "My story is none of your business." All the warmth she felt moments ago at the familiarity of the language has fled.

Badri continues to mash the deadly herb. Without looking up, she says only, "I imagine you are no stranger to fine jewels."

Is this another insult? Zo isn't sure. She doesn't like the way the girl seems to judge her. But then she notices a twitch at the corner of Badri's mouth.

"All of the women will be issued jewelry," she adds, still without looking up. She attacks her paste once more with the mortar. "Necklaces, bracelets, rings, and earrings, all with secret compartments."

"Secret comp—*oh.*" Zo recalls how often Alecta has said that even the strongest woman is unlikely to beat a man in battle if they are one-on-one. That they need other weapons to even the score: deception, surprise…and poison.

"We will also be given poison darts we will blow out of tubes made to look like flutes. If a man sees us pulling one out, he will think we are going to play music for him."

Very clever, Zo has to admit.

"So, where are you from?" Badri asks. "Near the west coast, from your accent, I think. Halicarnassus? Or no, Sar—"

"Sardis," Zo replies, putting down her mortar, astounded at Badri's ability to guess at both her rank and territory of origin in just a few minutes. The girl must be very studied, or—

"Don't stop!" Badri commands, glaring. "Not until I tell you to. The plant must be ground down while it is still moist."

Zo picks up her mortar and returns to mashing. They work in silence for a while, and Zo must admit to herself that this is easier work than the laundry, even if it does have the potential to kill her. When Badri judges the mashing to be complete, she and Zo spread the poisonous paste on wooden boards to dry, then set the boards on a table in the far corner.

"Over the next few days, it will turn to a powder," Badri explains. "Now, wash your hands in this basin," she commands, pointing to another table. "Very carefully."

After Zo has dried her hands, Badri hands her a painted clay cup. "Come, we have earned a bit of wine."

Zo looks into the cup, hesitating. Would the girl test her? Poison her just because she can?

"Personally, I prefer to be on top," Badri says.

Zo glances at her in embarrassed surprise, until she realizes Badri is commenting on the cup she handed her—on which a pair of figures are painted. The figures are very clearly having sex. Sometimes Zo is so exhausted she almost forgets that she lives in a brothel now.

Badri sets down the pitcher and starts to laugh, a pleasant, silvery sound at odds with her fierce demeanor and disfigured face. "That blush will get you in trouble, girl!"

Zo begins to relax. She sips the wine and happily bites into the honey cakes Badri offers, no longer worried about being judged—or poisoned. Badri becomes almost chatty, gossiping about Alecta and the other women she watches in the court-yard through a peephole in the door. Zo realizes that Badri is glad of the company—it seems she rarely leaves this room—and happy to speak her native tongue again. Zo begins to like her sharp humor.

"Where did you learn these skills?" she asks, gesturing to the poison drying on the planks.

"Ah," Badri says. "A long story. My family lives in Apasa. But my mother's younger brother, Kadmus, became a general in the Macedonian army."

Zo's heart skips a beat. *Macedon.* "Oh?"

"Great King Artaxerxes doesn't make all the decisions where our fine nation is concerned," Badri says, leaning toward Zo confidentially. "Given your status, you may have heard the whispers that he is under the thumb of other interest groups."

"Other interest groups?"

Badri rolls her eyes. "Have you really not heard of the Assassins?"

Some wine catches at the back of Zo's throat and she coughs.

"My uncle was made a spy against his will. If he didn't report on Macedon exactly as the Assassins demanded, well... My mother and I were their collateral."

Shaking, Zo pours herself more wine to calm her nerves—why does fate seem to twist around and around her no matter where she goes or what she does? How can this girl—hundreds of miles away from Persia, sitting across from Zo in her safe haven—be the niece of an Assassin? They say fate is a snake chasing its own tail, but this snake is swallowing itself whole.

"The Assassins took me as a hostage for my uncle's good behavior," Badri continues. "One of the higher-ups, Zand, forced me to become his lover."

"You mean he...he raped you?" Zo asks in a small voice. She still remembers her near rape on board the ship that took her to Macedon, by a foul-smelling sailor Ochus fought off her and then threw overboard. But if Ochus hadn't arrived in time...

Badri's eyes are distant. "He was ugly and cruel, but he had a soft spot for me. I grew used to him—enough to pretend. And, after a time, it worked; I became indispensable to him. He insisted they teach me a useful skill, the art of making poisons. I had been a skilled maker of medical remedies at home, you see. This work is much the same, only its purpose is to destroy rather than to heal."

Another sharp spasm passes through Zo's abdomen, like the harsh grip of a poison. She gasps, wincing. But Badri doesn't see it. She's staring fixedly into her past.

"It would have been all right, I think, if I hadn't fallen in love with someone else," she says softly. "Kazem. Tall and handsome and brave. We met secretly, when Zand traveled. But somehow, Zand found out. One night, as I slept, he painted my face with burning poison. I was two-faced, he said, laughing as I screamed in pain and tried to wipe it off. Now the world would see both my faces, he said. That same night, Kazem had an accident, it seems, and fell out of a high window."

Badri pushes her chair away from the table and clears the dishes. "I was closely guarded and had no choice but to stay on," she says, setting the cups and plates on a tray in the corner. "I worked hard making their poisons and never once complained about what he had done to me. Zand still wanted me. In some sick way, I suppose I should've been grateful for that. He said he was doing me a favor when he took me back, as no other man ever would."

Zo feels another sharp pain but grinds her teeth together to keep from crying out. Badri's story must be making *her* sick. Rape, murder, poison, disfigurement. She wonders if she is going to throw up.

"And then one night, after a banquet, I realized that Zand and all the guards were drunk. I stole their coin pouches and fled, heavily veiled. I went first to Pella, to find my uncle. But Prince Alexander had stabbed him in a rage, it was said, and Kadmus had dragged himself off somewhere to heal. I couldn't discover where. How can a girl with half a face support herself? No one would hire me as a waitress or shopgirl. Not even as a whore. And then I heard of this place and came here. I know the Assassins, and I know Zand. They are looking for me. And a girl with half a face is talked about. These past weeks, Alecta has kept me in here, hidden and safe, making poisons for the New Amazons."

So that was why Zo hadn't seen her before today.

Zo's heart starts to pound as she wonders if Badri knows Ochus, knows, perhaps, where he is. Yet how can she ask without giving away her own identity?

"Once, in Sardis," she says, knotting her hands. *Did she wash them well enough? Is she dying even as they speak?* She winces with another cramp, but tries to ignore it. "There was a sumptuous banquet at the palace. I looked down from the women's viewing chamber and saw the Great King. He was as tall and straight as a spear. I also saw his chief advisor, Darius, a small dark man. And Darius had a very handsome son striding around. I forget his name."

"Ochus," Badri replies, leaning back in her chair, still not observing Zo's discomfort. "Darius is chief of the Assassins Guild. Ochus works with him."

"Are they in Persepolis with the Great King?" Zo asks, hoping her voice is casual. She's not sure what answer she wants to hear. That Ochus died bravely? That he survived and was revealed to have been working in solidarity with his father the whole time?

Badri shrugs. "The last I heard before I escaped from Apasa was that Ochus was under suspicion for not following orders. That he had botched a mission and disappeared, obviously afraid of the Assassins' wrath. No one had heard from him. But I imagine he will appear soon," she adds, barking out a laugh.

"Why's that?" Zo asks, as something like hope flickers in her chest.

"For months, rumor has it Darius has been planning to assassinate the Great King, who has become a bit suspicious about what his advisor is really up to. If he succeeds, Darius will become the next Great King. And Ochus, as his only heir, will be brought back into the fold. I imagine Darius will explain that whatever it is Ochus did was, in fact, on secret orders."

Zo feels a warm flush spread through her—if Darius is king, surely Ochus, wherever he is—will hear the news and return. But what will it mean? Will he return to the umbrella of his father's protection? Become the new Chief Assassin himself? A pang of discomfort knots in her chest, making it hard to breathe. Will Darius, as the new Great King, force Prince Ochus to track Zo down and kill her once and for all, as punishment for escaping Macedon and ruining his plans?

The child within her gives a hard kick, straight into Zo's ribs, and she feels another stab of pain, this one unbearable—she cries out as hot water gushes from her.

Suddenly, without knowing how she got there, she is on all fours on the floor, panting in pain. Then it ebbs away, leaving her drained of strength. She tries to lie down on her side, but there are hands gripping her shoulders. "Lucky for you," a sharp voice says in Persian, "I am also a trained midwife. Let me help you over to my bed."

The next hours are a blur of grinding cramps slashing rhythmically across periods of utter exhaustion. Badri ties ropes to the top of her bed for Zo to hold on to when the contractions sweep over her. When she feels the discomfort start to rise, she grabs the straps and twists until it drains away and she goes limp as a rag doll. Her hair has become sopping-wet tendrils of sweat. Her skin is slick with it.

Sometimes, Alecta is there, mopping Zo's brow with cool mint water and offering words of encouragement. Badri gives her herbed wine to drink to keep up her strength, though once, when the pain becomes unbearable, she throws it up. At one point, lying motionless, waiting for more pain, Zo notices starlight filtering in through the smoke hole and flickering oil lamps set on the tables.

She has no idea how long this has gone on. Has it been days, or only hours? Each contraction leaves her weaker than the one before. The air smells thick and coppery. The sheets are soaked with blood. Is it too much blood? Is she bleeding to death?

She has been through so much during this pregnancy—captured and starved by slavers, riding hundreds of miles along the Royal Road as Ochus's prisoner, lost and wandering the Eastern Mountains, slashed by the claws of a Spirit Eater, falling from a Pegasus, drugged by Kohinoor—she wonders if it has all been too much. But despite it all, she has trudged on, endeavored to save herself so that she could save the child. Maybe it was all for nothing. Perhaps both she and the baby will die. Perhaps this time tomorrow their bodies will be consumed by flames in the funeral pyre, their ashes shoveled into a pot, and... She gasps as a new eruption of pain splays through her body like poisonous tentacles.

"It is time, Zotasha," Badri says, an urgent edge to her voice.

With a shriek, she finds the last vestiges of strength and pushes as hard as she can. Below her, Badri and Alecta wait, arms extended. "I see the head!" Badri cries. "Push harder!"

But Zo has nothing left to push with. Absolutely nothing. "I can't," she whimpers.

"Can we pull him out?" Alecta asks, her voice humming with fear.

"We'll have to do something, or he'll suffocate," Badri replies. Zo, eyes closed, feels prodding, tugging fingers. "Oh, goddess Anahita, he's stuck."

Waves of sickening pain thud through her, but they diminish as she feels herself sinking into unconsciousness. The voices around her fade, and she closes her eyes. She has never been so tired before. She will slip into blissful sleep. Nothing really matters anymore...

A bucketful of cold water slaps Zo's face. Sputtering and rubbing her eyes, she looks at Alecta's angry face.

"If you don't push now, your baby will die, and Badri will get her knife and pull it out in pieces. And while you will probably survive, it won't be for long, because I will personally feed you to the Spirit Eater," she snarls.

And yet it isn't fear that makes Zo push, but the knowledge of love and support all around her here, suddenly surging up within her, powerful, unstoppable. These women—total strangers—are fighting so hard for her. And her baby. Fighting with her *and* for her, in a world where sometimes even mothers leave you—like Zo's did.

Gritting her teeth, she pushes, thinking of the anguish and anger of her mother leaving when she was so young, of not being loved when she needed it, of constantly seeking love, of birthing love now, raw and real and beautiful love.

"Good girl!" Badri cries, as the child passes out of her, feeling like some enormous, wet sea creature. She sees the tops of the heads of the two women—one black as night, the other red as a fiery sunset—as they turn the baby over and examine it.

Zo lies back, stunned. She can see that the women are looking not at a giant sea creature but a tiny, pink-skinned baby. She wants to weep. But then she realizes something is wrong. It's the silence. The baby isn't crying. Why aren't the women saying anything as they look at the baby? Is it alive? Oh, all the gods of Persia and Greece, please let it be alive. After all this—

"A healthy girl!" exclaims Alecta, wiping Zo's sweat-drenched face with a cool moist cloth as Badri slaps the child, eliciting a fierce cry of protest from the baby, piercing the air with its pure, high sound.

A brief sob gushes out of Zo.

"Good thing, too, Zotasha," Alecta says, a joking edge to her voice. "We don't allow boys to live here."

"Can I see… Can I hold her?" Zo asks weakly, pushing herself up. Badri washes the baby with white wine and vinegar and swaddles her in a white blanket, then hands her to Zo. She peers into the tiny, crumpled red face. Wide dark brown eyes stare up at her.

"Oh, my baby," Zo says, her voice shattering into a million muffled sobs of joy. She nuzzles her—this child she has made, this new life, this new chance, this untouched one. The girl who was fated to come into her life.

And for the first time in nine months, she is truly happy.

Days of exhaustion pass, blurring into sleepless nights of feeding and dozing and soothing and pacing, of aching breasts crusted in sweet milk. Slowly, her body begins to return to its former shape, or some semblance of it. One day, when the child is a little over two weeks old, Zo looks into the cradle at the beautiful bundle sleeping peacefully for once, and is shocked by the sense of peace that descends on her. Even through her tiredness, she marvels constantly at her child's perfection. The silken dark hair, the curling fingers with perfect miniature nails, the smooth skin and sweet baby breath. It is as if all the beauty and sweetness in the entire world resides in this tiny girl, as if Zo has never known joy before the wondrous moment when she first held her in her arms.

Over the past two weeks, the baby has grown and thrived. This lucky infant has dozens of mothers; all of the women in the brothel have offered to watch her, bathe her, and change her diapers.

In Zo's family, it is tradition to name the first female child after her maternal grandmother, so she should have called her Attoosheh. But the very name makes Zo's hackles rise in resentment. Selfish and vain, the widowed Attoosheh ran off to marry a Bactrian king when Zo was only a few months old, leaving her behind in Sardis. The only thing Attoosheh ever did for Zo was to return twelve years later, widowed again, clutching another infant, Roxana, Zo's beloved half sister. Attoosheh ignored Roxana, too, and Zo was more like a mother to her than a sister.

Zo considered naming the baby Roxana as a way of making her sister live again. But she realized it would be unfair to burden this new soul with such painful memories. That first night Zo escaped from the palace to find Cosmas, Roxana had followed her. The slavers who captured Zo also caught Roxana, but at six years old she was too young to do hard labor or work as a prostitute. They had taken her behind a stand of wheat and killed her. Her little sister's screams still haunt Zo, still make her heart ache with the loss.

Finally, Zo decided to call her daughter Mandana, the name of the old nurse who raised her for over a decade while her mother, Attoosheh, was away. Loving, generous, and warm,

Mandana had nursed Zo when she was sick, played with her, told her stories, and listened to her problems. Zo has missed Mandana, too, and longs for her toothless grin and bright brown eyes alive with mischief.

"I can watch her now," says a throaty voice. Zo turns to see the stunning Ethiopian, Sophonisba, standing in the doorway. "Look!" she cries, holding up two tiny tunics—one blue and one green. "The girls have sewn some more!"

Smiling her thanks, Zo makes her way downstairs and across the courtyard. Her swollen breasts are painful at times. The rest of her is still somewhat sore and swollen, and she wonders if she will ever feel beautiful and young again. But it's been two weeks, and she has to get back to work. Her determination to contribute is no longer a silent appeal for Alecta to let her stay. It's a resounding thank-you to both Alecta and Badri for helping her through her labor and saving her baby's life.

As she approaches Badri's room at the far end of the service courtyard, she feels drawn to see the Spirit Eater. She opens the door, and sunlight falls on the blurring black form in the cage. But this time it no longer sits placidly when it sees her. It roars in rage and hunger, flinging itself against the bars of the cage, sending foaming flecks of spittle onto the floor. Its snarl seems to wrap around her, as if trying to pull her in and suck something out of her.

The natural fear that was absent in her before surges up now, and Zo leaps back, shocked. The creature has never done this in her presence before. What makes it so vicious today?

Could it be... It must be Mandana. All the times Zo came face-to-face with the monster before, she was pregnant. Today, the baby is upstairs in the house. Is it something about Mandana that tames the Spirit Eater? The creature continues to howl, shaking the diamond bars. Saliva continues to fling out at her in a sickening spray.

Zo stands perfectly still for a moment, stunned, trying to

figure out why it has changed its behavior. Then, by some un-
spoken instinct, she turns on her heel, races back to her room,
and takes little Mandana from Sophonisba's arms, causing both
the woman and the baby to each give a startled cry.

Moments later, she is back in the dim room below, standing
right in front of the Spirit Eater's cage. Sure enough, the angry
movement, the hissing and lashing, immediately stops, and the
creature seems to quiet, as if tamed. Zo, too, feels different with
Mandana in her arms—safer, somehow, and calmer, too.

There can be no denying the change.

Nor its cause.

Mandana. The baby.

Somehow her presence has an effect on the Spirit Eater. It
was never Zo's influence but the unborn child's that seemed to
tame the monster. Mandana herself seems peaceful, curling into
her mother and falling back to sleep with a soft buzz of breath.

Zo's heart races as she feels the tiny heartbeat of her daughter against her chest, held close. It *is* Mandana who has calmed
the creature. She's sure of it now.

Her mind runs in a million directions at once. This must have
something to do with why Kohinoor so desperately wanted the
baby. She remembers the ancient paintings in Kohinoor's cave
in the Eastern Mountains, a winged infant holding a wax tablet rose above the earth as darkness descended from above...

Suddenly, Zo is shivering uncontrollably. Because she sees
now that she was driven by fate to have this child, somehow.
For reasons she still cannot fathom. She cannot know what will
come, or how it will all take place, but neither can she shake the
dawning conviction that the sweet sleeping baby in her arms
may somehow carry the fate of the world in her tiny hands.

CHAPTER FIFTEEN

KATERINA

TORCHLIGHT FLICKERS OVER THE ROWS OF PIL-
grims bedding down for the night on the cool marble floor of
the temple. Kat bends down in front of Kephos, an old man
with a palsy and, smiling, helps him tip his sleeping draft into
his toothless mouth. Jacob and two priests attend to other patients, offering words of sympathy or a joke. This is the ritual
every night in the Temple of Asklepios, a sanctuary dedicated
to the god of healing, outside the ruins of Troy.

When they arrived from Byzantium, nearly five months ago,
they found no sign of the Aesarian Lords. Just a huge mound
of countless lumpy hills with trees growing out of them and
heaps of fallen stones. Surveying this barren landscape, Jacob
said, "Timaeus and the other Lords must have been delayed.
We'll have to wait for them."

But *where* to wait was the question. The midwinter wind
whipping off the turbulent gray sea whistled right through their
bones. And while they could have made a shelter on the fallen
citadel, the shepherds who grazed their flocks in the area told
them that at night the city was haunted, cursed. Demons and
dark gods lived in tunnels beneath the destruction, they said.
Those foolish enough to venture out at night saw smoke and

fire rising from the crevasses, and heard unearthly shrieks and howls. Some people disappeared, never to be seen again.

And they believed it, in a way. This city is the site of one of history's cruelest wars, defined and marked by savagery and flame and loss, where it had once been a rich city of bustling trade and refined culture.

Troy was safe only during the day, when visitors sacrificed to Achilles, Patroclus, Hector, and the other heroes who fell here. As the sun set, travelers fled, abandoning its ghostly ruins to the wind and the memories still trapped and echoing among fallen stones.

The nearest village was a two-day walk. But one of the shepherds pointed them to the temple on a hill about a mile from Troy. It was one of several Asklepions, or houses of healing, in lands dominated by Greek culture, even here in westernmost Persia.

"People come from Lesbos and Byzantium for healing," the shepherd said, his weathered face an intricate map of lines and spots. "You could stay there for a while, if you help them with the work."

So they traipsed across the plain and up the well-worn track on the hill. There, at the top, stood the little temple, its mismatched columns of black and pink and white marble clearly plucked from the ruins of Troy itself. There was something both tragic and beautiful in their reuse: hope always rises from the ashes. People reclaim what they can and make something new.

The temple was the heart of a tiny village of sorts, surrounded by numerous other buildings: offices, stables, a blacksmith's, a kitchen, a henhouse, latrines, and a laundry. After offering to work for their board, Kat and Jacob settled into one of the many sturdy single-room houses in the back, most of them used by families of the sick.

When Jacob asked the priests whether they had seen any Aesarian Lords, they smiled and shook their heads, misunderstanding. "They do not bother us here," said Iolanta, a strong-jawed, silver-haired priestess, standing between the columns of the sanctuary and gesturing to the entire compound. "We have no magic blood." And here she cast an amused look at the two priests standing with her, who smiled slyly back. "We merely help interpret the gods' instructions."

But despite their denial of any magic blood in the sanctuary, Kat found herself fascinated by the temple's healing rituals and wondered if some of the priests were secret Snake Bloods. For one thing, her normally numb golden fingertip—the one Princess Laila of Sharuna gave her to replace the injury Cynane had done—tingled almost constantly, as it did when in the presence of Blood Magic. For another thing, the sanctuary was dominated by a statue of a bearded, muscular Asklepios, three times the height of a man, holding a staff, around which a huge snake coiled. Sacred snakes slithered throughout the temple and often wound themselves around the patients, staring into their faces as their forked tongues darted in and out. Then they returned to the priests and priestesses and seemed to talk to them about the person's illness, just as they would to a Snake Blood, Kat noticed.

Every night, bedding down inside the sanctuary, the patients were given a bit of opium infused in wine to help them sleep. The following morning, they reported their dreams to the priests, who interpreted them and, together with messages from the temple snakes, developed a healing regimen.

At first, Kat and Jacob helped the priests and priestesses with cooking and cleaning. They washed sheets and tunics, filled lamps with oil, swept the fine silky dust off the porticoes, and hauled water from the sacred spring for patients to drink and wash with.

Then, one day, Kat, who had been collecting food bowls from the pilgrims lounging in the sanctuary, found herself face-to-face with a large black snake in a patch of sunlight. Its head hovered right and left, and its unblinking yellow eyes stared at her, silently beseeching her for…something. She set down the bowls and sat cross-legged in front of it.

Breathing deeply, she closed her eyes and emptied her mind. Her longing for Alex, her guilt about Heph, the spot she wanted to scrub off Jacob's best tunic—everything drained from her. Then she became aware of warm stone under her scales. She remembered the joy of gliding in dark secret tunnels and the freedom of shedding a too-tight skin. She was still in her body but also inside the mind of the snake. She slithered across the sun-dappled marble tiles to Briseis, a wealthy middle-aged widow with a raw, flaking rash over half her body, sitting on her pallet in the shadow of the large statue of Asklepios.

The woman's eyes were sharp and clear, though crust and redness disfigured her eyelids. She set aside a scroll she had been reading and murmured words of welcome to Kat as the snake, extending her hand, for it is a good sign when the sacred snakes visit those in need of healing. Kat curled up in her lap, raising her head to look closely at the diseased skin. Flakes and runny red sores, torn skin and raw flesh. Then she sank out of the snake and into the woman's skin, into the blood beneath it, and traveled through veins into muscles and organs. She pulsated with the rhythm of the woman's heart. She became the intake and exhale of breath. She lost herself in the swirling bloodstream.

Briseis was…imbalanced. Something was…off. Not seriously, not anything that could kill. But something to irritate and disfigure. Images rose before her. Of undigested meat causing internal swelling and bad blood. This woman shouldn't eat meat. Of honey, golden amber, sweet and healing. Of tangy lemons for cleansing. Of sunlight, warm and clear. For years, Briseis had lived in the shadows, fearing what the sun would do to her skin.

Kat was no longer Kat, nor was she the black snake. She was pure Mind inside the woman, thought only, without form or voice. She was…

Lying sprawled on the hard, cold sanctuary floor.

"Katerina," said a kindly male voice. Confused, she pushed herself up to a seated position. Clonius, a bearded young priest, squatted beside her. "Are you all right?"

She nodded, rubbing her eyes. "Briseis," she said, gesturing to the woman on the other side of the sanctuary. The black snake had wrapped itself loosely around the woman's neck. "She must not eat meat. She needs to eat honey and lemons, and the honey should also be applied to her bad skin. Also, she needs some sun every day."

Clonius looked between Kat and Briseis, his eyes wide. Then he grinned. "Ah," he said. "I think I understand." He picked up the silver lotus blossom pendant hanging around Kat's neck and smiled. Lotus blossom helps Snake Bloods recover from their trances, bringing them back to themselves if they have been traveling in animals. "Have you had these experiences with animals before?"

Kat nodded, unwilling to say anything about them. "You are right to keep silent on such matters," Clonius says in a low voice. "There are those who would gladly take us east for execution if they knew. But if we are careful, claiming we have been chosen by the healing god to work with his sacred snakes, we will be safe. The Aesarian Lords respect the traditional gods."

The priests of Asklepios were secret Snake Bloods. Kat had been right. And yet Ada had never told her anything like *this*.

She looked at Clonius. "How—how was I able to do that? To go into Briseis's body to discover what was wrong with her?"

Clonius grinned. "These are special snakes with powers of their own, Katerina. For many centuries now, we have bred them in our sanctuaries to work with us in diagnosing the sick. They act as a medium between our own minds and the bodies of the ill."

From that day, she has worked with the snakes to help the pilgrims. Some of them were beyond healing, with growths curling around organs. But even then, she learned what foods and medications reduced pain and increased energy. It was striking, she thought, that Jacob had healed those with injuries in Byzantium—he could not cure those with illnesses—and she, as a Snake Blood, could heal those with illnesses in the temple—or at least suggest the right path toward wellness. She and Jacob were truly two halves of a whole.

Though Kat's feelings toward the snakes at first had been wary but curious, she now found herself opening up to this new side of her magic. Ever since learning that the forefather of Snake magic himself, the corrupted and vengeful god Riel, was her own father, Kat has struggled with her powers—the gift in her blood seeming more and more like a curse. On Meninx, she totally rejected them, until Ada encouraged her to embrace her abilities once more, and she tried. They had led her to Byzantium and to eventually confronting—and killing—Riel. To saving her twin brother. To reuniting with Jacob.

She should have been thankful, then, to her magic blood. It had, all this time, been showing her the way home. The way to do what's right. To live in her own skin. And working every day to heal the sick helped dispel the blackness wrapped around her soul ever since she had been mauled by the Spirit Eater.

And yet, awakening to her true potential was still fraught with fear and uncertainty and a longing to understand—what is it she is meant to do in this life, with these gifts, with these powers?

Every few days, she and Jacob walked down to Troy to look for signs of the Aesarian Lords, and every time they were disappointed. But they loved climbing over the ruins, speculating if this mound of rocks had once been the bedroom where the beautiful Helen had slept in the arms of Paris, the Trojan prince who had seduced her away from her husband, King Menelaus of Sparta. Or if that hillock was the tower from which Helen watched Menelaus fight the Trojans to get her back. As they walked over the flat land between the mound and the sea, they imagined where, exactly, the valiant Prince Hector of Troy fell, slain by the Greek Achilles, and pointed out the likely path of Achilles's chariot as he dragged Hector's body seven times around the city, punishment for killing Achilles's lover, Patroclus.

Sometimes, braving the cold, she and Jacob strolled on the wind-whipped beach, imagining the thousand Greek ships anchored here on the wine-dark sea. Was it here—or over there— that the Trojans found the great wooden horse, filled with silent, secret warriors, and foolishly took it inside the city? After the Greeks climbed out and opened the gates, after that horrible night of looting and raping and burning, the entire beach must have been filled with the newly enslaved women, chained and sobbing, doled out to victorious soldiers as war-prizes.

Sometimes Kat felt the tortured history of the city seep into her bones and settle there. For centuries, Troy had been a place of thriving prosperity, of palaces and fountains, of gold cups and silver platters, of gorgeous women bedecked in pearls and rubies, of music, dancing, and feasting. But in the space of a single night it had burned and collapsed.

So, what was the lesson of this painful past? To never trust again, to never let your enemies close, to never love? To suspect that any gift might, in fact, be a curse?

And yet...

Over the years, the wind off the plains had covered the ruins with dirt, from which delicate grass and tall, spindly trees now grew, swaying like young bodies in the breeze. The crisp smells of salt and sea filled the air, and the lack of human activity made the sky curiously clear of smoke and noise, made the whole place both ache with emptiness and whisper of space, of peace. Nimble goats chewed their way across the fallen city, their staccato bleating like laughter at passersby. As if to say what folly it is to be human, to be stuck in the past, to live on in painful memories when you could live in the moment, from root to root and blade of grass to blade of grass. When, stone by stone, you could rebuild.

Still, as much as Kat enjoyed their excursions to Troy, it was usually a relief to return to the temple, to the cheerful priests and priestesses and hopeful patients, to the snakes that spoke to her of healing. And to Jacob's warm, strong arms every night.

Days turned to weeks, and weeks to months. The sharp bite of winter lessened. The wind off the water no longer stabbed; after a time, it gently caressed. The battering waves calmed and lapped meekly at the shore. And thousands of green shoots sprouted on the lumpy mounds of Troy. The goats and sheep had babies that gamboled and leaped among the ruins. Birds came to land on the grave mounds of Achilles and Patroclus and many other noble warriors, buried with their armor and horses and rich grave goods. Sites of tragedy, scars of the past, they were now sunny spots where you could imagine spending a whole day lying out, thinking of nothing but the open sky—where you could forget about the dark truth of this place.

Where you could trick yourself into believing that magic— and life—was pure and good and easy, and no secret despair clung to your soul.

Jacob has never been so happy, Kat knows. She can tell by the smile always playing on his face, and the sparkling of his dark eyes. He could probably stay here forever, delighted to be healing and, most of all, to be living with her.

As for Kat, she, too, is happy. It is as if the wheel of her life has come full circle, right back to where she started, with Jacob. And she loves the healing work at the temple. So many in this world devote themselves to destroying, so few to healing.

And she *does* begin to forget—what drew them here, what dangers may lurk beyond the walls of the temple, and to the east, where the monsters come from—the God Eaters, the Spirit Eaters, the destroyers of civilization that come with their fangs and their unending coldness and their hunger.

But forgetting, she knows, is a blissful and dangerous state. The Lotus Eaters on the island of Meninx wanted to forget, to suppress the true nature of their magic blood by ingesting copious amounts of lotus petals.

There are things Kat doesn't want to ever forget. Like Hephaestion, like their great journey to Egypt, like their time on Meninx, and the deep secrets they shared. Even though she never promised him anything, when she is lying close to Jacob at night, his arm loosely cast over her shoulders in protection, she feels as if she is betraying Heph somehow.

She misses Alex dreadfully, too. There is an aching hollow in her soul, as if some part inside her has been lost. But she can't go back to Pella—that much is certain—not with King Philip hoping to dangle her like bait to a royal suitor. Not for anything in the world would she allow herself to be married off to someone sight unseen. She'll never marry—this feels like a conviction that stems from some deep place in her gut, some place she can't quite understand and doesn't want to believe.

One thing she knows for sure: she loves using her Snake Blood to heal. Briseis returned home a couple of months ago, her skin smooth, a few pink marks the only trace of her hideous rash. Kat has healed many others, too, or at least made them more comfortable. She sometimes thinks she'd be content never to have children of her own—never to pass on the blessing and curse in her blood. Instead, the sick can be her children, and she'll remain content. She never has to leave this place.

And yet...

Tonight, torchlight washes across the brightly painted statue of Asklepios. Kat crouches down and pulls the blanket over a woman with the falling sickness. A small brown snake has curled up beside her, a very good sign of impending healing.

Jacob stands in the doorway, holding a torch. "Come," he says. "Let's go back."

They cook fish and vegetables outside their cottage. The air is warm; summer will be here again soon. It strikes her with fresh beauty, how—despite monsters, despite illness, grief, evil, loss—still, life pushes onward. Nature grows over ruins. We persist. We start again.

A crescent moon rises above a thousand glittering stars in the dark blue sky. Kat looks at Jacob across their small fire, admiring how the light plays with his face. The dancing flames illuminate his eyes, while throwing the rest of him into mysterious shadow. It's the perfect combination of familiar and new: the Jacob of her childhood; Lord Jacob, an Elder Counselor for the Aesarian Lords; and the all-powerful Earth Blood Jacob. Warrior. Healer. Lover. Friend.

He says little over dinner. Usually they talk about their day or reminisce about the past, before gradually curling in toward one another, discovering each other's bodies in the darkness, the places that make them cry out, shudder and gasp—the places in their hearts that are closed and tight but slowly, slowly, beginning to unfurl.

But tonight, Jacob is strangely quiet. The air pulsates with tension.

"Are you all right?" she asks, setting down her plate at her feet.

"I'm sorry," he says, his voice thick. "It's just... I have something I want to talk to you about. And I'm...nervous."

She scans her memory for something she has done or said that could have hurt him. He clasps his hands, then lets them hang, then places them on his thighs. "Those months, when we were apart," he says, his voice strangely deep. "I tried so hard to forget you. I figured you were in love with Prince Alexander." He laughs awkwardly.

"Good thing for me I never was!" she jokes, hoping to diffuse some of his nervousness.

"And then, to find you again, the day of the waves..." He shakes his head. "Surely the Fates wanted us to get back together."

Kat nods. She, too, has often thought the same thing.

"And then, since we've... Since our friendship has...*grown*," he says. Though she can't see his face clearly in the flickering firelight, she's fairly certain he's blushing. "Well, since then, I am more in love with you than ever."

There is a lump forming in her throat, impassable, and suddenly he is on his knees before her, gripping her hands in his. "Marry me, Kat. Let's tell the world that you belong to me. That I belong to you."

Her heart stammers, and for some reason she can't quite catch her breath. He asked her this question once before, on a late-summer afternoon, a hundred years ago—it can't possibly have been only ten months—after they had shared their first kiss in the pond outside their farm in Erissa. She didn't turn him down, exactly, just told him she needed to wait, but he took it as a rejection. The next day, he left the farm to compete in the Blood Tournament in Pella, and she followed him, and their lives changed. Jacob joined the Aesarian Lords, who soon after declared war on Macedon. When they were parted, she feared she'd never see him again.

So often, in the intervening months, she wished she had said yes to him that evening. That she had begged him not to go, told him he didn't need to become a king's guard for her to agree to marry him. That he could just be Jacob, the potter's son. His family would still be alive, and Kat never would have known that Queen Olympias, the woman Kat despised more than anyone in the world, was her real mother.

But no, that isn't right. It was her own fault—she is the one who followed Jacob to the palace, with dreams of revenge. She is the one who got everything wrong.

And if she hadn't gone, she never would have met Alex, her twin, or learned about the Snake Blood Magic fizzing in her veins. She would never have met Ada of Caria or Aristotle, or seen Persia and Egypt and Meninx. She never would have vanquished the Aesarian Lords, turning the tide of the fighting for Alex in the Battle of Pellan Fields. She wouldn't have killed

Riel, preventing the Age of Monsters from destroying the earth. She would never have become who she is now, stronger, wiser.

She would never have met Heph.

His image appears unbidden before her, his tousled dark hair, his sparkling brown eyes, his long muscular limbs and slight swagger. She remembers that kiss in the sea off Meninx, when the water lifted them off their feet and they floated in each other's arms. She thought then that he would be her choice. Before they left Meninx for Byzantium, Heph, too, had asked her to marry him. And she had told him she wasn't ready to give an answer.

She wonders now—how many chances will she have at love? If she risks this one, will it be her last?

Jacob fishes for something in his pouch and pulls out a ring. It is heavy, old gold, with a round center of mother-of-pearl that gleams in the firelight like fish scales glinting in water.

"Please, Kat," he says, his voice cracking. "Wear this ring as a pledge that you will marry me."

She cannot move and does not resist when he slips it onto her finger. It slides smoothly over the knuckle and settles snugly below. She feels a whisper of something travel up her arm and into her heart, a muted cry of yearning for freedom, along with determination and persistence. But not resisting is its own kind of answer, she realizes. How much of our lives may be determined, she wonders now, by what we do not voice?

"It is beautiful" is all she says. "Where did you get it?"

He laughs self-consciously. "From Lord Poseidon, apparently," he says. "The same god who cast us back together in Byzantium. I found it on the beach one day while you were running ahead. It looks very old. I wonder if some Trojan woman slipped it off, not wanting her captors to get it."

She stares at it, thinking about that unknown woman, wondering if she will feel her pain if she wears her ring. "Of course," he says quickly, "if you want something new, we can go to Lesbos. I hear there are many fine jewelers in Mytilene."

"No," she says, holding up her hand, unsure how to respond. Somehow it seems right to wear this ring. Fate has many surprises in store for us all, for Trojan women and Macedonian princes, as well as peasant girls and boys from Erissa. The unpredictability of fate requires strength. This ring will serve as a reminder of that. Of strength and also patience. Life is much longer and more varied than she ever could have anticipated. The threads of Fate weave in and out of one another, forming a tapestry we can never fully step back and see until it is too late to change.

She raises her gaze from the ring to the hopeful face of the boy who always loved her and smiles. She still doesn't know about marriage, but it feels wrong to say no when her heart is alive and singing. So, she says nothing, only draws him close and kisses him deeply.

Soon, Kat is no longer chilled but flushed with warmth.

She wakes. A slice of moonbeam from the open window illuminates Jacob, breathing deeply, a slight smile on his face as if he is having a pleasant dream. He must be dreaming about her, about the two of them together. But Heph… She remembers him telling her his story of murder and loss, of the secret pain he concealed beneath his confident attitude. She knows he is waiting for her in Pella, hoping she will come back to him. He promised, like Jacob once did, that he would wait forever. Will he?

She can't bear the thought of causing him more pain than he has already suffered. And she can't bear the thought of losing him, either, of never seeing him again.

But if she *were* to see him, would she be able to stop herself from wanting him?

Her heart is a coil of contradictions, writhing, snakelike.

There will be no more sleep for her tonight.

She grabs a light cloak and slips silently from the cottage. A walk will help clear her mind. She strides briskly down the hill toward Troy and turns to look back. The mismatched columns of the Temple of Asklepios glow silver in the starlight.

So far, Kat and Jacob have heeded the shepherds' warning not to wander about the ruins at night. But if she is stealthy, perhaps she can learn what is really going on beneath them. Most likely, there is nothing at all, and the story merely serves as ghoulish entertainment for bored shepherds around their fires.

Maybe she just needs to be reminded again of the epic love stories buried here, even if they all led, ultimately, to ruin. Even if all love, like this city, is doomed.

The mound looks completely different at night, heaps of jagged rock, silvery white in the moonbeams. She meanders around fallen stones, listening to the thudding of the waves on the shore, and the wind whispering ancient songs to the fallen towers of Troy. A small creature darts behind a rock. She breathes deeply, taking in the night air. There are no shrieks, no smoke and fire. She gazes around the ruins and wonders yet again what stories these walls could tell. That wall over there, standing upright about as tall as a man. Was it once part of a house? A gate? What lives were lived and lost there?

Suddenly Kat can make out a movement, as though the wall itself has rippled, or…

No, there is a form within the wall, or against it, in front of it.

No form: a girl, appearing as if emerging from the wall itself, or the air.

Kat blinks. Did the child step through an opening in the wall? Is she a ghost or phantom? Were the shepherds right?

Kat stands slowly, not wanting to frighten the girl, apparition or real. She half expects her to fade away, a figment of moonlight and imagination. But the child stands there, staring back at her, long dark hair framing a freckled face, round with youth.

"Hello," Kat says slowly, her voice sounding naked in the openness of the night. "Are you lost?"

The girl shakes her head. "Oh no," she says in accented Greek. "I live here."

Live here? Kat frowns. No one lives here. How many times have she and Jacob climbed over every bit of the ruins?

"What are *you* doing here?" the girl asks, coming closer. She's a pretty child of six or seven, in a dark tunic. "No one comes here at night."

"I...couldn't sleep," Kat confesses. "I'm staying at the temple and decided to go for a walk. My name is Kat. What is yours?"

"Roxana," the child says, extending a small hand. A trill of fear moves through Kat and she freezes as the girl reaches out, as if testing to see whether *she* is real. Then, in a voice that is wistful and distant, that makes her sound ancient, full of a sadness beyond her years, she reaches up to touch Kat's long hair and whispers softly, "My sister used to let me play with her hair."

"Your sister? Where is she?" Kat asks, hope rising that perhaps Roxana is not alone here, scrounging for food among the ruins. Her tunic is clean and fairly new, as far as she can tell in the moonlight. The child looks well-fed, her hair neatly combed.

"The mean men took her away," the girl says, her voice cracking. "They were going to hurt me, too, but I ran. And then other mean men found me and brought me here."

Kat has no idea what she's talking about. But her golden fingertip tingles. A sign of magic. Can this rag of a child be a Snake or Earth Blood?

"What are you doing here so late at night?" Kat asks.

"Practicing," the child responds.

"Practicing what?"

"Being the wall."

Kat shakes her head. "I don't understand."

Roxana laughs and goes back to the wall. And disappears.

Kat's jaw drops. Where did she go?

"I'm still here!" comes a laughing voice. Kat approaches, puts out a hand, and touches the girl's thin shoulder. Squatting, she realizes the child has altered the color of her skin to match the wall. She's a human chameleon.

Instinctively, Kat closes her eyes and stills her breathing. She senses powerful magic bubbling inside the girl, but it's not Snake Blood, for here is no kinship to other living things. Nor does she sense Earth Blood; there is nothing at all that reminds her of Jacob, and his oneness with earth and wind and water. This magic is dark as soot, burning as fire, cruel and hard. It is the opposite of life. It is…death.

With a chill, Kat lets go and backs away. Who—*what*—is this girl?

Roxana becomes herself again and wriggles out of Kat's mental grasp, breaking her exploration of the child's magic. The little girl stands in front of a hill covered with scraggly bushes. And disappears. Kat walks over slowly. "Where are you?" she asks.

"Here!" the girl says, suddenly appearing, her skin shedding the disguise of grass and dirt in the darkness.

"Who are you?" Kat whispers, wondering again if the girl is some kind of vision.

"Well, I was a princess once and lived in a palace," Roxana replies.

Despite her wariness, Kat smiles. Every little girl considers herself a princess.

"Then, like I said, some mean men stole me and brought me here. Kids can fit into the narrow passageways below the city more easily and bring back gold and jewels."

Suddenly a ray of comprehension shoots through Kat.

There are no demons or ghosts howling below the city at night, but *human scavengers*. Slavers forcing stolen children to mine the ruins for valuables.

Her heart pounds hard in her chest as understanding washes over her in waves. The Trojan people, she knows, hid their gold, silver, and jewelry in basements, under floors, and inside walls during the long war with Greece. When the city collapsed in the inferno, the invaders took what they could find above and sailed back home. The howls and shrieks the shepherds have reported hearing in the night must have been the slavers trying to scare people away.

Though none of that explains the girl's magic.

But one thing is certain: if the slavers find them… Kat curses herself for leaving her sword, the one Ada of Caria gave her, back in the hut.

"I can help you get out of here," Kat says quickly, in urgent, hushed tones. "And the other children, too. There must be more of you. I am with a very powerful warrior who can—"

Roxana laughs. "Oh no," she says. "I've already been freed. All of us have. We aren't slaves anymore. We are the Chosen Ones now."

Kat frowns again. *Chosen Ones.* "*Who* freed you? Where are they?"

Roxana takes her hand and leads her over a steep mound of fallen stones. They grab saplings to pull themselves up. The girl is as nimble as a monkey. She runs down the far side of the mound and stands still. A few feet away, Kat sees the flickering orange light of a torch and a wisp of smoke rise out of a hole in the ground.

"The Horn Men came and freed us all," she says. "They are down there. We sleep during the day and work at night."

So, the Aesarian Lords *are* here—have been here, perhaps, all this time, but hiding out below the ruins. That was why Jacob and Kat never found them. She shudders. At night, the Lords work in the tunnels. During the day, when shepherds and visitors climb the ruins, they are as silent as the tomb, sleeping beneath them, or scheming, plotting, hoarding, and hiding children. Why?

Fear, cold and pulsing, moves through Kat. She creeps silently toward the slice of fiery light in the earth. "How do you get down there?" she whispers.

"Oh, there are places we know," Roxana says. "Staircases and openings we block."

"What's down there?" Kat asks. "Tunnels?"

"Tunnels?" the girl asks, giggling so hard she bends over and cups her hands over her mouth. Spreading her arms, she says, "There's an entire city below."

Kat gasps. An entire city. When the tall buildings collapsed, there could have been entire streets left intact, especially after centuries of clearing rubble below to look for valuables.

Then it occurs to her that the Aesarian Lords, as rich as kings themselves, wouldn't need children to dig jewelry from the ruins.

Which means they are using them for something else.

"What do the Horn Men make you do down there?" she asks, her voice shrinking in fear of the answer, her heart wrangling to understand, to help.

The girl giggles again. "They don't make us do anything," she says. "They teach us things, and we practice them."

Kat stares at the girl. Moonlight dances on her long dark hair. "What kind of things do they teach you?" she asks.

"Magic," Roxana replies. "They teach us how to become magic."

CHAPTER SIXTEEN

ARRIDHEUS ("RAT")

THE SETTING SUN TURNS THE DESERT SAND AND the village behind him golden orange. Rat sits on a rock, playing with his little wooden puppets, working their strings so that they walk and talk, practicing his voices, and making himself laugh. Beside him, the Nile whispers softly; it has shrunk to a brown stream. But soon, Sarina says, it will be Inundation, and the Nile god will make the river rise and widen again, flooding all the fields. The temples and pyramids will be islands, reachable only by boat or raised walkway.

This year he experienced no winter at all. No smoky rooms with snow falling through the smoke hole and sizzling on the fire. No freezing days, when opening the shutter slats for a bit of light lets in the searing wind. In this strange land of eternal heat and blue sky, there is neither cold nor rain.

They have made him strong here, trained his tongue to speak and his body to use weapons. Still, he wishes he could go home. But he can't mention it. Or his real name—Arridheus, Prince of Macedon—or Yuf will beat him. But they cannot read his thoughts, and he often pretends Alex, his older half brother, is here with him, ruffling his hair and giving him sweets. And the nice beautiful girl he met shortly before he left his home, Alex's friend Katerina. She smiled at him so kindly, as if she didn't think he was stupid at all. And she was nice to his pet rat, Heracles, who liked her a lot, too. He hoped they would become good friends and always live in the palace together. But then the kidnappers took him away, to this hot, dry place.

At least he has Sarina, his beautiful dark nursemaid from that other life, the powerful priestess of Bast here. Sarina gave him the two wooden marionettes in his hands. They have jointed arms and legs and funny painted faces and wear little white kilts.

"You are ready now, my puppet," says Ramses, the bald doll with the wide smile. His voice is deep and loud—Rat likes making that voice.

"Ready for what?" asks the other doll, Sabu, in a high voice, his shoulder-length black hair and mouth like an O shape.

"Ready to kill Prince Alexander of Macedon," says Ramses.

"I won't!" cries Sabu.

"You will!"

"I won't!"

The puppets smash into each other again and again, screaming. Rat flings them on the sand, where they lie in a crumpled heap. He has to do it. He doesn't want to, but Sarina explained things.

It has been prophesied that Alexander will conquer Egypt. When the Persians conquered, they killed or sold into slavery my entire family. My people cannot allow this to happen again, little Rat. You must kill Alexander in order to save thousands and thousands of innocent lives. You will be a hero forever.

He doesn't want to be a hero. He just wants to go home. Sarina said he could go home if he does what they want.

A shadow falls over him. Worried, he looks up, fearing it is Yuf. But it is Sarina. She kneels beside him, smiling, as her sandalwood scent wraps around him.

"It is dinnertime, little Rat. What are you playing at?" she asks, adjusting her sheer blue veil so that the little gold coins on it shimmer and clink.

"Nothing," he says, scrambling off the rock to pick up the dolls. Smiling, she extends her hand, and together they walk back to the village.

But it's not nothing.

After all, he heard *her* saying it just this morning, telling Yuf and the village elders that the time has come. *The puppet is ready*, she'd said to them. *The puppet is ready.*

But Rat knows the puppet she meant was neither Ramses nor Sabu. The puppet is Rat.

ACT THREE

ATONEMENT

The gods, too, are fond of a joke.

—Aristotle

CHAPTER SEVENTEEN

PYROLITHOS

HE'S BEEN KING FOR ONLY A FEW MONTHS, BUT already the people grow restive.

And none more so than the Aesarian Lords.

Where *are* they?

Late.

Pyrolithos drums his fingers on the arm of his gilded throne and gazes down at the lovely women in whisper-soft gowns lounging on the marble benches along the sides of the throne room. Daylight streams in through the wall of open windows, along with fresh spring air tanged with salt, but nothing can reduce the tension coiled inside him.

The Lords have much to answer for. The king discovered that Ambiorix sent letters regarding diplomacy and treaties to neighboring kingdoms as if he himself were king. In return, Pyrolithos brought spies into the palace, a few of the girls most admired by the remaining Lords, to entertain them. So far, they have come up with vague information: that the bulk of the regiment indeed went east for reasons to do with the Spirit Eaters, and there seemed to be a plot developing between the Lords and General Georgios, perhaps to give him the throne.

The king has spent too much time with Alecta, that's the

trouble—training her in the cave for several months, and then, after the attack of the Spirit Eater, training the women at the brothel himself. There seemed no point in secrecy anymore, at least among his New Amazons. Once word got out that he'd captured the Spirit Eater, the women eagerly agreed to follow such a powerful and magical protector. As far as the Dardanians know, however, the new king is simply spending all his time pleasuring himself with whores instead of running the country. Not exactly a good look, if he wants to be taken seriously.

The deepest secret, though, the worry that worms its way through him in the darkness of the night, is his Smoke magic—more specifically, his weak grasp on it, the fact that it seems to be fading, leaking out somehow. Lately, he could swear his face seems softer, more feminine. He hasn't had to shave in three weeks. Even his hands seem smaller, not delicate exactly, but not as powerful as they were before. And he knows what he must do—knows the curse of Smoke Blood—how it requires more of itself, endlessly.

He will need to commit another betrayal.

Fortunately, he has one in mind.

But first he needs answers.

Finally, he hears boots marching toward him. Lord Ambiorix strides in with the five others, all of them grinning broadly, as if they had just heard a very amusing joke. Their eyes scan the women on the benches, and they laugh out loud. He can only assume the joke had something to do with Pyrolithos's womanizing.

They stop in front of the royal dais and give Pyrolithos the most perfunctory of bows. "My lord," says Ambiorix. "You wanted to see us."

Pyrolithos sits slumped on the throne, glowering at them until he knows they feel uneasy. Finally, he drawls, "Yes. How kind of you to come."

Ambiorix turns red, though the king isn't sure if it is due to embarrassment or anger.

"As you are aware," Pyrolithos says, sitting up, "there have been attacks here in Dardania by monstrous creatures some call Spirit Eaters."

The Aesarian Lords look up, their eyes wide. "Yes, yes, we have heard of such attacks," mumbles Ambiorix in his guttural accent. "A handful only. A couple of fishermen, some shepherds…"

"It is my understanding that the Aesarian Lords know a great deal about the Spirit Eaters," Pyrolithos continues. "Their lair is not too far from your headquarters in Nekrana, in the Eastern Mountains of Persia, is it not?"

Ambiorix's light blue eyes flash. "Not that far," he says vaguely.

"Why have these creatures left their lair?" Pyrolithos asks, leaning forward. "People say they have lived quietly enough there in the Eastern Mountains for centuries. Why now are they spreading out and devouring living things?"

"I don't know," Ambiorix replies, tossing his blond braids over his broad shoulders. He has a shifty look on his face, and his gaze doesn't meet that of the king.

"Did High Lord Gideon take the regiment east to deal with the Spirit Eaters?" Pyrolithos asks.

"Our orders are secret, my lord," the Gaul replies, straightening and looking Pyrolithos in the eye. "We are your guests, not your subjects, and as such we are under no obligation to reveal anything to you. Remember Zeus's law of guest-friendship."

The king cups his chin in his hand and tries not to smile. He knows that the gods decreed that hosts may not harm their guests, or even question them too intently. Anyone who did so would be committing an unforgivable betrayal against divine law.

"Have you ever seen a Spirit Eater, Lord Ambiorix?" he asks.

The Gaul frowns. "No," he says, shaking his head. "We never went that..." He stops.

"That close?" the king asks.

Ambiorix says nothing.

"Well, in that case," the king says genially, "I have a little surprise for you." He picks up a horn from the table next to the throne and blows a loud, clear note on it. A moment later, the double doors at the end of the throne room open. Alecta and Xanthe, both tall and muscular, enter wearing gleaming armor.

But the Lords don't seem to notice the two female warriors. Their eyes are glued to the diamond cage on the cart the women pull.

Inside, the huge creature snarls viciously, its dark, fractured form, shifting around in tight circles, all heads and wings and claws. Pyrolithos feels its hunger, its outrage. Ambiorix and the other Lords unsheathe their swords and creep forward curiously. They pad quietly around the cage as the Spirit Eater thrashes against the bars and roars, a sound of endless, anguished hunger.

"Lord Ambiorix," the king says once he sees all is in readiness. "I command you to tell me all you know about Spirit Eaters."

The men turn from the cage to find that the two dozen women in the room stand holding bows and arrows pointed at them. Alecta and Xanthe have drawn their swords and swung off the shields on their backs. More swords and shields, plucked from beneath the benches, stand at the ready for the archers.

"What is the meaning of this?" Ambiorix says, his face turning crimson.

"Quite simple," Pyrolithos replies genially. "You tell me everything you know about the Spirit Eaters, or I will feed you and your men to this one. It hasn't eaten in weeks, poor thing."

Two Lords lunge at the women with swords. The king hears the soft breath of arrows, sees their blur, and hears them thunk into solid flesh. The two Aesarians are so riddled with arrows they look like pincushions and fall to the ground dead. The other four form a tight circle. "You will pay for this!" Ambiorix screams. "Aesarians killed by women! You have dishonored us!"

"So sorry about the dishonor," Pyrolithos says, studying his fingernails.

He looks at the women and nods. More arrows fly through the air. The four remaining Aesarians are impaled in the right wrist and drop their swords. Then they are hit in their legs, and fall to their knees, gasping in pain.

The king says, "Now, tell me about the Spirit Eaters, or you will become this one's next meal. If you tell me what I want to know, I swear a sacred oath that I will let you live."

Ambiorix, on the ground, shakes his head. With a grunt, he pulls the arrow out of his thigh and flings it angrily on the floor. "It is an Aesarian secret only those in the Elder Council know fully. I would rather die than reveal it."

"Would you?" Pyrolithos asks coolly. "Take him to the cage."

Alecta and Xanthe prod him with their swords, and the creature, sensing prey, howls and slavers, its form fracturing into several Spirit Eaters atop one pair of spindly legs.

"All right!" Ambiorix says, his face a mask of terror. "May the gods forgive me. I will tell you."

Haltingly, the wounded Gaul tells an ancient tale of a magical fountain of forbidden water, of villagers who drank from it and turned into monsters craving divine flesh. Of the Aesarian Lords' true mission—to feed the monsters magic wielders, thereby preventing them from fanning out from their lairs to eat mankind.

Pyrolithos feels that a lamp has been lit in darkness. He finally understands why the Aesarian Lords search the known world for soothsayers and Blood Magics to send east. Not to execute them, but to feed them to the Spirit Eaters. Now he knows why they tried so hard to discover why Princess Cynane's grievous wounds healed immediately after their torture sessions, and why they wanted her entombed in a casing of hardened ash. They intended to send her to the monsters—to be devoured alive.

All this enrages him even more against the Lords.

And yet, the Lords had to placate the beasts, as they had no powers to control them. Pyrolithos, however, does have such powers. He proved that by capturing this Spirit Eater. He returns to the bold idea he has been formulating: that he could learn how to control the one in the cage—much as you could tame a vicious dog with the proper techniques. He and his army could capture more Spirit Eaters, forging an invincible battalion of the creatures. With the Spirit Eaters at his side, no army in the world—not even the Aesarian Lords—could vanquish such a force. He and his army of women would become the most powerful warriors in the history of mankind. Ruling this backwater kingdom of fishermen and goatherds—which had, up until he captured the Spirit Eater, been his life's ambition—now seems contemptible, unworthy of him.

Ambiorix falls silent, his story spent. His face is pale, and beads of sweat have broken out on his forehead.

"Where, exactly, in the Eastern Mountains do you take your magic wielders to give to the creatures?" Pyrolithos asks, his excitement rising as vast new possibilities unfold before his eyes.

The Gaul shakes his head. "I only went on such a mission once," he says. "The high command took us up secret paths in the mountains. That is all I know."

The king sighs. It might not be easy to find the information he needs. With an impatient gesture, he signals the women. Three of them drag Ambiorix, bellowing with rage and pain, toward the cage. "You liar! You have no honor!" he cries. "You said I would live if I told you!"

Pyrolithos takes out his dagger and slices his forearm, the pain causing what little is left of his Smoke Blood to rise and curl throughout him. The magic is weak. He must concentrate intensely on the Spirit Eater's diamond cage, imagining the bars in the center of the front dissolving to form a hole. Alecta— who, with three other Amazons, pulls a struggling Ambiorix toward the cage—looks utterly disgusted, but Pyrolithos feels exhilaration. Revenge is sweet. This man was involved in trying to do exactly the same thing to him as Cynane—feed him alive to such a monster.

The women hold the Lord's head just outside the opening in the front of the cage. And then he is sucked inside.

The man's shrieks as he is devoured alive echo off the marble throne room walls. Some of the women turn their heads or close their eyes and put their hands over their ears. But not Pyrolithos. This is the man who smashed his bones with an iron rod when he was nothing more than a girl. Such a man deserves this death.

Fire, smoke, and ashes explode inside the king's veins. For here is a double betrayal: betraying the law of guest-friendship and breaking his oath to Lord Ambiorix to let him go if he told him about the Spirit Eaters. Power floods through him, racing down his veins and into his muscles and organs. Flush with incredible strength, Pyrolithos concentrates on restrengthening the diamond bars to keep the Spirit Eater contained.

"Take the others to the dungeons," he says. "And dispose of the bodies." The women clatter out, some with the prisoners, others dragging the two dead Aesarians, leaving smears of blood on the marble floor. The doors bang shut behind them.

Pyrolithos sits on the throne, watching the Spirit Eater make quick work of the huge Aesarian Lord, spitting out the leather, the metal armor, and the large helmet horns, but consuming the entire body except for a few chewed bones. Sniffling, it licks up the pools of blood beneath it with a long black forked tongue, then stares at him with beady dark eyes that rearrange themselves here and there on two—no, three—blurred, moving heads, until they focus sharply into one. Now it hisses, a sound so terrifying that every hair on the king's body stands on end.

For all the horror of being so near the monster, there is something about the creature that calls to Pyrolithos, a kind of tugging on his soul. Could it have something to do with what

Ambiorix told him, that the Spirit Eaters want more than anything to devour magic beings, and he, a Smoke Blood, is now magic?

The king steps over puddles of blood and approaches the monster, who howls again, shaking the diamond bars with long black claws. He squats down in front of the cage, staring into the ancient flinty eyes, sensing its power, its hunger for magic blood, just as Cynane had been hungry for magic blood.

"You're still hungry, aren't you?" he asks quietly.

In response, the Spirit Eater opens its bloody maw and hurls itself against the bars.

The king holds his left arm directly above the cage. With his dagger, he reopens the slash on his left forearm. Blood, vibrant and bright red and full of Smoke magic, splatters between the bars of the diamond cage. The creature licks it up, ravenous. When Pyrolithos pulls his arm away, it howls for more.

A taste of what you crave will always keep you coming back for more.

After dinner, he slips back into the throne room. All the torches have been lit, casting shadows that seem to climb the walls and dance across the marble floor tiles, now cleansed of blood. He planned to study the Spirit Eater, to experiment with it, but a woman is standing in front of the cage, staring calmly at the creature who is curled up contentedly, like an old, well-fed family dog.

Pyrolithos doesn't know what surprises him more—that this woman isn't afraid of the creature, or that the Spirit Eater seems so tame. He's even more surprised when the woman turns toward him, and he sees she's carrying a newborn baby. It's the Persian girl. Zotasha.

"Why aren't you afraid of it?" he asks her. "The other girls keep their distance."

"Oh, at times I am afraid of it, my lord," she admits, and he notices the beauty of her large dark blue eyes. "But I am also oddly drawn to it. You see, a soothsayer once told me that these creatures can alter a person's fate, though I am not sure how. At any rate, I would like very much for it to alter mine."

Pyrolithos hardly has a moment to take in the girl's brazenness at speaking to a king so directly—almost as if she were royalty herself—because he has realized something. *That's* what he's been feeling as he looks into the monster's eyes—his *fate* being altered in some way.

"Wouldn't we all," he says now. "I want to capture more of them, learn about them, see if we can tame them and use them for our benefit." He doesn't know why he's sharing this with the girl, except that he instinctively feels he can trust her—an unusual feeling, as he has been trained all his life to trust no one. "But I don't think we can assume others will dive into our courtyards anytime soon. And I don't know where they live in the Eastern Mountains, which is a huge range.

"I suppose," he continues, walking around the diamond cage, "I could take the women east and explore. Persians might be suspicious of a regiment of foreign warriors but would surely let a man and his harem travel freely."

"I know exactly where they are," she says quickly, looking at him with intensity burning in her eyes. "I could lead you there."

His breath catches in his throat. "What?"

She shifts the sleeping baby from one arm to the other. "I have been to their cave," she says. "I have even licked that wall Lord Ambiorix was talking about, the one that trickles with drops of the diverted Fountain of Youth. At least I think it was that wall. I was so very thirsty, and one drop of that water gave me incredible energy, the energy I needed to survive."

Pyrolithos stares at her, suddenly taking in her many inconsistencies. There is something regal about her bearing and speech, despite her heavy Persian accent; clearly, she was not born in poverty. Yet she ended up in a brothel with an illegitimate baby, after wandering the Eastern Mountains. This girl—Zotasha?—must have an incredible tale to tell.

"I went to Persepolis," she continues, "and told Great King Artaxerxes about these creatures. I wanted to lead an army there to destroy them, but he didn't listen to me." She turns to Pyrolithos and says, urgency humming in her voice, "But perhaps *you* will listen to me. Perhaps we could all go there together. And if you can't tame them—somehow I doubt you could—we can destroy them."

The king is amazed once more. Zotasha had an audience with the Great King of Persia, all the way in Persepolis. She knows where the Spirit Eaters live. And she wants to fight them.

"Who are you?" he asks, putting his hands on her shoulders. "Where do you come from?"

He can see a flicker of uncertainty pass across her eyes. She says nothing for a long while, clearly considering how much to tell him. Then, as she opens her mouth, the door is flung open and Alecta storms in.

"I want answers," she says, tossing her mane of long red hair.

Zotasha, looking from Alecta to the king, hurriedly bows and leaves, closing the door behind her with a little click.

"We will not live in this palace with a monster among us," Alecta fumes. "We have taken a vote. We will go back to the Grotto if you keep this thing here, and you can forget about your New Amazons."

Pyrolithos turns to her and asks coldly, "Do you wish to resume your lives at the brothel?"

Alecta narrows her dark eyes. "Anything would be better than getting eaten alive. But now that you have taught us to be warriors, I think our whoring days are behind us. We will find Queen Cynane and follow her."

"You are following Queen Cynane by staying with me," he says, crossing his arms. "I am her proxy."

Alecta scoffs. "So you say. But what have you done to her?

We want to see her. Otherwise, we will no longer follow you no matter how many magical powers you have."

Pyrolithos looks at Alecta, then at the Spirit Eater in the cage. He didn't want to reveal the truth to Alecta, not yet, anyway. Will the truth ruin everything? Or will it make everything possible?

Finally, he stops in front of her, realizing he has no choice. For if he does nothing, she really will leave.

"Very well," he says. "I will bring her here."

Alecta looks around the room bathed in dancing amber torchlight. "Very well," she says, her voice hard but her expression softening. "Go get her. I will wait here."

Pyrolithos runs a hand through his thick black hair. "She is here already, with us."

Alecta rolls her eyes. "If you're playing some kind of a stupid..."

But she stops midsentence as the king, calling on the new Smoke Blood powers burning through his veins from today's double betrayal, feels his body shift and change. He grits his teeth, clenches his fists, and closes his eyes. And then, when he straightens, he sees delicate female feet in the now-overlarge sandals.

He stretches out his hands and sees the smooth, hairless hands of Cynane.

Alecta stares at him in shock. Her eyes are wide, her mouth open.

Then she draws her hand back and slaps Cynane hard across the face.

CHAPTER EIGHTEEN

JACOB

MOONLIGHT STREAMS SILVER WHITE OVER THE fallen stones of Troy, and Jacob could swear he can feel Kat's anger beside him, her frustration like a coiled heat, radiating outward. Last week, she came back from a midnight walk with tales of a magical child and an entire city hidden under the Trojan ruins. The Aesarian Lords were camped there and had been for months, she insisted, right under their noses.

Not only that, but she was convinced the Lords were teaching children a strange, dark magic. Jacob strenuously denied that this could be possible. Kat set her jaw in that mulish way of hers and said, "Let's find out, then."

Now, for several nights in a row, they have traipsed out here from the Temple of Asklepios, Kat carting the bag of Egyptian ushabtis, the statuettes of warriors she had taken from Princess Laila of Sharuna. "They could help us free the children," she keeps saying. "They have the spirit of a powerful ancient general inside them."

Every night, they have waited among the ruins, Kat squinting at shadows and walls, insisting it could be the elf-child, Roxana, practicing her magic. Jacob has begun to suspect that perhaps Kat only dreamed all of this, and tonight he is torn between impatience and worry. He has never known her to be delusional. Perhaps the overuse of her powers has put a strain on her.

"Time to go back soon, I think," he says, tapping the leather-wrapped lantern. "Unless you want to spend the night here."

Kat pulls away from him. Then, "Wait." She sucks in a breath and goes rigid. "Over there."

Jacob squints into the distance, across the thin pool of lamp-light, to where Kat is pointing.

A small girl, standing in front of a wall.

She wasn't there a moment ago.

It must be a trick of the moonlight.

No, that really *is* a child.

Kat is already moving toward her. "Roxana!" she calls out softly. "I am so glad to see you again! I've been looking for you."

Smiling a gap-toothed grin, the girl reaches up and touches Kat's hair. "I can't sneak out every night, you know," she says. "The Horn Men don't want us to go outside at all." Her gaze falls on Jacob and her smile fades. "Who's that?"

"That is my very good friend," Kat reassures her. "His name is Jacob." She takes the girl's hand and brings her over to Jacob, who smiles and stays seated. His height might frighten her.

"Hello," he says.

"Honey cakes!" Roxana says, pointing to the open basket he's carrying. "I haven't had those in ages. The Horn Men mostly eat meat."

Jacob has an idea. Long ago, in that other life, he had a sure-fire way of getting his little brothers to do things they didn't want to: feed the goats, pull the weeds in his mother's garden, sweep out the cooking hearth. "I could give you one," Jacob says, his voice playful as he reaches for the basket. "We could play a game."

"I like games," she says, nodding. He holds up a honey cake and she grabs for it, but he pulls it away as her small fist snatches the air.

"Well, let's say I give you a honey cake if you tell me a secret," he suggests.

The child considers this, then looks up at Kat.

"I think it would be a fun game," Kat says.

"All right," Roxana agrees. "What secret do you want to know?"

"Hmm. Well, I would like to know how you get into the city below these ruins."

Roxana looks hungrily at the basket of honey cakes. "But I would get into trouble with the Horn Men if I took you down there."

"We wouldn't tell them you showed us the way," Kat says quickly. "If they find us, we will say we found the way ourselves."

Roxana licks her lips. "All right."

She leads them around the fallen wall, over a hillock of stones and saplings, and pulls a covered lantern from behind a stone. After removing the leather cover, she and her light disappear into a crevice in what must have once been a turret. Kat bends over at the waist and squeezes in behind her. Jacob falls to his knees to push through. He angles his shoulders, the rough stone plucking at his tunic, and forces himself into a low, narrow passage, where his back scrapes against the ceiling. He removes the leather covering of his oxhorn lantern and holds it awkwardly as he crawls on three limbs.

A few feet ahead of him, Kat inches her way down the small tunnel. Finally, he sees the space open up. As he stands, the child, Roxana, runs down a narrow staircase, her own lantern a dull bloom of light in this rambling, pitch-black subterranean world. He and Kat run to catch up with her.

At the bottom of the staircase, Roxana stretches out her hand. "Honey cake," she whispers. He slides the bag off his shoulder, and before he has finished pulling one out, she snatches it from his hand and crams it into her mouth, eating greedily. Licking her fingers, she leads them on, down a dark corridor.

Despite his trepidations about seeing his brother Lords again after all this time, Jacob can't stop the tingle of warmth that flows through him upon entering the heavy embrace of earth and stone. Holding his lantern high, he realizes they seem to be in what was once a street, with elaborate doors and windows on either side. The wall on his left is made of finely hewed large stones. Was this once a home? A shop?

He places his free hand on the wall to draw in the power of the earth, but it seems he draws in something else: a whirlwind of sadness and horror that spins and ricochets inside him. He knows that Troy suffered ten years of siege, much of it in starvation. Men died on the plain below, Trojan sons and fathers and brothers. And then came that last awful night of fire and death. These are the facts that all men know.

It isn't the sadness of facts that has him in its grip, however, but the darkest possible emotions: heartbreak and rage, frustration and despair. The rock absorbs him and casts him down, down, spiraling into a place of such utter darkness he knows that neither light nor happiness could ever pierce it. The very walls ooze dark emotions. He is the wall. He is the sorrow.

He feels a soft hand on his arm and pulls away from the place of pain. It's Kat, her eyes shining with tears. "I can feel it through you," she whispers. "But don't take on this burden. This tragedy is not your tragedy."

"What are you doing?" Roxana asks, irritated and scampering back toward them. "Come this way if you want to see!"

He tears himself away from the black tug of the wall, of the song trapped in stone of loss and death, and puts his hand in Kat's before saying, "This is a place of ghosts."

Nodding, Kat squeezes his fingers and guides him forward. Silently, they follow Roxana through the underground streets. Sometimes Jacob pauses and holds his lantern up to an open door or window, but the pale light isn't strong enough to see more than a few feet. He catches only glimpses of brightly painted walls and mosaic floors. Periodically they see small dark openings in the walls, tunnels for scavengers.

"It's a labyrinth down here," Kat whispers. "Roxana, it must have taken you forever to learn these paths."

The child giggles. "I'm like Pegasus!"

"What?" Kat asks.

"Pegasus! She is never lost, you know. Pegasus knows the way."

"What do you mean?" Jacob asks.

"It's just something my sister used to tell me long ago." Suddenly, Roxana stops, turns to them, and thrusts out a hand. "Honey cake."

Jacob hands her one, which she eats only a fraction less quickly than the first.

The girl licks the crumbs off her hands, then puts a finger to her lips. "You must be very quiet," she says. "Not a sound." Jacob and Kat nod. They creep out onto a balcony and survey a scene below that Jacob doesn't understand, despite the light from dozens of wall torches.

The cavernous chamber holds perhaps thirty children in small groups. At a table, three boys stand before piles of sand, holding their outstretched hands over them. Two of them immediately change the sand into shards of highly polished metal; the third one takes a few moments longer, struggling, but finally transforms his pile of sand, too. At the next table, two children call smoke from a perfume burner into the shape of a small dog, then set it running across the room until it disappears.

Across the room, two girls practice camouflaging themselves. Jacob sees them disappear against the light brown wall, then walk, wall-colored, in front of a dark cupboard and suddenly take on the colors of the cupboard. He squints and looks closely at a little band of other children in the flickering torchlight.

These children are not camouflaging; there is no movement and change of color as they walk from one background to the other. They are truly disappearing.

Jacob's heart leaps when he sees Lord Turshu, the little bow-legged Scythian, in a knot of five children. His initial reaction is to call out to him, to find the stairs leading down into the chamber and embrace his old friend. But then he sees Turshu giving a vial of liquid to a boy of about eight. The boy drinks it, grimacing. Then he reaches into a nearby cage and brings out a pearl gray dove. The boy feeds it some grain in his hand, and the dove nestles lovingly against him. Obviously, it is a pet.

Turshu smiles at the boy and then puts two fingers into his own mouth and whistles. The other children stop what they are doing and gather around. "Arkan," he says, "it is time."

The child strokes the bird with a trembling hand. Tears shine in his eyes. Then, in a swift motion, he snaps its neck and drops it to the floor, a sad, broken heap of feathers.

Next to him, Kat gasps. Jacob puts an arm around her, though his eyes are riveted on the scene below. He has no comprehension of what he is seeing.

"I was right," Kat mummers. "They *are* magic."

Below them, the boy called Arkan falls to his knees, howling in pain and gripping his stomach as the other children retreat a few steps. After several long moments, he rises quietly, his eyes shining with unnatural brightness.

Kat, evidently, has seen enough. She gestures to Jacob and Roxana, and they walk back along the corridor through which they came.

"Roxana," she whispers urgently as she kneels to look the child in her eyes. "What are you? Some kind of Earth Blood?"

But Jacob knows even before the girl answers that she is no Earth Blood. He's never met another Earth Blood before—doesn't know if any others still exist—but he knows with his whole being that this is not Earth Blood. He could never change the shape of matter or transform smoke into whatever shape he chose.

Roxana looks up at Kat and Jacob, her eyes wide, her cheeks still holding a baby's curve, and shakes her head. "I'm not Earth Blood. I'm *chosen*."

Jacob glances at Kat, but she looks just as confused as he feels. Kneeling beside her, he asks, "What was it we just saw?"

Roxana lifts her chin. "The Horn Men choosing us."

"What do you mean?" Jacob presses. "How do they choose you?"

"They came in the night," Roxana says, playing with one curl. "They said we could be free if we drank the potion and cut off the hands of the masters."

Kat breathes in sharply, but Roxana doesn't seem to notice. "We said yes, and the Horn Men broke our chains, and then we took turns."

Jacob's mouth goes dry. "Turns doing what?"

"Cutting masters," Roxana says promptly. "That's when I became free and strong." Suddenly she is gone. Just not there in less than the blink of an eye. Jacob looks around for her, and she appears right in front of him, smiling.

A chilling understanding sneaks over Jacob. Strong and free... and *magic*.

"Have you ever heard of such a thing?" Jacob asks Kat. "Magic made, not born?"

Looking pale, Kat shakes her head. "No...but that does not mean it does not exist."

She looks the same way Jacob feels, as though her insides had been twisted, but Roxana seems unaware of the effect her story has on them. "I can do other things," she says, "turn into smoke for a few minutes, and hold my hand over fire for the longest time without getting burned." She prattles on, discussing her different strengths and favorite games, while Jacob's mind races.

He remembers snippets of Tim's letters. He remembers the

Aesarians' ultimate goal: to keep the Spirit Eaters at bay. To keep them full.

Magic made, not born.

What he and Kat saw back there weren't just children with unusual magic, but…

"A feast," he croaks out, staggering to his feet. "The children… *They're* the feast."

He can practically see the word trickle through Kat and then the horror it unleashes as she realizes his meaning. The Aesarian Lords have turned innocent children to magic…to feed them to the Spirit Eaters and keep them placated.

How could his brothers commit such an evil, disgusting act? When Jacob took the oath of the Aesarian Lords, he thought he was joining a brotherhood of honor and courage. A community that swore to guard mankind from the monstrosity of magic. And yet, here they are, practicing senseless cruelty, planning to murder the very innocents they had promised to protect.

"I need to find Tim," Jacob says hoarsely. Though he loves to play the fool, Timaeus is the smartest man he knows. Clever and witty and kind—Jacob *knows* this. It's why, late at night, he still sometimes feels the pinch of shame that he sent Tim to Dardania in order to protect his own secret. Jacob will tell him of the Elder Council's plan and, together, they'll find a way to stop this madness. But…

But how can he leave Katerina in an underground city full of Aesarian Lords, some of whom might recognize her as the one who defeated them at the Battle of Pellan Fields by catapulting pots of scorpions and snakes into their ranks?

Looking at her, he sees that her luminous eyes are no longer horror filled. Instead, they blaze with anger. "Go on, find Timaeus," Kat says, seeming to read his mind. "I can take care of myself."

"What will you do?"

Kat takes Roxana's hand. "Roxana, can you bring me some

of your friends, secretly? Do you think they'll like honey cakes, too?"

The little girl's eyes widen, and she nods. "Yes," she says. "Oh yes!"

Kat looks around, her gaze fixing on a doorway down the hall. "I'll wait in there, Jacob." She slips the bag of honey cakes off his shoulder. "Meet me back there. Hopefully, by then, I will have learned more from the children, and we can find a way to set them free."

"I *am* free," Roxana interrupts stubbornly.

"Of course," Kat says hastily. "Now, will you bring me your friends?"

The little girl smiles, sticks out her hand, and says, "Honey cake."

Worry gnaws a hole in Jacob's stomach as he watches Kat disappear into the dark room and Roxana skipping in the other direction, her lantern light disappearing around a corner. He trusts Kat, but still he wishes they had never discovered this horror—that they were instead curled by a hearth in the temple complex, limbs entangled, oblivious as they have been over the past few weeks. Thinking they were healing people, that they were helping, when all the while, right beneath their very feet...

He swallows hard. Right now he cannot be *that* Jacob, the healer. He must be Lord Jacob, the youngest member of the Elder Council in the long history of the Aesarian Lords. Counting to ten, Jacob squares his shoulders, picks up his lantern, and, no longer seeking stealth, marches boldly through tunnels that smell of pungent mildew, dank earth, and torch smoke.

"Lord Jacob! Is that you?"

Jacob turns to see Lord Gaius, the tan, charming Roman. "I didn't know you'd returned!"

"Well met, Gaius!" Jacob says, smiling. "It wasn't easy to find you, even with the instructions Tim—Lord Timaeus—sent. I'm looking for the blacksmiths. I need to speak with him."

"It's been a long time since Lord Timaeus has worked the fires, Lord Jacob," Gaius says. "He's now second-in-command to High Lord Gideon."

Second-in-command? Only a year ago Tim was the fresh recruit given all the worst assignments, from sweating over the blacksmith's forge to cleaning out the latrines. He has risen high—and quickly—indeed.

"We thought you had died in the great earthquake of Delphi until Lord Timaeus told us a few months ago that you had contacted him."

Was that suspicion in the man's voice? No. The truth is, Jacob *has* been gone a long time. Who knows how much has changed.

Jacob forces a smile. "I very nearly did. It's quite a story. I'll tell you all about it once I've met with Lord Timaeus."

Gaius returns the smile. "He is with High Lord Gideon, dining, I believe. Follow me. In these accursed tunnels, it's easy to become lost." Jacob sees the tunnel diverging into three paths. Gaius takes the left one.

"Did your sister marry that fellow?" Jacob asks. "Last time we spoke, you were worried the dowry negotiations would fall through."

Gaius's grin gleams white. "She did! And in a few months, she's going to give me my first niece or nephew!"

Jacob claps him on the back. "Wonderful news!" Though he's hardly listening—the thud of his heart threatens to drown out everything else. He must speak to Tim. He must understand. He must be wrong about their plans. He needs to hear it from Tim.

As they march down the corridors, Jacob hears greetings from his brothers as they recognize him. Lord Aethon, red-faced and barrel-chested, who can drink any man under the table. Melchior, the handsome Persian with the proud face of a hawk and a beautiful deep singing voice. Dexios, the Spartan, who can calm the wildest horse. As urgent as Jacob's need is to see Tim, he has to stop and greet his fellow Lords, men he has camped with, trained with, fought beside. Men who are, in a way, his brothers.

But even as his chest soars with something like relief to see their familiar faces after so many months, he asks himself how they could be complicit in what he suspects?

The murder of children.

He shudders. It simply can't be. Aethon has three boys of his own in Boeotia and spends a fortune on their tutors. Melchior has a beloved daughter by a beautiful courtesan in Sardis. Gaius is delighted that he is going to be an uncle.

There must be something he doesn't understand. Urgency courses through him. He must talk to Tim.

Finally, Gaius stops in front of a door. "They're in there." He smiles warmly. "It is good to see you back, Lord Jacob. We've missed you." Then Gaius continues down the corridor, leaving Jacob to enter the wide doorway alone.

He finds himself in a bright, torch-lit room. The staircase in the corner ends halfway up, but the walls are richly painted with scenes of gods and goddesses in white, blue, and red. The floor is of red marble, striated with white. Clearly, this was once a room in a rich man's house—nearly a thousand years ago. And in the center of the room is a table, where High Lord Gideon and Tim sit, dining.

There's a moment of silence while the two men take in Jacob, and then Timaeus leaps to his feet and strides around the table to embrace him. "By all the gods," he exclaims, grinning widely. "Jacob, you're back!"

Seeing Tim's comical face and bulging blue eyes, Jacob's heart leaps with unguarded happiness. After all these months of separation and danger, it is so good to see his best friend again. And Tim, he notices, has a new confidence, a spring in his step.

"Once we arrived here, I sent word to you in Byzantium," Tim continues, "to find us below the ruins. But I assume you had already left."

"Yes," Jacob says. "That must be what happened. I came weeks ago and have been waiting for you here ever since."

High Lord Gideon stands now, too, a bright smile lighting his dark face as he opens his muscular arms in greeting.

"Welcome, Lord Jacob," he says in his deep, rich voice. "I am so glad you have rejoined us at last. Eat, drink," he says, gesturing to the table. "And then you can tell us where you have been."

And while the scent of lentils and lamb is delicious, Jacob's insides twist. "I will, my lord, but first..." He hesitates. "I saw something strange in the tunnels. Children who seem...unlike other children I've seen before."

Gideon nods gravely. "The Smoke Bloods, yes. That was Lord Timaeus's discovery. Come now, sit, and Tim will tell you all."

Smoke Blood. Now Jacob has a name for it, but there seems to be no way around breaking bread with Gideon and Tim.

He joins them at the table while Tim spins a fantastical tale of ancient legends, a man of Smoke, the ambitious Queen Cynane, and a powerful potion. Of how, when he told Gideon of this new magic, the High Lord suggested they come to Troy, as the Lords had heard rumors of hidden, enslaved children here. There is something cocky in his behavior, something arrogant that Jacob has never seen before. In the past, Tim poked fun at himself. His foul jokes and curses could have stripped the hide right off a cow. Now he seems to be getting above himself, and Jacob realizes with a pang that he likes him less.

"In these mines," Tim continues, leaning forward, his pale blue eyes burning brightly, "are children who will never be missed when we take them east and, satiated with Smoke Blood, the monsters will return to their lairs for decades, harming no one else."

Tim smiles broadly, as if waiting for Jacob to congratulate him. But Jacob's heart sinks like a boulder catapulted into a pond. Tim isn't going to help him stop the Aesarian Lords. Tim is the *architect* of this great evil.

The disgust that roils in his stomach is enough to make him want to cough up all the food he has just eaten, but he manages to hold himself steady.

He is already telling himself he must tread carefully when Timaeus reaches for something on the chair beside him and holds up a large iron torch, about the length of a tall man's arm. Cruel spikes adorn the long handle. On top of the handle is a basket of twisted pieces of iron. The Hemlock Torch. Jacob's heart skitters in horror.

"We have been testing the children," Tim says, and something in his eyes tells Jacob he senses his fear and revels in it. "And the torch has shown increasing levels of magic. As you know, when lighted, the torch burns green flames when Earth Blood is nearby," he emphasizes the last words knowingly and gives a sinister little nod that makes a shiver run up Jacob's spine. "It burns violet for Snake Blood, and red for soothsayers and other types of magic. But the torch burns black flames for Smoke Blood, beautiful swirling black fire with silver and gold sparks. And the flames rise higher every time we test the children."

Everything in him screams to get up and leave. Race from the room, find Kat, and get out of these haunted tunnels. The Hemlock Torch can detect them both. And Tim already knows his secret. If Jacob disagrees with his plan, will Tim reveal it— reveal *him* for who and what he truly is? Yet how can Jacob allow him to sacrifice dozens, maybe hundreds, of children without even making a suggestion?

"It is a clever plan, Tim," Jacob stalls, "but one forged of desperation, don't you think? Are we really so low as this?"

Tim's watery blue eyes are cold as he slowly lowers the torch.

Gideon drums his large fingers on the table. "It is unfortunate we have come to this pass," he admits. "We know that. But we are forging ahead with this experiment, even as the regiments in Nekrana are working on their own solution. Supreme Lord Gulzar's engineers have created iron tubes that shoot long blasts of fire, which, they hope, will melt even the deathless soul of a Spirit Eater. They will lure the bulk of the monsters to a place with magic prey and then try to destroy them."

"We can only hope, then," Jacob says, "that the Supreme Lord's plan is successful."

Tim has taken Jacob's statement as an insult. His face has become as hard as the stone walls around them. "By sacrificing a few children, Jacob, we will save tens of thousands, perhaps hundreds of thousands of lives. The children understand that they have been chosen for a great purpose. Is there not dignity in helping to save mankind? Is not war a kind of mass murder all its own, especially war against the deadliest of history's monsters?"

Jacob's mouth feels dry. He is speechless at the horror of what Tim is suggesting, of what Tim has become. His old friend, a glimmer of dark pride on his face, continues, either oblivious to Jacob's horror or propelled by it. "Perhaps you, Lord Jacob, have another, better solution? Would you perhaps care to sacrifice… yourself?" He takes an oil lamp from the table and lights the Hemlock Torch.

Jacob's heart stops. Gideon, puzzled, looks between Tim, Jacob, and the torch, whose orange flames are starting to burn green. Jacob stands as his chair falls backward to the ground. His fingers are already around the hilt of his sword, when he sees the truth dawn in Gideon's face.

But even so, the large man surges to his feet, sword already bared. "A Blood Magic in our midst! Traitor!" Gideon bellows and hacks his blade down toward Jacob's sword—but the blades never meet.

A dagger suddenly blooms from Gideon's throat.

Timaeus's knife, thrown from the other side of the table.

Jacob's heart is racing in his own throat, and he desperately swallows back his shock as the High Lord's dark eyes widen in pain and surprise. Blood bubbles from his mouth. With an enormous effort, his shaking hands pluck the dagger out, and blood pumps obscenely from the ragged wound. A horrible, sick rattle rises from his throat. He covers the wound with his large hands but blood pours between his fingers. He falls forward, dead, knocking over his wine cup. Dark red wine flows onto the table, mixing with Gideon's dark red blood.

Jacob feels like he is going to vomit. He swings toward Tim. "By all the gods! What have you done?"

But Tim's eyes are shut. He grimaces and shakes. Something is happening inside him, Jacob realizes. He should kill him now. He raises his dagger and…can't.

Tim opens his eyes, which glow like twin blue flames. He seems different now, *stronger*. A slow, wicked smile spreads over his face. "A double betrayal is the best kind," he hisses, laughing darkly.

Jacob grips his sword tighter, but Tim doesn't attack. Instead, the man takes a whistle from his belt and blows it loudly three times. The signal for *a brother in danger*.

The truth rushes at him with a kind of stunning clarity: Timaeus has set him up. He will blame Jacob for Gideon's murder, and all the Lords will believe him. Jacob has been missing for months, while Tim is Gideon's trusted second-in-command, whose clever plan will save the world from the Spirit Eaters. And if any Lords were outside the door just now, they would have heard Gideon's bellowed accusation: *traitor*.

Rage rumbles deep inside Jacob. Tim has betrayed his best friend and his commander, has broken his vows of obedience, and has vanquished every vestige of ethics he ever possessed. Tim lunges toward him now, but Jacob slams his fist against the stone wall. Anger courses from his fist into the stones, and a shower of rock and grit falls between them as the earth trembles. Tim reels backward, his hands over his head, giving Jacob just enough time to run out of the chamber.

His heart hammers. He cannot believe what he just saw. He hears footsteps, urgent voices, sees the glow of torches coming around a bend in the tunnel. He runs into the dark shadows. His legs feel like lead. He can't see a thing, but his Earth Blood allows him to sense the right path—left here, right there, now straight.

Whistles and shouts follow him, echoing off the stone. Boots slap and thud. Finally, he sees a dull bloom of light from a lantern spilling from a doorway ahead and tumbles inside. She is sitting alone, her head against her arms, which are propped up on her knees.

"Where are the children?" he asks, but she shakes her head.

"They won't listen to me!" she says, her voice a cry of anguish. Tears track down her dusty face. "They don't want to leave. They keep saying that they are chosen to save the world! But, Jacob, what's happening? That earthquake, it was you, wasn't it? Where's Tim?"

"Timaeus…is not with us," Jacob says, not knowing how to tell Kat all that has happened in the last few minutes. "We need to get out of here, now!"

"But the children!"

Jacob grinds his teeth. Yes, the children. He has only hastened their deaths. With Tim now the head of the Aesarian regiment and knowing of Jacob's disapproval, he will most likely take the children east as soon as the sun rises in a few hours. This is their only chance to save Roxana and the others. But how? Even now, he can feel the stomping feet of the Aesarian Lords through the tunnels as they fan out to find him…and Kat.

"We would need an army to get out of here with all of us alive," he groans as the truth settles around him. He closes his eyes. This is the end. He has lived a life of impossibilities, but now he can perform no more miracles.

He feels a warm hand on his shoulder.

"Wait," Kat says, and he opens his eyes to see her bright with excitement. "We *do* have an army."

Quickly, she reaches into her bag and pulls out the proof

of her story: two dozen blue-glazed figurines shaped like tiny mummies, their arms crossed over their chests, their bodies stamped with strange signs. They look like normal Egyptian statues to him. There is nothing about them to suggest an ancient princess, a cursed city, and a powerful general whose soul split into countless pieces. How is Jacob supposed to transform the figurines into the warriors they once were?

He lets his fingertips brush over them and quickly pulls back his hand. "I do feel something powerful," he whispers. "But I don't know how to read those symbols. I can't do the right ritual. It's useless."

"Lord Gaius! Over here!" cries a deep voice from somewhere down the hall.

Kat's eyes sparkle in the semidarkness. "When I was on Meninx," she says, her voice tight with urgency, "I could no longer access my Snake Blood powers. But it was imperative that I do so to build the Atlantean Mechanism. Ada convinced me to swim into the ocean and not *try*, but do the opposite of trying. Relax. Our powers are always present. Sometimes we just block them with fear."

Her head turns at the thud of feet against stone. They are about to be found out. And he *is* afraid, so afraid—for himself, for Kat, for all those orphaned children—how could he not be?

Urgently, Kat grabs his hands, placing one of the doll-like sculptures into them. "Hold the ushabti and enter it, just as you can enter water and earth and rocks. The statuette is made of clay, of earth. And an Earth Blood created it. Your ancestor. You have his blood in your veins, his wisdom in your soul. You don't need Egyptian words or ancient rituals. You need only to relax and trust yourself. And *hurry*."

Relax. And hurry. Jacob wants to argue that doing both things is impossible, but he remembers his little brother Cal, all long gangly limbs and tousled hair, and how he couldn't save him from evil. How he would always regret not being able to save him. But there's a chance he can save *these* children. He must at least try.

He closes his eyes and takes a deep breath, blocking out his anger at Tim, his horror at Gideon's murder, his fear for Kat and the children. He floats, disembodied, into the earthen statue in his hands and feels the molten heat of the earth inside it. He senses the spark of life, the hum of thought, and he opens himself up to it. He lets the thoughts and sensations flow over him. He smells lotus blossoms and hot sand and...rotting corpses. He sees, rising from the desert, a lovely walled city, which catches fire as people flee and scream. He feels warm wind caressing his face...and unbearable pain searing through him. Light and shadows, laughter and screams, life and death...

It is too much.

He feels his head will burst from the strange sights and sounds and smells. But something tells him to keep holding the figurine. After a time, the images fade.

Blood of my blood, Earth Blood, calls a voice somewhere deep inside him. The voice is incredibly quiet despite its infinite power. It is ancient beyond measure and has always been inside him. He recognizes it as the center of his very being. And then he knows.

He sets the ushabti down, takes out his dagger, and pierces the inside of his left arm. A single drop of rich red blood falls onto the statuette and splashes. Kat looks expectantly from the ushabti to Jacob. The earth rumbles, and her eyes grow wide with fear as she looks around the room. But Jacob knows this is no earthquake that will destroy the underground city, trapping them all under tons of stone.

This is the rumbling of life coming into being.

There is a bang and a flash of light. Jacob, on his knees, looks up at a tall wide-shouldered warrior, his body made of cracked and flaking clay, the eyes in his broad dark face of orange flame. He wears strange armor, with a leopard skin thrown over his left shoulder, and a square helmet with long lappets on each side. In his massive right hand, he carries a heavy sword, and in his left a long rectangular shield.

He looks around, his thick neck muscles creaking, and his fiery gaze lights on Kat. "Princess Katerina," he says in a voice like thunder.

"General Wazba," she says, getting to her feet.

Now he stares at Jacob, who rises slowly. "You have awakened us," Wazba says to him, then turns to Kat, "though we were supposed to rest when Princess Laila destroyed her city. We toiled for her for centuries and deserved our rest."

Footsteps clatter in the hallway. A distant voice cries, "Turshu! He may be down there! Get torches!"

"We need your help," Kat says, "or the enemy will destroy us. Please, General, you served Princess Laila so faithfully. She thought enough of me to give me this." She holds up her golden fingertip.

He stares at it. "I remember. The princess was not known for her generosity once she was cursed. She must have liked you very much indeed."

"Can you help us?" Kat persists.

Wazba nods. "We will fight this enemy and then return to dust, to rest."

"Can you waken the others?"

Wazba tilts his enormous head. "My brothers and I are one. One soul, one spirit, one heart and mind." He raises his right hand, extending his sword, and mutters words that Jacob doesn't understand. The room explodes in bangs and bright light and is suddenly full of Wazbas.

"Down here!" calls a voice from the hall. "I see a light!"

"Kill the soldiers," Kat orders. "But save the children."

Wazba nods. He calls to his warriors, *"Ushbeth-ka-tark!"* and gestures for them to follow. They rush from the room.

"Retreat! Retreat!" cries a panicked voice. Weapons clash

in the corridor, metal on metal, metal thumbing on cowhide shields, grunts, and screams. Footsteps fading.

Jacob and Kat peer out. Two Aesarian bodies lie bloody on the ground. As Jacob approaches them, he recognizes Gaius, the Roman, so happy about becoming an uncle. And Phaedron, the Thracian, who bought each of his five brothers a large fishing vessel with his earnings from being an Aesarian Lord.

He feels his heart break. These were his friends, his colleagues. His brothers.

Kat, too, seems struck by the waste of it all. Tears well in her eyes, and she bites her lip. Then she deftly picks up Gaius's shield and hands it to Jacob.

"Jacob." Her voice cracks as she picks up Phaedron's shield. "I know this is hard for you. But we must make sure the children are unharmed."

Yes, she is right.

They run down the corridor and see more Aesarian bodies. Jacob forces himself not to look at the faces. They follow the sounds of battle to the little balcony overlooking the large room below.

The ushabtis and the Aesarian Lords battle viciously. The ring of sword on sword is so loud it is as if Jacob is in a forge with a hundred blacksmiths striking their anvils. He sees one Aesarian drive his sword deep into the heart of an ushabti. A stream of fire blasts out of the hole in the clay chest, burning the Aesarian's face. He screams, drops his sword, and covers his face with his hands as the ushabti, expressionless, runs him through.

Another Aesarian knocks the sword out of an ushabti's hand, then, in one clean sweep, slices off the baked-clay head. A spout of fire shoots toward the ceiling and the ushabti drops to his knees. He bends forward and blasts flame from his open neck, catching the lord's cape on fire. Howling in pain, he becomes a human torch, ricocheting off other soldiers.

It is an Aesarian who cuts off his head to put him out of his pain.

Jacob sees no children in the fray, thanks be to all the gods, but neither does he see Tim, who should be easy to recognize because of his slight size. What he does see is that, one by one, all his other Aesarian brothers fall, and each time his heart breaks until he wonders if the tiny shattered pieces can ever be put back together. Gone, so many brothers, so many friends— and it's his fault.

An explosion of heat, light, and clay shards forces Jacob and Kat to the floor, covering their heads with their hands. They rise slowly, looking down at the dust-filled room below.

Jacob turns to Kat and sees Tim standing behind her, his dagger against the back of her neck. Kat's eyes widen, and she straightens.

"So, I see you found your little lovebird," Tim sneers.

"Don't hurt her," Jacob commands. "She has nothing to do with this."

Tim's eyes blaze. "Everyone has always underestimated me," he says with an eerie calm. "Even you, who I thought were my best friend. You didn't trust me with your secret. You had me sent away to spy, to work as an acrobat and a fool. You were born with magic, and you don't want anyone else to have special powers."

The guilt that always sits in Jacob's chest finally splits open, slicing him in two.

"I am sorry for having you sent away." He hopes Tim can hear the truth in his words. "But, brother, this Smoke Blood has twisted your soul. The friend I knew never would have betrayed me with the torch or killed Gideon. Stop playing with this foul magic."

"Playing, is that what you think I'm doing?" Tim roars. "If I was as tall as you, would you say I was *playing*? Or would you say I was supervising? Experimenting? *Aspiring* to a greatness you could never imagine?"

Jacob searches for the right words to say and can't find any.

"Little did you know," Tim continues, "that in sending me to Dardania, I would attain powers beyond anyone's wildest imagination. Queen Cynane discovered Smoke Blood there, and I merely spied on her to learn about it."

"Cynane?" Rubbing her golden fingertip, Kat turns around slowly to face Tim. Now his dagger is poised to thrust through her throat, but she doesn't seem concerned. Her eyes almost seem to glow with sympathy, and Jacob wonders if she is trying to use Snake magic to reach him.

"Timaeus," she says gently, "Cynane was never someone you—or I for that matter—should have trusted. You are better than this. Jacob has told me much about you. You are clever, funny, loyal, a good friend. You can be those things again if you let this evil magic fade from your veins."

Tim blinks. "Can I?" he says. "We shall see."

And then…he vanishes.

Jacob thrusts out a hand to see if Tim is still there, camouflaging himself, as Roxana can. But his hand meets nothing.

Tim is gone.

A silence fills the secret city.

There are no more screams, no more footsteps.

Cautiously, Jacob and Kat look back at the room below.

Dead Aesarian Lords are strewed across the floor. Jacob doesn't want to look. But he has to look, if only to honor them with his grief. He sees Ervin and Farbod, cousins from the far reaches of Persia with amazing archery skills. Asdrubal, from Carthage, an amateur magician who could pull a coin from your ear or a rabbit from under your cloak. Tutmose from Egypt, devoted to a god with the body of a man and the head of a crocodile. Jacob looks at each one of them—Greeks, Persians, Gauls, Scythians—and feels as if his soul will split into dozens of tiny pieces, just as General Wazba's did so long ago.

They are dead.

And everywhere, there is a fine layer of clay dust that smells faintly of an endless river churning through sand, mixed with the delicate scent of lotus blossoms. All that remains of the ushabtis.

But then…through the billowing clouds, small forms begin to appear, wandering into the hazy, blood-soaked room. Some of the children hold hands, while others sniffle.

"Katerina?" They turn to see Roxana creep forward, picking her way through the dust and bits of clay. Her small fist grips a honey cake. She looks around at the devastation.

"Is everything going to be all right?"

CHAPTER NINETEEN

ALEXANDER

AS HE PACES UP AND DOWN THE SMALL ANTE-
chamber outside his mother's rooms in the Ambracian palace,
Alexander feels a kind of trapped tension in his muscles—he is
far better suited to battles on the field than in the home. What
could his mother and Philip be talking about all this time, just
on the other side of that thick door?

He should have gone to the guest quarters with Heph. But then,
there was a whole other kind of tension there, in their closeness, in
what almost happened but didn't in their shared tent near Chaeronea. Since then, they'd gone back to their old, easy friendship
and had vigorously celebrated the signed treaty of the League of
Corinth before packing up and heading here, to Epirus. Home
of Olympias's brother, King Xander. But still, when things were
quiet—in between feasts and strategy meetings and head counts and
recruitments, in between arranging for ships to sail west and navi-
gating not only the rough sea but also the storms of King Philip's
moods—there were moments when Alex knew, in his heart, that
things would never *really* be the same between them, at least not for
him. Something had awoken that he had hoped to leave dormant,
curled, and sleeping peacefully in the deepest part of him forever.

Now he paces, wishing there were a place to sit, almost—*al-*

most—missing the frivolous decor his mother always obsessed over back home at the Pellan palace. Everything he's seen of his uncle Xander's palace here in Epirus is old-fashioned and threadbare. When his entourage first rode into a courtyard and Alex saw the low-slung building with arrow-slit windows, he assumed he had approached the palace from the rear and was looking at the kitchens and stables. But it was the main entrance.

They disembarked in Epirus only an hour ago, and, after King Xander welcomed them, Philip insisted on talking privately to his wife. The two of them have been in her chamber for quite some time now, and it makes Alex nervous. The king has some plan afoot, a plan that he has hinted at but not revealed since the victorious Battle of Chaeronea.

Finally, the door bursts open, and Philip comes out, scratching his head. "I think her injuries from the flood have affected her brain," he says, then, possibly seeing the alarm in Alex's expression, adds, "for the better. I've never known your mother to be so calm. Pleasant, even. She doesn't seem to mind I brought Cleo, or that she is pregnant."

This last statement worries Alex even more. Either Philip is right, and Olympias's brain has been addled by her injuries, or Olympias is playing along with Philip because she, too, is plotting something and his plot weaves perfectly into her own. He wonders whether his mother will stay calm when his stepmother—who is only a year older than he is—fondles and kisses Philip in front of her, which she did with such nauseating frequency on the week-long journey from Athens that several times Alex wanted to jump over the side of the ship and swim to land.

"The oddest part was," Philip continues, rubbing his beard thoughtfully, "that she accepted my plan so quickly. I was sure she would fight it."

"What plan?" Alex asks.

Philip fixes him with his single dark eye. "Oh, you'll see very soon. You watch carefully and you will see a master strategist at work, boy." He beams broadly. "Well, it's your turn to see the witch. Enjoy yourself." And he marches off.

Alex inhales sharply as he places his palm on the door and pushes. How can he look into the face of the woman who both brought him into the world and almost took him out of it so she could be with her lover? Facing Olympias is more daunting than facing the Sacred Band of Thebes was. He squares his shoulders and steps inside.

He finds himself in a modest chamber with a low roof of oak beams, lime-washed white walls, and moth-eaten tapestries. Olympias sits in a chair by the open window, enjoying the warm spring breeze from the Ambracian Gulf. She turns to him, her face a strange mixture of delight and trepidation.

"Alexander!" she says, extending a thin white arm.

He approaches her, taking in how much she has aged—beneath her heavy makeup, her skin seems thin and wrinkling. A large pasty dollop cannot hide the thick red scar on her temple, the result, everyone thinks, of injuries sustained in the flooded Byzantine palace, but which Alex knows was caused by Jacob. He kneels for her blessing, and she puts both hands on his head. They feel like claws.

He looks up to find her studying his eyes, looking, evidently, for Riel's green ones. He forces himself to stare right back. She falters, looks away. Tears slide down her pale cheeks.

"Gone," she whispers. "Gone."

"Disappointed, Mother?" he asks, surprised that the tone of his voice is sharp enough to hew a tree.

"Do you know...everything?" she asks, her green eyes swimming with unshed tears.

He nods, clenching his jaw so tightly it hurts.

"I...didn't know," she begins, tears falling more quickly now, "that when I brought him back to human form, it would be *your* form. I swear, I didn't know. And after it happened, I thought... I hoped that, with his powers, he could regain his old form and leave yours. I wanted you to come back. I've always loved you. Don't you remember how I've doted on you, all these years?"

Alex rises and looks out the window. Clustered at the bottom of the palace hill is a tidy village, and beyond that the sea. Is she telling the truth? Probably. She has always been fiercely devoted to him as an extension of herself and, as he grew older, as a means of wielding political influence. Her selfishness alone should ensure her devotion.

"He was slowly killing me," he says, his voice tight, strangled.

"How did you…come back?" she asks.

Alex laughs harshly. "You did it," he says. "That much I can thank you for. By scratching Jacob with that hairpin. The prophecy said Riel could only be killed by Earth Blood, and, it turns out, Jacob is Earth Blood."

Olympias's eyes widen, and a skeletal hand goes to her throat. "What?" she croaks.

"Yes," Alex continues, enjoying her discomfort. "And Katerina, the daughter you tried to kill, was in the palace that day, searching for the Earth Blood. She found the hairpin, coated with Jacob's blood, on the floor, and when Riel, in my body, attacked her, she scratched him on the neck with it. He died so I could live."

What he doesn't add: *a part of me died, then, too.* His blood powers. In that sense, Kat really fulfilled two prophecies that day. She *did* kill Alexander, in a way, in order to free him, in order to vanquish Riel.

She sags into her chair. Alex expects her to pepper him with questions, but instead she just whispers to herself, "He's really gone, then. Forever." She's sobbing now. Large tears run down her cheeks, leaving white rivulets as they carry her cosmetics away with them. On the ship over here he had planned to yell at her, to punish her for allowing Riel to take over his body. But now, seeing this sick old woman crying like a baby, he cannot.

A small door next to the bed opens and a girl comes out, a look of concern in her large hazel eyes.

"My lady?" she asks, kneeling by Olympias's side. "Should I bring a calming draft?" Alexander recognizes her as a girl he had seen tending his mother's injuries in the Byzantine palace as soon as he and Heph returned from their horrifying night floating in the cold straits. Now, as then, he feels that there is something familiar about her.

"Yes, Patra," Olympias says, wiping her cheeks with the heels of her hands. "And when you return, light the perfume burner." The girl dashes from the room, and Alex finds his gaze following her slight figure until she has closed the door. Could Patra seem familiar because she reminds him of Kat?

"This palace is much worse than I remember." His mother sniffs. "Since Queen Heraclaia died, my brother has let it go. The mildew smell is awful. I've had a perfume burner put in your room, too, Alexander."

"Mother," Alex says, "mildew isn't the worst thing in this palace right now, I think. What is this plot you are hatching with Philip, or more accurately, against him?"

She smiles with such satisfaction that, for a moment, some of her former beauty returns, lighting up her face. "It's an alliance between Epirus and Macedon, Alexander. An excellent idea. I no longer have the strength to fight or plot. Philip can do what he wants." She looks at him with her old fiery intensity. "Except disinherit you for some brat that bitch bride of his gives him."

"He assured me he will not do that," Alex replies. "And I believe him."

"He assured me of that, too," she says airily, waving a thin hand so that her golden bangles clatter musically. "So, it seems we are all in perfect accord."

Words he has heard approximately never. Alexander shivers, uneasy, as he leaves his mother's chambers. Philip forced him on this side journey before promising part of his army to lead into

Persia. Alex doesn't like an errand he doesn't fully understand. Shoring up allies is all well and good, but Epirus should be the least of his concerns right now.

Anxiety eats at him as he makes his way up the winding stairs toward his own guest room. So much has changed over the last few months, and even weeks. Two great threats loom in the east: the armies of Persia and a migrating mass of legendary monsters. Rumor, confusion, and fear have stirred up a kind of restlessness among the people he has not seen before.

Meanwhile, Alex has spent the last six months trying to make amends for his behavior when Riel possessed him: convincing people he was ill, not in his right mind, and winning back their trust and approval, all the time knowing that his birthright is one of darkness and evil. He spent many years hating the man he thought was his father—Philip—when he should have saved his loathing for the truth. And now, on top of all that, when he thinks of his closest and most trusted friend in the world—Heph—he thinks only of the ache buried deep in his chest, and the knowledge of what cannot and will not be.

Not for the first time, Alexander wonders at the insidious, snarled nature of fate, which shows us that our fathers are not our fathers, our fears are not what we thought, and our friends are the people who have the greatest power of all to cause us pain.

After the midday meal, Alex and Heph enter the surprisingly small, dark throne room behind King Philip and Cleo to find King Xander sitting on his throne—not on the dais, but at an ivory-inlaid table that must have been exquisite hundreds of years ago. Now some of the ivory is missing, the rest cracked or stained. Next to him, on the queen's throne, sits Olympias. Xander rises and bids Philip and Cleo sit on the thrones across from him. Protocol, Alex knows, requires no king to be higher than any other king.

Tall and gaunt, with Olympias's silver-blond hair and pale

skin, Xander looks eerily like his sister, though his eyes glitter gray blue instead of green. To Alex, who takes his place with Heph standing behind King Philip, brother and sister, sitting side by side, seem like ghost monarchs from an ancient myth. The queen's handmaiden Patra stands demurely behind her throne.

It's a dim, ancient chamber with smoke-stained walls lined by old wooden benches. The fire pit in the center of the room is empty, and daylight streams through the smoke hole in the roof and small open windows on either side.

As Patra pours wine for the kings and queens, Xander's cold eyes linger on her lithe, graceful form, and then he and the others dash some wine to the ground as libations for the gods and ancestors.

"Congratulations, Philip," Xander begins, drinking deeply, "on your victory over the allied Greeks. My sister and I were so pleased to hear the news."

Philip nods. Cleo puts a soft, plump hand on his arm and squeezes it, looking up at him with big, simpering blue eyes. Her other hand rests against her swelling abdomen. Alex studies his mother. Her green eyes flash, but a slight smile plays on her ruby-red-painted lips.

"We need Epirus with us," Philip says. "We must show the Persians we are united against them."

Xander casts an appraising glance at Cleo, who has wedged herself so closely against Philip that they look glued together. "And yet, Philip," he says in his thin, reedy voice, "it seems you have discarded my sister as your queen and taken yourself a new one. Our old ties of alliance have, therefore, vanished." He snaps his long white fingers.

"I give Olympias all honor," Philip says defensively. "She is the mother of my heir, Alexander, who will remain my heir, and who has already proven himself in battle as a worthy leader. But we kings, who carry the burdens of our people on our shoulders, are allowed more than one wife."

"This is your eighth, I think?" Xander interrupts in an arch tone.

Philip frowns. "I have had more burdens than most," he says quickly. "And I still want ties of blood to bind Epirus to Macedon. It is time you, Xander, take another wife. You need an heir."

Alex stiffens at this. What young relative could Philip be offering Xander? He knows of no nieces or cousins of the right age.

Xander smiles, revealing long teeth that make him look like a rabbit. "Are you offering me some cousin of a cousin of yours?" he asks. "Because she would have to be very beautiful…" He leans forward with a passion in his face that surprises Alex, and says in a low voice, "Very beautiful indeed. And young. And a virgin. And sweet tempered. And I would have to see her before I agreed."

Philip leans back and laughs, slapping the table so that the wine cups shake. "By Zeus, Xander, you are more of a man than I thought. Yes to all those things. But the bride I offer you is not a cousin of a cousin." He examines a large iron ring on his left hand and says, "You have heard, I imagine, the rumors that the royal House of Macedon has a recently discovered daughter."

Alex's skin prickles. Has Philip managed to find Kat in Troy? Has he captured her and brought her here? Heph casts him a panicked, questioning look, but Alex does not betray his confusion, even as his mind races, trying to get a step ahead of Philip despite having clearly fallen two steps behind.

Xander casts a sideways glance at Olympias, who smiles congenially. Which makes no sense. Surely, she knows that a *new* alliance with Epirus would only further usurp her own political relevance. She would become practically disposable. "I think everyone has heard that gossip," he replies evenly. "And let me tell you, I would never marry my own niece. I won't help you out of your problems with public perception, if that's what you're looking for."

"It is not gossip, brother," Philip continues, "unless such stories cast aspersions on the virtue of Queen Olympias." Alex watches

his mother glow with pride; it must be the first time in ages anyone has called her virtuous.

"This daughter is not hers by another man, as is rumored
by vile scandalmongers," he adds, "but is mine, by a palace-
serving wench. No blood relation of yours." The queen smiles
even more broadly.

"Oh?" Xander asks, sitting up straight.

"A lovely girl, only seventeen, with royal blood flowing in
her veins."

Xander takes another gulp of wine. "Well, then," he says,
licking his thin lips. "That is different."

Alex feels another chill. Is Philip really about to promise Kat's
hand to this old king without ever having even met Kat or discovered her whereabouts?

Philip rises, pushing his chair out behind him with a scrape,
and holds out his hand. "Patra, my dear," he says.

Everyone's head turns as, timidly, Olympias's handmaiden
steps around the table and takes his hand.

Relief floods Alex. Not Kat, at least. But then he finds that
his head is reeling in confusion. What in Hades is going on?
What game is Philip playing? Alex looks to his mother, whose
face is a picture of equanimity. Why is Olympias playing along
with him?

Xander is speechless for several long moments as he studies
Patra. Her unbound hair gleams golden red, her large hazel eyes
are modestly downcast. The pale green gown reveals a slender,
shapely figure.

"Sister," he says, turning to Olympias, "your handmaiden is
King Philip's daughter?" His shrewd eye sweeps between her
and Philip, calculating. "Why didn't you tell me the truth?"

Olympias looks at her lap and says, "We discovered her last
summer, brother. King Philip made me swear on the vengeance
of the Furies to tell no one that he had recently put his bastard

daughter into my safekeeping until such time as he used her to craft a political alliance."

Xander rises from his throne and stares at Patra, whose pale freckled skin flushes becomingly. He walks over to her, drinking in every bit of her. He goes behind her, takes a long tendril of her thick hair and curls it around his finger, inspecting her as he might a prize horse. She has not raised her eyes and remains as still as a statue.

"Sister," Xander says, letting go of Patra's glossy curl. "What say you to this alliance? For I will do nothing that will dishonor or displease you."

"I am well pleased, brother," she says. "You need a queen and heir. This palace needs a mistress. And the future kingdom of my son needs an alliance. I do not resent Philip taking a younger wife. It is only natural." Here she beams at Cleo, who seems startled.

"And to prove my good will," Olympias continues, "I will bestow on Cleo rich gifts, worthy of a queen of Macedon, gorgeous robes, some of my best jewels, and other things. I understand she lost all of her bridal trousseau in the great flood of Byzantium, and I no longer need them."

Now Alex knows something is very wrong. He opens his mouth to say, "Mother…" when Xander interrupts him.

"Very well, then," the king says, his voice throaty with something like passion, and Alex marvels at what he knows he is about to hear—at the power of passion over men's capacity for reason. "I agree to take the beautiful Patra as my wife."

Bucephalus flies down the road toward the seashore, his hooves pounding the dusty earth into submission. As always when riding the big black stallion, Alex feels the horse's power as his own. He is no longer the prince with the weak leg, but a glorious being, perfect and strong, with the salty wind whipping through his hair and the soft golden light of the setting sun on his face.

Philip, thundering beside him, slows and veers toward a ridge overlooking the town below and, just beyond, the sun, like an enormous red ball, sinking into the choppy dark waters of the gulf. Alex, pulling up beside him, is mesmerized by the sight, and almost expects to hear the hiss of fire meeting water. The king pats his red mare on the neck and says, "It's good to be out of that dark old palace. An excellent idea of yours to go for a ride."

It is chilly out even though they are nearing mid-May—the capital of Epirus seems as inhospitable in climate as it is in personality. But the air *is* refreshing. It clears Alex's mind. He looks at fishing boats returning to the harbor on a slate blue sea, white caps rolling onto a sandy beach, and the red tile roofs of hundreds of houses, briefly wondering what the place was like for his mother, who grew up here.

"Father," Alex says, turning toward him. "I wanted to get out of the palace so we could have this conversation unheard by others. What happened in there?"

Philip grins mischievously. "That, my boy, was a diplomatic coup."

"What do you mean?" Alex asks. "Is that girl really your daughter?"

"Hades, no," Philip says, laughing heartily. "At least, not that I know of. Olympias tells me she was the oracle of Delphi. Ran off during an earthquake and ended up in Byzantium."

That bit of news startles Alex. Now he realizes why Patra seemed oddly familiar when he first saw her in Byzantium. As Riel, he had spoken with her on several occasions. Some cloudy memory of those conversations must remain.

"I needed to make an alliance with Epirus that eradicates your mother's position as liaison, to take her power away," Philip continues, watching a seagull cry and wheel. "Xander was right.

With his sister discarded, what connects us now? I was planning on using that real sister of yours, Katerina, but since you couldn't find her—" and here he turns to Alex, his eye narrowing a bit "—I had to improvise. The girl is young, beautiful, and devoted to your mother. And I thought perhaps Olympias might—after a huge row, of course—allow her new pet to become the queen of Epirus. But I didn't expect her to agree so quickly, to even suggest they marry immediately if Xander agrees."

Alex's mind whirls. Yes, his mother seems old, sick, and tired. But even if she was on her deathbed, thrashing in bone-shattering pain, he imagines she would still be plotting something. And her promise to give Cleo her jewels and gowns is like an alarm gong pounding in his head.

"Father," he says, his voice ringing with warning, "doesn't that worry you?"

But the king has already galloped off ahead of him.

Back in the warmth of his bedroom that evening, with the brazier blazing, lamplight casts soft shadows on the maps and charts littering the table. Heph tallies the numbers and says, "According to these latest reports, we will have five hundred and three ships. If the Athenians convince their allies on the islands to join, we might get thirty or forty more."

Alex nods. "Excellent. And we need to launch the invasion before the autumn storms can scatter the ships. Six more days here, Heph. To me, it feels like six more years. We should be in Athens now, not dillydallying in Epirus."

Heph straightens the papers into orderly piles. "Agreed," he says. "Though it wasn't a bad idea to obtain the Epirote alliance. That's three ships, eight hundred men, and two hundred horses."

It feels so right to be planning the invasion with Heph. Just like old times.

"Alex," Heph says, "Still no word on where King Philip wants to launch the invasion?"

Alex says, "Yes, he has decided to land where the Granicus River meets the sea." He doesn't add that the landing location is only a two-day ride from the Temple of Asklepios near Troy. Even though he no longer has his Snake Blood ability to read men's minds, he knows what Heph is after. Heph says nothing, but his face brightens.

"Let's give the king our new tallies right after breakfast tomorrow," Alex says. "Right now, I think we should get some sleep."

But hours later, the creak of a door pulls Alex from the darkness of slumber. He searches under his pillow for his phoenix dagger, dipped in the blood of the last phoenix. Its iron hilt is crafted in the form of a phoenix, its eye a glowing ruby, its long, pointed beak and wings raised skyward. The bird rises from curling flames of solid gold near the iron blade. It is a peerless heirloom, famed throughout the known world, and as soon as his fingers curl around the cold metal, his panic subsides, and he turns over to face the intruder.

His next thought is, *Heph?* But no. Standing on the threshold is a thin, draped figure holding a lantern, the dim light from the lamp inside casting a hazy glow through the oxhorn panels.

He rubs his eyes, wondering if he is dreaming, or worse—perhaps this is some memory of Riel's from thousands of years ago. Then she closes the door behind her and approaches him. His whole body relaxes when he realizes this is no memory of the dead god but a flesh-and-blood girl.

"Patra?" he asks, pushing himself up in bed. "Is everything all right?"

"Yes," she says, with a sad little laugh, "and no. Forgive me for waking you, my lord, but I thought I would die if I didn't have someone my age to talk to, someone who might understand."

Alex slides off the bed and gestures to a pair of chairs. "Sit down," he says gently, as he takes the oil lamp from her lantern and lights all the other lamps in his chamber. He sits across from her, pulling his sleeping tunic over the snake-like scar on his left thigh.

"I remember you from the temple at Delphi. You were different then," she says, tilting her head. "Your eyes were green, and you were…harsh. Impatient. Arrogant. You are much nicer without him inside you."

Alex massages his forehead. "I remember very little of that time," he says.

She smiles sadly. "Funny, isn't it? I was born a slave, then sold into a different kind of slavery as the oracle of Delphi." She tells him of life in the sanctuary, watched over by sharp-eyed matrons and strict priests, of a constant stream of rituals and festivals where she, the lead actress, was forced to faithfully follow a script written by others. Alex listens because it's all he can offer her, really. He can't renegotiate Philip's dealings or expose his lies for the sake of a servant girl, no matter how much he may feel for her position. And perhaps, after all, to be listened to is all she wants.

"I escaped in the great earthquake, thinking I would finally be free," she says, toying with the fringe of her shawl. "I wanted them all to think I was dead, my body buried under a heap of rubble. You see, I was in love." She looks up at Alex, and he feels the weight of sadness in her large hazel eyes. "In fact, I think I still am. But he didn't love me. I hoped he would with time, but one night I realized he would always love someone else, that there would never be any room for me in his heart. And so, I left. Well, I tried to leave. Boarding a boat in the harbor, I found myself washed right into the palace when the waves came."

Alex frowns. How many people's fates were changed that day of watery horror? Not just those of Kat, Jacob, and Heph.

Patra continues, "It's as if the gods themselves don't want me ever to be free and have placed me in a situation where I now face a new kind of slavery. Marriage to an old man." Her pale face has a haunted look.

"He's not really...old," Alex says, fumbling for the words to comfort her.

"He's more than twenty years my senior."

Alex sighs, thanking the gods that Katerina avoided this. Yet it seems a hard fate for this sweet girl before him. "You will be queen," he says, in a cheering voice.

"I would rather be free," she retorts, pulling her thin shawl more tightly about her.

She seems so like Kat in some ways, he remarks again, not just her appearance. "Women are rarely free, Patra," he says gently. "Most of them must marry, and Xander is not ugly and not unkind. I believe he was already half in love with you when he thought you were merely my mother's handmaiden."

"How nice for him," she says sarcastically, "to be in love with me. What about my feelings?"

But they both know her feelings don't matter. "Cruel as heartbreak is, it does fade, with time," he says carefully. "Or so I have heard." She sighs deeply, and he's not sure if he really believes his word, either. What *can* he say to cheer her up? Perhaps he should distract her. "Now, tell me," he says, "when you are queen of Epirus, what is the first thing you will do?"

She stares into the darkness beyond the lamps as if she is staring into her own bleak future. "It makes no difference," she whispers. In the glowing amber light, he sees in her profile the beauty of the woman she will become. And though his Snake Blood powers are lost, he has the strongest feeling, a kind of intuition, that she will be a beloved queen. A kind mother of many children. And, perhaps with time, a woman who loves her husband.

"No, really, Patra. Tell me. Will you go shopping for beautiful gowns? Have the jeweler make you a crown?"

Patra crinkles her nose. "The first thing I will do is clean up this palace. It smells mildewed."

"Yes," Alex says. "It most certainly does. My mother put a

perfume burner on the table over there, near the window." He points to a terracotta figure of a woman's head wearing a tall headdress.

Patra rises and, taking the oil lamp from inside her lantern, lights the coals inside the headdress, opens the incense box on the side, and sprinkles several golden rocks of myrrh on the coals. She is careful to step out of range of the smoke, Alex notes, and with good reason, given the fact that she is an oracle. Soon the room is filled with a sweet, delicate fragrance.

"I'm sure my uncle will let you do what you want with the palace," Alex says, crossing his legs. "You can order new furniture, tapestries…" Patra's eyes are riveted on the scar on his thigh, now revealed by his hitched-up sleeping tunic. He quickly covers the scar.

"That mark," she says, pointing, "What is it?"

"Nothing," he assures her. "I've had it since birth. The physicians say my twin's umbilical cord wrapped around my leg in the womb. My real sister, Katerina."

A cool night breeze washes in the open window, wrapping thick plumes of incense smoke around Patra, whose eyes roll back in her head as she starts to sway.

"The threads," she says in a deep, throaty voice very unlike her own. "The threads of Fate. You struggled with them even before you were born, and that is their mark. Unbound. You are the one to unbind us all. By untangling the knot."

Alex is chilled. This girl speaks in the voices of the gods. It turns his blood to ice.

As Alex listens to the swaying Patra mutter about knots and threads, his heart hammers in his chest. He tells himself there is no reason for fear. Perhaps he should view this as an opportunity for information.

"Tell me about the Spirit Eaters," he says. "Are these monsters real?"

She flings her long hair around her and says in a voice of brass, "Oh, they are real. And they are *hungry.*"

The hairs on the back of Alex's neck stand up, and he shivers. "Can they be destroyed?"

Patra stands in front of him, her chin on her chest, her eyes raised toward him. "Only he who is marked with the threads of Fate can destroy them."

"And who is marked by the—"

"You," she intones. "Only you, my king."

"I am not your king," he says, a kind of eerie dread filling his chest.

"No," she says slowly. "But you will be."

"How?" he asks, urgency thudding through him. "How do I destroy them?"

"Go to the Temple of Midas in Gordium," she says, pointing out the open window, to the sea.

Gordium? Alex learned about the city from Aristotle. It was founded by King Gordios of Lydia some three or four hundred years ago. Now it is part of the Persian Empire, though not nearly as far from Macedon as the Eastern Mountains. And there is a giant snarl of rope there, the famous Gordian knot. Long ago, a group of elders of the kingdom of Phrygia visited an oracle, asking for a new king. The oracle told them to return home and wait for the first man entering their town in an oxcart. He would be the man destined by fate to be their king. The first man to ride into town driving an oxcart was a farmer named Gordios. To memorialize the event, he declared the cart a holy object. To prevent anyone from stealing it, he tied it to a column with such a thick knot that no one thereafter could ever unravel it. He had to have used an ancient and forbidden magic, according to the stories—effectively, sealing his fate and that of his lineage forever to the spot.

"Gordium," Alex says, "is that where the hideous beasts have gathered?"

"No," she responds, her outstretched arm falling to her side.

"But—" Alex lets out a long, slow breath. Prophecies always fool you. They make no sense at all until after they have come to pass.

"You have only until the summer solstice," she goes on. "After that, their strength will wax beyond human means to destroy them. For, on the solstice evening, the new child of Fate will be theirs, giving them the power to devour the entire world."

"The new child of Fate?" he asks, trying to force this prophecy into clarity.

A man's low laugh bubbles out of her mouth. "Yes. Unless. Unless."

"Unless what?"

"Unless you slay the strands of Fate with the talisman of one who rises above mortal fate."

Alex rubs his forehead. She's talking in circles again.

"And only if you face them alone."

"Alone?"

"Alone, but not alone."

"You speak in riddles," he says, growing frustrated.

"You will need the help of one person only—a stranger. A stranger whose blood is destined to mingle with your own."

CHAPTER TWENTY

OLYMPIAS

QUEEN OLYMPIAS SITS IN HER FAVORITE CHILD-
hood chair—battered olive wood, tainted with years of bad memories. It's still somehow welcoming, like the arms of someone
who has hurt you but has come back to beg forgiveness. Patra
stands before her, and she surveys the girl from the top of her
gleaming golden diadem to the thick golden border of her yellow bridal gown. She is perfect—young, modest, beautiful—
everything a jaded, middle-aged king like Xander could want
in a wife.

Olympias knows Patra is a reluctant bride. The girl was horrified when the queen first told her of King Philip's plan to help
Macedon and Alexander by marrying her to Xander. But her
happiness does not really matter.

The queen could hardly believe her luck when Philip marched
in four days ago and announced his plan. *Pretend your new handmaiden is my daughter,* he said. *Marry her to Xander. Your favorite
becomes queen and will let you rule the roost here, unlike another woman
he might marry. And your son gets troops for our campaign.*

Yes, she said. *An excellent idea all the way around. Let's have the
wedding soon. You must, of course, attend and dole out your blessings
on the couple.* Philip was shocked at how quickly she agreed. He

had expected a fight, knowing he was rejecting her forever as his wife and queen, and taking away any power she might have in the alliance between Macedon and Epirus.

For Olympias, this marriage offers a greater advantage than Xander getting a wife or Patra becoming queen. Greater even than Alexander gaining Epirote troops for his conquest of Persia. This marriage will, most likely, give Olympias the dearest wish of her heart. For the oracle of Delphi—the girl in front of her, oddly enough—prophesied with the voice of gods that King Philip of Macedon would die at the wedding of Cleopatra. And yet, he didn't die at his own wedding to that stupid tart, Cleopatra Attalida.

But if there's anything Olympias has learned, it is that fate, and the prophecies, work in mysterious ways, looping in on themselves, offering obstacle and opportunity at every turn.

So, he did not die as predicted. As she *thought* was predicted. But he may still die soon. Perhaps they simply got *the wrong Cleopatra*. Perhaps instead, he will die at the wedding of *Cleopatra of Delphi* to King Xander. And if that doesn't work, Olympias will arrange for him to attend as many weddings of girls named Cleopatra as necessary until he does die at one of them.

For Olympias is not naive. She knows Philip could always change his mind and make Cleo's child his heir, disinheriting Alexander. But once Alex is king, Cleo's child will be nothing. Except for short-lived.

No, it has always been clear to her: Philip must die.

Malia, Olympias's brisk gray-haired handmaiden, adjusts the golden clasp pinning the gown on Patra's left shoulder and asks, "Cosmetics, my lady? She is a bit pale."

The queen scrutinizes Patra and quickly decides. "No. Xander wants a demure virgin bride, not a temple prostitute. Pale is perfect. Here, Patra, sit."

Visibly trembling, Patra dutifully takes her place on the footstool in front of Olympias. For a strange moment, a memory—silken and sad—sweeps over her, and it is no longer Patra kneeling there but Helen, her childhood friend, her *only* friend. Once. Helen was also an oracle, also modest, sensitive, and timid. Their friendship ended when both of them fell in love with Riel, so very long ago. She and Helen spent time together in this very room. There, against the other window, was Helen's loom, gone now. Like Helen.

But Olympias will not succumb to regretful thinking. Not after all that has happened. She did everything for Riel. Everything. And when he returned last year in her son's body, he didn't want her anymore. The natural aging of sixteen years, combined with the ravages of Lord Bastian's poison, had made her far less desirable. She denied her gut instinct, grasped at every compliment or kind word he sent her way, hoped the heavy makeup and false hair preserved the illusion of beauty. Alexander said Riel had come close to killing him, and Olympias wonders whether as king of Macedon he would have killed her, too.

She reaches to the table beside her and picks up the old lyre she found in a trunk. When her father gave it to her for her twelfth birthday, she had oohed and aahed at the shiny cow horns rising from the top of a polished tortoiseshell. It was dusty when she first pulled it out after her arrival here, the notes sour, and she struggled to tune the sheep-gut strings. Now her fingers move haltingly over them, teasing out the first song she ever learned to play.

Here she is, right back where she began. The same room. The same furniture. Over there is the table she hid under when her stepmother came to beat her. There is the bed in which she dreamed of her next rendezvous with Riel.

A sharp knock at the door interrupts her reveries, and Cleo enters, swinging her hips in an exaggerated way that makes Olympias's skin crawl. Perhaps it was seductive a few months ago. Now it is more like a waddle.

Cleo's black hair is piled in a tower of curls—much of it false, Olympias can only assume—and her heavy perfume is enough to choke an army. Little golden bells sewn on her robe tinkle as she walks as if saying, *I will not let you ignore me.* She's followed by a woman Olympias recognizes as her personal handmaiden, thin and olive skinned, her thick black hair coiled in a tight bun.

"Well," Cleo says boldly, a look of smug satisfaction on her painted face, "I've come for the gifts you've promised me." She clasps both hands over her pregnant belly.

"Ah," says Olympias, smiling warmly. "They are in that trunk over there, by the wall. You will find robes, jewelry, perfume, unguents, and cosmetics, including that red lip stain I gave you for your nuptials that always drove Philip mad with desire. I understand you lost it in the flood."

Like a greedy child, Cleo kneels before the trunk, throws open the lid, and starts rifling through the contents. Then she yelps with delight, holding up a dazzling silver-and-amethyst bracelet before thrusting it over her plump hand and onto her wrist.

"Sandalwood perfume from Egypt," Olympias continues, "an ivory comb from Ethiopia. A thank-you, Cleo, for treating my son as a prince and his father's heir."

Ignoring her, Cleo pulls out a shimmering blue-and-gold scarf and wraps it around her neck, then dives in for more. Watching the stupid girl, Olympias stifles a laugh. For months now—ever since Jacob injured her in Byzantium—she has felt weak and frail. But suddenly she feels as if she has been struck by lightning. Energy sizzles through her, sharp and tingling. She is alive again. *Alive.* Her life has an urgent purpose, even if that purpose is death.

She knows Cleo will test all her cosmetics for poison on her poor handmaiden, just as she did in Byzantium when Olympias first gave her the lip stain. But it won't make any difference, because the Persian mulberry pulp in the lip stain is harmless to everyone except Philip, who has a bizarre reaction to it. A hundred years ago, when she still loved him, she wore a skin cream scented with the berry's sweet essence. When he leaned in to kiss her, he began to choke; his eyes watered and his face broke out in angry red blotches. Palace physicians warned her that any further exposure to the berry could kill him. To Philip, it might as well be deadly nightshade, they said. She gave away the cream. But she tucked the memory away in her mental armory of potentially useful weapons.

Cleo slams the trunk lid down and leans on it heavily to stagger to her feet. She nods to her handmaiden and, without saying a thank-you, stomps out of the room, followed by the woman struggling with the trunk. Snorting in derision, Olympias's handmaiden Malia slams the door behind them.

"She doesn't bother you, my lady?" Patra asks, looking up at Olympias with concern. "She is not a nice girl, I think."

Now Olympias laughs out loud, a tinkling silver laugh that reminds her of being young and happy. "Not nice at all," she says, strumming the lyre. "But she has her uses."

She plucks a string hard, with purpose.

It snaps.

CHAPTER TWENTY-ONE

HEPHAESTION

HEPH TIPS HIS GOBLET INTO HIS MOUTH, BUT ONLY a single drop of wine falls on his tongue. He upends the oenochoe above the cup, but nothing comes out. His head is flushed with the warmth of the wine, which always has the strange quality of wanting more of itself. There's a meaning in that somewhere, he's sure, but he's too drunk to think of it.

Instead, he looks for another oenochoe on one of the dozens of tables set up in the palace courtyard. Around him, the wedding banquet is in full swing. Dancing girls in sheer costumes bend and swirl to the beat of drums and pipes. The gray-bearded man sitting next to Heph has already passed out. His head is on the table, his extended hands still grasp the bottom of his cup, and he snores loudly.

Two servants carry in a silver platter bearing a roasted peacock, its feathers sewn back on, deftly passing the krater, a bathtub-sized container where two other men mix wine and water with a paddle. But it's unmixed wine for Heph today. The bride, Patra, sitting on a throne next to King Xander's on the central wooden dais, reminds him a bit of Katerina. Who is not here. Who is with Jacob in Troy. Who is maybe in love with Jacob, maybe sleeping with him. Maybe in danger because she is Snake Blood and he is an Aesarian Lord, and Heph can't do a damned thing about it.

Frustration pounds in his head to the rhythm of the music. For months now, he has wanted nothing more than to leave Alex, go to Troy, and find her. Protect her. Convince her to love him, not Jacob. But he can't. Alex needs him. And he won't fail in his duty again, even if it means losing Kat.

King Philip's young wife, the appalling Cleo, approaches him and, to his horror, stops in front of his table. "Well, it's Handsome Hephaestion," she says boldly, smiling. He has drunk so much that she seems to be a blur of blue eyes, black hair, and dark red lips, moving into one another and then apart.

"Cheer up," she says, touching his cheek. He pulls back so quickly he almost falls off his bench as she laughs. "We'll find you a bride soon, Heph. We can't have you moping around the palace all...frustrated."

Is it so obvious then?

"If I weren't the king's most faithful wife, well..."

He's afraid she will stay and torment him, but she just laughs again and wanders off, thanks be to all the gods. While flaunting her position as the king's wife, she flirts with every decent-looking man in sight, even her own stepson. Even though she's pregnant. He and Alex have agreed that Cleo would never do anything to make Philip cast her aside; she values her position far too much. But she seems to want all men to desire her so she can turn them down, boasting about her own virtue.

Up on the dais, King Xander's narrowed, pale blue eyes are fixed grimly on Cleo, who is now laughing with a handsome young soldier near the krater. Then Xander turns to look at his own bride, the timid Patra, and beams. He leans toward her and whispers something that makes her smile shyly.

It could have been—should have been—Kat up on that dais married to the strange old man. The one thing Heph is grateful for is that she has avoided this fate.

A servant picks up the empty oenochoe on the table and sets down a full one. Heph grabs its slender neck, but a cool hand wraps around his wrist. "Not so fast," Alex warns.

Heph looks up at him questioningly. Alex's face seems to float above a sky blue tunic. "Where have you been?" Heph asks, trying to pull the pitcher toward him. Alex does not release his grip.

"All our lists of men, ships, horses, and equipment are on the desk in my bedroom," he says, straddling the bench beside him. "The list of battle formations, invasion plans, records of our meetings with Philip. It's all there, Heph. And the deciphered messages from our spies are behind the secret panel on the side of the desk. I showed you how to open it."

Heph laughs and pulls his wrist free from Alex's grasp. "Alex, this is a wedding, not a council of war," he says, pouring more wine. "You're a bit uptight. Should I pour some for you?"

Alex shakes his head and says, "I need to keep a clear head."

"I don't," Heph replies, taking a deep swig.

Alex puts a hand on his arm and says, "Heph, whatever happens, I know I can rely on you."

Yes, even though my heart is breaking, you can. But Heph just nods and runs a hand through his hair, which, he notices, is starting to get sweaty. Warm weather has finally arrived in this dreary outpost. The sky is a cloudless powdered azure, and the sun beats down mercilessly on the wedding guests. The breeze off the Ambracian Gulf is warm, hot, even, when it carries the heat from the fire pit near the gate, over which an entire wild boar roasts. The wine is warm. The people are warm. Heph mops his head and the back of his neck with his napkin.

When he looks up, Alex is nowhere to be seen. Cleo, however, is on King Philip's lap, passionately kissing him on a gilded throne set on a dais to the side of the newly married couple's. Across the courtyard, Queen Olympias, in a battered ivory chair on her own dais, stares at them, her eyes unblinking, her expression almost...eager.

Heph rubs his face and pushes his wine away. He's not seeing clearly. He will drink no more. He always found Olympias a hard person to like; at eleven, when he first came to live in the Pellan palace, he was terrified of this cold, selfish queen. But she accepted Heph as Alex's best friend and treated him decently. And, unlike Cleo, Olympias always behaved like a queen, in public, at least.

Phrixos and Telekles run between the tables up to the open area in front of the dais, pick up dancing girls, and swing them around to the beat of the music. Wedding guests clap and hoot. The actor Pausanias, wearing the grinning mask of Comedy, joins the dance. A tall, handsome man with riveting blue eyes and thick chestnut hair, he is Philip's latest male lover, according to palace gossip. Pausanias leaps and cavorts, the long multicolored ribbons on his costume fluttering wildly as he raps the dancers' rear ends with a beribboned stick.

The music, the heat, the smells of food and smoke wrap around Heph until he wonders if he is going to be sick. He pushes his slick hair out of his face and sees Philip, on his throne, quite red in the face, almost the same color as his scarlet tunic. He, too, must have drunk too much, Heph realizes, smiling. But then the king grabs the neck of his tunic and grimaces, as if he can't breathe.

Heph finds himself standing—a bit unsteadily—and looking around for Alex. The pale blond head is nowhere to be seen in the crowd. He looks back at Philip. Cleo has slid off his lap and stands beside him, bent over him and questioning. The king's face has broken out in huge red welts, as if he has the plague. He calls for something. Water, Heph thinks. As Cleo flags down a servant, the king, grabbing his stomach, keels over and vomits off the side of the dais.

Cleo screams, and the music stops. Phrixos and Telekles, still dancing with the girls in their arms, finally stop whirling and look around. On the central dais, Xander and Patra stand in alarm.

"The king is ill!" Cleo cries. "Where is his physician?"

Thrasybulus, tall and bald, pushes through the crowd. Now, in the silence, Heph hears how odd Philip's breathing is. How ragged and labored. Suddenly Heph's head is clearer. He leaps over the table and runs up to the dais. Philip has slid off his throne and is now on his back. His eye, lips, and face are grotesquely swollen. Thrasybulus opens the king's mouth and Heph sees an enormous swollen tongue.

"Help me sit him upright," the physician calls to Heph, and together they pull the wheezing monarch up to a seated position against his throne.

"Sire," Thrasybulus says, gripping the king's hand. "Sire, can you speak?"

Philip opens his eye—a dark slit in puffy flesh—and shakes his head. He's making strange, unearthly moaning noises that remind Heph of his near drowning in Byzantium, after Alex pulled him out of the water. Xander, ghastly white, has joined them.

"Is it poison?" he asks, his voice cracking with fear.

"No," Thrasybulus says, his long fingers on Philip's neck to check his pulse. "At least, I don't think so. The poisons I know attack the guts. His throat is closing up, suffocating him."

The king thrashes violently, a muscular hairy leg connecting with Heph's hip and nearly sending him flying off the dais.

"Hold him down," the physician says. Philip's favorite general, Parmenion, jumps onto the dais and helps Heph pinion the struggling king. Heph stares into the hazel eyes and battered face of the general, and they share a moment of pure panic.

Thrasybulus stands and cries, "I need a stick! Who has a stick?"

The actor Pausanias runs forward and hands the physician his smooth slender stick. Thrasybulus quickly tears off the many long ribbons, opens Philip's mouth, and thrusts the stick down his throat. The king gags, moves his head from side to side, and tries to push the stick away with swollen hands.

"I can't...get it...down," Thrasybulus says. He removes the stick and looks at Heph and Parmenion with a frightened expression on his face. "I need to open a passage for air. The king is suffocating."

Cleo starts to shriek like one of the Furies, bone-chilling sounds that stab the soul. "Take her away!" the physician commands, and two guards drag her out of the courtyard. Heph looks up and sees hundreds of shocked faces in the courtyard staring at the dying king on the dais. Every window in the palace is filled with faces. But none is Alex. His gaze slides to Olympias, who has risen from her throne and stands impassive and unblinking, her white face like that of a carved temple goddess.

The old physician looks at Heph. "Give me your dagger, son," he says through clenched teeth.

"Dagger? Why..."

"I need to cut an airway in his neck," Thrasybulus replies. *"Now."*

Hands shaking, Heph slides his dagger out of its sheath. The physician grabs it and, to Heph's horror, cuts an opening at the bottom of Philip's neck. Blood spurts wildly out of it. Air moans through it. Thrasybulus thrusts a finger inside, then withdraws it.

"His lungs aren't functioning," he says. "There is nothing I can do."

Helplessly, Heph watches the king twitch and go still. For a long time, no one moves.

Thrasybulus lays his ear against Philip's chest. When he pulls it away, half his face is smeared with the king's blood. "He is dead," he whispers. People in the courtyard gasp, cry out, and utter prayers to the gods. Some of them kneel, rip their tunics, and throw dirt on their heads, the ancient gestures of mourning.

The physician picks up the king's wine cup from the table between the thrones, sniffs it, dips a finger in, and licks it, then runs a finger over the rim and looks at it. "I see no trace of poison," he says, "but to be sure, let someone bring a dog." Parmenion races into the palace.

Heph scans the crowd again. Patra has rushed to Olympias for comfort and cries against her shoulder. Xander's expression is grim, and his servants look terrified. They know they may be tortured to death to find out who poisoned King Philip. There is absolute silence, except for, somewhere, inside the palace, Cleo's echoing shrieks. Heph must find Alex.

Alexander is now king of Macedon. And doesn't even know it.

But somehow, Heph cannot leave the horrific scene on the dais. His body is heavy, numb. He wonders if this is a bad dream and he will wake.

The crowd parts to let Parmenion through, leading a scruffy yellow dog on a piece of rope. "The cook's dog," he says. Heph sees a plump man following the soldier, tears running down his cheeks.

The physician descends the dais steps and sets the king's wine cup before the dog, who laps up the wine greedily and licks his chops. He looks around eagerly, hoping for more, while the cook throws his arms around him. They all wait.

The dog wags its tail. Its pink tongue hangs out and its bright eyes look around, evidently happy at all the attention. Meanwhile the physician cuts open Philip's tunic and examines the inside. "Though the king's skin has erupted in welts, I find no trace of poison on his clothing," he says. "Meanwhile, let us keep watching the dog for a time and feed it food that the king was eating."

"Where is Alexander?" comes a cool, clear voice. Olympias. "Where is the new king of Macedon?"

Heph pushes himself up to his feet. "I will find him, my lady," he says and races into the palace, his mind whirling. What did Alex say to him after telling him the location of all the invasion documents? *Heph, whatever happens, I know I can rely on you.* It's almost as if Alex was planning on running away. But no, he would never do that without letting Heph know. Heph will find him in his chamber. Alex, who doesn't enjoy drinking and feasting very much, is probably reading the latest dispatches.

But when Heph throws open the door, Alex is not in his chamber. All is tidy, and the prince's battle armor and sword rest on a table near the window. Perhaps Alex is with Bucephalus in the stables. But as Heph turns to go, a strange feeling scrapes at the back of his neck. Something isn't right. He throws open Alex's trunk and starts rifling through his tunics. The blue one is missing, but he was wearing it at the wedding. The green one is also missing. And the burgundy. And his dark red cloak. Heph sits back on his legs and runs a hand through his hair. Could they be in the laundry?

He glances around the room for some sign of where his friend has gone, if indeed he has. Then he sees a scroll on the desk with his name on it. Trembling, he unrolls it.

Heph,

It has been prophesied that if I am to defeat the Spirit Eaters, I must go to Gordium and do so without you. The Persian invasion must, at all costs, go forward. Work closely with my father. Tell him I have gone ahead to Persia to fulfill a vow to sacrifice to the Greek gods there. Take your time and focus on the invasion. If fate directs the Greek armies along the path to Gordium, meet me there. Hopefully, by the time you arrive, I will have fulfilled the prophecy. Heph, I know even a few months ago, you would have left Epirus immediately to search for me. But you have changed, grown in wisdom, loyalty, and duty. That is why I am trusting you with knowledge of my destination. I know I can count on you to do the right thing for Macedon and for all of us.

Alexander

No.

No.

Heph slams his hand against the desk until it stings. He shuts his eyes a long moment, then reads the scroll again, hoping it will say something different this time. It does not. He picks up the helmet, mystified. Why did Alex leave his armor behind? Perhaps he hasn't gone yet. Perhaps Heph can stop him.

Still clutching the helmet, he races along the dark upstairs corridor, down the winding steps, and across a narrow hall. Bursting into daylight, he passes the laundry, where tunics and sheets hang on lines drying in the sun, and flies around the corner to the stables. A skinny boy of about fourteen sweeps hay into a pile and looks up. "Is it true, sir, what they say?" he asks. "Is the king..."

"Have you seen Prince Alexander?" Heph asks, grabbing the youth by the shoulder. "King...Alexander?" he corrects himself. The words sound strange together, but he knows they must be said. The passing of the throne to the heir is immediate upon the king's death—soon, there must be a coronation, but fate does not await ceremony.

The boy's mouth drops open. "Y-yes, sir," he stutters. "Sometime ago. He went for a ride. B-but he did not take his usual horse."

Heph pushes past him into the corridor between the rows of stalls. There, in the largest stall at the end, stands Bucephalus. His enormous black head hangs over the gate. His huge nostrils widen as Heph approaches, and he whinnies and rears. Then he turns, and his back legs kick the gate. He seems to know Alex rode off on another horse, and he's furious about it.

But why would Alex take another horse? He never goes anywhere without the stallion. Except... Heph's heart sinks when he realizes Alex took another horse because he didn't want to be recognized. And everyone throughout the world knows that a blond young man riding a gigantic, wild black stallion with a white star on his forehead can only be Alexander of Macedon. And he left his unique golden armor behind for the same reason.

He sinks onto a low wooden stool in front of Bucephalus's stall, staring at the helmet in his hands, its intricate scrolls of goldwork, its jaunty red feathers. He's not sure why he puts it on his head. Does he want to be close to Alexander? Or does he want to hide from the world for a few fleeting moments before he takes it off and finds himself exposed and helpless in the face of all that has happened this morning?

He feels like he is teetering on the precipice of despair. At any moment, he can fall into its bottomless depths. He can't let that happen. The prince...no, the *king* has placed his trust in Heph to see things through. He expected Heph to work with Philip on the Persian invasion. But now Heph must do it by himself. Though how can he without Alex? Who is Heph, a nameless orphan, to invade Persia in the name of Macedon? Think. He has to *think*.

Running footsteps rouse him. "Lord Alexander!" cries Parmenion, breathless. "Thanks be to all the gods I have found you! Something terrible has happened!"

Heph stands slowly and raises his hand to stop the general, but he rattles on about King Philip's death, clearly thinking that the person wearing Alexander's helmet and standing next to his horse must be Alexander. Heph takes off the helmet. "It's me, Parmenion. Alexander is not here." The general's face falls, but without another beat of hesitation, he runs off to continue his search.

Heph, however, doesn't move. A plan starts to formulate in his head. A crazy, ridiculous plan that could never work. Or... could it?

In the *Iliad*, Homer's great song of war, love, and loss, the hero Achilles refused to lead the Greek allies against Troy, and the demoralized army lost battle after battle. Achilles's lover, Patroclus, begged him to return to the field and, when he refused, asked to wear his unique armor to pretend to be him and rally the troops. Achilles agreed, and Patroclus led the Greeks to victory that day.

Heph remembers the words every Greek schoolboy must learn by heart.

At his words, Patroclus began to clad himself in gleaming bronze. First, he clasped the shining greaves, with silver ankle pieces, about his legs. Next, he strapped Achilles's ornate breastplate round his chest, richly worked and decorated with stars. Over his shoulder he hung the bronze sword with its silver studs, and then the great thick shield. On his strong head he set the fine horsehair-crested helm, its plume nodding menacingly. With this, he put heart and strength into every man, and they launched themselves in a mass at the Trojans.

It didn't end well for Patroclus, of course. In the heat of battle, he forgot his plan and chased the enemy too far instead of retreating when he should have. But the new Patroclus Heph has in mind is the calmest person he ever met in a harrowing situation. He must see if his Patroclus is willing to take the risk.

Helmet in the crook of his arm, Heph walks slowly back to the courtyard. Thrasybulus, bent over the dog, says something to the cook, who gleefully picks him up and marches smiling back to the kitchens.

"No poison, then?" Heph asks the physician.

Thrasybulus scratches the back of his neck. "It could be a new kind, something from Persia perhaps. But I don't know how the king ingested it. Certainly not from his wine or food. The guards have arrested the actor Pausanias."

"Pausanias?" Heph asks, incredulously.

The old physician nods wearily. "Apparently the king and the actor got into a terrible fight last night. And he was found to have in his possession the king's gold signet ring. Well, if you will excuse me, I must prepare the body for burial."

Two soldiers carry the king's body on a shield, his fine red leather sandals poking out from below a tablecloth.

"Did you find the king?" Xander asks, his pale brows knit in worry. Heph looks back at the sandals disappearing into the palace.

"King *Alexander*," Xander adds.

Heph pulls himself up to his full height, squares his shoulders. "King Alexander left during the wedding celebrations to fulfill a vow to the gods and sacrifice at the tomb of Achilles in Troy." It is not *all* a lie, anyway. "The invasion will go forward as King Philip planned. We will leave in two days for Athens, pick up the allies, sail for Persia, and meet the new king at our first camp."

Xander nods and follows the body into the palace, with Heph close behind him. He has an urgent letter to write.

To Katerina of Erissa and Macedon at the Temple of Asklepios near Troy, Greetings from Hephaestion of Macedon.

The allied Greek army will sail soon for Persia. Alexander has gone ahead on a secret mission and wants you to help us. You will find our camp a two-day ride north from Troy, where the Granicus River meets the sea. Come to the camp cloaked on the night of the last half-moon before the summer solstice. Give the guard at the perimeter the enclosed pass.

On a strip of parchment, he writes:

Allow the bearer of this pass to enter the Greek camp and provide an escort to the tent of Lord Hephaestion of Macedon.

He stamps it with his signet ring in ink, wraps the letter around it, and seals it with red wax, which he also stamps with his ring.

In the courtyard, the scene of so much celebration and tragedy, Heph watches the messenger stir up a cloud of yellow dust as he rides to the port. He feels a strange envy of the letter, which soon will touch Kat's hands.

Unwilling to go inside the palace, which echoes with ritual wailing, he sits on a bench as servants silently clear the tables. He feels the sun on his head, the breeze on his face. The same sun and same breeze he felt moments ago.

But now the whole world has changed.

ACT FOUR

MONSTERS

*It is in our darkest moments that we must struggle to
see the light.*

—Aristotle

CHAPTER TWENTY-TWO

PYROLITHOS

RAGE. IT IS A GLORIOUS THING, FEEDING HIS VEINS, making him strong and alive. He hadn't realized just how trapped he'd felt in Dardania until he left, until he and the New Amazons took to the sea, bound for the roiling shores of Persia.

But Pyrolithos knows the truth: that without that rage, he is riding on a wind that could leave him plummeting at any point.

No, not wind—smoke.

He leans back in his chair, itching to move. Eating has become perfunctory. He lives now for movement, for the open road, for the skirmishes and the righteousness and the look of sickened shock in men's eyes just before they die.

For the blood—the spray of it against his skin, the way its heavy stench fills the air in his wake.

Alecta kicks at the leg of his chair. "Not eating this? I'll have it, then."

He watches the fig in her fingers as it moves toward her mouth, her lips as ripe and succulent as the purple fruit. She bites and a chill runs through him. Alecta raises her dark eyes to his and spits out a seed.

He never should have shown her the truth. Ever since he revealed himself to her as Queen Cynane, instead of the awe and gratitude she should have shown, she has berated him for lying to her. For lying still by not explaining the strange magic that transforms a woman into a man. Trust, she says, is more important than courage. Truth is the only real honor. Lies are badges of shame worse than cowardice. It is strange, Pyrolithos thinks, that a whore has a greater sense of honor than all the kings and queens he has ever known.

But she is wrong. Courage is more vital by far. It is not truth that will save your life, he knows, but the willingness to lie, to steal, to cut, to survive at any cost. To come out on top. It is ruthlessness alone that lets us win where others wither, that lets us vanquish instead of fall, that ultimately brings freedom.

He will not be trapped again. His power, his freedom—these are everything.

And besides, he enjoys Alecta's snark, her harsh words. He has known no other kind of affection except that of the men who succumb easily to seduction, women who become flustered and light-headed and lose themselves completely. He will not be like them, and he can never respect someone who is.

A warm breeze rolls in through the small window, barely dispelling the tavern smells of old wood smoke, fresh bread, and sour wine on the not-too-clean earthen floor. The heat of the day has passed; it is time to go. They have far yet to journey.

And the Spirit Eaters are waiting.

Waiting to be tamed.

So far, the New Amazons have cut a swathe of violent justice across central Greece and have at last reached Persia, pushing their way through the vast and varied territory, heading east all the while. And they have shown no mercy. Men who beat, rape, and abuse women have had their heads stuck on pikes in public squares at night. The heads sport paper crowns that say *Justice Courtesy of the New Amazons*. Their bodies have been fed to the Spirit Eater in the diamond cage.

Some of the women were afraid to travel with the monster,

no matter how hidden it is kept. But they desperately want what Pyrolithos has promised them—taming all the Spirit Eaters to command an invincible army and rule the known world. And even if they *didn't* share his vision, they know better than to cross it.

A waitress sets down a plate of bread. She's skinny and whey-faced, with lank, ash-colored hair. As she turns, a stream of sunlight catches her face, revealing a puffy black eye.

Pyrolithos is suddenly struck with hunger—or something akin to it. He grabs her slender wrist. "Who did that to you?"

"No one," she says nervously, looking over her shoulder at the door to the kitchen. "I...fell." She tries to twist out of his grasp but to no avail.

"Your husband?" He looks into her small light brown eyes. "Your father?" And then, with his voice lower, "I can help."

"No one can help me." It is more a moan than a statement. Her breath catches, raggedly. "The tavern owner. He calls me slow. But I have nothing. Nowhere else to go. Please don't make trouble, sir."

Fury lights Alecta's face. "We *can* help you," she says in a low voice. "You can come with us."

The girl looks around the tavern eagerly. There is a long table of loud men at one end, but all the others are occupied by women in modest robes eating quietly. "Who are you?"

"Travelers," Pyrolithos says, shrugging. "A man and his... *extended family.*"

"Oh."

She looks over her shoulder with a flinch just as the door from the kitchen bursts open and a fat, red-faced man strides up. "Efimia!" he cries, slapping her so hard across her face that she falls. "We have orders in the kitchen waiting to be picked up. Lazy, good-for-nothing piece of goat dung! Get back to work!"

He kicks her in the shin and Efimia whimpers as he disappears back into the kitchen.

Efimia picks herself up and holds a hand to her cheek. When she removes it, Pyrolithos sees red finger marks.

His eyes meet Alecta's, and they both nod.

They have their next mark.

"Go back to work, Efimia," Alecta says softly. "We will take care of things."

With a worried look in her eyes, the girl scurries back into the kitchen. Moments later, she shuffles back out holding an enormous tray of bread, meat, and salad, and sets it down on a long table of loud men nearby.

"Well, now, that took long enough," says a balding man with a long nose and droopy eyes. "I see your boss knows how to discipline you. I wouldn't mind a turn at it, you know."

Efimia bites her lip and quickly sets out the plates.

"Careful, Cyrus," says a bearded man with a thick thatch of black hair. "Or the New Amazons will come and get you." The men all laugh.

One man wipes beer foam off his beard. "I heard last week they cut off a man's head in Mittania."

The thin one, barely out of his teens, sneers. "Check your ears. Women are made for one thing only, and I'm sure it isn't that!"

The muscular man at the end of the table slams down his flagon of wine with another loud laugh, revealing missing front teeth. "I heard one of them carries a baby strapped to her back," he says. "Sounds more like a nursery on the loose!"

Fingers going tight around the base of his wine cup, Pyrolithos grits his teeth, glad he left Zotasha at the camp with the other women. Looks like there will be more work to do today than just the tavern keeper.

"Girl!" Pyrolithos pounds his cup down. The girl turns a frightened face his way. "Bring us an oenochoe of your finest wine and fresh cups! I want none of this filth." He knocks his cup to the floor with a clatter.

A cue, if you know how to read them.

And the New Amazons do—he can see their smiles of understanding, as, one by one, a few of them slowly take off earrings and rub their ear lobes as if they are sore. One removes her necklace as if to check the clasp. Others examine their golden rings or play with their bracelets. Moments later, he pours bubbling ruby liquid into the cups held by his companions.

"Gentlemen!" he says, walking to the men with the drinks on a tray. "I have recently received good news. How about some of the house's best wine on me?"

The six men gladly take the proffered cups, congratulating Pyrolithos.

One of them eyes him warily. "And what news?" he grumbles, taking a gulp.

"Oh, you'll know in a moment!" Pyrolithos says cheerfully.

They drink his health, clapping him on the back.

Sure enough, a few minutes later, the youngest staggers up from his chair and vomits all over the floor. "No," he moans, on his hands and knees like a dog.

Gripping his belly, Cyrus stands up, white-faced and sweating. "What the—" He looks around at the others. One of them pukes into his soup bowl.

"What's in the wine?" Cyrus cries, his hand on his dagger.

The dozen women around Pyrolithos push their chairs back and stand all at once, throwing off their cloaks to reveal breastplates, swords, and small shields on their backs.

Cyrus and two of his companions pull out their daggers as the Amazons place long wooden tubes in their mouths.

The fat one says, "Are you going to rob us while you play the flute? Well, I'm not so sick that—"

Darts fly across the room into the men's necks and faces. The fat man falls to the floor before he can finish his last word, gasping and writhing.

This seems to galvanize the rest to action. Several of the men are desperately trying to pull the darts out of their skin, and still others leap up. Benches and stools go flying. One man keels over with a sword thrust through his chest.

The skirmish lasts seconds.

All of a sudden, the remaining five stop fighting and fall to the floor nearly in unison. Dead. The women step back, lowering their swords. A few of them readjust their jewels—reclasping the hidden compartments where their poison is stored.

The wine—and darts—have done their work, and efficiently, too.

The tavern owner rushes out of the kitchen wielding a butcher knife. Alecta throws her dagger. It hits him in his right eye, and he falls forward as a rush of wet blood floods his face. He utters an unearthly wail, then goes still.

For a moment, there is silence.

"Take as much as we can carry," Pyrolithos says quietly.

The women set about gathering up food and wine into their packs. A moment later, Sophonisba comes out of the kitchen dragging a gangly straw-haired boy of about twelve. "What do we do with him?"

Pyrolithos sees pure terror in the boy as he gazes around the tavern at all the dead bodies. Alecta puts her boot on the tavern owner's face, withdraws her dagger from his skull, and wipes the blood on his apron before sheathing it. Calista quickly rifles the corpses, her curtain of long blond hair hiding her theft of their coins and rings.

"What is your name, son?" he asks the boy.

"M-M-Mikkos," he stammers. His whole body shakes. Pyrolithos considers a long moment, then rejects the idea. He's too young, and there's something about him that reminds him of Prince Alexander, when he was younger. Not that they were ever close. How could they have been? Alexander was lauded and celebrated, and trained in the military arts, while Cynane was ignored and neglected, and laughed at when she picked up a sword.

But time and distance have made Pyrolithos more levelheaded. Lately, he has found himself wondering what has become of Alexander, one of the few people in the Pellan palace who never did Cynane wrong.

"Well, Mikkos," Pyrolithos says now, taking a step toward the boy, who is shaking visibly. "We will not harm you. We will tie you to that pillar over there, see? Someone will come here soon and rescue you. And then you must tell them what I say, all right?" The boy continues to shake, too afraid to speak. "You will tell them the New Amazons were here, dispensing justice to brutal men. Will you do that?"

Wide-eyed, the boy at last nods.

Moments later, Mikkos is gagged and tied. Alecta, Agatha, Calista, and the others stream outside with hoards of food and skins of wine. Pyrolithos is ready to leave when he hears a whimper and looks beneath a table. It's Efimia, curled into a ball. He had already forgotten about her.

Well, she will serve his purpose.

"I promised I would protect you," Pyrolithos says, leaning over her. "Do you trust me?" The girl nods timidly, reminding him of a mouse.

The New Amazons have no need of a little mouse-wench, though.

"Come out," Pyrolithos says. Haltingly, the girl crawls out and stands.

"Close your eyes," he says. She squeezes them shut.

Yes, he feels confident of it: mice must be fed to the cats. He plunges his dagger into her heart.

Her eyes open in surprise, and then she falls to the floor.

"No!" Alecta, standing in the doorway to the yard, rushes forward and kneels beside the dead girl. "Why?" she asks. She rises and shoves Pyrolithos hard.

But Pyrolithos couldn't answer her even if he wanted to, because the flaming power of Smoke Blood is roaring through his veins, temporarily drowning everything else out. The ashes curl around muscles and organs. When the rising Smoke magic settles, he looks up, but Alecta has already stomped outside to the wagons.

The wind does little to cool his hot skin as he and the New Amazons ride back to their packed-up camp.

Even later, as they saunter back to the Royal Road with their renewed disguises, to all the world a small group of men riding beside several harmanaxas, he still feels the hot wave of power that moved through him at the death of the girl, and hardly notices Alecta's coldness, the way she rides at the far edge of the group, closest to the trees that dot the sides of the road.

Toward sunset, they veer off the road and make camp in the woods, erect their tents, and roast the stolen food, flames leaping high over all the pilfered flesh. Once again, though, Pyrolithos isn't hungry.

After making sure the first watch patrols the perimeter, he returns to his tent...and finds Alecta there, sitting cross-legged on his sleeping mat.

His heart skips a beat.

"Why?" she asks simply—the same question she demanded of him in the tavern.

"Don't question me," he says.

"You are strong and brave, Cynane, and yet you rely on deception and cruelty to lead."

That name. That former self. He bends to his knee, planting his hand around her mouth. "I've told you before not to call me that."

Using a move he taught her, Alecta flips him onto his back. He feels his Smoke magic flare up in a pillar of anger, but he controls himself, lets her stay on top. "Didn't we create the New Amazons to fight injustice?" she asks, straddling him, hissing close to his ear. "Didn't you commit a huge injustice to poor Efimia today, ending her life for... What? Some sadistic feeling of power? Some of the girls are talking among themselves, you know, asking if you will kill them next for the sport of it. This isn't what they signed up for."

Not for the first time, he wonders what Alecta would say if he told her about killing Taulus to obtain the Blood of True Betrayal. About using his own admission—that when everything else about him had turned to smoke, only his heart remained mortal—to kill him. The hot spray of bright blood that exploded out of Taulus's smoky form, even as he dissipated into the night air.

How disgusted would Alecta be if she understood his *need*...

That he *must* keep betraying innocent people?

Would it be enough to cause her to leave him? And would the Amazons follow her?

She's looking at him with flat dark eyes, waiting for an answer.

"You're right." A ball of tight emotion throbs in his chest. "I've always had to be deceitful. I've always had to be cruel." And it's true—even before Smoke magic. Long before it, in fact. "I don't know that I was born that way," he adds, trying to still the tremor in his voice even as visions of Audata fill his mind, her milky skin in the bath, her body floating in her own blood. "I think my life has made me cruel."

Alecta's air of ice seems to thaw somewhat. Her eyes soften. "You can stop, though," she whispers.

"No..." His voice breaks, and all the pain and injustice he ever suffered seems to bubble up from somewhere deep inside his chest.

"Cynane," she whispers, pulling him up to sitting, pulling him back into that old self, that old knowledge, the name like a surge breaking a dam.

He lets out a shuddering breath and finds himself telling Alecta the story of Cynane: how she was the daughter of Philip's lesser wife, Audata, whose authority in the palace had been completely stripped away when he married Olympias. How Cynane had always known of the rivalry between Olympias and Audata, and how it had made the more powerful queen vicious toward her. How she'd only been eight years old when she found her dead mother's body, black tendrils of hair waving in the red water like the tentacles of a sea creature. How, many years later, the Aesarian Lords had captured and tortured her before her desperate escape. How Olympias had laughed in the ruins of Knossos as her guards hustled Cynane onto a ship sailing straight for Dardania, to become the unwilling bride of a madman. How King Amyntas had proven even more terrifying and insane than anyone knew, hissing threats in her ears day and night.

How she had always, always been alone and had to learn to look after herself.

This is Cynane's story, and it is *his* story, his past, his truth.

There it is, he thinks. *The truth that can ruin you.*

Her hand warms his cheek, then wipes away the dampness there. His heart stutters, and he experiences a violent urge to pull away. To scream, *How dare you? How dare you touch me like that? How dare you touch me with kindness and threaten to undo everything I have built up to protect myself?*

But he doesn't pull away. He stays.

Because no one has ever made him feel like this before. And this isn't just a game like what he's played before. He no longer knows the rules.

And then comes a sick realization—a temptation both thrilling and foul.

If he truly needed to commit a great betrayal, one with the power of sustaining his magic for years and years…

Wrestling with the thought, Pyrolithos looks up, his eyes meeting hers. He grabs her and his hands meet her throat, feeling the gentle throb of her pulse, the allure of it, the power in it, the heat of her…

He leans in, not knowing what he wants—the power of betrayal or something else—the delicate, secret thing she offers him that terrifies him more than any Spirit Eater. That kindness, that care.

That word he has never once in all his life allowed himself to believe in: love.

It sickens and chills him but it moves him, too. Everything he comes close to loving dies. *You are not meant to love in this world. Love is a weakness. Love kills.*

His hand presses harder against her neck, and she inhales a short breath.

And then, before he knows what he is doing, and before he can stop himself, he leans in even closer, breathing in her scent, dragging his lips against the edge of her jaw, before finally they meet her mouth.

The kiss overtakes him. She doesn't push him away but neither does she succumb—instead, the kiss becomes a kind of sparring, a teasing that makes him want to fall into her more—forever. His arms are shaking, as though the powerful feeling Alecta is emitting is greater, even, than Smoke Blood. Impossible, and yet that is how it seems, as she takes control, pulling his hair and biting his lip and running her hands over his shoulders, pushing him back. She is taking him. Pyrolithos wants to dominate; even as Cynane, he was used to dominating, and can feel the spring and tension in his muscles. But it is impossible. He, who has always sought power, has found the greatest rush in the world: the sacrificing of it, an utter surrender. It is he who submits, inhaling the sweet scent of her skin, feeling the silken waves of her hair brush his face, making his mind and all its yearnings for greatness go slack, until all there is is this: heat and musk and the sweetness of two bodies in the darkness, skin against skin, souls opening into one another endlessly, until he is no longer Pyrolithos or Cynane.

He—she—they are no one.

CHAPTER TWENTY-THREE

KATERINA

SOMETIMES THE FATE OF A NATION RESTS SOLELY on the actions of one person.

In this case, it rests on the actions of one horse: Bucephalus.

If only Kat can get him to behave. Everyone knows, the demon stallion listens only to Alexander. But Alex isn't here—which is the whole reason Kat has come instead.

When she received Heph's letter in Troy and agreed to join him in battle, she expected something different. She'd felt stirred and excited—more than she had in a long time—by the idea of joining him and the rest of the Macedonian army, fighting side by side, like she had in the Battle of Pellan Fields. She felt her spirits lift out of the deep well of sadness that had been her constant companion since the attack of the Spirit Eater at King Philip's wedding in Byzantium. Perhaps, she reasoned, this sickness of the soul wasn't doomed to haunt her forever. She could get better, be her old self again. Feel joy unencumbered by the knowledge of death and suffering all around her.

She and Jacob had secured safety and healing for the rescued children with the priests in the Temple of Asklepios. The ushabtis had killed all the Lords beneath Troy, except for Timaeus, who had disappeared, and without their training, the children's magic drained from them like water into parched earth, until nothing was left.

And then, of course, there was the other cause of her excitement...the knowledge that she would see Heph again. It kept her up the night she received the letter and most of the two nights since then as she and Jacob rode to the allied Greek camp north of Troy, through hilly country with green fields and stands of olive trees, the salt breeze of the sea in their hair.

Then, last night, they heard the whispering of the Granicus River and followed it until they saw the torches and campfire of the Greek camp spreading out from the beach. Her face hidden by a large hood, she gave Heph's pass to the first perimeter guard she met, a tall man who, looking Jacob up and down suspiciously, recognized him as a fellow Macedonian guard who last year had become an Aesarian Lord, and Macedon's enemy. Reluctantly, she left him there, promising she would soon return with Heph to bring him into camp by order of King Alexander. The guard guided her through the chaos of soldiers and weaponry, forges and outhouses and fires, to Heph's private tent, decorated in the Macedonian royal colors.

Seeing him, she sucked in a breath as all the things that had happened between them in the past came flooding back: those long days on the island, working on the mechanism, growing closer to an answer for how to defeat the Spirt Eaters and growing closer, too, to one another. How he had taken her in his powerful arms and kissed her, told her everything about himself—all the fire and fury of his past. How he'd asked her to marry him.

How she'd never really given him an answer.

As soon as she stepped into his tent, Kat felt heat flood through her. She couldn't meet Heph's eyes but felt them blazing against her skin.

"You came," he said, his voice low and breathy.

"Of course, I did," she answered, wanting to step toward him but afraid to—afraid of how it might make her feel—aware that even one inch closer to him was one inch closer to a betrayal of Jacob's love.

"Be my Patroclus," he said.

"What?" She was thrown off. There were millions of things he could have said to her after their months apart.

"You know the story," he prodded.

And she did—Patroclus had been Achilles's lover, or so the myths told. Was that what Heph wanted from her?

She took a step back, uncertain how to respond.

"You remember what Patroclus did," he added, clearing his throat.

"He led the Greeks to victory wearing Achilles's armor," Kat answered. "You...you want me to wear your armor?"

Heph laughed, and she couldn't help it this time—her eyes were riveted toward his, and the heat of seeing him again flashed through her once more, dizzying.

"Not my armor, *his*. Alexander's. Don't you see? He couldn't be here in battle. But you can—in his place. His twin."

Kat balked.

He took a step toward her, reaching out to grasp her hands. She let him. "It is the only way we can keep the alliance together until Alex returns."

What he was proposing finally sank in. "We could never get away with it," she protested, her voice low and soft.

But Heph explained his plan. In mourning for his father, the newly crowned king wouldn't show his face or speak to anyone other than his most trusted advisors. The helmet's elaborate cheekpieces and nosepiece would hide her face. When she pointed out that she was several inches shorter than Alexander, Heph said she would only be seen riding Bucephalus.

It was a wild, dangerous thought. And yet, she had to admit, she wanted to say yes. It was politically necessary; she could see that. The soldiers would never follow Heph. They needed their leader. But it was more than that, too. It was as if Kat had been born to do this—as if she and her brother had been born twins for this very reason, and it was somehow her sacred duty not just to be there for him but to *be* him, when he could not.

And to be, even for a few days, a king?

Was it not every girl's dream?

And so, here she is, in the early-morning light, standing at the makeshift stable housing Bucephalus, Alexander's trusted steed. A beast no man has ever been able to control but him.

The Macedonians gather around her. Kat checks the tightness of her helmet strap, squares her shoulders, and approaches the horse. Jacob holds Bucephalus, who snorts and jumps, eager to get away. All around her, Macedonians stare at what they believe to be their new king in his golden armor. The king who, after sacrificing at Troy, rejoined the army and now stands ready to lead the Greek invasion of Persia. Kat senses the horse's outrage—at being stuck in a small ship's cabin for days, at waiting for his master to return. She keenly feels his distrust of her. While she might be able to fool the Greek generals and their men, she could never for a moment fool Bucephalus. Now, sniffing her, he brays his disapproval loudly, sidestepping away from her.

Hot panic races up her spine. This animal is a tense, dangerous muscle, ready to explode in fury at any moment. Before she can mount him, she pours all her Snake Blood Magic into calming him. She tries to settle into his mind—no easy task, as he resists at first, thrusting her out as easily as he'd toss an unwelcome rider off his back. Finally, she seeps in, just the thinnest strain of her thought, and begins to soothe him, sending the creature the same calm he gets when he smells the approach of Alexander. The horse seems not so much to have accepted her message as to be considering it. She wonders if he will throw her, proving to the entire Greek army that she is not Alexander.

But she must risk it.

She opens her eyes and swings herself deftly on top of the huge stallion. He shakes his head, nickering. Then Kat turns him toward the gathered soldiers. Sensing freedom, smelling moist earth and green grass, Bucephalus bolts like an arrow launched from a bow and gallops through the Greek camp. It's all Kat can do to cling to him. Men setting up tents, unloading wagons, and building fire pits salute their general, cheering wildly.

Around and around the camp she rides, then back to the wide white beaches, eyeing a sea that is black with ships as far as the eye can see.

Finally, sensing that Bucephalus is calmer, she finds the royal tent, its cupola dyed with Tyrrhian purple and embroidered with gold. Jacobs waits out front for her and takes the reins as she dismounts. He nods to the guards on either side of the opening, men sworn to allow only Alexander, Jacob, and Heph inside on pain of death.

In the cool darkness barred with light, she takes off her helmet again and finds her hair slick with sweat. Her stomach feels as if a horse has kicked it, and her head throbs with a nervous headache. Here she must stay, speaking in low tones only to Jacob and Heph, emerging only when needed for battle, in her golden armor, hot and sweaty in the summer heat, to ride the demon horse, fearful of discovery at any moment.

Unless…

Her body may be trapped in the tent whenever she is out of her armor, but that doesn't mean her spirit must be trapped.

A falcon flies over the enemy camp—and within the bird flies Kat's mind, analyzing, strategizing, observing. The Persian camp is like no Greek army she has ever heard of. To be sure, there are plenty of warriors—mounted and on foot. And a baggage train with tents, provisions, and weapons.

But at the center of the camp is a kind of traveling palace. Perched on a high tree branch, for hours she watches the Persians set up luxurious steepled tents and fill them with valuables.

She sees servants carry enormous silver platters, golden chalices, and inlaid tables into the banquet tent. In the gods' tent, bearded priests in orange robes and conical headdresses set up gem-studded altars and gilded incense burners.

Then there is the elaborate bathing tent. Whereas Greek soldiers wash in a leather bucket of water—or not at all—the Persians unload silver-plated bathtubs, gilded buckets, painted amphorae that must contain fragrant oils, and mounds of fine-spun towels. Next door, they set up the harem tent, fill it with rich carpets, beds with precious hangings, and plump tasseled pillows. Gorgeous women with heavily lined eyes and spangled veils wander in and out, seeing to the disposition of huge wardrobe chests.

Now an official emerges from the tent that holds wooden chests so heavy it took six men to carry each one using sturdy poles. Soldiers wait in front of a man at a little desk. The official opens a chest, and her falcon eyes are so dazzled by the sun reflecting off gold that she is momentarily blinded. She twists her head away, blinks, and then looks back. The official—who must be the paymaster—gives each man who comes forward a gold coin. If all those trunks she saw stored inside the tent also contain gold coins, it would be enough to buy a small kingdom.

Overall, there is good military order, she notes, but seemingly no worry among this army that they are facing a superior force. Perhaps they are overconfident they will chase away the barbarians from Persian soil, which the Greeks could use to their advantage.

She has seen enough. Beating her wings, she rises vertically from the branch, then thrusts herself forward, winging her way back to the Greek camp, cheered by the hours of soaring flight, golden sun, and bracing air high above fields blooming with early-summer wildflowers. She releases the falcon from her control with a heartfelt thank-you and feels the bird tear away from her, happy to be free once more as it soars into the impossibly blue vault of the sky.

With a start, she finds herself back in her body, sitting cross-legged in Alexander's tent. Jacob holds a vial of lotus blossom oil under her nose.

She blinks and looks around, confused. It is always a shock to be flying in the sun-gilded air one moment, feeling the breeze ripple through feathers, and the next moment waking in a solid fleshly body of arms and legs, heavy and earthbound. At first, her eyes—so used to scanning the distance as the falcon—cannot focus. She sees the blur of Alexander's camp bed and portable desk. Sunlight streams in through the open flaps high on the sides of the tent. Her vision sharpens as she looks at the two men who love her—and hate each other—sitting on low stools in front of her.

"Are you all right?" Jacob asks, concern etched on his broad face.

"Fine," she croaks. Her voice is always hoarse when she returns from voyaging with an animal host.

"What did you see?" Heph asks, his dark eyes flashing with interest.

"The Persian camp..." She swallows and coughs, and Jacob jumps up to fetch her a cup of watered wine, which she drinks gratefully. "It's about ten miles from here," she says, "along the banks of the Granicus River. It must be one of the coastal defense armies our spies reported. It's not the army of Great King Artaxerxes. It's not that big—maybe only fifteen thousand men—and among the leaders I didn't see a strangely tall, thin old man with a long white beard. I don't think he has had enough time to get here from Persepolis."

"Even if it is a coastal defense army," Jacob says thoughtfully, "I wonder why they didn't attack us on the beach. Their own scouts must have told them we landed."

"I think," Kat says, as the images of what she saw—the harem and bathing tents, the general feeling of the Persians being on a kind of holiday, "they are not terribly worried about us. They must think that we are barbarians they can squash like flies in their own territory."

"How much cavalry? Infantry? Catapults?" Heph asks.

"Maybe two thousand cavalry," she replies, her voice starting to resume its normal timbre. "Six large catapults, unassembled, left in pieces in their wagons for the moment. But the most amazing thing was the treasure wagons." She tells them exactly what she saw.

"I have heard of this," Heph says, nodding and looking at her, but not at Jacob. "The Persian armies do not travel as we Greeks do—light, flexible, and mobile. They believe their luxuries increase morale. And the soldiers fight not only for their homeland but also to guard their treasure and the commanders' women."

"All right," she says. "So, what would Alexander do?"

Heph runs a hand through his unruly dark hair and considers her question for a long moment. "He would divide our forces into three parts," he says at last, confidence blooming across his face, making him more handsome than ever, though Kat pushes the thought away. "The first part will act as a diversionary force, drawing off a good part of the Persian army. The second part will attack the treasure wagons, drawing in those Persians who remain to guard it."

"And when that battle is fully underway, the third part will move in and finish them off," Kat concludes.

Heph nods.

She turns her gaze to Jacob, whose chin rests in the palm of his hand as he contemplates. She knows Heph would never ask him his opinion. The tension between them is thick. Ever since they reunited, the two have barely spoken a word to each other. At first, Heph absolutely refused to even bring Jacob back from the camp perimeter where she had left him the night she arrived. An Aesarian Lord, he said, an enemy of Macedon, could easily betray them, betray *her*, no matter how well he had taken care of her in Byzantium. Because this was no longer about personal feelings, but war, victory, and the rise of empires.

"He will not betray Macedon or me," she argued, knowing, without proof, that it was true—that if she couldn't trust Jacob, then she couldn't trust anything, even herself. "Besides, he's no longer an Aesarian Lord." She gave him a brief outline of how Jacob had left the brotherhood during the earthquake of Delphi, resolved to find and kill Riel on his own, and how he had ended up killing almost his entire regiment in the tunnels beneath Troy to save the children. "But what he learned from them will help our army. The Lords are the deadliest fighting force in the world."

Even still, it was only when she threatened to refuse his offer altogether that Heph consented.

"What do you think, Jacob?" she prods, rubbing her eyes. She's still adjusting to the dimness of the tent after her flight within the body of the falcon. "What would the Aesarian Lords do?" She can't help but notice his arm muscles flex in a tense pulse in response, and she can tell it is going to require all her diplomatic skill to keep these two from punching each other.

"The plan should work," Jacob finally says, and she can tell by a tightness in his voice how hard it is for him to admit. "But it will be better if we can trap the army in one place, taking away much of their mobility when we attack."

"How can we do that?" Heph asks, irritation sharp in his voice.

Jacob looks coolly at Heph. "As you know, I have certain abilities. Kat says they are camped on the river's edge. Just before dawn tomorrow, we will encircle the Persian camp. I will cause the river to rise, trapping everything and everyone in the mud. The treasure wagons will be hopelessly stuck. Those that remain to defend them, we will pick off with our arrows. It will be like spearing fish in a barrel."

"And how do we prevent our own men from getting stuck in

the mud when we attack them?" Heph's question ripples with disdain.

Jacob's dark eyes flash, but his face remains impassive. "Easy. I channel the water only to their camp." He shrugs, a small movement but it doesn't go unnoticed.

"Hmm," Heph says. "Last time you caused water to rise, you killed hundreds, maybe thousands, of people. You almost killed Katerina."

Jacob's mouth sets in a hard line, and he practically spits his words. "I had just learned that my entire family, including my three little brothers, had been horribly butchered. I hardly think the incident is indicative of my capabilities."

"All right," Kat says, hoping her words can slice through the tension in the air. "So, we have a strategy."

"Even a good plan can be improved upon," Heph says, determined to have the last word. "Let's shoot flaming arrows at the tents. Between the rising water and the flames, they will not know what hit them."

The following morning, shortly before dawn, Kat leans forward on Bucephalus, peering into the darkness. Across the field, the torches on poles around the perimeter of the Persian camp flicker weakly, illuminating now and then a soldier patrolling in strange garb—polka-dot trousers and checked tunics. Something in her twists. Because of her, these men will probably die in the next few minutes. Do they have children? Parents? Brothers and sisters? She thinks of little Roxana, whom she left at the Temple of Asklepios to continue her healing along with the other children. "First my sister left me," the girl said, when Kat told her she must leave, "and now you." Pain, loss, and unbearable sadness wrap around Kat, weighing her down like a wet wool cloak.

She had been so excited to fight—to be driven forward by a purpose greater than her own. To get that much closer to facing off with the Spirit Eaters. She thought the sadness she had experienced was gone.

Why now are these thoughts—these sympathies—invading her mind and destroying her focus? Is the Spirit Eater venom still inside her, dragging her down? Will it never go away?

Suddenly, there's a drastic shift within her, and battle no longer seems as simple as brawn and strategy and victory. As with the divide in her own heart between two men, she sees now that there can never be a clear winner, never one side more deserving of victory than the other.

Beneath her, Bucephalus shifts his weight in frustration. He wants to race across the field, and it is all she can do to keep him in check. He galloped the ten miles from the Greek camp, his noble heart reveling in the freedom to run, and he wants more. *Soon.* She pats his moist neck. *Soon.*

The stars in the night sky are fading. A smudge of orange streaks the horizon. It is time. High up in the gnarled, knotty pine tree on her left, Jacob must be calling the Granicus River to overflow its banks and pour into the Persian camp. The thought of him like that—curled deep within himself in order to call up a power far greater than himself—sends a chill of terror and awe through her. Jacob understands her. Jacob is *like* her. There was a reason Helen raised her so close to his family—so that, one day, she might discover that she belonged somewhere, that she was not alone.

A bird trills, greeting the coming day, and all around her, others reply.

Now voices echo across the silent fields, punctuated by screams and loud orders in Persian. Soldiers run along the perimeter, lighting fresh torches, which they carry inside the camp. Horses whinny. The guards have all completely disappeared. After a time, Kat sees something large move out of the camp and stop. Hears the crack of a whip and the bellowing of oxen.

"It must be the gold wagon," Heph whispers, leaning in from

his bay mare. "They would want to get that out first. But it must be so heavy, it's already stuck in the mud."

"Time for fire arrows," she says. Ignoring the rising horror inside her, she takes the bird whistle on the thong around her neck and blows into it. Up and down the Greek line, the sound is repeated. Heph and the other archers open their containers of glowing coals, insert a tar-tipped arrow, and bring it out burning brightly. Moments later, flaming arrows arc through the dark blue sky. They stick in the proud turrets and domes of the distant tents, which burst into flame. High-pitched screams erupt, followed by shouts and orders. Flames leap from tent to tent, and from this distance, it all seems like a strange fairy tale come to life, the bright colors of the camp igniting in a burst of fire and dawn.

Horses shriek. Kat feels their panic as if it were her own fear—instead of her own doing. Moments later, dozens—no, hundreds—of horses run out of the camp, their long legs sticking in the mud. In the shimmery rose-silver light, she sees them twisting, struggling to free themselves, heads raised, huge teeth exposed. Panic—fueled by the roar of flames and the thick haze of smoke—helps extricate them. Once outside the circle of floodwater, they hit solid ground, pound their way in different directions across the fields, and disappear.

People, too, stagger out of the camp. Kat sees women holding hands, helping each other navigate the goo, and servants carrying silver platters that reflect the rays of the rising sun, flashing and blinding. More horses appear, but these are saddled and carry soldiers. The Persians are launching a counterattack. But the weight of the riders makes it more difficult for the horses to pull their legs from the muck. A new round of Greek arrows sinks into the soldiers, who scream and fall off their mounts. Kat wants to scream, too, but clenches her jaw so tight it hurts as she watches the horses, freed of the burdens, struggle to safety and vanish.

Some of the horsemen, however, make it to dry land, followed by a steady stream of others. Kat nods to Phrixos, on her left, who raises the battle horn and blows. The signal for the attack. Kat kicks Bucephalus, who jolts forward almost as fast as any arrow. Horses' hooves pound, men shout, and people in the camp scream.

She raises her spear. She is supposed to be King Alexander of Macedon, after all, and must show no weakness. Beside her, Heph fires arrows one after the other. And then the two sides meet in a furious clash of metal and leather and flesh.

Ada taught her to use her Snake Blood to feel what is coming—the sword blow, the arrow, the spear—and veer away from it a moment before. It doesn't work if she's distracted, which is what happened last summer in the Battle of Pellan Fields, when an Aesarian Lord stabbed her. Now, instead of feeling fear or aching despair, she just feels what is there. An arrow is whizzing toward her, though she can't see it through the billowing smoke. She swerves Bucephalus and hears the arrow pass a finger's breadth away from her left ear.

The smoke clears, and Kat sees a Persian horseman riding straight for her, straight for King Alexander of Macedon, he must think, curved sword raised, a malicious gleam in his cruel dark eyes, his mouth open in a laugh or shout. Kat raises her spear—Alexander's gilded spear—and urges Bucephalus into a gallop toward him. But just before they meet, an arrow enters the Persian's mouth. Blood spurts from his throat. He tumbles backward off his horse, which runs away in a panic.

Heph pulls up next to her, his bow in his hand. "Excellent target practice," he says coolly. But she can see by the flush on his face that he is not as cool and collected as he pretends. Behind him, Kat sees a Persian headed for him, spear raised shoulder high, ready to throw. She throws hers first, using her mind to send it straight and true into the man's chest. It pierces right through, a good foot of it coming out of his back, and as he falls to the ground, Kat feels part of herself falling with him.

The Greek armies, waiting on dry ground, quickly dispatch the Persian soldiers spilling from the camp. Kat notices that Heph stays by her side, to protect her, of course, but probably also to gall Jacob, who is still stuck up in the tree, channeling the water. She signals him to follow her, and they ride to the river, where hundreds of heads bob, desperate to get away from the flames and enemy swords. Probably any Persians who could swim have jumped in, paddling for their lives. Greek archers send arrows zooming toward the heads, which hit them as if they were bobbing melons used for target practice. Horsemen on the banks throw spears at them, laughing as they hit their mark or people dive under the water. This killing of unarmed, fleeing men and women is a game to the soldiers. Kat is so disgusted she can barely move as the lifeless bodies float downstream.

When the flames have burned out and the battle is over, it is time for her to blow three long wails on the battle horn: the sign for Jacob to drain off the water. But she finds she doesn't have the air in her lungs to do it and hands the instrument to Heph, whose blasts echo loudly across the field. Even after the water drains, there is still mud, of course.

She and Heph pick their way through the remains of the once-magnificent Persian camp.

The tents, rugs, furniture, and chests are ashes, once-bright colors now caked in dirt, dust, still-wet blood. Glorious fabrics shredded and limp, like flags of surrender, sway in the breeze, forming the only movement in the camp.

But the silver bathtubs, mounds of gold coins, and jewels are intact. In their first battle, King Alexander has not only won a decisive victory, but a huge pot of plunder for the Greeks to distribute to their men. If only Kat could be pleased about it.

Carting the valuables out of the camp and rounding up the fine Persian horses takes the rest of the day. When the sun has set, she and Heph ride into the Greek camp, which is alive with singing and feasting on rich Persian food and wine. She hasn't seen Jacob all day. She wants to thank him for his amazing feat of Earth Blood, but also to confide in him the sinking despair settling into her bones.

To tell him about the daydreams that threatened to drag her to her death out there on the field today—fleeting visions of being back on Meninx, an uninhabited island of wind and waves, trees and birds, with no bloodshed, no war. A place where magic, once thriving, was put to sleep forever, leaving in its wake an emptiness, a kind of relief.

"Come to my tent for a drink," Heph says in that charming way of his. People were surprised young Lord Hephaestion no longer shared Alexander's tent, but he put it about that this, too, was part of Alexander's mourning ritual for his father. "I have an amphora from the Persian general's tent that I want to share with you and only you. The finest Persian wine, made in Babylon, I hear."

She leans toward him and whispers, "I should always stay in my tent when not exercising Bucephalus or leading the armies," she says. "That was what we agreed."

Heph yanks off his helmet, runs a hand through sweaty dark hair. "I know, but Jacob is always there. His tent is closer to yours than mine. I bet he is waiting for you now. You and I haven't had a moment alone. Please come. For old times' sake. For Egypt and Meninx and all our adventures on the sea. Please. Just a few minutes."

He smiles hopefully at her. How can she say no? It would seem cruel, childish. And perhaps she can open up to him about the dark feelings caused by this battle, the death and suffering. She confided in him on Meninx, didn't she? And he confided in her.

"All right," she says quietly, as if whispering makes it less a crime.

No, there is no crime here, she tells herself—or if there is, it is only inside her chest, where no one can see it.

They slide off their horses in front of Heph's tent and tie the reins to a tent pole. Kat slips between the canvas flaps and finds a camp bed, camp table, a couple of folding chairs, and a trunk. It's smaller than hers—Alexander's—with no luxuries, no plush carpets, no gilded perfume burners, and no large desk for maps. But his servant has lit the lamps, which hang from poles driven into the earth, and it looks tidy and comfortable.

"It seems I am doomed to always miss those I love," Heph says sadly, pulling out the two chairs from the wall and opening them. "I miss you, even though you are here. And I miss Alexander. Wonder what he's doing. Pray that he is safe."

"I do, too," she says, sitting. She unstraps her heavy golden helmet and removes it. The feeling of cool liberation is much like taking off a sweaty, blister-causing boot. It is nothing less than sweet, blessed relief. She rubs her hands through her damp, tangled hair.

"Can you...feel how he is?" Heph asks, pulling the amphora out of its circular stand and releasing the wooden cork. He pours two cups of wine, hands her one, and sits across from her. "Many twins, I hear—without Snake Blood—have a kind of connection. There were two old women in the Pellan palace who were twins. One was a cook, another a laundress. One day the cook ran screaming through the palace that her sister was dead, and everyone laughed at her. They had just seen the sister walking to the laundry with a basket of soiled sheets. But the cook was right. Her sister had had a fit and fallen over dead. They later found her in the garden. How did the cook know?"

Kat doesn't answer. She drinks deeply. The wine has a spice to it that she has never tasted before, something exotic and eastern. It slips easily down her throat, sore from smoke and soot. "There was a similar case in Erissa with a miller and his twin sister," she says at last. "But as far as Alex and me, well, I do sense that he is alive. Or maybe it's more that I know I would sense if he were in trouble or...or no longer..." She pauses. "I would feel the loss, the emptiness."

Heph seems to understand. "Well, I'll take that over nothing."

"And after our victory today, I think," she says, "the Greek allies will praise the strategy of young King Alexander. The fire, the flood—it will all seem as though even the gods are on our side." The words prick at her and she flinches.

For all his bluster and pride, all his charm and passion, at least he notices. "What's wrong?" he whispers.

"Ever since I was attacked...by the *thing*, the Spirit Eater, I mean." Dark waves, clawed and fanged. The shuddering cold, more soul crushing than the chill of the freezing waves. "I've felt..." But how can she tell him? How could he—or anyone— possibly understand?

"When we were on our summer campaigns with King Philip," Heph says quietly, "the prince and I would stay up late forming battle plans until we fell asleep together." He looks at her, his eyes suddenly dark with something she cannot read. But if she had to guess, she would say it was longing.

"I wouldn't mind doing that with you, my king," he says, his voice a whisper now, so low it rumbles through the air, al- most like a caress.

For a moment, she feels hot and chilled at the same time. She leans closer to him. But then, just as quickly, anger, hot and bright, flares up in her, forcing her back—anger at herself for feeling tempted these last few days whenever Heph is near. Anger at his inability to really understand her, the pain she has gone through, the loss she has felt—even when they were back on the island of Meninx together and she first learned the evil of her true father. Both then and now, it's as though some inner piece of her has broken into shards that even love—his or Ja- cob's or both—can't seem to fix. An indefinable lostness that she'd hoped to drown in battle but instead it has become only more piercing and more pure.

She sees it now—even before the attack in Byzantium. How she has been floating, at a loss, with no direction. Ever since learning the truth—that her mother was the evil queen of Macedon, the very person she'd sought revenge on her whole life until that point. That her father was Riel, the Last God, a terror to the very earth.

She sees now how she floated, lost, even on Meninx, trying to bury that sense of directionlessness in Heph and their quest to create the mechanism. How she'd floated again, just as lost, with Jacob during the past weeks they spent in Troy—helping the sick but ignoring the sickness that tugged at her own heart, twisting up inside her like a pit of snakes.

How even coming here and pretending to be her brother— how just last night their plan had seemed euphoric and thrilling but had then come crashing into reality this morning as nothing more than another disguise.

Who is she now?

No man can answer that.

And if they cannot, then the last thing she needs is to get lost in either of them.

She stands abruptly. "This was a mistake," she says, setting down her goblet and picking up her helmet. "I'm going."

"No," Heph says, grabbing her arms. His flirtatious charm has vanished, replaced with an urgency that almost frightens her. "We need to talk, Kat. And we can't with that—with Jacob always hovering around you. All I ask is honesty. What happened between you and Jacob all those months in Byzantium and Troy? Did you... I mean... I know what you once were to each other. What I must know is what you are to each other *now*. I deserve that much, Kat."

"It's none of your business," she flings back at him. Her whole body is shaking. With fury. With the lack of answers. With hatred at herself and the confusion that has overwhelmed her ever since they launched the battle this morning.

"It is my business to ask the question," he counters. "You know where I stand, Kat. Nothing has changed for me. I still—" His voice breaks and she wants to run away but can't. She wrestles with the heavy helmet in her arms and the emotion welling up in her throat, threatening to choke her. "I still feel the way I did on the island. I still…love you." His voice, wavering, drops back to barely more than a whisper. "And I will wait for you, if you let me. But…"

He reaches for her but she holds her ground. They both stare at his hand, floating in the space between them.

"But while you told me Jacob gave you that pearl ring you always wear, you won't tell me what it means. Tell me, Kat. If you have chosen Jacob. Just one word, and I will back off forever." His hand goes to his heart as if in vow.

Kat opens her mouth to speak but can't find words. Because the fact is she hasn't chosen Jacob. Not really. Fate pushed them together, yes, and after he had done so much to heal her, it felt right to be with him. It had always been the two of them together since she was six years old. Still, she can't bring herself to say it, or to lose Heph—or if she must lose him, then it would be more than she could bear to lose him by her own doing.

"You want honesty, and that is a fair request." Desperately she tries to steady her voice. "The truth is I just don't know. Until I know who I am and—and what my true purpose is—I *can't* know, and all I can do is play these games, breathlessly trying to keep up, to seek meaning where there is none, forcing myself to see victory where I know there is only loss—everywhere. On both sides."

Heph shakes his head. "Does Jacob know how you feel? Because if so, he doesn't show it. He acts like he owns you. Maybe you should tell him he doesn't."

"There are more important things on my mind than which

man to choose," she says angrily. "Today I commanded a victorious army. I am probably the only person in the world who has killed a god. Why are you pushing me, Heph? Jacob is patient with me, understanding. He knows I need time to…to figure things out."

Heph's dark eyes narrow, becoming slits in the lamplight. "Those soldiers out there might think you are Alexander, but you are really nothing like him. Alexander is decisive. If you had his spirit, you wouldn't dangle Jacob and me for months, torturing us both. You would make up your mind and be done with it."

"As we both know, I am *not* my brother!" she cries, hating how thin her voice sounds in the thick, hot air of the tent. "Maybe you would prefer it if I was?"

Heph's face floods with pink.

She crams the helmet back on her head so she can run outside and get far away from Heph. But as she turns, she glimpses a man's startled face peering between the tent flaps.

She cries out. The face has vanished.

"What is it?" Heph comes up beside her.

Kat stands rooted to the spot, panic gnawing her stomach. "Someone was standing there, looking at us," she says, her voice trembling.

"Jacob?" Heph smirks. "Are you worried it was him?"

"No! Not Jacob," she snaps, her nostrils flaring. "I wish it had been. It was a servant, perhaps. Or a soldier. I couldn't see his face clearly. Fairly young. Clean-shaven." Her gaze slides from the doorway back to Heph. "Don't you see what this means? Someone saw me standing here in Alexander's armor, putting on his helmet. Someone knows Alexander isn't here leading the armies. That the person riding his horse and wearing his armor is an imposter. And not just any imposter. But a girl. If word gets out to the armies, they will probably go home in anger and disgust. We just won a battle, but now the whole war is at stake—at the mercy of our ruse."

Quickly she stuffs her long hair under the helmet and dashes out of the tent before he can contradict her or tangle up her thoughts once more. *Stupid, stupid.* If they had argued in her own tent—Alexander's tent—surely the guards would have prevented someone unknown from entering. Was the person she saw a servant or soldier hoping to speak to Heph? Seeing Kat in Alexander's armor, did he become afraid and run away? Perhaps, fearing for his life, he will never tell anyone. Or perhaps it was a spy from one of the allied armies following "Alexander" to find out what was really going on.

As she mounts Bucephalus, she thinks of the other generals and her heart sinks. Chares, the Athenian, lean and dark, was reluctant to be led by Philip, even less so by his teenage son. The Theban leader, Theagenes, red-faced and quick to anger, will probably never forgive Macedon for killing his Sacred Band of Immortals. Either man would pay generously to learn the real reason that no one can talk to King Alexander on this campaign or even see his face.

Kat walks the horse around Heph's tent and sees five men sitting on logs around a fire, roasting an entire lamb, courtesy of the Persian army. Three of the men are bearded. The other two don't have the right features to be the man in the doorway. Who was he? Panic fills her head, thudding in her ears.

By the light of a torch, two men play golden dice on a silver game board, another bit of Persian plunder. One of them could be the man she saw. Couldn't he? They don't even look up as she passes. Frustration nearly explodes inside her. About half the clean-shaven young men in the army could be the intruder.

A strong hand grabs the reins and Bucephalus rears. Calming him, Kat looks down into the worried eyes of Jacob. "What's wrong, sire?" he asks. "You look upset."

She gazes around the camp in despair. Men sitting around fires, polishing swords, sewing ripped tunics, playing dice, carrying wood and water. Because of one mistake, she could have lost everything for Macedon. For Alexander. She wants to kick Heph for inviting her into his tent. Mostly, she wants to kick herself for going, for wanting to be near him, for needing *either* of them.

"Come with me," he says. "I can see you don't want to talk here."

A few moments later, Jacob has led Kat through the phalanx of guards and into Alexander's royal tent. The lamps are lit, making strangely shaped shadows on the walls and roof.

"What is it?" Jacob asks. "Tell me."

"Someone saw me take my helmet off," she hisses, flinging the helmet onto the carpet. "Someone saw that I am not Alexander."

"What?" Jacob asks, aghast. "Who? How?"

"A few minutes ago. I don't know who. I just saw a face."

"But why didn't the guards..."

"There were no guards, Jacob. I was in Heph's tent."

Jacob crosses his muscular arms. His face sets in a mask of control. "And why were you there?"

"We were...talking. About Alexander. I didn't think, that one time, anything bad would happen. But that's not the point. Don't you see—"

"It's clear he wants you, Kat," Jacob interrupts. "And you're not being fair to him or me. You haven't told him you and I are together. Have been together as man and wife. That we have a future together. You accepted my ring, after all. That was a promise."

Was it? She didn't think so at the time.

But clearly Jacob did.

"Seeing him again has confused you," he continues. "I understand that. You still have feelings for him. But let me tell you this. You will *never* be first with Hephaestion, Kat. That much I know."

"What do you mean?" she asks. Why are they even discussing this? They should be searching for the man she saw. Or strategizing what to say to the Greek commanders if they come barging in, demanding to speak to Alexander.

"Hephaestion will always put his relationship with Alexander first, especially now that your brother is king," Jacob replies.

"We all put Alexander first," she says angrily.

"I don't." Jacob looks at her steadily, his brown eyes sad. "I put you first." She pulls in a shuddering breath as his words tumble over her, the truth of them. "I always have, and I always will. If you and Alexander were trapped in a burning building and I only had time to rescue one of you, it would be you. Do you believe that?"

Her head is suddenly so heavy she fears she may fall, her chest so full that it is hard to breathe. "Yes." It comes out like a whimper. How can someone's love feel simultaneously like joy and like a crushing weight? What does it mean to feel that way, to love him back and yet to yearn for a freedom she can't even define?

"Do you think Heph would do the same?" he whispers.

She tries to picture it. Smoke, flames. She and Alex both injured, unable to move. Heph racing through the fire to grab one of them before the roof collapses on the one he leaves behind. The fact is, she doesn't know which of them Heph would save.

"What a silly question," she says, waving her hands as if to physically push the thought away. "That will never happen. You're not talking sense."

"I'm just saying it's what you deserve. You deserve someone who will always choose you first. Who lives for you and would be willing to die for you. I am that man. And Hephaestion is not."

"I need—" She stops. What she needs is Alexander, her brother, her twin. But he is not here. "Jacob. A man saw me. We must do something about that first—before…before anything else can be discussed. We need to find him, and I don't know how, and I don't know what to do."

"Then do this," Jacob says, his hands warm and strong on her shoulders, his dark eyes intense. "Keep leading the armies to victory as we follow the Royal Road east. Today's plunder has made every soldier in this army a comparatively wealthy man. If you keep giving them more, they won't care if Alexander is really someone's maiden aunt." And then, as if reading her thoughts, Jacob says softly, "Perhaps we will find Alexander in Gordium. It is only an eight- or nine-day march, by all accounts. Our scouts say there is only one Persian cohort in our way, the Third, just outside the city."

Eight or nine days. To Kat, it feels like eight or nine years.

But if she finds Alex at the end of that march, it will be worth any price she has to pay.

She just has to make it that long. While her body fights battles in her brother's armor and her mind soars in the sky above, Kat herself just has to float, like she has been doing all this time. Float and wait and pray that answers come.

CHAPTER TWENTY-FOUR

DARIUS

DARIUS URGES HIS HORSE FORWARD TO COME UP
alongside the imperial harmanaxa. Sunlight reflects off the gold-
plated winged bulls on its red leather sides. The wheels are plated
with gold. The leather traces and bridles are studded with golden
rosettes, and the horses' bits are solid gold. The whole contrap-
tion has the effect of a giant gilded beetle traversing the sparse
and dusty landscape—desert as far as the eye can see.

He signals to the driver, perched on a small chair in front, to
stop the eight white horses, and the carriage grinds to a halt. He
dismounts and hands the reins to one of the numerous bodyguards riding alongside. Another guard opens the door, and he
climbs inside.

Great King Artaxerxes reclines on a heap of brightly colored
pillows, his long white hair and beard a stark contrast to the
shades of scarlet and purple all around him. The sweet, cloying
scent of incense rises from a perfume burner on the wall.

The eunuch Bagoas is already there, of course, sitting cross-
legged on a rich carpet next to the king's heap of pillows. A block
of light—coming from an open panel in the ceiling—illuminates
him, as if he is the lead actor in a theatrical production, while
the Great King is a bit player in the shadows. The sight discon-

certs Darius, the brief flash of some divine omen. But then the impression is gone. This is simply the way the Great King's carriage allows light and fresh air to enter while preventing prying eyes and ears from discerning what happens inside. In the shadows lies freedom and invisibility—this much Darius knows better than anyone. It is in the shadows and not the broad light that the slyest and most effective strategies play out, after all.

Darius and Bagoas nod curtly at each other, keeping up the pretense of their old hostility. Artaxerxes must never know they have combined forces.

The harmanaxa lurches into motion, and Darius folds himself neatly onto the carpet in front of Artaxerxes.

"My king," he says.

The black glittering eyes fix on him, aglow in the dim recesses of the cabin. "News, Darius?" he asks.

"I have received word that the Greek forces have achieved a victory against General Gardashasp's army on the coast. They burned the camp and have taken all our treasure and our horses."

"Did they now?" The king's thin lips spread into a smile under his long hooked nose. Ah, so he has already heard from his own spies. "My messenger tells some tale of wizards who conjured the river to flood our camp. As for me, I think it is an excuse for a poor defense. Gardashasp burned to death, I hear, trying to save the treasure. But I will execute his lieutenants if they are found."

The Great King snaps his long crooked fingers, and Bagoas unstops a flagon, pours some wine into his own cup, and then some into the king's. Bagoas drinks first, swishing the wine around his mouth, then swallows, and nods—no poison.

Artaxerxes drinks deeply. "This early defeat could, actually, have a positive outcome for us. The easy victory will give the Greek forces overweening confidence, more than they should have taking on the Great King of Persia. We will arrive in Gordium in eight days and prepare to give battle there. We are a much greater force than that under the command of Gardashasp. I am curious to see if the Greek wizards will vanquish me. Especially since I already have my priests working on counterspells." He drinks again.

Darius steadies himself for a moment, takes his time, listening to the crunch of wheels, the rhythmic clomping of horses' hooves, and the voices of soldiers, an unassuming backdrop for the astonishing news he is about to share. "I have placed a spy in the Greek camp as a servant. As you may have heard, the young king Alexander has been behaving mysteriously, staying in his tent, emerging only in his armor to ride his horse and give battle."

Artaxerxes rearranges the pillows behind his back. "The boy pretends to mourn for his father, I should think, to disguise the bloodlust that drives him on. Perhaps he even killed the old king himself. Is that the theory you were hoping to surprise me with, grandson?"

"There is more to it than that, my lord," Darius says, leaning in. "King Alexander did not lead the Greeks against Gardashasp. It was someone else masquerading as Alexander." He lowers his voice. "A girl, no less."

Now that catches them both off guard. The king starts, spilling some wine on his bejeweled purple robe. Bagoas's wily dark eyes open in shock.

"A girl?" The king blusters. "Perhaps one of these New Amazons terrorizing their way across the empire. Are you sure your man hasn't succumbed to the Greeks' wizardry himself?"

"I assure you my men are reliable."

The king leans back on his pillows and looks up at the ceiling, staring at the square of light as it jolts and sways. "Some say King Philip died of poison. Is it possible someone poisoned the prince, too, and is pretending to rule in his name? Pity none of our spies know where the *real* Alexander is, then—or if he is even alive."

"The young king is on his way to Gordium," Darius says, his voice smooth and confident.

The Great King raises his eyebrows but says nothing, clearly not wanting to reward Darius with his surprise this time.

"Gordium?" Bagoas asks, speaking for the first time. "What's for him there?"

Darius shrugs. "The impersonator spoke of it. Perhaps Alexander himself is on a spy mission. Perhaps he wants to try his hand with the famous knot."

Darius continues, "Anyway, Alexander's purpose doesn't matter, really. If your majesty agrees, I will send word by our fastest messengers to all our men to search the environs of Gordium for a young blond Greek with a slight limp, a snake birthmark on his left thigh, and eyes of different colors." But he has already sent word to all his Assassins to fan out across the Royal Road to search for the new king. *He* must find him first.

Artaxerxes tugs at his beard thoughtfully. "Send word not to kill Alexander if they find him, but to bring him to us alive. If we can prove to the Greek armies that we have their leader—that he is not leading their troops in his golden armor—their morale will plummet and their ranks will be ours."

"Yes, my liege," Darius agrees. "And we must send word to the Ninth and Twelfth Cohorts to surround the Greeks on the road. They have a large force, but they are on our soil, and when we collect our forces together, we will have more. We can crush them before they get too much farther into our territory."

Artaxerxes smiles. "No, Darius. We will let them come deep into Persia. Too deep to turn around and flee. Let them come east. Our great empire will wrap them in its snare like a cobra, squeezing and squeezing until every last one of them falls prey, and we are fattened on the taste of Greek meat."

Darius fumes silently. Why let the enemy come so far when they could stop them near the coast? "Yes, sire," he says smoothly. "But I would also like to suggest we send an advance force to lay waste the land through which the Greeks march. Prevent them from foraging for food, water, and wood. Poison the wells. Evacuate the villages and burn them. Destroy the crops and orchards. These Greeks may be much stronger than we imagine, and we will weaken them through hunger and thirst. Even powerful wizards need food and water to survive."

Artaxerxes waves a hand, his rings glinting in the golden block of light pouring in the opening above. "The farmers and villagers will evacuate to the fortified cities, but we will not burn their homes or poison their wells. Do you know how long it takes to cleanse a poisoned well? As for food, I imagine the Greeks will pluck the harvest from the fields and the fruit from the trees as they pass, anyway. Let us not destroy the orchards entirely. Next year our people will need that harvest. How many years does it take for an olive tree to produce good fruit? Twelve?"

Anger pumps through Darius at the old man's stubbornness. The very survival of the empire is at stake and Artaxerxes hesitates because of olives. "Very well, my liege. But I have crafted a plan to surround the enemy with fire in battle. If their wizards use water, we can use fire."

"We need not concern ourselves with Greek wizards," the Great King replies wearily. "I have notified the Supreme Lord of the Aesarians in Nekrana about the purported magical Greek, and I expect him to move his men west to search for him. The Lords are already fanning out across the empire, desperately looking for even one powerful magic being as part of a plan to destroy the monsters. This supposed wizard will certainly interest them."

He takes another swig of wine from his glistening golden chalice studded with emeralds the size of robins' eggs. "That map you gave me, Darius," the old king says, "the one your Macedonian spy, Kadmus, sent you that gives the location of the Fountain of Youth, near which the monsters live…"

"Yes, my lord?"

"I sent a regiment there to investigate for ourselves, and it never returned."

Darius is not surprised. "We must hope the Aesarian Lords are able to stop the creatures, Great King. For, in the end, the Spirit Eaters are far more dangerous than the Greeks, who are, after all, only men."

Artaxerxes rubs his eyes. "Amazons. Spirit Eaters. Wizards. Invading Greeks. A missing king. It is too much for an old man like me."

Darius locks eyes with Bagoas. This is one point on which they both agree with him.

The king looks up. "Bagoas, I want a woman. Fetch me that Olbian redhead."

Bagoas raps sharply on the ceiling with his ivory walking stick, and the carriage rolls to a halt. As Darius remounts his horse, he realizes that he will have to move to the next part of his plan sooner than he thought.

King Artaxerxes imperils the entire empire with his hesitation. He is too old, too careful to rule a nation with so many disasters facing it at once.

And Darius's plan is not just for Persia, but also for himself. For two decades now, he has been waiting, plotting, and planning. The richest, largest empire in the history of the world is just a finger's breadth beyond his grasp. Only one thing stands between Darius and his magnificent destiny.

The beating heart of Artaxerxes.

CHAPTER TWENTY-FIVE

RAT

RAT TRUDGES FROM THE RIVER INTO THE CAMP, two heavy buckets of water suspended on either side of the yoke around his neck. Yuf, he knows, is somewhere nearby, watching him.

It was Sarina who decided Rat and Yuf would join the great Greek army Alexander was assembling to invade Persia. Rat and Yuf would work as laborers, would become familiar faces to the soldiers and the king's guards. They hired on in Athens and joined the Greek transport ships sailing east. After the victory near the coast, they have been marching through empty fields and vacant villages as people who are afraid of the army run and hide.

But it has been hard for Rat to get near King Alexander. Ever since he joined the army on the Persian coast, the king has appeared only in his golden armor for the long marches east. Rat cannot stab through armor. The rest of the time, the king spends in his tent mourning his father.

Father. Rat has the image of a burly, one-eyed man with a red-brown beard and a loud voice. But Father was never kind to Rat and always called him bad names because he wasn't smart like the others.

No, Rat is not sad that King Philip is dead.

But he will be very sad when King Alexander is dead.

Even if it means that it will be *his* turn at being king. The Rat King. It has a kind of ring to it.

But Alexander always was nice to him...

Several times Rat tried to carry fresh water inside Alexander's tent, but the guards in front of it merely took the buckets from him and sent him on his way. The only ones allowed to enter the tent are Hephaestion, who was also nice to him, and another man they call Jacob.

But Yuf is getting frustrated at the delay. *You must kill the king soon*, he says. He has threatened to kill Heracles, Rat's pet rat, when he gets back to Egypt. Rat left Heracles in the care of Sarina.

Today, Rat has a new idea. Sarina and the Egyptian physicians healed his mind to make it more like those of other boys, and now he can come up with smart ideas, too.

He passes the medical tent, where doctors treat not only battle wounds but also the stomach ailments and fevers of an army on the march, and around the pens of baaing, grunting livestock, where the butchers prepare meat for the men. The wooden yoke, even though it is padded, cuts into the sores on his neck, and he sets the buckets down a minute, then picks them up, and walks unsteadily past the blacksmiths, who hammer damaged armor back into shape, the black smoke from their portable forges heavy in the hot summer air. Going around a large tent, he stumbles into a merchant rolling a cart filled with weapons, capes, and boots for sale, and falls to his knees. He thanks the gods the buckets didn't tip over. The merchant curses him, but a pretty young laundress, sets down her basket of soiled tunics and helps him up with a kind word.

Finally, he approaches the royal tent of King Alexander and sets down his burdens, removing the yoke from around his bruised neck. One of the guards calls back through the closed tent flap, "Lord Hephaestion! Fresh water for the king!"

The guard turns back to Rat and says, with a dismissive flick of his hand, "Well, boy! Be off with you!" But Rat doesn't move.

The flaps part and Heph comes out, eyes on the buckets. Rat cries, "Heph! Don't you recognize me?" The guard pushes toward Rat with the shaft of his spear. "Get out of here, you little—"

Heph stays the guard with a hand on his shoulder, looks at Rat, and frowns. Rat realizes he must look very different. He is tanner, leaner, and taller than he was last year when he was kidnapped. He is also dirtier, his hair unkempt and stringy, his tunic ripped and soiled, a far cry from the pampered little prince of Pella.

"Arridheus?" Heph says, his eyes opening wide in disbelief.

Rat has to force himself to remember the name. It feels heavy and foreign, like a suit of armor he has not worn in years and has outgrown. "Yes! Yes, Heph! It's me!" Rat says at last. Just looking at Heph, he remembers so many good times in that other place where he always had enough to eat and his body wasn't sore and throbbing.

Heph puts his arms around Rat's narrow shoulders. "Arri, what happened to you? We looked for you for so long!"

"I was…taken by bad men," he gasps. "I got away. I heard Alexander was marching here and joined the army as a water boy. But I couldn't get near him. I tried so many times."

Heph stares at Rat. "Arri, I don't believe I have ever heard you talk so much at once."

Rat beams. "A priest healed my mind and tongue and made my body strong." He frowns. Has he said too much? And he shouldn't be happy. He has come here not to be happy, but to kill Alexander. "Can I see my brother?"

Heph frowns, as if something is wrong, and Rat wonders if he knows what Rat is planning. "Wait here, Arri. I will tell him we have found you, at last." He turns to the guard. "Borus, don't let this boy out of your sight. He is indeed the king's younger brother."

The guard looks at Rat with new respect. In the hot sunlight, Rat shivers.

He hears low voices in the tent and, after a time, Heph parts the flaps and leads Rat inside. Rat feels the dagger in his belt. Yuf makes him sharpen it every night.

The sun was so bright outside that inside he cannot see for a few moments. It is cooler, too, and his dirty bare feet feel a soft carpet beneath them. Alex stands at the far end of the tent, in his golden armor, his arms outstretched.

"Brother?" His voice sounds thin, muffled by the helmet.

Rat runs toward him and feels strong arms wrap around him.

It is so good to be in his brother's arms again. But how is he going to stab him in his golden armor? Then he sees the back of Alexander's neck, soft and vulnerable, below the helmet. Slowly, he takes the dagger from his belt and puts his arm around Alex's neck. He will push it in very hard and run.

He *has* to do it.

But he cannot, for it feels so good to be hugged, to be loved again.

No, he *must* do it. What will happen to Heracles, otherwise? He cannot let his pet down, or all the people who helped him, even if they were not very kind about it.

He positions the dagger just above the soft flesh of the neck, but he hesitates. He can't do this. He can't. Alex pulls away from him, and the moment is gone…but his helmet gets caught in Rat's arms. Rat's dagger falls, and the helmet falls…and a tumble of long golden-brown hair falls.

Rat stares in astonishment. This is not Alex. This is someone else.

Alex's friend Kat. Who was always nice to him and Heracles.

Kat looks stricken, and he watches her neck as she swallows.

The neck he almost cut with his knife, which now lies useless on the floor of the tent, staring up at him like an accusation.

"Ah, Arri," she says, his real name sending a shiver through him, a current of some old feeling starting to reawaken. She bends to her knees. "Now you know our little secret."

But Heph pins Arri's arms behind his back so hard that pains shoot up into his shoulders. "You were holding a knife!"

"Heph, let him go!" Kat cries.

Rat feels the mean hands let him go. He hangs his head.

"Arri," Kat says, "you weren't trying to kill me, were you?"

"No," Rat says. Kat casts Heph an accusing glance. Then Rat adds, "I was trying to kill Alex."

It takes Rat a long time to tell them—and the man called Jacob, who joined them—about everything that happened to him. About the puppets he'd been given and how he'd also become one. He didn't know people could be puppets, too—that was a thing he'd learned in all this.

How he had been kidnapped on the road from Pella and taken to Egypt, how the priests had cured his mind, how Yuf had trained his body but also beaten him, and how Sarina had wanted him to kill Alex to save Egypt from more bad men and promised that one day he would be king and a kinder ruler than any of the others had been before him.

Heph, Kat, and Jacob talk a great deal about this, all at the same time, until it hurts Rat's head. Then Heph runs out of the tent, while Kat gives Rat roasted meat and bread. When Heph comes back, he says, "The man called Yuf has been arrested. We are questioning him."

"You are safe, Arri," Kat says.

"My name is Rat," he says. "I am not allowed to be Arri anymore. Yuf said so."

"You are Arridheus, Prince of Macedon," she says firmly,

"Brother to King Alexander, who will be here soon. But you must tell no one that he is not already here. Do you understand?"

He nods, wondering if Yuf will come in the tent and beat them all. Though these two men look strong, Rat has the feeling that only Alex could save them from Yuf. "Where is Alex?" he asks.

"On very important business," Heph says. "Secret business. The army must think he is here, which is why Kat puts on his golden armor."

Rat nods and eats an olive. He hopes Alex will be here soon. Maybe Alex can get Heracles back. He misses his little rat, who never hid anything from him and never pretended to be anyone he wasn't.

"We can't trust him," the big man named Jacob says. "You say he was never right in the head. And those people twisted him. How do we know he will keep our secret? How do we know he won't kill us all?"

Heph pushes his hands through his hair. Rat looks between the two young men, both strong and broad and handsome, men who use all of the most impressive words and stand as though the world is theirs. Men that Rat will never grow to be like, no matter how hard he tries. Some things just aren't fated for all of us.

That was another thing he learned about in his time away. Fate.

"Agothacles, the blacksmith's assistant, is deaf and has a way with children. We will put Arri in his care when we are not looking out for him," Heph says.

"Heph," Kat interjects. She nods gently in Rat's direction. "There'll be others to watch for, surely?"

"Sarina and her clan don't know this one has failed," he says. "Eventually, someone will have to go to Egypt and disarm her one way or the other. But we can't worry about her now."

Rat tugs at Heph's sleeve. "When you see Sarina, will you get Heracles from her?"

Jacob asks, "Who is Heracles?"

"His rat," Heph and Kat say.

"Zeus help us," Jacob says. And Rat hopes that Zeus will.

That night, after a hot bath, Rat slips into a clean, soft-woven tunic and tumbles onto a soft feather mattress in Heph's tent. For a moment, he feels a shiver of fear, remembering that he failed in what he promised Sarina. But then he remembers that he did the right thing. So perhaps he is not a failure but a hero, after all. The one thing he has managed to learn about fate is this: you can never know what yours is.

So tomorrow, he will awaken as Arri. There is no more need to be anyone else, and that in itself is a wonderful thing.

CHAPTER TWENTY-SIX

ALEXANDER

GORDIUM DOESN'T SPRAWL OUTWARD, AS MOST cities do, but upward, walls and towers curling around a massive gold-gray rock at its heart. As he approaches it, Alexander feels a profound sense of relief. The first part of his quest, at least, is nearly at an end. And he has two days left. Two days until the summer solstice. After that, no one will be able to defeat the Spirit Eaters, if what Patra spoke was true.

After many delays due to storms, last week his ship at last landed in Apasa, on the Persian coast. There he rented a horse at a posting station and set off on the Royal Road—a marvel of the modern world—sixteen hundred miles of hard-packed, well-maintained thoroughfare, wide enough for two carriages at once, with ferry crossings over rivers. He has spent every night in a comfortable room in posting stations, fortified hotels with baths, a tavern, and stables, situated every fifteen miles along the road. One day, when Alex becomes king, he would like to copy this system of moving goods, soldiers, and messages quickly and efficiently throughout his lands.

When he becomes king. According to tales he heard on the road, spread by royal couriers from the coast who ride like the wind, he might already *be* king. Philip was dead, they whispered in posting station taverns, from poison, from apoplexy, from a knife wound. No, he was alive. The death had been that of his brother-in-law, King Xander of Epirus. Or Philip's new, young wife, poisoned by his older one. Though Alex questioned everyone he could, all he could ascertain was that someone important had died at the wedding, but the retelling of tales had jumbled it.

And then there were Patra's words to him before he left. *My king.* When he'd said he was not her king, her reply had been, *Not yet.*

If Philip really is dead, all their work in assembling the allied Greek army would be for nothing. Only Alexander himself could lead them now.

But the summer solstice cannot be forestalled.

Looking at the city rising before him, he wonders about the object he needs to destroy the Spirit Eaters, the talisman of one who is above mortal fate. The fate of all mortals, he knows, is death. Who doesn't die? A god? A spirit of some sort? Where can he find this object? And what if he doesn't? Not only that, but the oracle said he required the aid of a stranger whose blood was destined to mingle with his. Will it be a woman with whom he will have a child? Will he even know when he has found her? He has looked carefully at every person on the road, in the posting stations, in the towns he visited, expecting some sign telling him, *That's the one.* But none has come.

He never imagined making this journey alone. Always he had envisioned Heph by his side. A year and a half ago, when he and Heph were studying at Aristotle's school in Mieza, they rode out exploring and found a cave with an altar of sorts at one end, and above it, gleaming from the light of their torches, a large painted eye with a bright blue iris. On the altar was an ancient vase, and inside was a scroll of thick parchment. Out in the sunshine, they unrolled it and discovered it was a map. The ink was faded, the language archaic, but they eventually deciphered it.

In the province of Asia in the Persian Empire was marked,

Fountain of Youth, Well of the Gods, Providing Physical Healing and Spiritual Power to All Who Drink of It. As soon as Alex read about the fountain, he felt hope rise inside him, utter joy at the thought of healing his weak leg and becoming a perfect king for Macedon. Perfect people don't have physical disabilities, which are punishments given by the gods to those who deserve them— or so everyone says, and sometimes, what people think matters more than what is true.

Next to the fountain were the words *Spirit Eaters*, though he had no idea then what it meant, and he and Heph had joked about it. They had planned to find the Fountain of Youth, using the bag of gold Heph would win at the Blood Tournament. But Heph, against all odds, hadn't won. A peasant named Jacob had won, and a girl named Katerina showed up at the palace, and suddenly all their plans changed. Heph should be by his side now, but the oracle prophesied that to defeat the Spirit Eaters, he must do so without his friends.

Alexander isn't used to putting this much trust in the unknown; he is a planner, a strategist, a deep but decisive thinker. And yet here he is, putting his journey into the hands of Fate itself, and the flimsy few words spoken by a young oracle who might have simply been choking on too much incense when she uttered the prophecy that he ought to come here. And yet, the prophecies about him, Kat, and Riel—even those that seemed to conflict— ended up being absolutely true. He can no longer shrug off oracular predictions. His very existence is a testament to their validity.

Truth be told, it isn't only saving mankind from the monsters that has driven him forward. There are private, personal reasons, too. For one, he wants to prove that he is not a weak boy with a crippled leg, but a man who is stronger *because* of his weakness. For another, there is Heph himself—the space Alex needed from his friend, and from the confusion of intimacy that has been brewing in his chest, threatening to unravel his clear thinking and good sense.

And there's something else. It's as if, stripped of the magic that colored the way he saw the world all his life, everything seems starker and simpler to him now. There seems to be a knowing deep inside him of what to do. To trust the prophecy. To go east. To vanquish the Spirit Eaters.

He nudges his horse into a gallop and races toward the rocky citadel ahead. All around, as far as he can see, giant rocks rise from lush emerald plains and smoky blue-green woods. He passes a temple carved out of living stone, with stairs, columns, and a pediment—perhaps the tomb of an ancient king.

Just outside the city gates is a posting station, where he turns in his horse and receives his deposit. He approaches the steep, crowded city on foot. At the gate, two burly, black-bearded guards block his way.

"Your business?" asks the taller one, gruffly.

"I am on a pilgrimage to the Temple of Midas," he says in his best Persian.

The guard grins, revealing sharp white teeth. "There is no Temple of Midas here. In Gordium, the Greeks go to the Temple of Zeus to worship their gods. By your accent, that is where you should go, too."

The other guard sees Alexander's confusion and adds, "But there is the Arch of Midas up on the old citadel, by the knot. Perhaps that is what you seek."

"An arch?" Alex asks, hope fluttering in his chest, even though it is not what Patra told him to find. She said he must go to the *Temple* of Midas.

"Yes," the first guard replies. "An arch put up many centuries ago by King Midas, next to the oxcart of his father, King Gordios, founder of this city. Perhaps you have heard of the famous Gordian knot?"

Alexander nods, remembering that Aristotle told him some

men had lost their minds trying to solve the puzzle of the knot. They starved to death or were dragged away unconscious.

"It is a strange courtyard," the second guard says, stroking his black beard, "reportedly haunted. The townsfolk keep away from it, and it stands empty other than visitors who try to untangle the knot and children who dare each other to walk through the arch. I have done so many times, and believe me, it is just an arch." The two guards chuckle.

A cart groans to a halt behind him. Alex turns to see an ox-cart filled with huge, bulbous amphorae. "What do you have there?" barks the first guard, moving toward it.

"Olive oil" comes the fatigued reply. The driver wipes his sweaty brow with a dirty piece of cloth and pulls out a wax tablet to show the guard. "My master already calculated the tax."

"Ardashan! Come and help!" shouts the first guard.

"You'd better go," the other guard says to Alex. "The arch you seek is in the Courtyard of the Winged Genies, off Leather Street, high up on the citadel. It's no temple—at least I don't think so—but you can pray there if you need to fulfill a vow."

Perplexed by the strange statements about the arch, Alexander passes through the city gates and begins to follow what seems to be the main street, curling upward toward the palace high above. The noon sun reflecting off the golden palace roof is blinding. He learned in his schooldays that everything inside the Midas palace of Gordium is covered with pure gold—tables, chairs, beds, floors, and walls.

Either the stories of Midas's magic touch are true, or he had even gaudier taste than Olympias.

Legend has it, he even turned his *daughter* into gold—by mistake, it is said. It's a cautionary tale, though Aristotle argued there are too many men in this world who believe a daughter of gold more valuable than a living one.

The streets are crowded with pedestrians, ambling riders, and donkey carts of merchandise. Dozens of shops boast carpets, jewelry, furniture, and weapons—enameled, curved swords that dazzle as he passes by—and little marketplaces burst with booths offering cheese, wine, and olives.

The street opens onto a square, the Temple of Zeus at its far side, painted in blue and gold stripes. Like everything else he has seen in Midas City, it is small and centuries old, but beautiful. A pink-cheeked boy marches past rolling a hoop, and when Alex asks where Leather Street is, the boy points to a narrow lane off the square.

Alex walks past shops and booths displaying sandals, boots, belts, bridles, and pouches. It is stuffy on this tiny street, and perspiration trickles down the back of his neck and into his tunic. Finally, the street ends at a tall set of stairs, cracked and crumbling. Dangerous, but he climbs them. At the top he sees a small square, bounded by a wall on one side, on the others by abandoned buildings. All the walls are engraved with the figures of muscular winged gods in profile, their long beards plaited. Persian genies. In the center stands an arch.

And on the side, tied to a column in a colonnade along a once-grand building, stands a rotten oxcart, its front pole and yoke hidden by a thick tangle of knotted rope. It's a decrepit thing, useful only for a few minutes as fuel to warm those sitting around a bonfire. Is this really the famous Gordian Knot? He approaches it and runs his hand over the tight jumble of rope, feeling a spike of something that makes him withdraw his hand immediately. It's as if the ropes contain fear, frustration, anger, and sadness all balled together.

He steps back in shock. Then he squats down to examine it from below. He can't find an end, and even the knots have knots.

He turns his attention to the arch in the center and walks slowly around it. It is a doorway without a door: a triangular entablature over two flat pillars flanking empty space. The Arch of Midas. But not the Temple of Midas. He walks over to the edge of the little square and looks out over a winding street in the city below. The residents have beds, chairs, and tables set on the roofs of their houses to enjoy the fresh air outside of stuffy little rooms. On one roof directly below Alex, a man sweeps the floor. Next door, a woman sits carding wool under a striped canopy.

A cool breeze wafts up from the valley, washing away some of his heat but none of his frustration. He had expected something here. A mysterious woman, perhaps, holding out an ancient amulet of some forgotten god. If only he still had a vestige of his Snake Blood Magic, he would know what to do. But it is gone, sunk into nothingness with Riel, the father-god who had given it to him. Without it, he is nothing but a silly schoolboy sent on an adventure by the wild riddles of a girl in a trance. He's a man now, perhaps even a king. He should be with the Greek army doing a man's work, not out here on this fool's errand. He needs to get another horse and ride straight to the coast. He turns to go.

No.

The voice is inside his head, but loud and clear. For a moment he panics, wondering if Riel is back—Riel, who used to sit in the rafters of his mind like a watchful crow, cawing out his comments from time to time.

Stay here. You can do what needs to be done.

But it is not Riel. Nor is it Snake Blood Magic with its visions of others' lives. This is something else. Something new. Some deep part of him that he has never known.

What had Aristotle said? That men relying on magic lose the chance to test their own abilities, find their own strength.

How? he asks himself. *How can I do what needs to be done?*

He feels a tug—he can't explain it as anything else—and turns around. It is as if the arch is pulling him toward it.

He slowly walks closer and studies the carved stone again. It is, as the guard said, a normal arch. Then why does he feel he must walk through it? He will find only himself on the other side, here in the hot, deserted square near the top of the citadel. Now the feeling is stronger than a tug. It is nothing less than a demand. He takes one look around him, up at the heartbreakingly beautiful canopy of cloudless sky, and over at the yellow cliffs and green hills. In the distance, a cloud of large black birds wings its way toward him.

Inhaling deeply, he steps through.

And into a temple.

Light from a hundred torches dances off golden columns and walls. The paving stones are covered with gold and edged with rubies. At the far end is an altar of sorts, though he cannot see the god honored there, because an old woman is standing in front of it, pouring libations of wine into bowls on a golden table.

Alexander looks behind him. There is no door to the outside, just a wall a few feet beyond the same stone arch. There are no windows. Panic races through his veins. Is he in a cave? Has he slipped into a different world? Is he trapped here? How can he ever get back out? On either side of him, in between tall glittering columns, are looms of solid gold instead of wood, with threads of gold instead of wool, and loom weights of gold-speckled rocks.

"What is this place?" he asks in Persian, as he approaches the altar.

The old woman turns. Alex sees stringy gray hair, a crooked toothless grin, and cloudy violet eyes.

"This temple," she says in Greek, in a voice that sounds like wooden wheels rolling over gravel, "was built by King Midas and is accessible only to those born with Blood Magic. Anyone else passing through the arch will simply walk out the other side." She turns back to the altar, feels for a bowl, and pours wine into it.

Now Alex understands why only a few individuals could enter the temple.

He has rarely, if ever, heard anyone speak so openly about Blood Magic.

"But my—" He stops himself from admitting the truth: his magic is gone.

He hears something like the repeated slamming of a door and realizes the crone is laughing. She turns to him again. "You will always have a kind of magic all your own." It's as though she has sensed the truth—or read his mind. Perhaps *she* has Snake Blood.

"What did King Midas know about Blood Magics?" He approaches her cautiously.

The old woman goes back to pouring the libations. "Midas was an Earth Blood who used his abilities for his own gain, sniffing out minerals in the mountains and earth. After his death, the legend developed that everything he touched turned to gold, which was not quite true."

"And who, if I may ask, are you?" he asks. It is a relief to speak his native language again, to feel the words sliding from his tongue without worrying about tenses and grammar and sounds his mouth can't quite make.

She sets down her oenochoe as a smile lights her wrinkled face. For an instant Alex thinks he can see that she must have been very beautiful, a thousand years ago, when she was young.

"Merely a servant of Fate," she says, shrugging crooked shoulders. She seems like a bundle of ancient bones beneath her rough-spun gray robe. "Since fate decided you must come east, it was I who put the ancient map of the Fountain of Youth in that cave back in Mieza, for you to find. I have been waiting for you ever since."

Alex's heart judders and skips. *She put the map in the cave?*

He asks quietly, "Why? Why was I supposed to come east?"

She turns from him, arranges the bowls of wine, and bows to the figure above the altar. It is, he sees now, a winged baby holding a tablet. He has never heard of any god or goddess—Persian or Greek—taking such a form.

"It is your destiny, young king." She twists her head to look at him, her lips curling into a smile.

King? His heart sinks. Philip is dead.

"Yes," she says, her violet eyes shining strangely in the dim light. "Your father died the day you left on your quest. Before you were even out of the city."

Alex feels tears stinging his eyes. He last saw his father striding around the Epirote palace in excellent health, issuing orders about the royal wedding, bellowing with hearty laughter about dry, bloodless King Xander taking such a luscious young wife.

"How?" His voice is a ragged whisper.

"He received the kiss of death," she hisses.

"Mother," he says, but it is more a groan than a word. Olympias found a way to kill him. Only she would arrange for him to be killed with a kiss. At a wedding. He knew it. He knew she could never truly accept Philip's rejection of her for an obnoxious new wife half her age.

"The queen, yes, in such a clever way no one suspects her."

Alex's mind reels, memories overtaking him. When he was seven, Philip took him to the tallest tower in the Pellan palace on a cold, clear night and pointed out the stars, including that of Ares, god of war, the deity all soldiers must worship. When Alex shivered, the king took off his own thick cloak and gently wrapped him in it. It was a simple gesture, and yet, at that moment, Alex had never felt so convinced of his place in this world.

Philip had always been a larger-than-life figure, hurting him, irritating him, and, in his way, loving him. There is such a huge, empty space in Alex's world without him that Alex is at a loss at what to put there.

He should go back. Macedon is without a king. The Greek armies are without a leader. Urgency pulses through him like a hammer ringing on iron.

"Has the alliance fallen apart?" he asks. "What is happening with Macedon and the Greek allies?"

"You have good friends," she says in a singsong voice, "who have seen to everything as you would desire."

Heph, yes. Who probably sent for Kat as soon as he landed in the empire. Yet the Greek allies would never follow Heph and Kat into war against Persia.

"And yet they have," the old woman says, evidently reading his thoughts. "And won a great battle. Still, your twin is in terrible danger from enemies and allies alike."

Alex winces. He needs to be in two places at once. "I cannot go back until I defeat the Spirit Eaters," he says through gritted teeth.

"Are you *sure* you want to do that, young king? After all, all those who have grappled with Fate have failed. And the Spirit Eaters are the children of Fate."

"What do you mean?" he asks, his head beginning to throb. "I don't understand."

The woman hobbles toward him. Her head comes only to the middle of his chest. She seems so thin and frail, and yet he senses a frightening power in her. If he grabbed that knobby wrist, she would probably fling him across the sanctuary.

"Midas's father, King Gordios, was also an Earth Blood," she says, staring not at him with those blind eyes, but *through* him. "A descendant of the god Brehan. Unlike his son, Gordios cared nothing for wealth but wanted to battle the goddesses of Fate. Men and women, he said, should make their own fates, and not, like puppets, have fate determine the course of their lives. Gordios failed, and succeeded only in hopelessly tangling the strands that connect fate to mankind."

Alex frowns. "You mean those ropes on the oxcart out in the courtyard? He tied those there to prevent anyone from stealing the thing that gave him his throne," he says.

"In this case, the myth is not nearly as exciting as the truth," the woman says, giving him a sinister smile. "The knot came when he fought against the threads of Fate. He wanted to leave the palace and take the cart back to his farm, for he was far happier being a farmer than a king."

Alex's blood throbs with impatience. "What does that have to do with me?" he asks.

"Everything." The deep voice rings throughout the temple, bouncing off golden walls, penetrating his mind like daggers.

The tiny figure before him smiles, blinks, and adjusts her gray head shawl with bent fingers. "You and Gordios have much in common, young king. You have already grappled with Fate. In the womb."

Alex just stares at her.

She reaches toward him and he steps back, alarmed for reasons he can't explain.

"The mark," she mutters, staring not at him but at his pants— at his leg.

At his scar. As though she can see right through the fabric to the scar that winds its way around his upper thigh.

"The mark," she says again.

"M-my twin's umbilical cord," he stammers, unsure why he has become so unnerved. "It was wrapped around my leg when we were born."

"A lie," she croaks.

"What?"

"That mark. It was caused by threads. The threads—"

He shivers, suddenly cold.

"You," she barks out, and he is rooted to the spot by the power of her low voice. "You wrestled with Fate. Before you were even born. You wrestled with the threads of Fate. In the womb. It damaged you, didn't it? Made it hard to walk like other men." Her words send an icy chill through him, seem to choke him from the inside.

"I did what?"

She ignores him and goes right on. "Why would you want to grapple with Fate again, boy?" she presses. "Go find your friends and resume your battles. You and I will meet again."

After the summer solstice, it will be too late. He can't lead the army against the Persians, he can't help Heph and Kat, until he is finished here. *Two days.*

He wonders if he can get out of this place, with its windowless, doorless walls, wonders if he is trapped in here, considering that the stone arch is next to a wall. He has a sudden need to get out, to feel the sun on his face, the breeze in his hair. But first, he needs answers. "Where is the stranger whose blood will mingle with mine?"

"Close," the crone says. "Closer than you think!"

Anger pumps through his veins. He is tired of riddles. "Where is the talisman I need?" he asks, more loudly now.

"Closer than you think!" she repeats gleefully, her laughter echoing off the walls.

His head is spinning. She won't help him. And Philip is dead. Even though he heard the rumors along the road, he still can't really process what she has told him. That he is now king.

"And the Spirit Eaters?"

She laughs, her blind eyes rolling upward. Smiling, she pushes an oily lock of white hair away from her face and says, "When the time comes, you will find them...where all the knots of fate are tangled together."

That much, at least, is clear. "I thank you, servant of Fate," he says, turning toward the arch, urgency pumping through his veins now. He's got to get out of here or he will suffocate. He needs fresh air. He needs to think.

"Don't thank me yet, young king," she croons, her eerie laughter ricocheting off the golden walls.

He hurries under the stone arch in front of the rear wall...and onto the windswept little square at the high edge of the citadel.

Clouds have filled the sky. How long was he in the temple? There is something in the air that is...different. He walks to the wall and looks down into the little street below. What he sees is so unreal he turns away and rubs his eyes. Surely his time in the golden Temple of Midas has addled his mind. The news of becoming king. The strange words about fate and its threads.

He turns back. No, this is real. The furniture on the roofs below is scattered, broken, the mattresses and pillows shredded. The woman who carded wool is a heap of bloody rags, a hand, a foot. The man who swept is a skull with dark hair and some ribs.

Spirit Eaters.

He reels, gripping the stone wall to prevent himself from collapsing. This is their work. It must be.

Heart in his throat, he dashes down the crumbling staircase. More bones and body parts. Doors and window shutters have been ripped off houses. Roofs and walls have been torn open. He stops to look through the gaping hole in the wall of a house. The furniture has been thrown around and broken, and the floor is smeared with blood.

Down and down the curling streets of the city he runs, frantic, in search of a single living soul...someone he can save, someone who can tell him what happened...

Until, nearly out of breath, he hears something behind him, soft as a whisper, chilling as an old wrinkled finger tracing up the back of his neck.

He swivels around.

No one's there.

A flash of darkness.

One of the creatures, left behind? Or something else...

A shadow.

A figure?

He could swear there's a human darting between the fallen rubble and remains.

He pivots again, but before he can see what has been following him, a sack goes over his head and a heavy weight tackles him to the ground, turning the whole world black.

CHAPTER TWENTY-SEVEN

ZOFIA

ZOFIA HAS A CHOICE.

She could choose to believe that she is helpless. That all of the desperate decisions that have governed her life have only entangled her further in an unseen web, a preordained plan over which she has no control. She can choose to believe that Fate is a trap, a curse, a slow-unfolding terror into which she has birthed an innocent being, who now, too, will become inextricably entangled.

She can choose fear.

Or.

She can choose, instead, to believe in something else. She can choose to believe that her choices matter, that evil like the Spirit Eaters can be conquered.

That humans can prevail, even if the gods could not.

That love can take many forms, that it can surprise us again and again, and when we are at our lowest, offer us a hand and a way out.

Zo has chosen hope. It is the only way to go forward.

But as they've traveled the Royal Road, unreeling before her like the snake of fate, bringing back eerie memories as though from another life ago, though they are shockingly recent, it has been hard. She has clung close to Mandana, always keeping her strapped to her body, not just for the ease of nursing her while traveling, but because feeling that tiny heartbeat against her own is sometimes the only thing that keeps her from slipping into the dark thoughts and fears that threaten to overtake her at every stop, at every cruel memory.

But when the New Amazons had settled into their hidden camp this afternoon, not more than a mile from the Royal Road, the air was filled with terrible, wrenching screams. Zo's heart nearly stopped, and for a moment, she forgot to choose hope. Fear came rushing back in, cold and splintered. Ugly and strangling. Trembling, Zo emerged from her tent, holding the baby. Those who had been stacking firewood or feeding horses had stopped and looked fearfully at the sky.

For Zo, the screams—the sheer horror of them—were not unfamiliar. They brought back the terror of that day at the brothel...

The day the Spirit Eater descended.

The day they lost a sister to its fury, its unfathomable hunger, its reckless, violent power.

So when they turned to their leader, perhaps they should not have been surprised by his response. Stepping from his tent, alongside Alecta—who had taken up sleeping with the warrior king every night despite the censure she received from the other women for doing so—Pyrolithos scanned their camp, then the sky. Then he looked each woman in the eye, and Zo knew what he was going to say before he said it.

"It is a sign. We have come closer than we thought."

The Spirit Eaters had come again. Somewhere very near.

And so, in stark silence, they mounted their horses and rode straight toward the direction of the horrific sounds and blackened sky: a city rising high into the air, curled around a steep and massive gray rock.

The city of Gordium, famed, Zo knows, for once having

been the home of King Midas, a center of uncontained greed and power. A place, too, known for drawing out the foolish pride of men who traveled there to try to prove their prowess by taking a turn at untying the Gordian knot, though none has ever succeeded.

They'll probably keep trying until the end of time, Zo thinks. Men are all slaves to their pride, and it will forever be their weakness.

The same could be said of Pyrolithos, who leads their party from several horse lengths ahead. He does not look well of late, and Zo must wonder what illness is eating away at him. An illness, surely, of the heart and not of health. For he has been even more ruthless than anyone had imagined when they first set out.

They all have. They've had to be. Fierce and unforgiving. That is the whole point of their band. And yet. Pyrolithos has been more than ruthless—he has been blood hungry and vacant. And now that darkness seems to be taking its toll. He is less animated, narrower somehow, where he used to take up whole rooms with his presence. It occurs to Zo that Pyrolithos looks far too weak and ill to create any more diamond cages for the beasts. Yesterday, when she brought Mandana to calm the creature before the Amazons went to sleep, it seemed the once-glowing adamantine bars had turned to iron or even—in some places—smoke. She wondered whether the creature would break out and kill them all in their sleep.

Yes, some angry fire inside Pyrolithos is burning dangerously low, and that gives Zo almost as much trepidation as the thought of facing the Spirit Eaters.

When they arrive at the base of the city, though, it is clear the damage has been done, and they are too late. There is no time for relief in it: the women stare in shock and disgust at the disaster that lies before them, towering along the sides of the rock city, and Zo tightens the straps of her sack, pulling Mandana in closer.

It is as if a great fire has ravaged the place—a fire with teeth.

Heaps of bones—human and horse, as far as Zo can tell—litter the road near the gate. She shudders, looking at the tall city before them. No, it is no longer a city, vibrant with people living, working, buying, and trading goods. It is a tomb full of chewed bones.

Everything in her screams to protect her child, to flee. But if she fled, she'd be considered a traitor, and possibly beheaded if caught. She has little choice but to hold her ground, to refuse fear even as it rattles through her.

Alecta looks nervous, too. As for Pyrolithos, it's impossible to say.

"We have to get supplies, anyway," he mutters to Alecta, just loud enough for the others nearby to hear.

And it's true that they're running out of food, though the idea of pillaging this haunted, tortured place is sickening. Zo can't help but wonder if it's not their need for food but the king's desperation to find another Spirit Eater that drives him to dismount, stepping over the ripped-open corpses that must have once been the city guards, and shove open the gates himself.

All the women, including Zo, reluctantly follow, their backs straight, admitting no fear, though Zo knows they are feeling it as much as she is. Their horses, however, smell death and roll their heads in protest rather than enter the city. They struggle to turn around, neighing loudly as their hooves dance sideways. Only with difficulty are they forced forward, over piles of bones and puddles of blood at the city gate.

They ride up a street circling the outer city, past ravaged shops and homes, their nervous mounts stepping over body parts. The coppery scent of blood is nauseating. The silence is so loud that it hurts Zo's ears. There is no sign of life. No barking dog. No crowing chicken, bleating goat, or crying baby. And memories of the village she passed through in the Eastern Mountains flood back to her, causing her whole body to shake and baby Mandana to mewl softly against her chest.

Zo notices up ahead something shining on the street. A broken wooden casket has spilled its contents—dozens of thick gold coins—into the street in front of one business. Next to it is a skeletal arm.

Pyrolithos nods, sliding off his mount.

Alecta, too, dismounts, and the two scoop up the gold and throw it in their saddlebags. Then they enter the shop nearby— a moneylender's.

Zo slips off her horse and stands in the shadows, straining her ears for any indication of Spirit Eaters. But all she hears is the sounds of Pyrolithos and Alecta throwing furniture around in their search for loot.

The other women boldly disperse, after more of the same.

Zo doesn't want gold. Or wine. Or food. She wants to leave this place with her baby. The revolting smell of blood and organs on hot stone rises in the humid air. Then, for the first time in this city of death, she hears some sign of life: the buzzing of flies that have come to drink dead blood and devour dead flesh. She puts her hands over her mouth, willing herself not to be sick.

She moves apart from the others, trying to get a view from one of the city walls, a reminder that the rest of the world is still thriving, that there is green and hope and life beyond this terrible place.

She takes several turns down abandoned roads when she hears something else. She stops abruptly.

Men's voices, loud and arguing, coming from around the corner. Survivors! Her heart leaps with hope and she kicks the sides of her horse.

But as she trots closer, a dangerous feeling winds up her throat. What kind of men might they be, and why are they arguing so violently? More looters, probably. Like them. And potentially just as lethal.

She should call for reinforcements, prepare to attack.

First, she needs to know for certain. She cannot stand the loss of more innocent lives on her hands.

She ties her horse to a post and looks for a place to hide Mandana, who has drifted to sleep in the eerie quiet. Across the narrow, curved street is a destroyed shop, whose mattresses and pillows for sale have been torn to shreds. Silently, she removes the baby from her back and sets her down on a soft heap of feathers. Mandana moans softly, yawns, and falls back to sleep.

Staring at her for a moment, Zo considers whether it is safer to carry her. No, she'll be fine here just for a moment or two.

Zo darts back out of the shop and creeps closer to the men, flattening herself against the corner of a stone house, and holds her breath.

"On what grounds?" a man says in Greek-accented Persian. "Unhand me! Do you even know who I am?"

"We know who ya' are," replies a deeper voice, a Persian voice. "There's not many who look like ya' in this land."

A higher, edgier voice joins in. "We been trailing you for two days. Ran away from your army, did ya? Left a girl to take your place in battle."

"What?" the captured man says, sounding truly flustered. "I know not of what you speak."

"You've a funny way a running your country," says the first man. "Like no king I ever heard of. First, you kill your father. Then, you put a girl in charge of your pathetic little mishmash army."

Zo wonders which king could be the soldiers' prisoner. There are dozens of Greek kings. Every island has one.

"I've done no such thing. If I am a political prisoner, then I demand you take me to the Great King."

One of them laughs wickedly. "Oh, we don't work for the Great King—and yer hardly in a position to demand anything of us."

"Ain't you heard of us, then?" says another, snickering.

The first shoves him and the man lets out a grunt.

"What? He don't even realize he's reckoning with Assassins, does he? Some king."

"Shut it," says the first man.

Zo doesn't hear the rest because, with a gasp, she steps back and away from the wall.

Assassins. The word wrenches through her with a slicing fear. The sinister group of murderers who have tried for the past year to kill her: unbelievably, they are here, in this remote, devastated city where everyone else is dead.

Another trick of fate, coiling itself ever tighter around her neck.

Steadying the tremor in her fingers, she removes her blow dart tube and three poisoned darts from the pouch at her belt. Two of the darts are tipped with deadly nightshade, the poison she and Badri made that kills almost instantaneously. The other is laced with scorpion venom, a toxin that paralyzes the limbs and relaxes the mind for several minutes before killing, often causing its victim to tell truths they might otherwise have wanted to hide.

Holding her breath, she tiptoes back to the wall and peers around the corner. Three men dressed like civilians—two Persians and an Ethiopian from the looks of them—are holding a handsome young blond man. One of the Persians has tied the Greek's hands and holds a long length of rope. The others hold curved daggers.

She inserts the truth-telling dart into the tube, aims, and blows hard. The tiny winged dart strikes exactly where she wanted it to—in the neck of the Persian with the weapon.

He slaps at it as if it were a stinging insect, pushing it more deeply into his neck. He drops the dagger, pulls out the dart, looks at it, and screams. Panicked, he flails his arms, sending his rust-colored cloak to the ground as he topples beside it. The Persian holding the prisoner's ropes drops them, pulls out his dagger, and races toward Zo, along with the Ethiopian. She has readied the second dart, the killing one. She blows hard, and it sticks in the cheek of the Persian. He shrieks, pulls it out, and keeps coming for her. Behind him, she sees the blond prisoner pick up the first man's fallen cloak with his bound hands and throw it over the Ethiopian from behind, tackling him to the ground. Straddling his neck, he wrenches it hard with a sickening snap.

The man coming toward her is more than twice her size, with murder in his dark eyes. His face is beet red with rage. She blows a second dart at him; it hits him in the shoulder. He raises his dagger—it seems like it is in slow motion—and she wonders how long before the poison fells him. Too long. She turns to run, feels the tug of his knife on the loose material at the back of her robe, hears the sickening rip of linen, and feels the soft air on exposed skin. She is going to die.

A thud resounds behind her. She can't stop running. She needs to… At the top of the tiny street, she realizes there are no footsteps behind her. She stops, turns, and sees her pursuer flat on his face, a dagger in his back. The young blond king has his foot on the man's shoulder. He looks at her, pulls out the dagger, and wipes off the blood on the dead man's tunic.

"I won't hurt you, you know," he calls to her, in Greek-accented Persian.

Slowly, still breathing heavily, she approaches him. When their eyes meet, she realizes that his are unusual, one sky blue and the other dark brown, which reminds her of…

But no, that couldn't be. Though, he would be about the right age, seventeen or eighteen, and athletic. His wavy hair is the color of sunshine, his skin a golden tan.

Silently, she cuts the ropes binding his wrists, marveling at how well he fought bound. What could he do with both hands free? "I don't know what a beautiful girl like you is doing here alone," he says, "armed with poison darts in this city of bones, but I am lucky you are."

Averting her gaze from his, she kneels beside the Assassins she shot with the truth-telling dart. The Greek comes over and helps roll the man over. He is still breathing.

"Hey!" She shakes him by the shoulders. "I have questions."

"Huh?" he asks sleepily, his eyes shut. "I will never reveal…"

"You will answer me," she insists, knowing he will not be able to fight the poison coursing through his veins. He will tell the truth before he dies. Badri, mistress of poisons, said they all do.

"Tell me the location of Ochus, the Chief Assassin's son," she says.

The man laughs feebly, his eyes still tightly closed. "Ochus," he mutters in disgust. "No one knows where the traitor is. He disappeared after killing many of his brothers in Macedon."

Kneeling on the other side of the Assassin, the Greek tenses at this. His strange eyes meet hers with questions. She refocuses on her prisoner. "What brothers did he kill in Macedon?"

The man smiles. Clearly the poison is having the desired effect: that of intoxication. "When the Persian princess was sent to Macedon," he says, slurring his words, "Ochus was supposed to kill her and make it seem as if Alexander did it. To start a war. We wanted war with Macedon, not a marriage alliance," he says and stops. Zo wonders if he has fallen asleep.

She shakes him again. "Yes?" she says. "Then what?"

"But his father, Darius, didn't trust him," the man continues, his voice sleepy and hoarse. "He had Assassins among the Persian guards that escorted her. Even among the Macedonian guards at the…" He is drifting off. "At the palace." He falls silent and, a few moments later, starts to snore.

She slaps him. "What did Ochus do to them?" Though she suspects she already knows.

"Killed 'em," he murmurs.

Zo suddenly understands what happened that horrible night when she lost both men she loved. Ochus didn't kill Cosmas. The Assassins did.

In retaliation—and to protect *her*—Ochus killed them all.

Ochus didn't abandon her on a whim. He had to disappear beyond the reach of the Assassins, including the most powerful one of all, his own father.

If what she suspects is true, it means that Ochus was acting out of loyalty. *To her.* He really did love her. The knowledge is like a sudden spring after the most bitter winter—a crisp hope inflates her lungs.

The Assassin is snoring loudly again. She pinches his nostrils and puts a hand over his open mouth. He winces and shakes his head. "What are your instructions now?" she asks. "Why were you arresting this man?"

He purses his lips. "Instructions…in the hidden pocket…of my cloak."

The young Greek king helps her roll the man off his long brown cloak, and together they examine it, but they cannot find a pocket.

"Where?" the prisoner says.

"Button." The man gasps. "On the…back."

The Greek holds up the cloak, and Zo sees a decorative button on the pointed bottom of the back. The thought occurs to her that Ochus's cloak, which she left back at the camp, has one, too, which she thought was merely sewn on as a decoration. But when she looks more closely at the button, she realizes the cloth of the border has been slipped around the button. Slowly, she unbuttons it. And finds a tiny pocket. Inside is a scroll with Persian writing.

She unwinds it and reads aloud. *"Find King Alexander of Macedon and bring him alive to the Chief Assassin. Blond. One blue eye, one brown eye. Slight limp. Snake birthmark on left thigh.'"*

She looks up, the truth of the situation dawning on her.

"Are you…"

He nods. "I am. And I will arrange for you to receive a royal reward, when I can."

So her hunch was right. The man standing before her is none other than Alexander of Macedon. The man she was supposed to marry last summer when she ran off to be with Cosmas instead. The man she hoped, last fall, to convince to come to Persia with her, to seek and destroy the Spirit Eaters.

"You are king now?" she asks, her voice a whisper.

He nods, sadness shining in his eyes. "I've only just learned of my father's death."

She gapes at his beauty. The golden hair and golden skin. The straight nose and square jaw. The perfection of his slender yet muscular body. If he does limp, she has not noticed it. And the mismatched eyes—which she thought of as a deformity—are arresting, hypnotizing. This is the creature she worked so hard to avoid marrying, this tall, strong, gloriously handsome person. She was enslaved by rogue slave traders, and nearly died from starvation and a fall from a Pegasus, all to avoid marrying...*this*.

She starts to laugh—a long, loud, uncontrolled bellow. Her belly aches, and she bends over it, unable to stop herself.

A kindly hand touches her arm. "Are you...all right?" he says.

"Yes." She wipes away tears. "Yes."

"I would like to know the name of my savior," he says, "so that in future I can suitably reward her."

"Zofia." She gasps for air. "Princess...Zofia of Sardis."

He tilts his head and blinks in confusion. "Surely you can't be... Are you the Persian girl I didn't want to marry?"

"I didn't want to marry you, either!" It comes out like a cry of glee. "Last summer, I ran away from my family in Sardis to avoid it. And when a soothsayer said it was fated for my blood to mingle with that of Prince Alexander of Macedon, I did everything I could to change that fate."

He inhales sharply. "What did she say exactly?"

"Just that—that my blood was destined to mingle with...with yours." She has stopped laughing as his face goes pale and serious.

"An oracle told me something, too, recently. That I was to

accomplish something great, something unthinkable—but only with the help of a stranger *whose blood is destined to mingle with mine.*"

She eyes him. "What thing? What great thing are you—are we—destined to do together, then?"

He pauses, as if trying to read her face. Finally, he opens his mouth and says something she never expected. "Defeat the Spirit Eaters."

They stare at each other in wonder. Then he says, "But you did come to Macedon to marry me, last fall."

"I wanted to tell you about the Spirit Eaters. I know where their lairs are in the Eastern Mountains. I've been there. I hoped you and I could lead an army there to destroy them."

"Have you seen them?"

"I—" Where to start? How to tell him?

"Yes, last year. Now I am with the New Amazons. Out of Dardania. Perhaps you have heard of them. Of *us*."

Alexander's eyes open wide in surprise. But before he can respond, a cry resonates through the air.

The baby.

Zo is already racing around the corner as panic slices through her. Mandana.

Wordlessly, she runs to the mattress shop.

Mandana has awakened, wriggled out of the blanket, and lies, clad only in her diaper, on a heap of feathers. As Zo starts to pick her up, she freezes, staring down at her child.

Coming up beside her, Alexander sucks in his breath. "By all the gods," he says.

"What?" Her voice comes out in a harsh whisper. Is he seeing what she's seeing?

"The baby…with wings."

Slowly, she nods. Mandana gurgles and coos. All the mattress feathers sticking out from behind her back look just like the image she saw on Kohinoor's cave wall—like *wings*.

"I saw a statue just like that in a temple I was in not an hour ago," the young king says.

"What temple?" Her voice has gone tense with horror.

"Here, in the city, but to most people it looks like an arch. Only Blood Magics can enter."

Zo wrenches her gaze from the baby and stares at him in wonder. "Are you a Blood Magic?" Of all the strange tales she heard of Alexander of Macedon, this was not one of them.

"I...was," he says. "But I still have something that allowed me to get in. At least, that's what the old woman who worked there said."

"What old woman?" she shrieks, her heart pounding. "What did she look like?" She bends down to pick up Mandana, letting the feathers fall away as she holds the baby to her chest. Fear and panic and *knowing* rise in her like bile. She needs to get away from here. Far away.

"Ancient. Stringy gray hair. Cloudy purple eyes. Blind, I think. A voice like an oxcart rolling over gravel."

Now Zo's heart beats so fast she wonders if she is going to faint.

Kohinoor is here.

Kohinoor wants her baby.

The baby with wings.

"We have to get out of here. Now." She can hardly get her breath. As Zo quickly hurries out of the shop and around the corner, she explains over her shoulder, "That old woman's name is Kohinoor, and she has been stalking me for a year now. I don't know why, but she will do anything to get her hands on my baby." They must find the other Amazons. Surely the army of women would protect them from Kohinoor, from other Assassins tracking them.

"What do you mean she's been stalking you?" the king asks, following her. "If—"

"There's no time!" she cries, panic rising inside her. "We need to find the others!"

"The others..." he says slowly, hesitation in his voice.

"You cannot stay in this city of the dead," Zo says, making the decision on the spot. "We'll find the New Amazons. They're here, looting. We will find our leader, Pyrolithos. You will come back with us to our camp. It is less than a mile from here. And if we are truly fated to...to work together...then we must not be parted, not yet."

Alexander pauses, looking up at the highest part of the city. Then he lowers his gaze to Zo, and she feels the burning intensity of his mismatched eyes. A blush rises hot and red on her neck and cheeks as she stares at a crack in the ground.

"All right, then," he says at last. "Let's go."

CHAPTER TWENTY-EIGHT

CYNANE

PYROLITHOS CAN FEEL THE HEAT OF ALECTA'S gaze on his skin, on the back of his neck, on his sweating, tensed muscles, as together they pick their way carefully through the abandoned Midas palace crowning the citadel of Gordium. But he doesn't turn around. Can't look her in the eyes. Not right now.

The other women have scattered throughout the ruined city, gathering and pillaging what they can. But the palace is eerily silent, save for his and Alecta's footsteps. The building itself is ancient, the rooms smaller and ceilings lower than any palaces built in the last two hundred years. Yet every surface is plated with thin sheets of hammered gold—almost blindingly so. Though he can appreciate a spectacle, Pyrolithos has never been one for gaudiness. Still, he can't help but feel temporarily dazzled by the patterns gleaming in the gold—here rosettes, keys, meanders, waves; there palmettes, ivy, hanging lotus buds. The furniture, too, is wrapped in gold and studded with emeralds, agates, and carnelians—in stark contrast to the singed bones that lie scattered about in pools of blood and bile.

He enters what must have been the king's bedchamber, brightly lit, now, by sunshine streaming in through the broken roof. At its center sits a golden pillared bed studded with ame-thysts and covered in dark silken sheets. Next to the bed stands a life-size golden statue of a girl of about eight years old. She is so realistic—including the look of surprise and pain on her pretty round face—that the question springs from his lips with-out pause. "Could it be her? The daughter Midas touched and…"

"Turned to gold," Alecta finishes. She walks around the statue slowly, a flicker of sadness playing across the angles of her face. "It must be. Though perhaps it is just a reminder and not re-ally *her.*"

What would it have been like for King Midas to know that he killed the person he loved most?

Pyrolithos's palms are sweating; he drags them across his pants, lets out a breath.

He hadn't *planned* on doing this today.

He's been waiting for the right opportunity, as his strength subsides, and his body softens, and the bars of the Spirit Eater's cage weaken…all the while hoping it would never come, and yet knowing it had to come.

The leaden realization that today is the day causes his heart to stutter and his head to throb.

If Alecta can tell, she makes no show of fear. "Should we take her?" She sets a hand on the little golden girl's shoulder.

"No," he says quickly, putting a hand on Alecta's arm, then pulling it away again. He could not bear this reminder of what he will have done. "We have enough."

This is it. He must do it.

The ultimate betrayal, to obtain the ultimate strength. He has to keep his goals in mind. The promises he's made to the other women. If he takes the right steps, they could become the most powerful fighting force in the world.

Make the Aesarian Lords cower before them.

Before him.

And all it requires is a simple movement of his hand, the flash of his dagger.

Mere seconds. Glimmering silver. The heat and pulse of blood when it's first released from flesh. The look of shock that will fix in her eyes. The hurt. The knowing.

He has only been truly known once: by Audata. But she died a terrible, forgotten death.

And he is no longer a child, no longer a woman, no longer weak.

No—he won't think of his mother, won't let the memory sink him, drowning his will.

Love comes and goes or turns to hatred and disgust. Glory stays forever, even long after men die. A thousand years ago, the proud warrior Achilles was given a choice by the gods: a short life and everlasting glory, or a long, happy life, with friends and family, and ignominious obscurity after death. He chose the former.

Which is why we know his name.

"We are alone," Pyrolithos whispers. *And I will be more alone, soon, than I have ever been in my life.*

"That we are," Alecta says, her voice carrying a current of emotion he finds hard to interpret. There is too much of it. He wonders, sometimes, how she can feel so much, so powerfully, and still stand.

How she can take it.

Her hand slips into his, pulses once. Then, gently, she pulls him away from the child statue. And though he knows exactly what he must do, what he *will* do, he allows himself, one last time, to be tugged slowly, gently, downward.

The royal bed, laden in gold and silk, catches them as they fall.

Alecta's dark lashes curl from her pale cheek. He decides to remember her like this, warm and content, one lean arm flung out over her pillow. He stares at her a very long time, and she stares back.

Then slowly, quietly, he reaches over for his belt on the floor and takes out his dagger, honed to a deadly point. There will only be a little pain. He gazes at the gleaming iron. He tests it first on the pad of his thumb. A drop of red blooms there.

"What is it?" Alecta asks. Her fiery hair spills over the sheets as she sits up.

"Do you remember, along the way, those innocent people I killed?" he asks, his voice shaking. "The farmer in Paeonia, the waitress in Pessinus, the fisherman in Athens…"

She pulls a sheet up to cover herself.

"I am not cruel by nature. I wasn't born this way. But nor was I born with…power. Not like this. Not magic. Do you understand?"

She shakes her head, but by the flicker of fear in her eyes, the sudden stiffening of her muscles, he guesses she *does* understand.

"I needed to do it," he whispers.

"No."

"Yes. To keep my powers. To stay like this—a man. To keep the Spirit Eater contained in its cage."

Alecta stares at him through narrowed eyes. "Then stop. Stop pretending to be someone you're not."

"And the Spirit Eaters?" Pyrolithos asks, his voice breaking with desperation as he turns to look her in the eyes again. "Without Smoke Blood, we will never be able to have an army. I could never control them."

"We are already formidable," Alecta says, her voice holding steady. Perhaps he was wrong—perhaps she is not afraid, only prepared to face him, to fight if necessary. The thought sends a shiver down his spine. Does she not fear him because she trusts him? Or because she knows exactly what he intends to do to her, and is still willing to stare him down, unblinking?

"We don't need them," she says, touching his arm. "The beasts. The creature can go. I would rather have you. *You*."

Gently, he shakes off her grip. "You don't understand. All my life I wanted power. I wanted to lead. And I needed to be a man to do it. Now I have everything within my grasp. And everything to lose…"

He can do this. He is strong. He can be cruel when necessary. He has been practicing for as long as he can remember.

For a moment, she is silent.

"Very well, then," she says at last.

He turns again to look at her, to study her features, so glorious, all hard angles and mournful eyes and angry mouth and wild hair.

"If all you want in the world is this—is power—if you choose that over me, then you have made *my* choice, too." Slowly, she lets the sheet drop away from her body, revealing herself to him.

He is overcome by the power of her body—not the desire that awakens inside him all over again, and not her fighting strength either, but the simple miracle of her existence taking form before him, so human, so unfathomable. His and yet not his. No one's.

Free.

All her life, Alecta was a prostitute. And yet she is the freest person he has ever met.

Her hand pulls at his—the one holding the dagger. "I choose," she says again.

Pyrolithos holds the knife so tightly that his knuckles turn white. His hand aches. Everything he has ever wanted is at his fingertips.

He remembers the lost, motherless little girl everyone laughed at for wanting to learn the use of arms. Of all her dreams of commanding an army and ruling a nation, dreams that could never come true.

How can he hesitate? How can he disappoint the girl he was,

the girl who did everything she could, sacrificed everything, to be where he is now?

He forces himself to push the tip into the side of Alecta's neck, just over the large vein. A pearl of blood blooms on the pale skin. Alecta's full lips are parted. Her eyes stay focused on him, the calm flooding her features so profound that it shakes him.

With a growl, Pyrolithos flings the knife across the room.

It falls to the floor with a clatter.

He is shuddering uncontrollably. The magic rages up in him, hot and smoky and choking, craving more of itself. Hungry. So hungry. Never satisfied. His head hammers with a beating, relentless sound of screaming and tearing, as though the Spirit Eaters have found him and are sucking out his soul through his skull. The Smoke magic wants what it wants. He must betray. *He must betray.*

No.

He must resist. He can resist. He *will* resist.

He doesn't know how it happens, but somehow he is on the floor, curled in on himself, panting for breath, arms over his head to block out the glare of the setting sun through the windows, ricocheting off all that gold.

Gold, gold, gold.

Light, light, light.

But no. The fire, the smoke, the blackness, the hate, the hunger. These things keep rising up and demanding the last of his strength. He can't even pry open his eyes.

He understands now the truth: that if he doesn't betray Alecta, he has chosen to betray himself instead, to betray his magic. And the magic is angry. Unrelenting.

How much time passes, he cannot say—he is feverish, shaking, sweating, and sick.

Strong arms wrap around him. Maybe they have always been there.

"Shhh" is all she says. "Let it go. Let it all go. The hate and pain and anger."

How does she know? How *can* she know? His mind is alive with torture. His body is dying from the recoil of the magic. He won't survive. He made a mistake and now it's too late. He is weak. He is nothing. He will surely die.

"I am here," her voice says, and a sob opens up inside of him, a well of sound and water and fear he knows will drown him—of sadness, loss, and hurt that has been held underground so long, swelling and falling, he had forgotten it was there.

Tears run down his face.

"I will never leave you," her voice says.

Her voice is a rope. Pulling him up out of the waters, out of the depths, out of the darkness, out of the hurt.

I will never leave you.

In that moment, she is his mother and his lover. She is his own self, past, present, and future. She is everything. She is the only way forward, the only way up.

Her words, such simple ones, really, change everything. They cut through the smoke.

He can breathe again. Months—no, *years*—of rage are draining out of him. He is weak, but now it is a good kind of weak. Tired. Spent. But cleaned out. Purged. Renewed.

Steadying himself, he revels in the release of tension as even his body begins to change. The convulsions are akin to what birth pains must feel like—racking and whole. And yet, euphoric. He is birthing himself anew.

Alecta gasps, pushing his sweaty hair out of his face.

"Cynane," she whispers.

And that's when he knows. He is no longer a he. He is no longer Pyrolithos.

He—*she*—is Cynane again.

Her hands find their way to Alecta's shoulders, her fingers graze the cut where her knife barely punctured Alecta's skin, just at the base of her neck. She wants to weep. How could she have done that?

"It's all right," Alecta whispers.

And this time, when she kisses her, the kiss is a whole other kind of experience. Sweet and salt. Slow and intentional. Cynane sees now how touch isn't just a replacement for love, or even a trigger for its release. How, in that moment, touch *is* love. They are forming it from nothing, like gods.

The miracle of it is so consuming that for a few seconds they don't notice the way the walls and floor thrum with vibration, as though the world itself is changing beneath them and because of them.

And then the rest of the New Amazons are pouring into the room, and the women pull apart. There are gasps and murmurs as the Amazons see what has become of their leader. Still in the clothing of Pyrolithos.

Now Cynane.

One by one, they kneel down before her.

Zo kneels, too, bringing her child down to the floor with her.

The person beside Zo is no woman warrior, though.

The last person standing is a man. And not just any man.

Cynane's brother.

Alexander.

CHAPTER TWENTY-NINE

HEPHAESTION

THE FOREST HERE IS DIFFERENT FROM THE ONES back home. The trees are scrubbier and more densely packed—and the scents: rich and cedary and so sweet. Everywhere, fat bees hover, abuzz with the warmth of coming summer. Hephaestion, too, is buzzing with something—urgency, or perhaps fear—fear of losing Kat. No, it's humiliation, or frustration, or perhaps just a cloying, syrupy impatience. Kat is so near and yet so far. It has been nine days since he asked her the question he could hardly bear to ask—nine days since he demanded the status of her feelings for him. Nine days since she once again told him nothing, gave him no assurance. Is he crazy to think he still has a chance?

He rode this far into the woods, at first, because he needed to be alone. Needed the cool of the forest shade and the time to clear his head, to escape the heat of her always watching him with those big, unreadable eyes. If she doesn't want him, so be it. But the torture of not knowing is too much.

Only once he was surrounded by the hum of so many low hives, throbbing and spinning with active bees, did the idea come to him: if Kat wants someone big and dopey and thoughtful like Jacob, Heph can do that. He can impress her, bring her back some of Cimmera's precious honey. There is a saying about honey, isn't there? That it's the best way to catch a fly.

Kat is no fly. And yet she is a thing he cannot catch. That much is true.

She is more like one of these bees. Innocent, hardworking, full of impossible sweetness, and only a sting of pain away.

The harder he tries *not* to think of her, of her sweetness, of her sweet mouth, of all the parts of her that are infinitely, unbearably fragrant with the scent of her, the less he is able to stop himself.

He slaps away another stinging bee.

This idea to gather honeycombs came to him in a heady rush, as though he had tilted his head back and swallowed a rich, golden mead—it left him dizzy and elated. Something soft and sweet for her. Something to remind her he is more than just Alexander's right-hand man, more than a soldier, more than a fling. To show her he is steady and that she can trust him, that he's not going anywhere.

Of course, however, he *has* gone somewhere. He has ridden so far from their camp, in fact, that it takes him the better part of the morning to find his way back, and by the time he does, his victory over the bees seems to have intoxicated him completely. In fact, he is light-headed with victory.

Something isn't right. He is *too* light-headed, he realizes, as he dismounts, stumbling into Kat's—the "king's"—tent. The world tips around him, the basket falls from his arm, and he collapses onto all fours like a dog. He is sick—somehow his desire for her has driven him to madness. That must be it!

No, that's nonsense. He must have a fever. Heatstroke.

He was stung many times—could that be it?—but bee stings never bothered him before.

"Heph!" He feels her long hair tickle his face, and from deep within him, a demented laugh bursts out.

"He's drunk, the fool," Jacob growls. Heph hates Jacob, his too-broad shoulders, his too-wide smile.

"It's not yet noon. Heph doesn't drink unwatered wine in the morning," Kat says, her voice tight with worry.

Heph rolls onto his back, heavy and helpless.

"Then explain this," Jacob says.

Heph would like to explain it with his fists, but he can't seem to sit up.

A thin boy's voice cuts into the dimness of his mind. "Is he sick? Egyptian priests can heal him." Arridheus.

Cool hands touch his face. "Heph," Kat whispers. He half opens his eyes, and her face goes in and out of focus. "What happened?"

He gestures to the basket he dragged in with him, now on the floor. "Honeycombs. I was in the woods and found so many honeycombs. I brought you some, Alexander." He chuckles and closes his heavy eyelids.

"Don't touch it, Arridheus!" Kat commands.

A bee lifts out of the basket, hovering nearby. Heph shudders, suddenly cold.

"Hold on," Kat whispers, and then goes quiet.

Heph wants to know what she's doing but he cannot keep his eyes open or his mind working, and gradually his world goes dark.

When he rises into consciousness through the pounding of his head sometime later, orange light slants through the tent flaps and glints off Kat's golden breastplate. She sits beside him on her bed, dabbing his forehead with mint water. Outside, he hears men issue orders, horses whinny, carts creak and roll by. Is the army moving camp? At this hour?

"What happened?" he asks, his voice a raspy whisper.

"Our salvation, I think," she replies, "even though it comes at the cost of a splitting headache." A cup of cool water meets his lips. He drinks greedily.

"The honey…" he says, wiping his chin.

"Yes, the honey. It took me a while to sift through the bee's mind—hectic and…and frenzied. But then I saw what he was after. The pollen from a flower with a beautiful purple bloom."

Heph rises to his elbows, and the world swings heavily to one side. He slips back down onto his back and groans.

"I think their honey is highly intoxicating to humans." She wrings out the cloth in a basin. "Though the bees themselves have gotten used to it."

He opens his eyes again. He needs to get up, but somehow his body doesn't follow his instructions. Why is Kat talking about bees? They have to craft a strategy to battle the Persians camped just a few miles away. After the battle of the Granicus River, their army was left unmolested as they marched east along the Royal Road. And now, only half a day's march from the city of Gordium, their scouts have told them that the Third Persian Cohort waits just ahead, blocking their path.

A man's voice just outside the tent calls out. "We'll pack King Alexander's tent soon, Kaunos! We're just waiting for his signal. Bring the cart around."

"Are we breaking camp?" he croaks. "Moving ahead? I thought the Persians were blocking our path."

"We're retreating."

Retreating? His head throbs. "Why?"

"Listen, Heph. I instructed the bees to vacate the hives."

"Instructed?" He knows better than to question her.

"Coaxed. They will do it." There's confidence in her voice. Her magic has evolved, even since their time on Meninx.

"Jacob has already led the men to collect the honey. Hundreds of baskets, Heph. The entire Cimmerian forest was filled with hives."

"I know," he says, his throat dry as a husk. "But why gather the honey when it is obviously poisonous?"

"We gathered the honey *because* it is poisonous," she says.

Of course. Now he feels like a bigger idiot than before.

"Not lethal, but highly intoxicating. As if you had drunk several oenochoes of wine."

"I can attest to that."

"So we're retreating a couple of miles, leaving behind half the tents, some of the treasure, and all the food..."

"Including the honey," he fills in.

"Exactly. The Persian army will think we became afraid and ran off. After they've gorged themselves on our leftovers, that's when we come in for attack." She tucks her helmet against her side and rises.

Heph forces himself to a seated position. His vision swirls, then steadies. Her shining green eyes bore into him. The last rays of the sun strike her golden-brown hair, setting it alight, setting his heart to pounding. "Beautiful," he says, appreciatively, though he is not sure if he is talking about Kat's plan or Kat herself or, most likely, both.

The next morning, as dawn brightens and warms the sky, Heph and the Greek army edge their horses back toward the very camp they vacated only yesterday. The sounds of laughter and singing echo from the site, long before it comes into view. Someone is banging a drum; others play flutes.

As the advance force approaches, he sees Persian soldiers, who have thrown off their armor, doing cartwheels and somersaults. Several dance wild jigs. Many have passed out among the tents. There must be hundreds of them acting like drunken buffoons at a wedding.

The honey has worked its magic.

Kat, in Alexander's golden armor, sits low on Bucephalus.

"What's wrong?" He tries to gentle his voice, as if approaching a skittish horse. "Don't you see? Your plan is working."

"Yes," she whispers, but there is no victory in her voice. Finally, she looks at him. "I thought coming here had cured me of...of this darkness. But now, seeing those men... Knowing what's going to happen... How can we fight them like this? It will be like slaughtering lambs in a pen. It's not fair somehow."

Heph frowns. What is she talking about? Wasn't this the whole point of their strategy?

"Yes...my lord," he says carefully. "But they would gladly slaughter *us* if they could. This is, after all, a *war.*"

Jacob, on the other side of Kat, looks at her with compassion in his eyes. "We must crush this army before Artaxerxes comes with his much larger one. If they join up, we will have no hope, and we will all be massacred. Your sadness—that...that darkness you speak of. It, too, will pass, Kat."

Heph doesn't understand what sadness Kat is talking about, nor why this girl who reveled in winning the Battle of Pellan Fields a year ago is suddenly afraid of hurting a fly. Finally, a deep sigh breaks from her as she nods and raises the battle flag. Behind them, the eerie notes of the salpinx rise, announcing imminent attack. A few of the Persian soldiers look up and laugh. Most do not even notice. And perhaps it is for the best. Heph wonders if he'd rather be boldly awake when he dies or half in a dream, already on the verge of surrendering to the endless sleep.

But before he can ponder the question, the command is sounded again and he urges his horse into motion, every thought burning away but one: *win.*

The Greek army thunders into the camp, spears outstretched, swords raised. Heph cleaves off the head of a Persian still dancing a jig. His horse crushes the bodies of countless slumbering soldiers. A soldier in baggy Persian trousers staggers out of a tent, trying to lift a spear, and Heph impales him with his own. It's a bloodbath, a massacre. Heph's arms blaze with heat and power and movement. He is all weapon, all focus.

Several dozen soldiers race toward him now from the other side of the camp, weapons at the ready; clearly, these men must not have come near the mad honey. But they are outnumbered by the Greeks, who ride systematically through the camp, killing every Persian they meet. Hundreds flee into the woods, and the Greeks gleefully hunt them down and butcher them as if they were stags.

As Kat, Heph, and Jacob return to their camp, General Chares, the Athenian commander, strides out of his tent and blocks their path, spooking Bucephalus, who whickers angrily and bucks.

"I demand a word with King Alexander," the general says. Under thick black brows, his bright blue eyes flash in a way that Heph finds unsettling. "We must discuss the equitable distribution of spoils from the Persian loot. The Boeotians have taken more than their share of gold."

"Speak, then," Heph says.

"In private." Chares grins. "Or is there a problem with that?"

"You know the king has taken a vow to mourn his father…"

"Has he now?" Chares asks, taking a step closer. "What mourning vow would prevent us from getting a glimpse of his face?"

"We will discuss this later," Jacob says gruffly, allowing his horse to take a few steps toward the general. "Move out of the way, Chares. We are exhausted from the battle."

"I say I want Alexander to take off his helmet now!" Chares pushes toward them. "Because if this man is not the king, then *I* will take command of this army. And *I* will distribute all the rich booty we have won." Greed and ambition gleam in the Athenian's eyes as he slowly unsheathes his sword.

Heph's jaw clenches and his muscles, exhausted from battle,

go hard and ready. The moment has come, the challenge they knew they'd eventually meet.

"Chares," he says calmly. "Step. Back."

But just then a man pushes his way through the crowd, crying, "King Alexander! Another regiment is coming!"

Heph whips his horse around to face the man. The men they just slaughtered, he knows, were an advance brigade of the army of Great King Artaxerxes, a much larger force.

It's impossible the full Persian army—and the Great King himself—have already reached them. His mind races. He will have to line up the infantry…

"No, my lord! Women!"

The crowd parts as he, Kat, and Heph ride to the other side of the camp, their men following. A line of Greek archers, arrows nocked, stands poised to shoot at a group of about fifty well-armed, mounted women surrounding a cart bearing a howling black beast in some sort of dully gleaming cage. A chill goes up Heph's spine. These must be the New Amazons, a group of ruthless, highly skilled female warriors he has heard about. Have they allied themselves with the Persians?

The long-limbed, black-haired woman who appears to be in charge slides off her horse, as does another tall, athletic woman beside her. Their faces are hidden by the nose and cheek plates of their helmets, but the woman beside the leader has a few locks of pale, wavy blond hair escaping her helmet. Beside Heph, Bucephalus strains against Kat's reins, nickering loudly, twisting his huge head and pawing the ground. It is all Kat can do to keep him from bolting toward the visitors.

There is something strangely familiar about both women. Their posture, perhaps. The way their bodies are knit together. The way they ride a horse.

The leader removes her helmet. Her dark eyes sparkle with merriment as her handsome face slides into a wide, white grin.

Despite all he's seen in his life, Heph's breath catches for a moment.

It's Cynane. Once his lover. The girl who tried to kill Kat and succeeded in cutting off her fingertip. The girl who acquired strange and horrifying powers when married to the mad king of Dardania, before killing the lunatic and escaping.

Seeing her now, tall and tan and smiling, Heph's heart jumps, though he has no idea if it is fear or joy at such an unlikely reunion. As trustworthy as a snake, he must remind himself.

He must keep her away from Kat at all costs.

"Greetings, Lord Hephaestion." Cynane strides up to him, spreading her arms wide to show she bears no weapon in her hands. There is something different about her. She beams with a deeply rooted confidence he has never seen before and has certainly never felt himself. She almost glows with it.

"I, General Cynane of the New Amazons, Princess of Macedon and Queen of Dardania, have just learned of your presence here and have come to offer the Greek allies my military support." She looks at Kat in Alex's armor, grins again. "Dear brother, I would recognize you even without your armor."

The Greek commanders nearby murmur to one another.

"I would like a word with my brother," Cynane says.

"I think...not," Heph replies archly. "Say what you have to say here, in front of us all." He gestures to the well-armed men around him.

Cynane shakes her head. "The information I have is for the ears of King Alexander and his most trusted advisor, Lord Hephaestion, only."

Kat turns to Heph and nods. "Let's hear what she has to say. If these Amazons are only a fraction as ferocious as reports indicate, they could be an excellent addition to our army."

Heph leans in. "She tried to kill you. Betrayal was her weapon of choice even before she delved into that pit of darkness."

Kat considers this and studies her golden fingertip. "I sense that there is a little magic there, but not much. And if she wished to disappear and kill us, she could have attempted so before now."

Heph can't argue with her logic, but he doesn't like this. He can't forget how Cynane drugged his wine and seduced him in Egypt, then raced to Kat's room to murder her. With Smoke Blood powers, however weak they might be, she must be infinitely more dangerous.

And it's not just her newly dark magic—it's the power she has always had over him, to make him lose himself, to make him forgo his honor with the arch of an eyebrow.

So it is against his will that Heph turns to Cynane and says through gritted teeth, "All right. In the king's tent. With one more of his advisors, Lord Jacob." He eyes the other women. "You will come alone."

"I must bring my lieutenant." She gestures to the oddly familiar blonde woman beside her. The woman is tall and muscular. She walks like a man.

Heph hesitates. That will be three of them, armed, and their guards right outside the door, against two unarmed Amazons. "All right. Just the two of you, then."

Moments later, they dismount in front of Alexander's tent, Bucephalus rearing and kicking as two grooms lead him away with difficulty. The women hand over their weapons and enter.

"Say what you have to say, then," Heph orders, hand on his sword, wary of any sudden move.

"First, let me introduce my lieutenant," Cynane says.

The blonde woman next to her removes her bronze helmet.

It is no woman at all.

Heph utters an embarrassing sound of shock.

Alexander. Safe. *Here.* He wants to throw his arms around him, but Kat has already thrown her helmet on the ground and leaped into her brother's arms. The two of them swing each other around as they laugh, and for a moment, the ground seems to shift beneath him and Heph feels as though he is standing on a boat, already setting sail away from the two people he cares most for in the world. But at least Kat will be happy now. Surely whatever darkness she was talking about will be gone.

Now Alex is in front of him, his hands on Heph's shoulders. "Dearest friend. I have much to thank you for. And we have much to do. Quickly."

"Welcome back, sire" is all he says.

CHAPTER THIRTY

DARIUS

AN ABANDONED ORCHARD IS NOT, NECESSARILY, a fruitless one. Even in a land believed to be cursed.

Decades ago, this area of Persia thrived, known for its figs—until a plague forced the farmers to leave. Fearing the spot to be ill-fated, no one has returned since. Now it is abandoned, overgrown. Darius pushes his way through the high summer grass as Bagoas, at his side, points out a variety of beautiful old trees that have somehow survived without tending, growing twisted and wild. Great King Artaxerxes nods calmly, all the while, as if the orchard had sprung up purely for his own pleasure.

"Ah, sire, that is a most excellent specimen!" Darius plays along, pointing to a leafy tree, wider than it is tall, its branches heavy with round dusty-purple figs. They trample a narrow path toward it as rows of bodyguards make their own tracks on either side. Smiling, the Great King wanders around the tree, searching for the most delectable fig, then plucks a large, glistening one. Darius and Bagoas twist off smaller ones and bite into them. Over their heads, the sun beats down. The trees are too stunted to cast much shade.

"Pity that we leave fig country behind tomorrow," Artaxerxes says, biting heartily into the fleshy pulp of the fruit. Juice dark as blood runs into his white beard.

Yes, today is the last day Darius and Bagoas can execute their carefully constructed plan. This is the last day of fig trees. And in a few days, this army will meet the Greek invaders for the first time. They must do so with fire and fury. Not with the plodding, old-fashioned strategy of an eighty-year-old king. The empire needs a new king—a younger, more ruthless king, willing to burn crops, poison wells, do whatever is necessary to repel the invaders, and then launch a punitive invasion of its own in Greek territory. A king who will make these barbarians feel the agony of Persian wrath.

A fat fly buzzes around his head, darting in and out of the branches of the nearby tree. Bagoas swallows, wiping his hairless chin with the back of his hand. "We will have some packed for you, sire, from this very tree." His tone is obsequious, as always. The king does not seem to notice any smugness in the man's smile.

Darius spits out some seeds and takes a second bite of his fig, savoring its sweetness. It tastes rich—like the future. "Four days until we meet up with the Third Cohort."

"Even if the Greek army attacks before we arrive," Artaxerxes says, throwing down his fig and twisting another large, shiny one from the tree, "the Third will keep them at bay."

They stroll around the abandoned orchard for a time, discussing their strategy, until Artaxerxes winces and grabs his stomach. "I must go back to camp," he says, striding purposefully forward. Sweat glistens on his tan forehead. Suddenly he stops, leans forward, and vomits. Then he falls on all fours, moaning like a wounded animal.

Bagoas's eyes lock on Darius.

"Call…my physician," the Great King says, his voice threaded with pain.

"I think—" Darius kneels beside him in the hot sun "—that there is nothing your physician can do, sire."

Artaxerxes turns his head, a knowing look in his glinting, obsidian eyes.

"How?" His voice has gone ragged. "How did you do it?"

"We knew your propensity to choose only the fattest fruit on the tree. Last night, our men crept out here and painted only the biggest figs with poison. We knew you wouldn't have your tasters test fruit on the tree."

The king grimaces and clutches his stomach, panting heavily.

"Don't worry," Darius says smoothly. "Persia will be safe in my hands. Safer, actually. Perhaps if you had only listened to my advice. We must meet the Greeks with deadly fire. But you refused. You are too old, my king. You have become soft. It is time to pass the scepter on to stronger hands."

Artaxerxes collapses completely, whimpering and writhing.

"Bagoas and I have already planned your funeral. A very grand one in Persepolis, once we have trounced the Greeks. We will build you a huge mausoleum."

The king whispers something through tightly clenched teeth.

"What?" Darius leans in. "I didn't hear that."

"The gods punish traitors and cowards," Artaxerxes manages to hiss out. "You have written your doom—and that of Persia."

He closes his eyes, shudders, and is still. Darius looks impassively at the face as finely carved as a cameo: the noble brow, the hooded eyes, the hooked nose, and high cheekbones.

As he turns, a pair of viselike hands grabs the neck of his robe and pulls him down with astonishing force for a dead man. "You...will...never...be...safe," Artaxerxes whispers, his face contorted. Darius tries to pull the hands away from him. He pries them loose and flings the king back. His dark eyes are open as air rattles out of his throat and his body goes limp.

Darius stands and claps the dirt from the front of his black robe.

Bagoas prostrates himself on the ground in front of Darius.

"All hail the King of Kings, Darius of Persia!" The words echo all around them as men throughout the orchard—secret Assassins working as soldiers and servants—take up the refrain.

At last.

And now this land can burn.

Now he will show the Greeks what they are really made of.

Fire.

CHAPTER THIRTY-ONE

KATERINA

IMAGES FLASH BEFORE HER CLOSED EYES. A LAKE
of shimmering, magical water that doesn't slake her thirst but
increases it, changing her human form over time. Wings black
and wide as night. The glowing golden flesh of gods—fang
torn. The devouring, all-consuming hunger of a canyon, an
abyss that can never be filled. Animal fury, but human memories. And everywhere, ropes of light, harnessing her, yanking
her, entrapping her in a massive unseen web.

"What do you see?" Cynane whispers from close beside her.

Kat flings open her eyes, and the sensations fly away, dissolving in the light.

They are at the rear of the Greek camp, guarded by a wide
perimeter of Macedonian soldiers, spears at the ready. They
believed Alexander when he said the Spirit Eater was a deadly
weapon against the Persians, a sure means of victory, and completely under control.

Alex lied.

Jacob and Heph flank her sides, ever protective.

The sun has just risen, spreading a lovely rose-amethyst glow
over the land. And before her, beyond the bars of its glimmering cage: the hard, dark eyes of the trapped Spirit Eater.

She can't answer Cynane. She's still overcome by the beast's ravaging hunger for magic blood, for her blood. She cannot understand what makes it seem to shift, to expand and contract as the light hits it. Sometimes, it looks like several creatures crammed into the diamond cage; a moment later, only one.

She shakes her head, unable to fully escape the murky pull of the creature's mind.

Jacob holds a vial of lotus blossom essence under her nose, and as she breathes in, her head begins to clear.

"It was human once," she says slowly.

"Did you sense anything that would help us to destroy the rest?" Alex's arms are around his little half brother, Arridheus, who stares in awe at the monster. "Today is the summer solstice, Kat. At sunset, we've run out of time."

"I'm not sure," she says slowly. "It was more like… I felt something. Ropes…"

"Ropes?" Cynane asks sharply.

"Threads. Something binding me. Invisible. But I could feel them."

"That hardly helps us," Cynane says quietly. "And I am getting weaker by the hour. I won't be able to contain it forever. And we can't exactly rely only on *her*." She nods toward the baby in the arms of the Persian princess.

Mandana is a beautiful baby with wide dark eyes, a fringe of black hair, and dimples. She reaches a chubby fist toward her mother, and Kat wonders what it is about the child that calms the Spirit Eater. Looking at the lovely girl who saved Alexander's life in Gordium, Zofia, Kat is struck once again by how strange the workings of fate can seem.

"There is only one thing to do." She sighs, steeling herself for what lies ahead. After all the sadness she suffered after the Spirit Eater's attack in Byzantium, what will this do to her? Will it sink her even deeper into horror and despair? Still, it's the only chance they have.

"I will become the Spirit Eater."

"Kat." Alex takes another step toward her.

She glances up at him. "It's the only way. I must enter the creature fully this time, so that I can control it. Cynane can dissolve the cage. Then I will guide it, and we will fly away, as far as I can, before..." She trails off, knowing how dangerous, how ill-advised the suggestion is. Her personal darkness aside, what if she isn't able to control or persuade it? Every creature is different in how it responds to her Snake magic.

Silence hangs heavily around her. "What if it won't release you, Kat?" Jacob puts a hand on her shoulder. "It's not...natural. Not like a falcon or a fish, or..."

She doesn't know what to say. He's right.

"It's our only choice," Cynane says, and her eyes trail to the cage itself. They are all aware of how dull and faded the diamond bars have become, no longer quite solid. It is as if they are becoming smoke and, with a gust of wind, will blow away, liberating the ravenous monster within.

Kat stands. "I can do this. I'm ready," she lies.

From the still place inside her, she slides once more into the creature's consciousness, before anyone can stop her.

Another onslaught of images. A deluge. A screaming, howling pain.

She is dizzy with it.

A frenzy of muscle and movement.

This body is only part body, part something else, made of spirit or smoke, or somehow cut from the fabric of evil itself.

And yet. Her mind is drawn toward something at the core of its being, something burning but solid, like an orb.

She imagines holding the glowing orb in her hand.

And suddenly, she can feel what has happened, can feel the transference click into place as her body becomes the creature's body, its darkness *her* darkness, its torment hers, too. She can see through its eyes—the familiar faces of those she knows, grown distant and strange, cloaked in expressions of disgust or fear.

Her first feeling is that of sheer rage at all of them for keeping her cooped up in this too-small space for so long. Her second feeling is that of ravenous hunger for the magic blood so near, the blood that has been tantalizing her with its delicious smell. The blood of the warrior man-woman, who lassoed her and put her in this cage. The blood of the broad-shouldered warrior man, and the others nearby.

A force inside her commands her to tear open their soft bellies, to devour their organs, to taste the raw magic flesh, to make the blood her own. A roar rips through her, and the bars around her begin to shake. The worried faces around her retreat. Swords and spears point at her. She laughs, but it comes out as a howl.

A glimmer of Kat comes back to herself, enough to realize this joining is nothing like those she has had in the past with jellyfish, birds, whales, and scorpions, when she slipped inside unopposed, easily experiencing the creature and herself at once, merging together into one wish, allowing her to both guide and observe. This being is powerful beyond measure, perhaps impossible to control. She fights to dominate the roiling spirit of the creature, to assert herself as master. It is as if she is wrestling with a large black demon in a place of utter darkness, writhing and twisting for the upper hand. Her weapons are not fists and feet and teeth, but fear against love, despair against hope, beauty against horror. She is sprained and wrenched and clawed, her Kat-ness dripping out of her wounds like blood, and so exhausted it is tempting to just sink into the darkness and let the monster take control.

A mere breath of herself remains, but it is enough to know that she must fight. She focuses on all the love she has ever felt—for Helen, her true mother; for Jacob's generous family, who took her in; for Jacob himself; for Alex and Heph; for Aristotle and

Ada of Caria. She calls on all that love to surround and protect her, spiritual armor against the ancient horror of the Spirit Eater.

And in the darkness of the creature's soul, something golden gleams, and the rage of the monster recedes—just enough.

Just enough.

She calms herself, aware that even now she is not fully in control. The creature's fury stirs just below the surface, and she senses an unendurable longing to be out of this prison, to be free, flying in the clean crisp air, searching for prey, since she knows the invading spirit inside her will not permit her to eat this prey standing around the cage.

The golden-haired male approaches her, staring intently. She cannot understand his words—Spirit Eaters long ago lost the use for such clumsy things—but in his tumble of sounds, she hears one thing over and over again. *Katerina? Katerina?*

The humans exchange more words, then each lights a torch from the campfire nearby. They reform in a circle around the cage, holding a spear or sword in one hand and a torch in the other. The black-haired man-woman closes her eyes and utters a deep sigh.

The darkness around her seems to melt and sigh, too, and then the shimmering bars of the cage begin to flicker, turning to dust, to smoke.

The cage is gone.

She is free.

Her brothers and sisters are nearby; she can feel them.

She flies.

It is unlike any flight she has ever experienced before. The flight of birds is calm and focused. It is as grounded as walking is for a human, or swimming for a fish. But this. This is something else altogether, as though the sky is folding and unfolding around her, as if all of time and space are not fixed things but morph as she moves through them, vulnerable, as all life is, to influence, to change.

Below her, treeless hills push up from the earth, and patches of woods, then a silver stream sparkling over plains of grass.

In the distance, she sees them: dozens, perhaps hundreds, of the others, wheeling over golden cliffs in a dark mass.

Far below, an enormous white-winged horse is tied to a pole with a thick rope.

Pegasus.

A magic creature that could sate the hunger for many years.

The Pegasus rears and bucks and whinnies, rolling its huge black eyes and pulling its lips back to show large white teeth.

Its fear makes her hungrier.

All around the horse gather men with horned helmets. The sight brings Kat to the fore as she pushes back down the hunger of the Spirit Eater. Because these are Aesarian Lords. They've come, most likely, from the headquarters of Nekrana to the east. Her glance lingers on the faces. One of the men has long iron gray hair and a helmet with golden horns, and she wonders if this is Gulzar, Supreme Lord and Commander. He is talking to a short Lord beside him.

Timaeus. She shudders. After he left the underground city of Troy, he must have sought out the Aesarian headquarters and joined a new regiment.

Her gaze shifts from Timaeus to the Pegasus. All around the animal, the men have positioned long metal tubes, engines of some sort, atop wheeled carts. Men pump enormous bellows attached to the end of each tube, and near the front is a cauldron of fiery pitch and sulfur.

Ah, so the Pegasus is a lure. She understands now. A lure for her, for all of them.

The little Lords are trying to outsmart the Spirit Eaters once and for all.

The Pegasus twists and shrieks as the monsters spiral down, ready to tear out its living flesh, and flames roar out of the tubes...

She inhales sharply.

She is lying on the ground, familiar faces gathered around. Zofia is massaging her temples while Alex holds the lotus scent beneath her nose.

Tears spring to her eyes.

She realizes her whole body is shaking. *Her* body. She is Kat again.

She has shaken off the Spirit Eater.

And yet.

The darkness of it still tugs at her, a turbulence stirred up somewhere deep inside of her. Months ago, its bite had infected her with despair. And now her journey into the soul of the monster has magnified the sorrow. Black tendrils wrap around her heart, squeezing.

Thunder rumbles nearby. Raindrops hit her forehead, as if the gods are weeping for her, or perhaps trying to wash away the filth that has befouled her soul. But nothing can wash her clean.

"Where did you go?" Heph asks, kneeling beside her, caressing her hair.

She knows he means, where did she leave the Spirit Eater? Where did *it* go? To the mountains. To the others. To the Pegasus—bait.

The Aesarians. Their plan.

Yes, she knows what he is asking. But all she can think is, *Where did I go?*

What happened to *her*?

No, she will never be Kat again. But there is a battle to fight.

Mere hours later, still weak and exhausted, Kat sits on the hill overlooking the plain of battle. Below her, the Greek forces are massed, tens of thousands of men on foot and horseback, archers and spear throwers and swordsmen. Every regiment has catapults on wheels. Facing them are tens of thousands of Persians, mounted and unmounted, with catapults of their own.

The three men she loves are down there: Alex, Heph, and

Jacob, leading the Macedonian army. Alex was torn. He wanted to go back to Gordium, to the knot, the place where he was prophesied to defeat the Spirit Eaters on this—the last possible—day. Would Katerina take his place once more, he asked himself, to fight the Persians as she had already so ably done?

No.

She can't stomach more bloodshed, more slaughter, see the light fade in the eyes of good young men on both sides, hear the screams of the horses, smell the blood. She thought she had shaken off the worst of this melancholy by pretending to be Alex, to help her twin by keeping the alliance together until he could join them. Then, seeing him, knowing he was safe and she could stop the nerve-rattling pretense, she was even happier.

But the journey she had just taken into the soul of the Spirit Eater brought all the darkness back and more. The dead and injured at the Battle of the Granicus River weigh heavily on her once more, but it's the unmitigated slaughter of honey-mad Persians at Cimmera that haunt her like vengeful ghosts. Even now she sees them dancing…and dying. She wonders if she can ever be happy again, knowing she did that.

Knowing the army would never fight without him, Alex grimly nodded and said only, "We will do what we must."

Even if Kat couldn't take Alex's place, there were unique and vital ways she could help him. She has already told them the de-tailed battle formation of the Persian army, gained from enter-ing the mind of a kestrel and flying over the enemy lines. And she will continue to do so throughout the battle, waving flags from the hill to signal a change.

The rain, barely a sprinkle, left the air thick and misty, though the occasional wind from the valley below cools Kat's cheeks.

The ghostly moan of the salpinx rises over the battlefield, along with the echoes of men's cries as the armies race toward each other and clash. There is a scrum of warriors and horses, the flash of sunlight on swords and shields. She cannot see clearly what is happening, even from the hill. Down on the plain, the Greeks will be lost in the fog and chaos of war.

Calming her breath, she sinks into herself, transferring her thoughts to a raven flying along the side of the fighting. The bird was flying home to her young, a stomach full of worms to regurgitate into yawning beaks, but she relinquishes control easily to Kat, who flaps broad black wings to arc back over the battle. On either side of the melee, lines of Persian infantry are running around the Greeks.

She opens her eyes, rubs her forehead. "Zofia! Pincer movement. Blue flag."

Zofia picks up a blue pennant and waves it back and forth for several minutes.

Kat looks for the raven, but she is gone, home to her chicks. A sparrow is flying almost directly overhead, however, and she enters it, dipping lower to take a closer look at the flanking Persians, who seem to be kneeling.

Flames catch in the dry grass. A line of Persians has flanked the Greeks and are setting fires.

She snaps out of the sparrow, gasping.

"What is it?" Zofia asks, kneeling beside her.

"Red flag," Kat says. "Fire. Circling us from behind. We will be trapped."

Zo picks up the red flag and waves it in a semicircular motion, first one way, then the other, to indicate the fires being set around them. Suddenly she cries out and falls to her knees. An arrow has pinned her hand to the flagpole.

A Persian archer must have spotted them.

"We need to get back to the trees!" Kat pulls Zo away from the front of the hill as the wounded girl gasps and clutches the flagpole with her other hand. Arridheus, who had been watching Mandana in the safety of the trees, steps out of their shadows. "What is it?" he asks.

"Get back!" Kat cries. When they reach the trees, Kat yanks

the arrow—and Zo's hand—from the pole as Zo shrieks. The tip has gone clean through the girl's palm. Kat takes out her dagger and chops the arrowhead off the shaft, then pulls the shaft out of Zo's hand. She wraps it in the bandage all soldiers keep rolled in a bag on their belts.

"Arri," she says to the wide-eyed boy, "look after her. Both of you, stay back here."

Throwing a shield over her back, Kat crawls to the front of the hill and sees, to her horror, flames licking a giant U shape around the Greeks, wafting waves of smoke over the embattled soldiers. She looks right. Left. Where is the Persian archer? Behind a rock on that hill over there? In that tree?

She sees movement below, three Greek soldiers climbing the steep path up the hill. "Watch out for archers!" she cries. One of them takes the shield from his back and holds it over them. Heph and Jacob clamber over the crest, supporting Alex.

"Get down," she says, momentarily grateful that the first clouds of black smoke hide them from the archer. She coughs—and then her heart stutters as she realizes Alex is bleeding profusely from a head wound. "Oh, great gods, what happened?"

"I'm all...right," he mumbles, his eyelids fluttering.

"A Persian sword came down hard on his helmet, splitting it in two," Heph says, examining the wound with deft fingers. Alex's pale golden hair has turned scarlet. "Cynane killed the Persian who did it. I think it's just a flesh wound, but he's disoriented. I thought Jacob could heal him if we had some peace and quiet, a place where he could concentrate."

"Drag him back to those trees," Kat commands. "And, Jacob," she says as he casts her a searching look, "help Zofia, too."

Sprawled out on her stomach, Kat studies a moving plain of men, fire, and smoke. Catapults lob flaming, tar-dipped stones through the air. Smoke obscures her view of the plain at times, then clears.

"Kat!" Zofia's voice reaches her through the din and smoke.

Kat crawls between the trees. Zofia, cradling a fretful baby, holds up her blood-slick hand. "Jacob healed the wound," she says. "Alex's, too, but he's still dizzy."

Kat approaches Jacob, Heph, and Arridheus, who kneel beside a prone Alex.

"I'm really fine," Alex says woozily, his eyes closed. He puts his bloody hand on his bandaged head.

"I think that's the best I can do," Jacob explains. "It will take some time for the dizziness to fade. Right now, I should be dousing the fires."

"Yes." Alex sighs. "Douse the fires. We must save my men. And women."

Their shields slung over their backs, Jacob and Kat creep to the front of the hill. Now smoke billows across the battle below, wafting over the hill and making the two of them cough. "See that stream? I'm going to channel that water to the fires." She nods.

He lies absolutely still, but she can see the effort it takes by the set of his jaw and the lines in his forehead. Below the shifting clouds of smoke, she can see the water spreading toward the roaring fires. Some of the flames, those farthest away from the hill and nearest the stream, go out.

Jacob groans. "There's not enough water here."

Kat sees that now the stream is empty. But then she sees something else, something that strikes fear into her heart like a blade of ice. Black figures wheeling over the battlefield, diving down to pick up struggling soldiers, eating them in midair. Their sharp, piercing screams make her want to cover her ears.

Spirit Eaters.

They've come.

"My men," Alex says. He's crawled out to join them, as have the others. He's white as a sheet, his hair matted with clumps of blood.

Heph grabs his arm. "You couldn't make it through the fires at this point. Look, they have almost encircled this hill."

As Kat looks down, she sees two Greek soldiers leaping over flames to the hill, then scrambling up. Cynane's head appears first, followed by Alecta's.

"What's going on down there?" Alex asks, rubbing his forehead.

"Total chaos," Cynane says. "The Spirit Eaters have caused a rout. The Persians have fled, the Greeks and the New Amazons running after them as the fires have blocked their own retreat."

"Cynane," Jacob shouts urgently. "In the tunnels below Troy we saw Smoke Blood children taming flames and smoke. Can't you do that, even a little bit?"

"Don't you think I tried?"

Alecta puts a calming hand on her shoulder.

The wind shifts, and thick clouds of black smoke cover the hill, choking them.

"Get down!" Heph commands, coughing. "It'll be easier to breathe."

Jacob puts his arms around Kat as they lie flat on the ground. "I'm going to try again to draw out water from under the ground. There has to be some nearby. An underground spring, something." He closes his eyes. His jaw tightens. After a time, beads of sweat form on his forehead and a little vein throbs in his temple. But water does not flood the burning plains. All is smoke and the screams of men and wheeling black figures diving and shrieking over the battlefield. Now a baby's cries join the cacophony. Next to Kat, Zo arches over Mandana, shielding her from the smoke with her body.

"Jacob will put out the fire," Kat says, wishing she were more certain. "Don't worry. He'll..."

A piercing shriek rends the air, echoing over the plains below. It comes again and again, bloodcurdling, unbearable, as those on the hill put their hands over their ears. Is it a cry of pain? No,

Kat realizes, seeing the black shapes take to the sky in a rain of blood, flapping away in the same direction, toward Gordium. The monsters are answering a call.

Just then, a dark winged shape flies over the hill, obscured by the thick clouds of smoke.

Cyn draws her sword, taking up a position next to Zo and Mandana, with Alecta right beside her. Kat and Heph also leap to their feet and draw their swords. Kat's eyes sting and water, and her throat is raw from the smoke. Alex tries to stand but is too weak. Heph bends to help him up.

The figure wheels around and around the smoky hilltop. Kat begins to sense it is not a Spirit Eater, not something hungry and evil. It is...

"Pegasus," Zo breathes before her. "She is never lost."

"What?" Kat shouts, as a huge winged horse thunders through smoke onto the hill and gallops in a circle until it stops, neighing angrily, its sides heaving with exertion.

The same creature Kat saw tied as bait for the monsters, but soot has blackened its hide, the feathers on its enormous wings are singed, and a nasty red burn oozes on its shoulder.

"Pegasus is never lost," Zo repeats, holding Mandana close to her chest. The phrase reminds Kat of something. The little girl she met in Troy—Roxana—had said the same thing.

Zo is approaching the restless creature, and now she puts out a tentative hand. "Vata," she says, as if calling it by name. And sure enough, the horse whickers a warning, then sniffs at her. Recognition enters its large dark eyes, and its breathing calms.

No one moves for a long moment as clouds of black smoke waft over the hilltop. Kat hears the crackle of flames now and looks over the side. Fire is licking its way up the dry brush on the hill, inching toward them.

When she looks back, the beast is kneeling, and Zo, tying Mandana firmly to her back, climbs on top. "Please understand," she says, "I have to save my baby."

Before any of them can respond, Heph drags Alex toward the creature. "He's wounded," he pants out. "The king is wounded."

Alex has barely been slung onto the back of the Pegasus before, neighing in anger, the creature flaps its wings. Through wisps of smoke, Kat sees Zo grab the burned length of rope around its neck and quickly wrap it around Alex's waist behind her. "Hold on to me!" she shouts, as the Pegasus bolts in circles around the hill, then leaps over the edge, into smoke and fire. Kat's heart skips a beat as the horse and its passengers sink, but then they rise, climbing above the smoke and into a clear blue sky.

But the smoke and heat of the flames still comes ever closer, and there is no path for the rest of them to make a run for it now.

They are trapped here, by a wall of fire.

"We should be fighting—like warriors—not waiting, like lambs for the slaughter." She turns to Alecta.

Alecta nods, then clasps Cynane's hand.

And then, together, chins down and shields raised, they run headlong—

Into the flames—

Only, instead of screams of agony, instead of disappearing into the thick smoke, something happens.

Kat gasps as the smoke seems to part, separating around the two women, forming a billowing black wall on either side.

Then it separates again, now into individual columns.

No, not columns. Enormous soldiers of smoke, three times the height of a man, all of them holding smoke shields and swords.

A small column of black smoke glides toward them, and it slowly forms into a man. A small, wiry man wearing a horned helmet.

Timaeus.

CHAPTER THIRTY-TWO

JACOB

JACOB IMMEDIATELY UNSHEATHES HIS SWORD, though part of him wonders if this is some trick of the smoke, some fantasy borne of his exhaustion from trying to draw water.

"Ah, some old friends, I see." Tim walks up to Jacob and makes an exaggerated bow. "Lord Jacob. Savior of the children of Troy. Ah, and here we have his childhood love, Katerina."

He turns to Heph, who eyes him as if trying to remember where he saw him before. "Don't remember me, Lord Hephaestion? It was I who bested you in the Blood Tournament, tumbling out of your sword's path, hitting you in the head with a slingshot pebble. Oh, how the crowds roared with laughter to see a funny little acrobat from a flea-bitten fishing village beating Pella's noble champion!"

Comprehension dawns on Heph's face, but he says nothing.

"And here we have Princess Cynane. Pardon, my lady, *Queen* Cynane," Timaeus continues, bowing before her. "Blamed for murdering her husband, the mad King Amyntas of Dardania, an honor that should really have gone to me."

"In that case," Cynane says, pulling herself up to her full height and looking down on him, "I owe you a debt of gratitude, Papari."

Jacob can see the anger ripple like a smear of oil across Tim's face. Before he can react, Jacob steps forward. "Why are you here, Timaeus?" he asks.

"Since you killed my entire regiment, I journeyed east to headquarters," he says, shrugging. "I am already rising high with the Supreme Lord. It was my idea to capture the Pegasus as bait for the Spirit Eaters. And I was the one to catch her as she was grazing. She never noticed the figure of smoke approaching her."

"But why are you *here*?" Jacob asks.

Tim grins. "You mean you really don't know?"

And then, of course, he does.

Tim wants another betrayal—a great one.

"Take me," Jacob says. If Timaeus takes the bait, at least the others might be spared.

"You can't trust him." Cynane takes a step toward Jacob. "No matter what promises he makes to us, he will break them."

Timaeus smiles. "She's right, of course. But you are all going to die up here, anyway. So it doesn't seem like you have much of a choice. Besides..." He glances sneeringly at the others. "I have no use for the rest of you. Or this little war of yours. Perhaps some of you would like to leave?"

Jacob looks at the towering clouds of choking black smoke taking the form of enormous warriors, and the racing flames charring the brush along the edges. "Kat..." he begins.

"I'm not leaving you." Kat has stepped up beside him, slipping her hand into his.

"Please." Heph reaches out toward her.

She shakes him off. "Don't touch me."

"This is no time to be a martyr. Even the enemy has fled the fire." Both enemies—the Persian army and the monsters.

"He's right." Jacob clears his throat, unable to look into Kat's eyes. For the first time ever, he and Heph completely agree on something. "Kat, go with him."

"No," Kat says, low and hard.

"You would choose to die with him rather than live with me." Heph's face is unreadable, smoky, ashen wind billowing his dark hair into his eyes, his mouth set firm.

She doesn't answer, but her grip on his palm tightens.

And for Jacob, that small signal is everything.

She *has* chosen him.

The knowledge of it, that she has done it, has finally chosen him, here, at the end of all things, makes everything suddenly settle into clarity inside his chest. Resolve burns clear and bright, and he knows he can do anything—even vanquish an impossible enemy.

"A lover's quarrel," Tim says, eyeing them. "I won't wait forever. I don't need to, you see." He gestures to his army of smoke and darkness.

Heph says at last, "I won't leave you without a fight. Your brother would never forgive me."

For Heph, it will always really be about Alexander.

But Kat says, "Alex will always forgive you, Heph. I know it."

"But I won't. Like I said, we don't go down without a fight." Cynane's sword is drawn, and before Jacob can stop her, she attacks Tim.

He could turn to smoke and vanish, but he parries her blow, disappears only to reappear behind her.

Alecta joins in, and Tim releases his hold on the smoke army. They descend on the group below, embracing them with sooty arms. Smoke coils around Jacob, forcing itself up his nostrils, into his mouth. His eyes water and sting, and he can't breathe. Through the smoke he sees Tim fighting Cynane, their swords ringing out, then dancing over to Heph. Tim is enjoying this, like a cat toying with doomed mice.

Anger rises in Jacob, fury that his friend, one he loved and trusted, is doing this to him, Kat, and the others. The earth trembles with his anger, but Jacob channels it out of the earth and into the air. Gusts of wind scatter the forms of the smoke soldiers for a few moments, enough, at least, for everyone to cough out the soot and breathe clean air. He looks for Kat. She is nearby, her face blackened, gray ashes in her hair. She wipes at red runny eyes, then meets Jacob's gaze, and nods grimly. Tim is fighting Alecta, who stabs him in the shoulder, in the groin, her sword merely pushing through smoke as he laughs at her frustration.

Now the smoke returns to the shape of soldiers, black and churning. And Jacob realizes that his wind has merely fanned the flames burning the dry grasses around them. The conflagration is unbearable. Heat and flames pour forth from all around the little hilltop—a fire flung with deadly swords, a fire stoked by the breath of hate and rage. Heph is on his knees, coughing. Alecta has fainted. Cynane crawls on top of her, convulsing.

Wind. He needs the hilltop to become a vortex of wind to push the flames and smoke out and away, over the plains, so those here can breathe. Exhausted as he is, he must do this, or they will all die in the next few minutes. He thinks of Tim's betrayal of his friendship, of Olympias killing Jacob's family in Erissa, and fresh rage pulsates through his veins, out of his body, and into the air, swirling in rapid circles, pushing away the fiery fingers of flame, the poisonous clouds of black smoke, causing even the smoke soldiers to dissipate.

But one figure of smoke does not dissipate. Timaeus marches up to Jacob, fury in his pale eyes.

"Why are you doing this, Timaeus?" Jacob asks, gulping in the fresh air. This is only a respite, he knows. He is drained of energy, drained of Earth Blood powers. Tim is far stronger. Tim will kill them all. If only he can reach that part of Tim he used to know, his humor, loyalty, and good nature. Surely, that must still be there, somewhere, folded into all the smoke and darkness?

"Power" comes the response. "But I think you know that, already, don't you? You, who were so desperate for it yourself."

Jacob shudders. "Promise me you will let her live."

Tim's sword sparkles like crystal.

"Promise me."

Tim's sword plunges into Jacob's abdomen—tearing through flesh and muscle.

A searing pain.

Blood bubbles up, soaking his tunic below his breastplate. He drops his sword. Both hands clutch the gaping wound.

He would heal himself, would save himself, but all of his powers have gone to form the whirlwind that has kept the others alive and fighting.

"Jacob!" It is Kat's voice crying out to him through the darkness and chaos.

He can't see her. He tries to reach out but crumples to one side, sitting lopsided on his legs and arm, pressing one hand against the wound, slick with hot blood.

"Open your eyes, good friend. There is one last thing I want you to see."

Jacob tries to squint through the blaze of heat and choking black smoke. A Timaeus of smoke stands before him, holding Kat by the wrist. "You will see her die, slowly and painfully." Tim shoves her to the ground and conjures a ray of dazzling light.

No, not a ray, a rope. A rope made of fire and soot, which lashes out and twists around Kat's neck. Jacob wants to pick up his sword and save her—she is so very close—but as he rolls onto his knees, he falls forward, dizzy from blood loss. He cannot reach his sword. He cannot save her.

He cannot save her. The others are unconscious, or dead.

He can only turn his head and watch Timaeus choke the life out of her slowly as she gasps and writhes on the ground. With his last strength, Jacob reaches out with one hand toward the sword that lies between them. It seems so far, and his hand is so heavy. He picks it up, his hand trembling with the weight of it, and reaches toward Kat.

"No," she growls, trying to slip her fingers under the unforgiving rope around her neck. "I will not...let you...do this." She pulls the length of rope hard, bringing Timaeus close to her. He's clearly enjoying this, laughing in her face. "I battled a god last year," Kat says, between coughs. "My own father, and killed him. And believe me, you are no god!"

With her free hand, she takes the sword from Jacob and plunges it into the place where Timaeus's heart would be. Bright red blood explodes all over Kat, some of it splattering onto Jacob. The smoke face is a portrait of utter shock, eyes wide, mouth gaping. The smoke dissipates, all except the protruding eyes. They look at Jacob, and then they disappear, too.

And as the smoke of the man called Timaeus blows away, up into the sky, it sucks with it the smoke warriors surrounding them, and all the smoke and fire on the plains below.

A stunned silence follows.

A vortex of cold air swirls in circles, lifting the soot and flames higher and higher until they disappear into dark clouds.

Watching it, Jacob wonders if he is dead.

And then, it begins to rain.

He slides against wet, charred grass as someone drags him slowly—one step at a time—under the protective canopy of the trees, still smoking with soot and embers.

Soft hands are pulling at his tunic. He hears a gasp, then the ripping of cloth. Someone is stuffing bandages into the gaping wound as he grits his teeth.

Kat.

"Channel your Earth Blood now, Jacob. You are tired, wounded. But it is still there. You can do this."

"Kat," he says, his head spinning, "I don't think I can."

"You have to," she says, quiet and determined. "Don't give up! We have a life, a future together, children..."

He feels a smile play against his face as the images move through him, and the pain in his abdomen redoubles. His smile turns into a cough. His whole body shakes with the effort.

"It's true," she insists. "Because you were always right, from the very beginning. That last day in Erissa, when you kissed me in the pond, do you remember?"

He nods, though he can barely move his head. He could never forget. He finds the strength to open his eyes to look at her. There's not much more time to look at her. He doesn't want to waste it.

"And you asked me to marry you," she continues, her eyes shining in the rain, her hair, undone now, pressing damply against her face and neck. "I should have said yes. I should have begged you not to fight in the Blood Tournament. But I wasn't ready. I needed to…"

"Kill Queen Olympias," he finishes for her.

"For killing my mother," Kat says. "Little did I know, Olympias was my real mother. The woman I hated more than anyone in the world."

"I tried to kill her, too," Jacob says, closing eyelids that suddenly seem too heavy to hold up. "And yet, she lives."

"I don't even care anymore," Kat says, holding his hand tightly. "She can be queen of the entire world for all I care. The only thing I really care about now is you, Jacob. You always put me first, you were right about that."

"What about…"

She knows. "Hephaestion will always put Alex first. You were right about that, too. Alex needs him by his side to advise him and protect him. They have a love that can't be broken. And I need you by my side. Stay with me, Jacob. Don't leave me here alone."

It is getting so dark, Jacob notices. He had forced his eyes open a bit so that he could see the light for the last time, but there is very little.

"Kat," he whispers. "I—I don't know if I can." She is flickering, like Tim did, only it is not because of any Smoke magic.

It is his own vision going, he knows. It is so hard to see, to think, to feel.

Her voice comes to him in the ebbing light. "We will return home, Jacob. To Erissa. Can you see it? Hunting and farming. We could build our own farmhouse, free from prophecies, kings, and battles. Jacob, can you see it?"

He does. He sees it all now. The courtyard of his family farm back in Erissa. He's confused, at first, because someone told him it had burned down. But here it is, just as it always has been. His little brother Calas chases a chicken around the well. He hears the clatter of pots and dishes as his mother prepares food inside the house. The mouthwatering smell of freshly baked bread mixes with the smoke from his father's kiln in the field beyond.

He is so happy to be back here, with them, after all the terrible things he thought had happened. But his happiness is complete when he looks down the lane and sees Katerina, her long limbs sun bronzed, racing toward him beside a gazelle, her wavy golden-brown hair flying out behind her. She smiles, waves at him, and runs toward him with her arms wide-open. And he feels love, such pure love, that the pain fades, and he's not afraid anymore. Because wherever he is, if there is love such as this, there is absolutely nothing to fear.

ACT FIVE

THE MUSES

No evil can happen to a good man, either in life or after death.

—Plato

CHAPTER THIRTY-THREE

ALEXANDER

IT IS COOL UP HERE, NEAR THE CLOUDS. FAR below him, hills roll through the dappled light of the setting sun like a distant ocean, and to either side spread the wide white wings of Pegasus, as if in a dream.

That's it. This must be a dream. That would account for the dizzy feeling.

But no. Alexander's head is still spinning from his wound, from the brisk air, from the incredible height.

His arms tighten around Zofia's waist, the baby between them. He has no idea where they're going, or how long they've flown—only that the others he left behind are facing certain death, and he should have stayed to help them or die in the attempt.

Heph.

Kat.

All his men.

After the Spirit Eaters routed both armies, leaving both sides fleeing, hiding, being devoured alive… Will this mean the end of the war, or that it is only just beginning? He withdraws one arm from around Zo's waist to feel the comfort of his sword. But its sheath is empty, a useless shell, like a snakeskin without the snake. Then he remembers. He dropped it when the Persian nearly split his head open. His hand fumbles for his dagger. That, at least, is still there.

He closes his eyes again, hoping to quell the sickness rising in his stomach. After a time, it seems to him that Vata's wings angle downward. They are descending. With a clatter of hooves, the Pegasus hits the ground at a gallop. Alex opens his eyes and realizes the horse is circling a familiar plaza, high up on the citadel. There, in the center, stands the Arch of Midas. Chained to a column of the arcade, along the side, is the Gordian knot, lengths of tangled rope wrapped around the pole of a rotting oxcart.

Pegasus is never lost.

Against all odds, he has made it to the place where he can defeat the Spirit Eaters. The realization is like spring after a bitter winter, like balm to his soul.

The giant winged horse kneels, and Zo carefully slides off, then takes Alexander's blood-smeared hand to help him down.

"My lord," she says, looking at the bloody bandage on her own hand. "Our blood."

"The prophecy."

She nods.

The stranger whose blood is destined to mingle with your own. Perhaps not in the way they'd thought.

Yes, he thinks, feeling a bit dizzy again. First one part of the prophecy has come true, then the other.

Zo's dark blue eyes slide from his to the square. "Where are we?"

"Back in Gordium," he says. "Remember I told you about a temple with an old priestess? One that only Blood Magics can enter? I entered through there."

As he speaks, a small, bent figure creeps out of the arch, appearing where once there'd been nothing, only a vacant opening between stones, revealing the sky.

And indeed, it is the same priestess he saw within the impossible, hidden temple, only now she holds an enormous golden chalice in her small hands. A toothless grin stretches across her face as she shuffles toward them.

"Welcome, beloved ones." Her cloudy violet eyes peer out between loose locks of gray hair. "We have been waiting for you."

Zo takes a step back, and Vata whinnies nervously. There's a coldness in the air—and a shadow, a piece of moving darkness, comes into view along the skyline, muting the golden rays of the setting sun.

A Spirit Eater.

Silently, the shifting creature lands on the roof of a house across the square, nearly doubling its size as it hunkers down, seeming to fold in on itself. He and Zo stare in awe and terror as others follow, serenely calm as they land, until all the roofs and the wall overlooking the city below are filled with the monsters. They cast long shadows on the paving stones.

"Do not fear," Kohinoor says. "They will not hurt you or the Pegasus. They are under my command." Vata, however, has backed up into the shadows of the arcade, whickering in fear.

"Our command," says another old figure, emerging from the arch.

As the second one steps forward, Alex shudders and blinks. It is as if Kohinoor has doubled, the second woman a nearly exact replica of the first.

"They cannot be destroyed," says a third, coming behind her sister. "They will always be."

He stares. There are three of them. Three Kohinoors. Eyes and voices and small, hunched forms each exactly like the other.

"Who are you?" His voice commands the air.

The women laugh, a series of soft rustling sounds that scurry together, impossible to locate, as if their laughter is made of the wind itself. A new wave of sick dizziness descends over him. Perhaps the question he should have asked is not who they are but *what*.

"Fate," one of the women says.

"Fate," the others echo.

"Fate, fate, fate." A dark, whispery chant.

Zo clears her throat, coming to stand beside Alex bravely, though he can see that she is trembling. "What do you mean? We do not understand you. What do you want?"

"We are the Fates," they say, their voices misaligned with one another just enough that the words come in rippling waves.

Zo's face has gone as white as parchment.

"And these?" Alex sweeps his arm toward the hovering Spirit Eaters, forming their own layer of night laid down atop the city.

One Kohinoor smiles, waveringly. "Everything comes at a cost, my dear boy."

"Fate is beautiful," says another.

"Beautiful," echoes the third.

"But," says the first, "all beautiful things must have their price."

"Enough riddles," Zo says, her body going rigid beside his.

"They," the second Kohinoor explains, gesturing above, "are the byproduct of Fate's elegance. Fate cannot exist without its other side. Without chaos. That is what they are. Chaos embodied."

"Chaos," coos the third priestess.

Alex swallows, trying to focus, even though their words have a lulling effect over his mind. "How can they be destroyed?"

"They can't," say the old women, gesturing to the setting sun. "The solstice is upon us!"

The first Kohinoor steps even closer. "Here," she says, looking into the goblet. "See for yourself."

He begins to move toward her, but Zo pulls his arm back. "Don't," she warns.

Kohinoor ignores her, her blind eyes glittering at Alex. "Here lies the greatest fate we have ever woven for any man."

She holds up the sparkling goblet. "Drawn from the Fountain of Youth. Drink, and your body will be made whole."

Made whole. His scarred leg. His imperfection. This is it. This is what Alex has wanted every day of his life since he was old enough to know he was not quite like other boys. Without knowing how, he has come even closer, and now he stares into the broad goblet. The water shimmers like glittering diamonds. He is suddenly so parched he wants nothing more than to slake his thirst with the cool, sparkling water.

But there is always a price to pay. They said so themselves.

"What do you want in return?" It is a whisper, as if to speak more boldly would be to break the enchantment.

"The baby," she coos, so gently Alex almost doesn't hear her.

The other priestesses stretch their gnarled fingers toward Zofia and the small bundle still on her back. "The baby, the baby."

"Give us the baby. Then you can heal yourself with this life-giving water, take the princess, and fly away from here on her winged horse, on to your great destinies, for we have woven one for her, too. It is not much to ask, is it? A tiny infant, a mere girl. The princess will have others."

"Why?" Zo's voice breaks through Alex's reverie.

The violet eyes look kindly at her. "She is one of us," Kohi-noor says.

"The newest."

"The next."

"Through her, our powers will wax strong."

And understanding dawns in Alex, just as it must in Zofia. "No," she says, low and hard.

"Fate must go on," Kohinoor says. "It must be woven by the fated fingers of the future. It is her. *She* is the fate of Fate. We do not live forever. We will raise her, train her. When the time comes, she will become us. She will become three."

"The fate of Fate," echo the others.

"Why, though? Why her?" Zo's voice is throaty with anger.

The Kohinoors whisper-laugh. "We pick our replacement at the moment of her conception," says the one in the middle.

"We were there that night," says the one to her left. "We came to you. We felt the powerful pull of you—of your desire."

"Your desire to change fate. To weave your own."

"Do you recall," asks the third, "the black cat in the palace basement, where you met your handsome lover?"

Alex has never seen an expression of such horror as Zo now wears. A dark red blush. Or is it the last rays of the setting sun?

"We arranged for your capture," says the third one.

"The slave traders," Zo whispers in shock.

"We tried to watch out for you on your journey."

"We sent the Spirit Eater to chase your Pegasus that day in the Eastern Mountains," says the second one, "to cause you to fall, so that we could find you there and nurse you back to health. We caused the Pegasus to escape the Aesarian Lords' fire and the Spirit Eaters' hunger today, so she could bring you here, to us."

"Give us your baby willingly," the third one says, "and we will make sure you will find the man you love again. He is waiting for you even now. And the two of you will, quite soon, rule over all Persia."

"No," Zo says, backing up toward the nearest column. "Not if it means giving you Mandana."

A question has been forming in Alex's mind. "Why do you need to ask Zofia to give you her baby if it is fated for her to become your replacement? Why do you need to ask me to drink from the Fountain of Youth? Why don't you just make it happen?"

The Kohinoors look at each other questioningly. Finally, the first one says, "There is, among the countless threads of Fate, a tiny breath of..."

"Of what?" Alex asks, thinking he knows the answer. The old women stand uneasily, looking at one another. Is it his imagination or do they seem to flicker, just slightly?

"Of free will." It is Zo who names it. "That's it, isn't it? All of us have free will, and if we choose to fight against the Fates you have woven for us, maybe…"

"We can break them," Alexander finishes.

A sunbeam breaks through the thick clouds, illuminating the three women, who seem to shift in and out of the threads of golden light, bringing to mind what Aristotle once told him. *We are all connected, and controlled, by invisible strings of energy. We cannot see them but if we are wise enough, we can feel them—and alter them.*

Above the old women, the Spirit Eaters shift, restless.

"Many men before you have tried to undo fate," warns one of the Kohinoors.

"But they cannot untie the threads. You are bound to us forever. All of you."

Untie the threads. Patra's prediction returns to him. *Unbound. You are the one to unbind us all.*

Suddenly, the truth flows into him so directly he wants to laugh with the simplicity of it, of why they've come here, to this legacy of Midas, the Earth Blood with the touch of gold. Home of the Gordian knot.

"Men have tried," they repeat, "but it rarely makes any difference, in the end."

"It does with me," Alex says, stalling.

He must untie the fabled knot.

It is as easy as that.

As impossible as that.

For no one has ever been able to.

The world still spins around him. He needs to think, to figure this out. He's not ready when the first Kohinoor walks toward him, smiling. "Look into the water, young king," she says, "and see the glorious destiny we have woven for you."

He cannot help it. Though he knows he should not look, the temptation is too great. He moves toward her as if he himself is a mere puppet, controlled by invisible strings, and looks into the sparkling crystal liquid, dappled in the scarlet rays of the setting sun. At first, he sees only the reflection of his face surrounded by crimson. But then the liquid swirls, and when it clears, he sees himself at the head of victorious armies, crossing mountains and rivers, deserts and fruitful plains, and sailing the seas in battleships. He leaves behind shining cities in all his new lands, all of which he calls Alexandria so they will remember his name.

Brides sit beside him on queenly thrones: sloe-eyed Persians, shapely dark-skinned Ethiopians, golden-haired Gauls with sapphire eyes. And playing at their feet are strong sons who will grow to be kings in their own right, and lovely daughters who will marry kings and sire yet more kings. He sees Hephaestion and Katerina by his side, helping him rule his empire as the three of them grow old. And Princess Zofia, a new friend, but one he knows he will grow to love, sits on a great throne, allied to his, beside a handsome, amber-eyed warrior.

He sees that all of mankind, thousands of years from now, will know his name, will call him great. Warmth spreads through him like hot spiced wine on a snowy day. All his dreams will come true.

"Drink it now," Kohinoor croons sweetly, pushing the cup toward his lips, "and you will be healed. Then all that I have showed you will come to pass."

He hesitates, remembering what Aristotle said about his birth injury. *You have strengthened your leg with exercise. You have run with weights on it in the face of tremendous pain. Would you have tested yourself so, mentally and physically, if I had uttered an incantation and miraculously healed it?*

And the answer, clearly, was no. It was through his weakness that he found his strength. Aristotle said something else, then, that stuck with him. *The only true magic is human ingenuity. Search for answers to your problems within yourself, Alexander. For in yourself all problems and all answers lie. Not outside. Magic is an illu-*

sion. So is perfection. So is power, unless it is the power an individual wields over himself.

He pushes the cup away. "I don't want it."

It is only part a lie—he does want it, but not like this.

"It is your fate to drink it and be healed," the old crone shrieks. Gone are the strange smiles and gentle crooning. Her eyes glow with dark purple fire. "Drink the water."

"No." Remembering he has no sword, he draws his dagger.

"How dare you hesitate, you ungrateful wretch! Yours is the greatest destiny we have ever woven!" the third Kohinoor says, her face twisting in rage.

But he turns from her, an eerie calm descending over him. "We live and we die," he says to all of them, "and in our brief spark of light, we deserve to make human choices. Human mistakes, too. We deserve an Age of Man." And didn't the ancient prophecy state that he could bring such an age into being?

He approaches the oxcart, examining the knot, understanding now why he felt such sinister energy when first he touched it.

In a flurry of wings, a Spirit Eater flaps down from a roof and onto Zo, who screams and falls as it plucks her baby off her back and swoops over to the Kohinoors. Mandana howls her fear, wailing high and loud. Zo scrambles to her feet and lunges toward them, but Alex holds her back. He needs time to think. To figure this out. He knows the monster won't harm the baby.

The Spirit Eater, who seems to be three laughing heads now, squats down, holding the child in front of him to face Alex and Zo as he spreads his black wings. Alex blinks. It is a similar image to what he saw in the Temple of Midas, a winged baby. Like the first time he ever saw Mandana in the ruined mattress shop, with feathers splaying out beneath her arms and shoulders. He feels suddenly dizzy again.

Mandana looks uncertain, but she has stopped crying. One of the Kohinoors hobbles forward and hangs a tablet around her neck. There is strange writing on it, symbols of stars, the sun, a crescent moon, rain, and lightning. "Let her fate be written," the old crone says, "that she will become Fate."

"She will become Fate! She will become Fate!" cry the others. The baby opens her mouth and shrieks in protest as the old women cackle. Zo reaches futilely toward the child and cries.

No, he cannot allow this to happen. What did Patra say? That on the summer solstice, the new child of Fate will be theirs, giving them the power to devour the world. And the only one who can stop it is he who is marked with the threads of Fate. Alexander himself.

The prophecies buzz in his head. He stands in the city where Patra said he could destroy the monsters, and at the place where the strands of Fate are all tangled together. He has by his side the person whose blood has mingled with his. All he lacks is the talisman. Well, he can't wait any longer. He fingers the cold steel of his dagger, ready to brave the Spirit Eater's claws and fangs and take the baby back by force before the sun dips below the horizon. A ray of orange sunlight glints off the glowing ruby eye of the phoenix on the hilt of his weapon, off the curling flames of gold that surround it.

And then he knows. He knows exactly what he must do.

Because the phoenix doesn't die as mortals do. It has no mortal fate. It bursts into flame and rises from its own ashes. The talisman he needed was with him all the time, in his belt. *Closer than you think*, the Kohinoor in the Temple of Midas had said, laughing.

He turns to the knot, and with a roar, he raises the dagger.

A white light radiates from the cart, so bright he can barely make out its shape. The three Kohinoors scream out. The dark shapes of shrieking Spirit Eaters swoop around him. He can feel their cold, killing breath, their rage and hunger—*chaos itself*—even as his dagger slices down on the knot before him.

Heat and light and screams erupt all around him. He is blown back from the cart, landing hard on the pavement, his dagger sliding away from his hand.

When the blinding light fades, he finds himself looking up at a sky dark with clouds. Rains falls gently on his face as a baby's sobs rend the air. He scrambles to his feet and sees that the Kohinoors are gone, leaving behind three heaps of gray rags. The Spirit Eaters, too, seem to have vanished. The cart is gone, blown to splinters and a few fibers of rope. And the arch has fallen, its golden stones scattered and cracked.

Zofia is crawling toward Mandana, who is on the ground, kicking and screeching in outrage. "My baby," she says, picking her up and comforting her. The tablet Kohinoor hung around the baby's neck has disappeared.

And in the distance, just as the sun sets on the horizon, Alexander sees the Pegasus, winging its way toward the horizon.

SIX MONTHS LATER

CHAPTER THIRTY-FOUR

KATERINA

ADA, THE NEW QUEEN OF CARIA, LEAPS AT KAT
with her curved sword as Kat parries her blow and twists out of
her way. A crisp winter breeze off the sparkling, white-capped
harbor of Halicarnassus cools the sweat beading on Kat's brow.
She is tired. No, more than tired. Stifled. Ready for whatever's
next.

Alexander's army conquered the kingdom of Caria and freed
it from Ada's unstable brother, Pixodarus, a week ago, fulfilling
Alex's vow to Ada and carving away another prosperous western territory from Great King Darius of Persia. It was an easy
battle, as the whole city rose up to aid the conquerors, eager to
be free of the cruel king's tyranny.

Kat throws her sword onto the ground in a haze of dust. "No
more." She walks across the lawn to the little beach, looking
across the water from the island palace to the hilly city of red-
tiled roofs. Halfway across town rises the Mausoleum, a stone
tower twenty times the height of a man, with an enormous temple on top. Sunlight glints off the golden figures on the roof.
It is the tomb of King Mausolus, built by his wife, a poem, in
stone, of love and loss.

"You were doing so well." Ada comes up beside her, sheathing her sword. "What's wrong?"

Kat shakes her head. The world of men is one of war and power. Always, someone must fall so that someone may conquer. Life is predicated on death. She knows that. And yet...

The pearl ring Jacob gave her glimmers on her finger, and she wraps her other hand around it to feel the love it will always contain.

"I am afraid I have played a role in all this tragedy," Ada says, watching a merchant ship ply its way to an empty pier. "It was I who sent Helen to Erissa to hide from Queen Olympias. But she was an oracle, and her child was prophesied to be a Snake Blood. I thought it would be somehow safer—sweeter—to be near a family of Earth Bloods, even though Jacob's family had little idea of the extent of their abilities. Olympias found her anyway and killed her. And now Jacob's death has broken you."

"I am not broken, Ada," Kat says, rubbing her thumb over the smoothness of the pearl. "Though I am changed. And it's not just losing Jacob that hurts. It's all those whose deaths I was responsible for. The Persians whose tents we burned. Those I drove mad with the honey so our troops could slaughter them."

Ada stares at her. "That's war, Katerina."

"Yes, it is. And every one of those who died was a son or brother or husband or father. Their faces float before me in my waking hours and haunt me in my dreams."

Ada is silent. "Well," Ada finally says, "if this life isn't for you, then what will you do?"

"That is the question, isn't it? Alexander has no need of me. He will make his mother—our mother—his regent. It is what Olympias always wanted, and she is suited for it. I've already told him."

Ada's dark eyes glisten as she touches Kat's silver lotus blossom pendant. "Alex has had a disappointing day indeed, then. I hear Princess Zofia has turned down his offer of marriage."

Kat looks at Ada in shock. Over the last few months, she has grown fond of the pretty Persian princess and her beautiful baby—and it had warmed her to see how much time she and Alexander spent together. "Why?"

"Here she comes now," Ada says, nodding toward the palace. "You can ask her yourself. As for me, I have an appointment to train young Arridheus in how to wield a sword. I'm looking forward to a more eager pupil, even if he will never be one of your skill." Her voice carries a mix of disappointment and levity—and Kat knows that she has been forgiven for pulling away. Though Ada may never understand how she feels, she will always respect her.

Zofia, in sparkling dark blue robes, smiles at Ada, who disappears into the palace. Zo greets Kat with the same warm smile. "Well, I finally have a moment to find you," she says. "Mandana has just agreed to take a nap."

"Let us walk," Kat says kindly, curious what the girl will have to say. They march along the little beach, toward the stone bridge connecting the island to the town. Oxen slowly pull a cart of amphorae toward the palace.

"Ada tells me you turned down Alexander's offer of marriage," she says, after a moment of quiet.

Zofia smiles sadly and looks to the distance. "Yes."

Kat kicks a shell on the sand. It falls into the water with a little *plop*. "I am sorry," she says, "because, of all the women I've met, I think you would have been the best wife for him. You are so alike, so brave and clever and good."

Zofia's face is contemplative. "If I had met him before all of this, yes, I think we could have been happy, even though he's not in love with me."

Kat raises an eyebrow.

"Oh, he likes me well enough. And perhaps with time..." Zo trails off. "But I am in love with someone else. Someone who risked everything to save my life."

This is news. Zo told Kat about running away from Sardis to avoid marrying Alexander and to find Mandana's father, who was later killed. But she has never told her of loving another man.

"Do you know where he is?" she asks.

The princess's eyes sparkle. "I have an idea." She reaches into her pouch, takes out a small scroll, and unrolls it. Kat can't read what it says; the letters are Persian.

"The last night I ever saw him," Zo says, running her fingers over the writing on the scroll, "he asked me where, of all the places in the world, I would like to go. And I said the royal library of Babylon." She looks up at Kat and her smile radiates across her whole face now. "I was pregnant, and wanted my child to learn more than I ever had. I was a foolish, silly girl who never paid attention to my tutors. And I thought, if I could go to that center of learning in Babylon, I could understand science, astronomy, philosophy, engineering, so many things to teach my child. Even women can study there."

Kat studies the strange little symbols on the scroll, like trees with lopsided branches. "What does it say?"

"It says, *'Meet me at the Great Library of Babylon. I will wait until you come, no matter how long it takes.'* He left this for me hidden in his cloak, though I didn't find it until just before the Battle of Gordium."

"Do you think he will still be waiting?"

She runs a hand through her hennaed dark hair. "I don't know." She pauses. "I can't be sure what will happen, only of what I must do. Now that Great King Darius is retreating into the heart of the empire, I think I may eventually be able to safely travel along the Royal Road again."

Kat feels a wave of warmth for this girl. "So you are leaving, then," she says, grasping her hands. "I wish you weren't. I wish I knew that you would always be here, waiting for Alexander. But I understand why you will not. And I—I admire you. You have conviction. You know what you want."

"Yes," Zo says. "And, Kat? I understand you, too. I know the pain of loss. A beloved little sister. She was so young—just a child—and she died trying to rescue me and bring me home."

"I'm sorry. I didn't know."

Zo's eyes fill with unshed tears. "Roxana. She was only six and followed me out of Sardis the night I ran away. The slavers who captured me took her into a field of wheat and..." Zo pulls a hand out of Kat's grasp to wipe away a tear.

Kat is speechless. Transfixed with shock. With hope. A trickle of realization moves through her. The pretty little girl in the ruins of Troy. Disappearing in and out of the wall.

Her name was Roxana, too.

Kat can still remember her saying, *The mean men took my sister away. They were going to hurt me, too, but I ran.*

I was a princess once and lived in a palace.

Kat hadn't believed her. All little girls like to pretend they are princesses.

"Zofia." Her voice cracks with emotion, with the impossibility of it. "Roxana. I—I may have found her."

Zofia's expression is blank. She blinks several times. "Wh-what?" she asks. "But I heard her cry out. The slavers said..."

"She got away!" Kat says, jubilant now, more sure than ever that she is right, that it was fate that brought her to Troy and to Roxana.

Perhaps it has always been her destiny to help instead of hurt. Perhaps that is the lesson she has learned about herself. After so much of her life spent plotting revenge against the queen who turned out to be her own mother, seeking a path full of darkness and anger, violence and blood. Perhaps, in that way, she was far more like Olympias than she ever realized.

Only, now she has a choice. A chance to be different. To be more like Helen, who was a hero in her own right, though she never fought a battle in her life, never likely even lifted a sword.

She didn't have to. She served others through humility and patience. Through personal sacrifice.

"But…how can you be sure? What if you're wrong?" Zo asks, clearly unwilling to have her hopes raised and dashed.

"It's like you said, sometimes you can't be sure what will happen, only what you must do."

Zo nods, her face full of wariness and hope.

Kat puts her hands on Zo's shoulders. "Roxana told me once that Pegasus is never lost. Like you, she has conviction. I know that you two will find each other again. I'm going to help."

"*Pegasus is never lost,*" Zo whispers. Then she puts her face in her hands and sobs.

Alexander paces around the council chamber table filled with maps, his hands clasped tightly behind his back. "It is a day of goodbyes," he says, his voice tight. "First Cynane, just when I was beginning to like her for the first time."

Kat smiles. She, too, liked the new Cynane, to whom Alexander granted the satrapy of Lydia, where she will rule in his name with her army of Amazons. They left this morning, riding like the wind out of the gates of the city.

"And Princess Zofia," he adds, sighing. "I hope she finds those she seeks."

He stops in front of her and puts his hands on her shoulders. "But it is parting from you, Katerina, sister, twin soul, that breaks my heart. Why do you want to leave me alone?"

"You won't be alone." She hates to hear her own voice breaking. "You will have Hephaestion. The love you two have for each other is far greater than any feelings you will ever have for someone else."

Alex pounds his fist onto the table. "Are we only allowed to have one person we love, then? Why can't I have you both at my side?"

She looks out the window. A Greek military trireme, its red sails round bellied with wind, heads toward a pier. Sunlight glances off the helmets and spears of soldiers crowded on the deck. "Those who stay by your side must constantly live with battles and wounding and death."

After a long pause, he says, "Please, just tell me where you are going."

"I will let you know."

"And not just where you are, but if you are happy."

"Always."

A tear slides down his cheek. "I have a feeling we will never meet again."

She, too, has that feeling. "We are in each other's hearts and souls, my brother." She smiles through tears. "We can never truly be parted in life or death."

She finds him in the stables courtyard, currying his dun-colored stallion, Ares. Briskly, he brushes the yellowish hide, taking care to avoid the thick scar from an arrow wound on the horse's back.

She hesitates in the shadows of a doorway, giving herself time to drink him in, knowing she must make this memory last a lifetime. The messy dark hair he pushes impatiently out of his face. The lean, muscular body that bends down agilely to dip the brush in a bucket. A sob threatens to rise in her throat. A moan of what she is giving up, mixed in with the temptation to grab what happiness she can.

She pushes it all back down, squares her shoulders, and marches into the sunlight.

He looks up, his dark eyes flashing something for a moment. Hope, perhaps, that she has changed her mind. Then he turns away from her. "So. You're going."

She says nothing. *Goodbye* is too hard a word.

"I could never compete with a dead man," he says, not looking at her.

"Heph, listen to me." Now she's standing only inches away.

"I loved you. Maybe I still do." The words are hard to say, their sting of truth. "But I also *know* you. I know you have only one great love in your life. And that is not me."

She doesn't have to say her brother's name. He knows exactly what she means.

"The two of you will have eternal glory."

"That is ridiculous!" He kicks the bucket of water hard. It flies a few feet, crashes down, and rolls on its side as Ares steps sideways in fright, straining at the rope tying him to the post. Kat watches the hot water seep between the cobblestones. "Why? Why can't it be both? Why must you make everything an impossible choice?"

She lets out a breath, then reaches out to touch his arm. There's a part of her that wants never to let go. And another part of her that knows time will not be good to them. That if she stayed for him, she would resent being trapped, and that entrapment would put reins on her love.

"The truth is, I don't think I ever want to marry."

Heph looks at her with dark eyes rapidly filling with tears. "I love you, Katerina of Erissa. I will always love you."

She strokes his cheek. "You know where you belong. Now it's my turn."

He nods, swallowing hard.

"Thousands of years from now, everyone will remember your name."

There is much more she wants to say—that she will always love him, that she will never forget their time together on Meninx, that in leaving him she is breaking off another part of her already broken heart. But she cannot see him cry. She, too, would cry. And they would comfort each other, with whispers and touches and sighs...and then she might not be able to go.

And so she steps away, back through the door, and into the shadows of the courtyard.

In a rush of feathers, she transforms into a kestrel. Beating her wings, she rises rapidly over the palace complex. The buildings grow smaller, as does the dark-haired young man standing next to a yellow horse, his right hand raised in farewell.

Before she flies west, to the place that calls her, she heads north. For there is something she must see, something to gladden a heart aching with loss.

Once she is there, she waits among the ruins of Troy, flying in circles as shepherds and their flocks perform their slow, ancient dance. Rich foreign visitors pray ostentatiously before the funeral mounds of the heroes. The sick and the lame limp toward the temple of healing high up on the hill, the place where she and Jacob found happiness, for a time. And at night, the tunnels beneath the ruins are silent and empty as the grave.

On the morning of the fourth day, wheeling over the beach, Kat spies Zofia's ship dock. Men lead a brown mare down the ramp, followed by Zofia herself. Within minutes, she is riding like a Fury toward the Temple of Asklepios, its mismatched columns gleaming pink and white and black on the hill. Children are playing on the lawn in front of it, chasing each other in a game of tag. Zofia pulls up some distance away as a little girl stands stock-still, staring openmouthedly at the approaching visitor. Zofia jumps off the horse and runs toward the girl, arms outstretched, calling her name again and again. Roxana runs toward her and throws herself into Zo's embrace, crying out her name. The two whirl around and around in a frenzy of pure joy.

Satisfied, Kat angles her wings and continues on, over the sea and toward the setting sun.

CHAPTER THIRTY-FIVE

DARIUS

"WINE, SIRE?" BAGOAS KNEELS BEFORE HIM.

Darius nods, pushing the maps and military scrolls off his sandalwood desk to clear a space. The eunuch, now the wealthiest man in the empire, except for Darius himself, pours wine into a cup, sips it, swishes it around in his mouth, and swallows. He nods, fills the royal chalice, and hands it to Darius.

Briefly, the king imagines there might be poison in the royal cup itself. Or in the wine, and Bagoas has already taken an antidote. It has occurred to Darius lately that Bagoas agreed rather too quickly to help him kill Artaxerxes with the poisoned figs. And after that, the remaining Assassins—anyone who might have questioned his loyalty to the throne.

Darius can never forget the last words of Great King Artaxerxes. *You will never be safe.* Was it a curse? A prophecy? The words seem to pump through Darius with every beat of his heart. The birds in the trees seem to sing it. The wind whispers it. Can others hear it? Sometimes he wonders if he is going mad.

He stands and looks out the tower window over the sprawling palace of Persepolis, its famed courtyards and gardens far from the continued battles in the empire's west. At least he is safe from Alexander's armies here. The Persian forces were routed at the Battle of Gordium. The fires Darius set to trap the Greeks proved ineffective when creatures of darkness winged their way through the sky, devouring Persians and Greeks alike, and then the rain came. Since then, Alexander's armies have conquered the western provinces along the Aegean, his success made easier by promising they could keep their local rulers and ways of life. Formerly Greek colonies, they submitted cheerfully, many of them opening their gates as the soldiers flocked to join him.

But Darius has set up a wall of armies in Cappadocia to protect the east. He has withdrawn his forces from Egypt and Palestine to fortify the heart of his empire, which is wide, and rich in people and in resources. The young king's successes in the west are no indication of what will happen if and when he marches farther east. Darius knows he is safe here. He has hired many former Aesarian Lords as his personal bodyguards, the brotherhood dismantled now that the very reason for their existence—to protect the world from the Spirit Eaters—no longer exists.

No, his main concern is not the Greek invasion, but the fact that he has no heir to give stability to his throne. For despite his extensive spy network, he has not been able to learn what happened to his only son, Ochus. He sent spies to search all the mercenary armies in the known world for someone with his son's appearance—broad-shouldered, muscular, with a lion's mane of tawny hair and unusual honey-colored eyes. Perhaps Ochus is dead of a fever or a brawl. He always was prideful to a fault.

"Sire?"

He turns to see Bagoas, his heavily lined dark eyes intense, holding out the royal chalice brimming with wine. Darius removes the tall gem-studded conical crown and sets it on the table. Before becoming Great King, he never understood how heavy it was.

ONE YEAR LATER

CHAPTER THIRTY-SIX

ZOFIA

BABYLON: A SPRAWLING COMPLEX OF TOWERS, domes, and gardens, all undulating in a violet haze through the modest veil covering Zofia's face. It is breathtaking, a place she has often read about and dreamed of before, but in person it is more alive—birds dart through a cerulean sky, and the sounds of chanted prayer fill the warm air.

And there, in the center of it all, stands the royal library.

Zo's heart flutters as she approaches.

She already has so much, she reminds herself. Mandana, now a toddler tripping over her own robes, curious and full of laughter. Then, the miracle of her sister, Roxana, who seemed to come back from the dead, saved by Katerina. And her old nursemaid, too, the original Mandana, plucked from the Sardisian palace when Alexander conquered it, to look after both of them. She knows that she could easily trundle them all back west over the Royal Road and settle down in Alexander's newly conquered territory on the coast. He has promised her whatever riches and property she wants.

And yet...

Zofia has always been determined to create her own fate.

She pushes open the double doors, twice the height of a man, and steps into a large, shadowy hall with a round pool below a circular opening in the roof. Corridors and doors lead off the hall, and beyond another set of open doors is a large colonnaded garden. Scholars in white robes, arms full of scrolls, bustle about.

For a while, she wanders, hesitant to make a disturbance, in awe of the power of knowledge that fills the air. There are uncountable libraries within the library, rooms heaped with scrolls and windows overflung with lush plants and flowers. She moves through the first garden with its splashing fountains and lounging scholars, and past the domed astronomical observatory. For a moment, she almost forgets why she has come, but the parchment folded into her robes rustles gently against her thigh, reminding her softly of its presence. The note she found in Ochus's cloak, hidden in the secret compartment she hadn't known of until Alexander pointed out in Gordium that all of the Assassins have them.

She enters a doorway at the far end of one hall—to the philosophy library, a cool, high-ceilinged room. Men and women reading at the long tables look up at her in surprise.

Light streams in high windows, illuminating an old man painstakingly copying a text.

A young woman reading a scroll absentmindedly drums her hennaed fingers on the table, each tap a subtle drumbeat that momentarily lulls Zo.

In the far corner, a white-robed figure holding scrolls descends a tall ladder. Her heart stops. The wide shoulders. The tawny hair. The indescribable confidence of his every movement, the ease of a trained killer, the elegance of a wild cat.

When he turns, he sees her and drops the scrolls.

His mouth opens and closes. His amber eyes widen, as if to let her in.

"You...came," he says, his voice hoarse.

"It took me a while to find your message," she says, tears already falling down her cheeks.

He comes toward her, reaching out to touch her tentatively, like she might turn to dust and blow away. His hand lands gently against her cheek, and he inhales sharply, as if surprised to find her warm and real and alive.

His arms open, and she falls into them.

TWO YEARS LATER

CHAPTER THIRTY-SEVEN

ALEXANDER

ALEX CASTS A LOOK BEHIND HIM. HIS VAST ARMY fills the fields as far as he can see. Tens of thousands of men, some mounted, most on foot. Thousands of carts bearing tents and weapons, cook pots, medical supplies, and dismantled catapults. Entire herds of livestock. They are ready to march. For the army is moving eastward, ever eastward, until they surround Persepolis itself and Great King Darius. But he never sets out without Heph. He will wait.

Behind him, men on horses move aside, allowing a rider to pass.

Heph pulls up beside him.

"She's settled, then?"

Heph nods. "I never thought I would be like the Persians, taking my wife with me on campaign."

Alex smiles. "Who knows how many years it will be until we return? You and Sarina need to start working on our next generation of warriors."

Heph grins. "Oh, we're working on it, my liege."

Alex is glad Heph has found happiness with Sarina. After Kat left, two years ago, he seemed so heartbroken that Alex wanted him to have a complete change of scene. And someone had to deal with the Egyptian agitators led by the sultry, dark-skinned priestess, who had kidnapped Arridheus and attempted to assassinate Alexander. And so Heph sailed down the Nile on a diplomatic mission to promise that Alexander would not brutally conquer their land and enslave their people, as the Persians had done. He returned not only with a treaty, but with a bride to seal the alliance.

At first, Alex wondered if Heph had married Sarina to forget Kat. And even though he seems quite happy in his choice, perhaps he did. Sometimes Alex catches a shadow in his eyes. Alex suspects Heph will never quite love his wife as much as he loved Kat, which is exactly as it should be. The love between a man and a woman, Aristotle said, can drive a man mad.

Kat sent word that she is living on the isle of Meninx, also known as the Island of the Lotus-Eaters, off the coast of Carthage. She explores the sea, searching for the inhabitants of Atlantis, Snake Bloods, she says, who long ago intentionally sank with their entire civilization below the waters, where they still live. During those wonderful months of togetherness between the Battle of Gordium and her departure, she once told Alex of her fleeting vision of a city on the bottom of the sea, with many-columned temples and palaces, markets and roads, and people gliding forward, their long hair and full robes trailing behind them in the sea currents.

Since then, Alexander has heard strange tales of a siren off the coast of Lotus Island. Only, this siren doesn't lure men to their deaths, as sirens are wont to do; she swims out to sinking ships and rescues them. The sailors call her Thessalonike and worship her as a goddess of the sea.

Some parts of the vision the Fates showed him in their goblet remain yet to be determined. Will he have the wives and many children he saw in the sparkling water? He does not know. And the long life? It doesn't matter. For, one thing he does know; one thing does matter. He will have the glory he always dreamed of. He will conquer all of Persia. But he will not stop there. He will continue east, to that legendary land where brown men dye their hair green and ride tusked beasts as big as houses. Perhaps he will march to that fabled place far beyond the known world, where worms spin shining threads on trees, and where the earth ends at an endless ocean. And in his path, he will leave justice, thriving trade, and peace. Dozens of new cities called Alexandria will spring up behind him. His name will truly live forever.

And, always at his side, he will have Heph. He looks at him now; they smile at each other and nod. Then he blows the horn, and the army moves forward.

★ ★ ★ ★ ★

ACKNOWLEDGMENTS

ALEXANDER THE GREAT DIDN'T CONQUER THE known world by riding east alone on his horse. He was assisted by a devoted, talented group of generals and countless others who strategized, negotiated, and polished weapons to a burnished brightness. Together, they slogged through mud, desert, and a fair share of horse manure into luminous realms of glory.

As with Alexander, so with this fourth and final installment of the Blood of Gods and Royals series. It would not have been possible without the assistance of an extraordinarily capable team: Lexa Hillyer and Kamilla Benko at Glasstown Entertainment; my agent, Stephen Barbara of Inkwell Management, and his incredible team there; my editor, Natashya Wilson at Harlequin Teen, and her excellent team as well, including Gabrielle Vicedomini, Lauren Smulski, Amy Jones, Bryn Collier, Evan Brown, Krista Mitchell, Laura Gianino, Shara Alexander, and Linette Kim. To all of you, it has been great ride. I'm so glad I had you by my side.

AUTHOR'S NOTE

WRITING THIS SERIES HAS BEEN AN EPIC JOURNEY of its own. In doing so, I have traveled to a time and place often more real to me than the here and now, and certainly more interesting! I have dug deep into my soul to channel Alexander's brilliance, Hephaestion's loyalty, Jacob's courage, Katerina's independence, Cynane's resentment, Zofia's determination, and Olympias's endless manipulation. These characters are all pieces of myself and I will miss them.

It has also been a joy to write about the ancient world, blending a great deal of fact with fiction. For instance, the Asklepions of the sort Katerina and Jacob encountered outside Troy were healing temples sacred to Asklepios, the Greek god of medicine. Sacred snakes really did wander the site, communing with patients and priests. Asklepios—who I believe was a real medical practitioner with amazing skill—was known to walk with a staff, and the symbol of a snake twisting around a staff has been used by medical practitioners for centuries, including the American Medical Association.

The epic saga of Troy greatly shaped Alexander's world. Warriors wanted to be like Achilles; women compared their beauty to that of Helen. For centuries, Greeks visited the ruins of Troy on the northwest coast of what is now Turkey to sacrifice to the heroes who died there, including Alexander himself in 334 BC. While we don't know if Achilles, Helen, and the host of other unforgettable characters were real flesh-and-blood people, we do know the site was devastated around 1200 BC, as were most coastal cities in the eastern Mediterranean around that time. The end of this advanced civilization was due, experts now believe, to a combination of climate change (resulting in earthquakes, droughts, tsunamis, floods, and famine), epidemics, large-scale migration as people tried to escape these cataclysms, and invaders taking advantage of them. In the wake of this massive destruction, people moved to the hills and, while focusing on survival, forgot how to read and write, build elaborate palaces and temples, craft gold and silver, and make sophisticated pottery. The *Iliad* and the *Odyssey* were, I believe, love songs to a vanished golden age, a mythical explanation of unendurable loss, and a light in four hundred years of darkness.

The story of the Gordian knot is much as I have written it. When the kingdom of Phrygia found themselves without a king, the elders visited an oracle who told them that the next man driving an oxcart to enter the city should be their new ruler. A peasant named Gordios must have been shocked as he drove his oxcart into town and was immediately proclaimed king. To commemorate the historic event, the oxcart was tied to a post with an intricate knot. Another oracle proclaimed that any man who could unravel the knot was destined to become the master of all Asia. When Alexander arrived in Gordium, he tried to untangle it without success. Frustrated, he pulled out his sword and sliced it open. He went on to conquer Asia, thereby fulfilling the prophecy. These days, the term *Gordian knot* refers to a particularly thorny problem that requires creative thinking to solve, just as Alexander did with the real knot.

The tale of mad honey is one of my favorites from the ancient world. In 67 BC, Roman soldiers in Asia Minor marching against the wily King Mithridates near the Black Sea unexpectedly found luscious, gooey chunks of honeycomb strewed in their path. The hungry men dived into the sticky, sweet stuff, became wildly intoxicated, and were killed by the enemy army lying in wait. Bees make mad honey with nectar from a certain kind of rhododendron flower that contains grayanotoxin, a highly hallucinogenic substance. Even today, hikers and tourists in that part of Turkey are periodically treated for mad honey poisoning.

In the Battle of Chaeronea in 338 BC, King Philip of Macedon led one wing of the army, entrusting Alexander with the other. Philip retreated, but it was a trick to draw the enemy in as Alexander's wing whipped around and attacked from behind. The prince clashed with the Sacred Band of Thebes, one hundred and fifty pairs of gay lovers known as the fiercest warriors on earth, killing them all. When Philip surveyed the battle after his victory, he encountered corpses "heaped one upon another," according to the ancient historian Plutarch. Understanding they were members of the Sacred Band, he wept and said, "Perish any man who suspects that these men either did or suffered anything unseemly." He erected a memorial on the battlefield in the form of a lion as a testament to their courage, which was discovered in the nineteenth century and stands today. Beneath the statue, archeologists found hundreds of skeletons, human ashes, shields, helmets, and spears. After the battle, Philip formed the League of Corinth with his former enemies and prepared to march on Persia, but he was assassinated before he could set sail.

One of my favorite characters is Queen Olympias, Alexander's mother, who was what we today would call "a piece of work." Her marriage to King Philip was quite stormy, especially after he married a girl half Olympias's age, Cleopatra, the niece of Attalus. At the wedding of another Cleopatra, Philip's daughter, Philip was murdered by a former lover, Pausanias, though

Olympias was believed to have had a hand in the deed. She returned to her brother's court in Epirus, where she organized the murder of Philip's young widow and their infant son. In proving the old adage that only the good die young, she survived just about everyone mentioned in this story.

The eighty-eight-year-old Great King Artaxerxes III of Persia was reportedly poisoned by his eunuch, Bagoas, and a physician. While details of his death are unknown, I borrowed from the reported poisoning of the seventy-seven-year-old Roman emperor Caesar Augustus in 14 AD. According to one version, his wife Livia painted figs on his favorite fig tree with poison, knowing he never had a taster test them.

Regarding the fate of Katerina—fierce, smart, independent, and a fictional invention of my own—it seemed impossible to me that she would settle down with a man, have kids and a traditional life. There is a legend that Alexander, in his effort to find the Fountain of Youth, found a flask of immortal water he used to wash his sister's hair. Years later, hearing of his death, his sister tried to commit suicide by leaping into the sea. But instead of dying, she became a mermaid who passed judgment on sailors who came her way. To everyone she met, she asked, "Is Alexander the king alive?" If the sailor replied, "He lives and reigns and conquers the world," she would permit the ship to sail on safely. But any less pleasing answer would cause her to become a monster and send the vessel and its entire crew to the bottom of the sea. I borrowed from this story to paint Katerina's fate—it seemed fitting for her memory to take on mythic proportions, just as Alexander's did.

Nor did it seem realistic for Alexander's half sister, Cynane—another of my favorites—to settle down to bake honey cakes for a husband and children. And history agrees with us here. After her disastrous marriage to her cousin Amyntas, she never remarried but remained a warrior until the end. As the ancient Macedonian historian Polyaenus wrote, "Cynane, the daughter of Philip, was famous for her military knowledge: she conducted armies, and in the field charged at the head of them. In an engagement with the Illyrians, she with her own hand slew Caeria, their queen; and with great slaughter defeated the Illyrian army." It seems right, somehow, for her to ride off into the sunset with Alecta and her own battalion of female warriors.

There has been much speculation about the nature of Alexander's relationship with Hephaestion. No ancient sources state that the relationship was sexual, either because it wasn't, or because it was and gay relationships were so commonplace no one cared or thought that was unusual. Whatever the case sexually, Alexander was so close to Hephaestion he considered him to be his other self. When a captured Persian queen mother went up to the two gorgeous young men waiting to receive her and bowed down before Hephaestion, everyone burst out laughing, causing the queen to turn bright red. But Alexander reassured her, "You were not mistaken, Mother; this man, too, is Alexander." When Alexander poured a libation at the tomb of Achilles at Troy, he remarked how fortunate Achilles was to have had such a faithful friend as Patroclus, clearly a reference to Hephaestion.

Whether they were gay or not, both Alexander and Hephaestion married women, Alexander three times to secure political alliances. His first wife, the one he truly loved according to all accounts, was named Roxana, daughter of a Bactrian king. Though Zofia is an invention, I imagined Roxana might have been her own sister, lost and then found again, who, later in life, met and fell in love with Alexander and fulfilled our prophecy of Zofia's blood mingling with that of Alexander, but in a whole new way.

Throughout this book, a major thread—pardon the pun—is that of fate versus free will, a question that has intrigued writers from ancient Greek dramatists to Shakespeare. Many of us ask ourselves, "Is everything in our lives fated and we are just going through the motions of what must be? And if so, what's the point?" I look at it this way: some things are indeed "fated." The bodies we are born with. The parents who welcome us into the world—or not. The people we meet. The situations that appear before us. Free will is what we do with these things. Free will is the essence of what it means to be human, and while genetics and circumstances may set up the playing field, it is our own choices that define who we are and how far we run.